GW00836328

BOBBYJACK

A.E. Snelling-Munro

Michael Terence
Publishing

First published in paperback by
Michael Terence Publishing in 2017

www.mtp.agency

ISBN 978-1-549-51764-8

Dedicated to my DNA, ancestry and parents, to include Mary and Brother Roger who died March 2016 and who remained a true believer in my work(?)

BOBBYJAC

A.E. Snelling-Munro

CHAPTER ONE
Another Day, Another Night

Within the dark confines of the mansion, a shadowy figure appeared, slowly descending the wide staircase. A gloved hand trailed the bannister. The dull thud of heavy boots was scuffing the thick carpet, echoing the sounds in the darkened hallway below.

From outside, light illuminated the hallway, making a silvery glow through the stained glass window. As the wind bellowed and raged among the treetops, the strong winds shook the trees and cast constantly changing shadows on the pale walls. The man's blue eyes were bright like animal's eyes in the glow.

Reaching the bottom tread, the man stopped. His gloved hand momentarily caressed the wooden newel post, while his eyes grew more accustomed to the half-light around the open door of the lounge. Moving quietly, he pushed back the door.

In a black balaclava and black leathers, the man stood bathed in the milky light. A crash helmet swung to and fro from the fingertips of one hand, his eyes focused on the dishevelled form cradled and twisted in the reclining chair by the niche at the fireplace. Tommy Sands burnt with anger as he studied the sleeping figure of his friend, Lenny Burns.

It was another day, another night. Tommy felt the onslaught of his loneliness. Lenny had sought the comfort of another drunken stupor. His hand clutched the neck of a whisky bottle. Tommy took a deep breath through gritted teeth turned and closed the door.

He quickly left the house by the rear door. He paused for a few moments in the darkness of the rear porch. Drawing deep breaths from the fresh blowing breeze, he gathered his senses before he walked slowly down the gravelled pathway at the side of the house.*

For many weeks he had followed the same nightly

ritual, leaving the house before midnight and going to his private haven in the grounds. It was a sad reflection on their long friendship. Lenny was becoming an alcoholic. Tommy felt guilty for not doing more to help him, but he had been preoccupied with other matters.

Arguments had been commonplace and extremely bitter and had for several days at a time they wouldn't even speak. He realised some action was going to be needed if their friendship were to survive.

For five years they had lived together in the big house, buried in an isolated part of the West Country and they now faced conflict. Tommy found solace driving through the countryside until the early hours. Tommy continued to focus on the past. Living on the edge gave him the adrenaline and excitement he craved.

He needed to be alone, to think clearly about his options. He was already scheming for new ways of making money. He had avoided telling Lenny that their investments had withered on the stock market. Something had to be done to put some money in the bank.

On reaching the rear of the house, Tommy strode across the lawn and disappeared into the bushes as he climbed the embankment into the copse. As he reached the trees he heard noises from the lane below. Camouflaged by the bushes, he dropped down and crawled to the edge of the trees, where he heard muffled voices. His eyes strained for the slightest movement in the dim light cast by the moon.

Tommy saw two figures shuffling up towards the brow of the hill, their swirling breath making it possible for him trace their line of movement.

"Christ, bloody gypsies," he murmured to himself, as they came closer.

He wondered where they had been. They sounded bloody drunk, he thought, and that was the last thing he needed: Drunk Gypsies, he scrambled into the heart of the copse until he found the manhole cover that lay half hidden in the undergrowth. Lifting it open, Tommy climbed down into the black hollow beneath the ground. Clutching at the ladder, with his head below the rim, he reached up and closed the cover. As he reached the floor level of the hollow, his hand fumbled in the dark for the light switch. He flicked it on and a dim light appeared in the narrow tunnel.

Within months of taking possession of the house, Tommy had laid four steel lorry containers soldier like behind the embankment at the front of the house. Linking the four containers, he used scaffolding, supported by shuttering plywood to form the basis of a wall and passageway. He obtained topsoil from a local motorway construction site, which he bulldozed up over his construction. Tommy had planted shrubs to form the landscape of an enlarged copse adjacent the mansion.

He had always entered the tunnel by this route when he felt low and despondent. Pungent smells wrapped around his nostrils as he drew breath. Easing through the passage, Tommy arrived at a control panel and pulled down hard on the lever and a series of ceiling lights flickered on. Leading off the corridor was a series of rooms housing a workshop and metal lathe, a large assortment of tools and an array of electronic equipment? Tommy was ready to return to crime whenever the need arose. With echoing footsteps drowning an eerie silence he walked away from the entrance. Stopping only to remove a dustsheet from a large object, with a flick of the wrist he tossed the sheet to the floor, revealing a black Range Rover with darkened windows.

Seeing his own darkened reflection in the door panels, his sudden lack of concentration in the dim light made him panic, his stomach churned and with a violent reaction he punched the wall.

"Damn the fucking thing," he uttered, "Jesus Christ!"

Immediately grinning at his stupidity, he then

grabbed the sheet off the floor and tucked it away.

Seating himself in the vehicle, Tommy pressed a button on the control panel. With only a slight vibration an opening appeared in the wall in front of him. On with the ignition, the engine sprang into life; lights dimmed and faded in the tunnel. He pulled on the helmet as he watched the garage door rise up and over, exposing the open centre of the man-made dungeon and the blackness of the night outside.

Emerging out from the entrance, radio playing, the black finish of the bodywork shimmered against the backdrop of flickering moonlight. Tommy waited for the garage door to close behind him, then slowly, and without lights, drove from the copse onto the shingle bed of the dried up river, travelling for some distance before reaching the edge of the field and road beyond. With its tinted windows, the vehicle was like a strange mythological bird with bright shining eyes and where a soft orange light glowed from the dashboard outlining the silhouette of the driver as it came into view from below the pastures of the valley, a haunting presence that he loved to drive. Still without lights, Tommy approached a wooden gate at the same time giving an electronic signal from the vehicle. The gate swung open. Checking his instruments and pulling tight his seatbelt, he was ready for the off. With gloved hands, he turned the wheel and slowly edged out into the country lane, before accelerating. The engine roared and the vehicle thundered away from the mansion house.

Tommy now had the bit between his teeth, the adrenaline pumping through his veins as he drove hard. Zooming around the many bends, he felt the breeze pushing hard into the open visor of the helmet from the open window. Only an orange glow from the dashboard lights gave the interior a warm tint of colour. From an outward appearance, a vehicle purposely without number plates that remained nondescript to anyone who may have seen it, Tommy presented a frightening figure.

He continued to drive hard, fast and furious for the next fifteen minutes when finally he followed a detour. Another route would take him up and over the approaching hill towards a ridge and the valley beyond. Then rounding a tight bend, Tommy slammed down hard on the brakes, holding steadfast as he gripped the driver's wheel with arms locked and straight to avoid skidding. Fucking hell, there in the headlights lay a prostrate figure. Stopping, he remained at the wheel, his watchful eyes peering through the tinted glass looking for a sign, any sign of others. Switching the lights onto full beam, he continued his wary examination.

He listened to the blast of symphonic music blaring from the vehicle's audio-speakers; the prone figure remained lifeless on the ground. Tommy felt tense and uneasy. He turned off the music and, with the engine purring in tick-over, he leant out of the driver's window and strained his ears for the slightest sound above the throb of the engine. He then checked the interior mirror for any movement from behind. Finally, he left the vehicle.

Standing by the open door he called out, then again. He finally removed the key from the ignition and the night fell silent. Tommy approached the figure; the helmet still covered his face, as he loomed in the headlights like a knight in shining armour. His elongated shadow cast a dark evil over the figure, cautiously Tommy reached out and touched the figure lying there. With no response, he moved closer and knelt down. Tommy saw then that it was a young man, scruffily dressed Tommy pondered on what to do next. There was no blood or marks, he realised, and that was strange. Tommy looked at the boy's face and hands more closely and concluded he was a gypsy. Taking hold of his chin, he squeezed the mouth open, the sight of the bad teeth was sickly, the tongue coated in grime.

"Christ, that's bloody awful. No kiss of life for you mate, you're bloody drunk," he said.

At the same time, Tommy saw a shadow appear in the headlights of the vehicle as someone came towards him. He quickly got to his feet and moved backwards, but the man was quicker and punched him on the arm, a fast, powerful blow.

The attack came without any warning, at close quarters. Without hesitation, Tommy let fly a punch in defence he felt his fist connect.

"Come on, you bastard!" Tommy screamed.

He lunged forward, again and again, repeating a combination of fast blows to the assailant's body. With his visor down, he saw the pain he was inflicting on the attacker, and then abruptly he took hold of the man's clothing and lifted him off the ground, tossing him onto the nearby hedge. Tommy watched the man land crumpled, caught on the branches. He remained motionless and suspended off the ground. Tommy seethed at the attacker's intrusion, his anger boiled over as he went for the attacker again, with two further blows to the suspended body. Tommy heard him cry out, again in pain.

Tommy returned to the unconscious youth and pulled him by the legs on to the grass verge at the side of the lane, and left him there. Now tired and sweaty from his altercation, Tommy lifted up the visor for gasps of air; his hands ached as he pulled the gloves from his fingers. Already tense, his mind in turmoil, he leaned against the front of the vehicle. He wanted to be violently sick; his stomach muscles were now in knots, bile rose in the mouth.

In panic, he pulled roughly at the helmet, breaking free in relief as he felt the night chill on his face. Moving to the side of the lane, he grabbed hold of a wooden fence post in the hedgerow. For awhile he just held on for dear life, he breathed deeply, sucking in large gasps of air as he regained some composure.

Finally, he returned to the safety of the vehicle and

with one turn of the key the engine roared back into life and moved off, slowly passing the two motionless gypsies. A mile down the lane, Tommy stopped in the entrance of a farm, sliding the vehicle up against the wooden bars of a gate; the headlights beamed through the spars and illuminated the pasture ahead. Tommy was about to reverse back when he caught a glimpse of movement from the field. He sat for a moment as he realised that he had seen a crouched figure. Curious, Tommy left the vehicle and stood by the gate, peering over. He was astonished to see a man, naked from the waist down and mounted over the rear of a sheep, his extended arms grappling two fists of fleece, whilst holding the animal between his legs.

Tommy was rooted to the spot; he couldn't believe that anybody could do such a thing to an animal. He let out s deep-throated roar of verbal abuse, but his shouts went ignored.

"You bastard, you animal, get off!" He shook the gate in temper, and then kicked it. "God, what the fucking hell's going on here? I just don't believe this!"

Forcing open the gate, Tommy ran back to the vehicle and accelerated fast as he roared into the field towards the crouched figure with all wheels spinning and sliding on the grass, left, right, left, right, his arms locked as he steered towards the man. Finally sliding to a halt he quickly clambered from the vehicle, almost slipping to the ground in his rush, and at that moment the man released the bleating animal from his grasp. Tommy raced across the ground towards the man. He was now attempting to escape, but Tommy lunged at him grabbing his ankle as they both fell to the ground. The man kicked out with his other foot, and Tommy fought back. Clawing at the ground, the man anxiously trying to break Tommy's grasp, but Tommy was quick to anticipate the man's next move. He scrambled back on to his feet and towered over the figure on the ground, Tommy rained a series of powerful blows to the half naked man, and then three fierce blows to the head. The man let out a cry for help, but Tommy had lost all sense of reason, and he was ready to tear the man apart limb-by-limb. Tommy realised by the man's accent that he was another gypsy, a thought that sent a wave of doubt through him. He placed a heavy boot against the man's neck and pressed down hard to keep him trapped on the ground. Tommy felt every squirm and wriggle as the gypsy tried to fight back, yet at the same time, he felt vulnerable. He could see across the moonlit valley a blue flashing light. The gypsy saw his chance and wriggled free and quickly scurried across the open ground to freedom.

Tommy snapped back into life with a half-hearted attempt to restrain him, but really, it didn't matter. What was he going to do with him, after all, his thoughts had been interrupted by the presence of the blue flashing light and the sick panic he felt. He raced for the Range Rover. Ramming into first gear, he headed back towards the open gate, then into second gear as he began to gain speed. Not stopping, he thundered on through the entrance and raced down the lane. He then made a quick right turn, heading for the ridge and the valley beyond.

Tommy maintained a high speed around the tight bends and narrow lanes, passing through a large gypsy encampment situated on both sides of the lane. Unrelenting, he drove on, at gaining speed, leaving churning dust clouds in his passing wake.

Unbeknown to Tommy he had become the focus of attention of wise 'Old Ben Witney'. Ben was tucked in the shadows of the last caravan in the lane, whilst he puffed and fingered on his pipe he saw the Range Rover speed past. He was familiar with the driver and vehicle, he knew that Tommy was the squire from the big house in the valley below, but this knowledge was Ben's secret and not one to be shared with the fraternity.

CHAPTER TWO
First Tuesday – Headlines

The rays of the rising sun had not quite reached the shadows and shelter of thick undergrowth which lined the sides of the quite, lane that led up from the village below. Swirling mist and vegetation laden with the morning's dew were brushed aside as the speeding cycle passed by. The wheels strained against the turning pedals as the fresh-faced paperboy tackled the steep gradient. He fought determinedly with the handlebars as he fought to steady the heavy canvas bag from unbalancing the bicycle.

He was earlier than usual on this Tuesday morning, his clothes looking as though they had been thrown on rather than put on; the collar of his jacket turned inwards, revealing the worn green jumper back to front.

(He was always rushing out of bed each morning dog tired and always dishevelled as he could be seen each morning racing through the winding country lanes with his bicycle laden with the morning papers)

The boy's journey was to take him to Tommy and Lenny's impressive mansion, set well off the lane in idyllic surroundings. It was a place noted for intrigue and mystery, as little was known of its residents, a house of tall stories told by the people from the village.

On reaching the top of the rise and the open gate overshadowed by two large trees, the boy slowly ambled through, while gazing into the morning paper. At the same time, his grubby hands brushed off the beads of water that dripped from the branches above.

The boy hunched his shoulders to repel the drips and looked up at the overhanging canopy of foliage with the sun coming up behind the leaves. He was unaware that from the kitchen window at the front of the house, watching eyes were upon him, noting every movement he made.

Tommy Sands had returned to the house after his night skirmish some hours before and catnapped on his favourite armchair. His body ached and he felt all of his forty-five years as he watched the figure approaching the house.

Tommy was always suspicious of any visitor to the house; at the same time, he realised what good cover the thick undergrowth provided against unwanted guests at the front of the house – most of all Coppers. In truth, just the thought of coppers was enough to scare him, sending unwanted shivers down his spine.

Unaware that the boy was now out of vision, a sudden thud and the noise of running feet attracted his attention. He smiled as he watched the youngster from the window kick the morning dew off the grass at the edge of the driveway, spraying up with each swipe of the foot.

"Little sod," he thought.

He remained fascinated, following the boy's departure. Finally, he watched the boy wobble and scoot as he sped back down the hill in the direction of the village.

The kettle blasted Tommy's eardrums and he bounced back to earth, shaking his head and grinning from his daydream. He reached for the teapot and yawned as he tried to shake off his drowsiness. The brightness and penetration of the morning sun through the window stung his eyes and brought unexpected warmth to the kitchen. Removing the lid of the teapot, Tommy noticed that the steam from the kettle was misting up the window, leaving a grey haze that blocked his vision to the outside. With a shrug of his shoulders, he rubbed absently at his morning stubble, then turned and went back into the hallway. Stooping in jeans a size too small, he let out a loud grunt, his aching torso straining at the waist as he gathered the paper from the floor.

Back in the kitchen, it wasn't long before Tommy was

holding a mug of scalding tea against his lips. Peering through the rising steam, he read the paper; a wry smile forming on his lips as his eyes caught the headlines.

"Christ – I don't believe it," he laughed. "Cor – bloody hell, that's it, this is the one, Tommy you are a clever boy."

His laughter remained long and loud as it echoed through the house, and disturbed the sleeping figure of his lifetime friend Lenny Burns.

Feeling like a traffic accident and with only one bleary eye open, Lenny gazed around the room. Hours earlier, Lenny had groped his way from the ground floor, on all fours, upstairs to his bedroom, collapsing fully clothed on the bed.

Slowly, he raised himself up onto one arm and scratched at his face in annoyance. He slowly eased his aching legs off the bed. His tongue felt like leather from the excesses of the previous evening and he grumbled obscenities in response to the noise.

"Tommy, for Christ sake, is that you? Tommy bloody answer me, will yeah."

Not hearing a reply, Lenny pushed himself off the bed and moved across the carpeted floor. He cautiously opened the door and stood listening; he was aching from the exertion already. His stomach was full of butterflies and his head full of prickling needles.

A branch tapped sharply against the window springing back and forth in the wind. Lenny quickly dropped to the floor, thinking it was a gun going off.

"Oh, Jesus," he muttered.

He was becoming confused and extremely nervous as he took hold of the doorframe. Remaining quiet, he listened for other sounds. With no further intrusions again he shouted for Tommy. On the third call, Tommy answered.

"Lenny, get your arse down here, we're going into

business again."

Lenny was slow to pick himself off the floor, he felt like squeezed lemon.

With one hand scratching his stubbly chin, he staggered and fell along the landing, heading for the stairs. Never agreeable at that time of day, Lenny cursed as he descended the stairs. Reaching the kitchen, he shouted at Tommy,

"Why can't you bloody wait until I wake up properly? You always know how to get me going, don't you? I'm pissed off with your jokes, Tommy."

"Lenny stop being a bloody old woman, grab a cup and just bloody listen to me for a moment."

"That's been my life story, Tommy, and you bloody know it."

"Look, please just sit down and listen; please, Lenny."

Following Tommy's order he slid the mug of tea across the pine table; moving then to the pantry he fetched a bottle of whisky. He unscrewed the top and poured a generous amount into the mug. He faced Tommy from across the table, whilst he sipped the tea.

Tommy held up the local newspaper, and squinting Lenny tried to read the headline.

"What is it? I can't see clearly, bring it here."

Tommy placed the paper down in front of Lenny. The headline read, 'PUBLIC OUTRAGED BY POLICE PHONES'.

"So what...what's this got to do with us – Tommy, for Christ sake?"

Tommy leant over the pine table and held both of Lenny's wrists.

"Read it, it's given me an idea for another job. Just read it, that's all I'm asking, then I'll explain."

"Jesus, Tommy have you gone off your bloody rocker? We've been away from it for the past five years, we're out of touch, we're both past forty; we're gone soft and anyway, I've come to enjoy the good life. I don't want any more prison, so sod off with your big ideas. Find someone else. I'm not bloody interested."

"Alright, alright, just stop getting nasty will yer, you're always bellyaching about something and I'm getting pissed off with it. I want you to understand this, our money won't last forever, and you bloody remember that."

They both remained silent. Lenny clutched his mug and thumbed the rim, his eyes fixed on the window. Tommy snatched back the paper. Not really concentrating, he flicked through it. He wondered would he be the first to break. Neither of them did.

It was a strange argument to be having, Tommy could feel the tension between them; odd, he thought for lifetime friends. As neighbours, they had lived in Stepney in the East End of London. Terraced houses lined street after street, with deep basements and grilled windows at pavement level. Stacked like playing cards, houses fell and crumbled under the onslaught of German bombers. Daily news reached the neighbouring families of those lost during the raids, and Tommy and Lenny were to see their surroundings dramatically change during their younger years in the 1940's.

It was by school association that their friendship blossomed – it was as if their destinies were made to cross in pursuit of another life together. Each had been the eldest of four children; both their fathers had worked as Dockers in the East India Docks, and in similar surroundings they too were friends. But this was not enough for Tommy and Lenny. Times were changing rapidly and there was action to be had on the black market. Both earned a few bob on the side acting as runners for some of the traders that operated around the docks. Stepney was a breeding ground for young criminals and both boys were no exception. They were both arrested for stealing, neither incident's related, but in time a habit became greed, and their lives now entwined like a Dockers rope.

Tommy always had the ideas and Lenny was more content to be ordered around. It wasn't long before they received their first prison sentence.

As the years passed they were getting caught more often and spending more of their lives in prison. During their years of incarceration, the two still continued to earn good money from the firm. With good management and investment, a tidy nest egg had built up. Their exploits had often been outrageous but small-time and they always awaited the big one, always the last job that would make them their fortunes. That had proved fruitless and their final sentence had jolted their systems. So it was that, five years previously, they had left prison together for the last time, vowing never to return to their former lives.

Their journey brought them to the West Country and the mansion house, bought many years previously, had been a sound investment. During their years of freedom, they remained reclusive and never socialised with their neighbours.

Minutes later, Lenny was the first to move. Without uttering a word to Tommy, he placed the empty mug on the draining board and left the kitchen; Tommy twisted round in his chair and sighed. Rising, he slowly followed Lenny with the offending newspaper tucked under one arm. He peered from the doorway into the hall; Lenny was not to be seen. Tommy hovered in the passage, deliberating on his next move. He crossed to the open door of the lounge and peeked around the doorframe, again no Lenny. Turning on his heels, Tommy scanned the twisting staircase, the long wooden balcony and balustrade towered over him as he looked up from the hallway below. Believing that Lenny had returned to his bedroom, Tommy climbed the stairs. Standing at the end of the corridor he knocked gently on Lenny's door, deciding to apologise as he realised that he had been out of order. His knocking went unanswered.

He was feeling lousy about the tension between them it was becoming unbearable. After a few minutes, Tommy returned downstairs. On his way down, he could hear movement coming from the kitchen. Stopping, he looked back upstairs, shaking his head and frowning, he muttered,

"What's going on here?"

His fingers trailed the bannister rail as he quickly hastened from the hallway to the kitchen, the smell of frying food hitting his nostrils as bacon sizzled on the stove, fresh coffee was on the boil, toast jumping from the toaster as he entered the kitchen. Seeing the rear door open, he moved and stood in the doorway, looking out. He saw the hunched figure of Lenny, standing on the grass some yards from the house. Tommy felt a lump in his throat as he stepped out into the garden.

Lenny turned his head. He began to move further away as Tommy approached, Tommy called for him to wait. Ignoring his call, Lenny swung to his right and turned back towards the house, brushing Tommy aside as he swept past and headed for the kitchen. Tommy stood gesturing with an outstretched hand but was ignored as he watched his friend pass by. Still clutching the local newspaper, Tommy returned to the kitchen, stepping silently through the open door.

He stood watching Lenny from behind as he stood poking bacon on the stove; approaching Lenny with a saddened face he placed an arm around his shoulders.

"Lenny I'm sorry for the way I started on at you this morning, I didn't mean it the way I said it, it was watching the kid, the paperboy, he got me wondering about a number of things and reading the headlines in the paper just switched me on. Only I.ve got this idea for another job," said Tommy

Lenny swung round to face Tommy, his face looked stern.

"All right, I know what you're going to say Len, but just hear me out, mate."

Lenny gently slapped Tommy's face with both hands and said:

"Do you want some breakfast, because it's gone eight and it's ready?"

Tommy smiled and sat down at the table. Lenny placed the food in front of him.

"Where is the paper?" he asked. "I'll read the story myself later, but I suppose I'd better hear you out."

"Lenny you are going to like my idea, you wait and see; I wanna screw a whole town in a night, no violence, just show our class, just like the old days."

Before he went any further Tommy was tucking into his breakfast.

"Yeah, I'm bloody hungry as well," said Lenny, joining him at the table. "The day looks nice, I've got to pop down to the village later, do you want to come Tommy?"

"Mmmm, I'll have a run down with you mate," Tommy said.

"Listen to this story," he passed the paper to Lenny, "It's about the local Police, they've had a new phone system put in and apparently there've been loads of complaints from the public since it was installed, everyone's doing their nut. All the stations are linked together with nothing in between and every now and then the phones go down. The phones can't be used by the local police or the public, the Old Bill is closed down. This is technology at its best, can you believe it? It can last for hours."

Lenny was still working on his breakfast as he listened.

"And you don't think we're out of touch?" he broke in "All right, so what have you got in mind, you said something about screwing a town and our money's running out. Now the money bit does worry me and I'm not prepared to see all this go either," Lenny said, gesturing and looking around him.

"We know," Tommy said, "That's right, now you're seeing sense mate' I'm not trying to brainwash you but we've got to do something, Lenny, Look at the politics, crime pays today and gives real benefits because no bugger gives a sod. Every bleeder is on the take. If you remember a few years back, the Old Bill lost a lot of good coppers, they don't look after them like they use to do, so what happened, many of them left. The poor sods out there today are still learning their trade and that takes years of experience. The cream's gone; they don't bother to keep the old coppers. They are political pawns they know more than the management, it's obvious they can't wrap the old copper around their finger can they, knowing more than them on this fast track promotion, graduates or whatever they like to call them running up the bloody ladder for the big money and position. Many jobs today are with Union people; young girls, the call civilisation. You've got to fight to speak to a copper today, it's like catching a bloody bus, when you want one it's gone past, when you don't there are dozens of them."

Lenny by this time was smiling. Tommy was in full flight and he saw a flicker of his former brilliance.

"But Tommy, you said about screwing a town, now that takes money and staff, remember, you were the one to put the old firm on ice. Oh! Christ, I can't believe that we're in such a state with our money, what's bloody gone wrong?" he said angrily.

"Look mate, for the last couple of days you've been on a bloody binge and for months you've been a bit regular with your drinking, you've got to admit. The last year has been very boring for both of us. We haven't done much, have we? We've let things slide and the recession hasn't helped with our investment. Look we've lived the life of Riley and you can't argue with that."

Tommy left the kitchen; Lenny sat and pondered his every word. He then spread out the paper, brushing the pages flat across, the table and read the article, it was obvious to Tommy that a change was on the way for both of them. Neither over the years had spent any real time away from the house that they had been idle, Tommy had kitted out the underground bunker, which housed his pride and joy, a high specification Range Rover. At the other extreme, Lenny spent most of his time with his four German Weimaraner dogs, believing himself the Country Squire. Neither had married – women had not played a major part in their lives for many years.

In Lenny's absence, Tommy had walked the ground floor of the house, browsing from room to room; his mind was preoccupied with the charm and character of the house. The house appeared sad in its reflection of the present owners; he felt ashamed and saddened by the neglect that had taken place, It was a house that cried out for a feminine touch, a tranquil embrace that would give warmth and joy to any family life. A rambling house set in a picture postcard setting, each room was clearly marked by its own character of the period and it had been a shooting lodge, obviously. Around the 1800's the servant quarters had been absorbed into the structure of the house for greater accommodation.

Tommy and Lenny had originally purchased the house prior to leaving prison. They had made a joint commitment and an arrangement was secretly formulated for their future. On their release from prison, they withdrew from family and friends and remained in self-imposed exile.

Tommy had been oblivious to the time, and now the chimes of the hall clock ticked, ticked, ticked in anticipation on the strike of nine. Not wanting to enhance any further the tension with Lenny, he returned to the kitchen. Lenny was still seated at the table and was so deep in thought that he was unaware that Tommy had returned.

Tommy, with arms folded, rested against the sink, staring down at his chum. Lenny stood, picked up the newspaper, and folding it once, he handed it to Tommy as he left the kitchen.

"Look, I don't know how you feel about things, but I've been thinking about this a lot lately and well, to put it bluntly, do you fancy a good fuck?" Tommy called.

"Say that again," Lenny said, startled.

"Do you fancy a good fuck?"

Lenny started to laugh, "Christ, you're off your bloody rocker, are you making me an offer?"

"No, damn it, I'm not."

"The dogs then?"

Tommy burst out laughing, as he reached out and gently pushed Lenny by the shoulder.

"No, you bloody fool; women, what do you think?"

"You got me going there for a minute mate, what have you got in mind."

"Well, I don't know really, but I was thinking earlier about our abstention from life and what we both need is female company. It's never too late to start over again, is it? We could organise some women down here." Tommy suggested.

"I see what you mean, you dastardly bastard, you've been getting horny in your old age, is that it?" joked Lenny.

"Well, if you must put it like that, yes I bloody well am, and I feel it's about time we turned the clock back and had some fun. Don't you agree?"

"Mmmm, yes I would agree with you on that, So what are you proposing then?"

"Well, I thought about an escort agency. I know a fellow who could fix us up, I could try him for starters."

"Yeah, I do like the idea. Christ, isn't it bloody funny after all these years, we're now wanting to go a – rutting."

Together in their excitement, they shadowboxed.

When Lenny went into the Village, Tommy made the first of two phone calls to the escort agency. The first was an absolute cock-up on his part. What with this strange sense of humour and flippant manner falling on deaf ears, he was soon disconnected for his troubles.

"Cheeky cow. What a bloody cow she was – bleeding hell," his words uttered in anger as Tommy paced the lounge in irritation.

"Blanked off by some bloody tart," he moaned.

"Eh! Jesus Christ hasn't she got a sense of humour?" he shouted.

A little over an hour's drive from the mansion house lived Toni Harris. On this particular morning, Toni appeared to be in high spirits. From the kitchen window of her spacious third floor flat, She waved to her neighbour in the car park below.

Sipping coffee, Toni remained by the window as she heard the click of the answer phone. Tommy's strong voice echoed out impatiently, almost to the point of demanding. Toni laughed out loud as she heard his words.

"Stupid man, just wait," she said.

Tommy reeled off his words into the answering machine, unaware that anyone could be listening as he struggled to express himself.

Moving away from the window, Toni entered the hallway. She leant against the wall listening as if she had intimate knowledge of the caller. Toni became more curious with every word spoken. Who was this brazen man? she wondered. How did he get my number? She became more puzzled by the minute.

"Two of us, he wants two of us – today, right this bloody minute. He sounds a cheeky sod," she muttered to herself.

Toni felt a buzz of excitement, as she churned his words over in her mind. Tommy's accent and banter held a greater attraction for Toni than she immediately realised. Whispering to herself, she turned away and climbed the stairs to her bedroom.

Dressed in briefs and sweater, Toni sat on the edge of her king-sized bed and pulled on a pair of tight fitting jeans.

Toni decided to contact her agency on the pretext of collecting any messages. Her appointment diary was empty for the remainder of the week, confirming that by some quirk of fate Tommy's call had been misdirected by her agency. She knew the call should have been stored and entered into the stacking system for the agency's later attention. Whatever the reason, Toni's empty diary had been pre arranged some weeks before. She intended to take a short break away from home and work with her friend Karen Black. Thumping down the stairs, Toni became more fascinated by Tommy's distinctive London accent. Repeating, who is this man? Over and over in her thoughts. She did not recognise the voice as a previous client.

In her amusement, Toni remained listening as she fumbled with her glasses in concentration.

"Gotcha mister, I'm on your wavelength – let's see how big a boy you really are."

Toni shrieked with excitement at the prospect of Tommy's invitation. God, Karen. I must ring her, she thought, having scribbled Tommy's details down. Toni was very determined to follow through with his request. "Yes, I'm sure we might do some business, my friend, if you check out. Oh! bloody hell, Karen that's it, I'll ask her to check him out." She thought.

Toni phoned Karen, "Are you finishing at midday as planned?"

"Yes," Karen replied

"Before you leave could you do me a favour?"

"And what favour would that be Toni?"

"Could you check out a credit card for me?"

"Toni, bloody hell – can't do this, I just can't, I'll speak to you later, must go – bye."

Toni was annoyed, "Damn, what can I bloody do now," said Toni muttering to herself. Her mobile phone then rang out from the bedroom and she rushed back upstairs, It's me," said Karen as she answered, "I've got to be quick, I am sorry about earlier."

Toni said, "Can you check out a credit card – please, please, please just see if it's legit, I'll explain later when I see you."

"Be quick then, I'm in the loo at the moment, right, give me the details," said Karen.

Toni did so and immediately the line went dead.

"Bloody hell, she's gone," Toni muttered, she smiled as she tapped the mobile against her cheek.

Over the years, Toni's middle-class background, grammar school and university education had offered her a different lifestyle. She had found a taste for adventure, with parting knowledge from a worldly travelled father who focused the greatest attention on his youngest daughter. An executive who worked in the motor industry, her father was now in retirement, giving Toni the opportunity to flit between the sedate lives of her parents and the motherhood of her two older sisters and their children, this she enjoyed most of all as she could come and go as she pleased, without the kind of commitment other family members expected from her circumstances; albeit single, she liked the acquaintance factor more, as she could flit like a butterfly without revealing too much of herself and her work from delving questions of those closest to her. She was happy with what she did with high financial rewards and the freedom of choice she chose.

It suited Toni to be the aunt; because she enjoyed being with the children and the comforts and cuddles they each offered her. From Toni's point of view, it was an excellent arrangement knowing that her responsibilities to the children ended when she left her sister's home. Her freedom was priceless and the pinnacle of her delights. Her flat was to be the most important commitment that she had made. Furnished with soft trimmings and expensive furniture Toni was in her element. She knew from experience that she needed to cope with her independence and by that she adopted a more aggressive attitude towards money, men and business. But nevertheless, she sometimes felt the downside to her life of travel and how loneliness can be such a bitch at times.

It was during her early twenties and the last 18-months of university that Toni's attitude changed towards the male species. With an ever-changing social scene and frequent weekend invitations that took her the length and breadth of Britain, Toni was becoming more and more disillusioned at the way her girlfriends were being treated at the hands of their boyfriends – with inevitable chop and change of relationships and the many tears that had been shed in the ensuing break-ups. Romance was fast becoming a dirty word. Toni was left cold, angry and resentful towards men. Becoming more of a target herself from the boyish approaches, she had to endure the narrow male egos she rubbed shoulders with.

By the time she was twenty-one, Toni had not had a full sexual relationship with any man, other than the occasional grope. Her dates lasted no more than a few days to a few weeks of petulance on the part of her male partners in wanting more than she was prepared to give them. With the odd kiss and snog, the unwelcome attention of the wandering hand squeezing her breasts and the persistent hand trying to delve into her panties was where Toni drew the line. She had no desire to be the next sexual topic on the agenda of the male dormitories.

It was after her graduation that she accompanied

both her sisters and their families abroad for a summer break. Then by a chance meeting with a Frenchman ten years her senior brought the question of romance into her life for the very first time, Toni lost her virginity to an unconstrained passion that had long awaited her feelings, indeed, the experience was to be the opening of a new chapter in her sexual life; as her sexual desires and fulfilment had become more overwhelming and more powerful than she could have ever imagined from her first sexual encounter. Quality and experience had replaced youth and their fumbling clumsiness for the sensitivity of touch, and attentiveness that Toni sought in her sexual awakening. To taste and feel her first man, fulfilled her desires in wanting more from her sexual conquests of the future; and where quality could not be replaced by quantity and why she chose the older man to appreciate what nature had provided for us all.

Over the years, Toni had kept in touch with her old school friend, Karen Black. With a similar background to Toni's Karen had entered the Civil service, where for the past four years she had followed a successful career in a secondment post. Being extremely secretive, Karen's work was never divulged when in the company of others, Toni was always on hand to be protective towards her friend, especially as she was the one to have encouraged and introduced a reluctant Karen to the world of female escorting, albeit on a very occasional basis, as she always partnered Toni on her liaisons.

Karen had been more focused on her career than considering marriage. Karen's self-interests never bounded to open affairs of the heart or the tryst that Toni expected. It was much easier for her to find the occasional sexual relief among Toni's business clientele without having to provide the emotional energy and commitment to a proper relationship. Karen felt more in control that way and was happy to fulfil her role as Toni's companion and nothing more.

CHAPTER THREE
House Visitors

By ten o'clock that morning Lenny had arrived in the village. He manoeuvred his blue metallic Jaguar into a parking space. Still with the engine running, he played his usual game of hide and seek, which he hadn't been able to break since his days of criminal involvement – always careful, always suspicious, he remained motionless in the driver's seat as he waited for the all clear.

Feeling confident he secured and left the vehicle on the High Street. A motorbike roared past, the noise disturbing his concentration. Looking around after the bike, Lenny shouted:

"You noisy bastard!"

A passing old lady said,

"Quite right, they are a bloody nuisance in the village, they want their arses kicked."

Lenny grinned, "You're right there darling," he said.

He had dressed casually, for the day's business shopping. Forty minutes later he was weighed down with shopping bags as he watched the traffic crawl past. His eyes caught the same old lady juggling with the gear stick of her car, and becoming flustered, even more so as a passing builder's truck with a half-naked torso hanging from the window shouted obscenities and made a V-sign at her. It was no fun getting old, he thought.

The sun was up with shadows cast across one-half of the street, the warmth of the morning's breeze felt pleasant. It made Lenny feel good, and raised his spirits; he was already sporting a slight tan from his recent excursions with the dogs. Before unlocking the car boot he realised that he hadn't got the booze.

"Bloody hell, I nearly forgot," he muttered.

Leaning against the boot lid he scanned for any

prying eyes. Lenny felt confident that he hadn't lost his touch, always careful; he smiled and shook his head. He still couldn't come to terms with Tommy's suggestions, perhaps deep down he believed the problems would go away in time and let them be. Entering the off-licence he was soon in action, the teenager on the till watched him from the oval security mirror on the ceiling, the lad couldn't understand how anyone had that kind of money to spend on drink, let alone have the time to drink it.

As Lenny struggled with the weighted baskets up to the checkout, the young lad looked numb as he began stacking the drink onto the counter.

"You having a party?" he asked

The broad West Country accent made Lenny laugh.

"No son, I'm going to give my old lady a good bath, I've got to get her wrinkles out."

The lad blushed and smiled.

"You think I'm kidding you," said Lenny

The lad didn't know what to make of him, he just kept stabbing away with his finger at the till keyboard. The baskets now empty, Lenny said, "Well son that's it, I suppose you want some money now?" the lad nodded.

"Well I've got no money on me, so what can we do about that?"

The lad looked nervous and agitated.

"I can't do anything about that, Sir."

"I'm fascinated with your accent, are you local son? Does your family live in the village?" said Lenny

"Yes, I'm from these parts, are you, Sir?"

Lenny stopped to think about the answer,

"No son, I don't come from around here, I'm just visiting. Here, I was only pulling your leg," said Lenny, placing down a wad of notes on the counter from which he promptly counted out the amount needed. The lad looked relieved and offered to help Lenny carry the booze to the car. After a short struggle Lenny opened the boot, and placed the boxes into the vehicle, Lenny pushed down the lid of the boot, "Bloody hell!" he said, shocked, the lad had been there all the time. He watched him running his hands along the bodywork of the Jag.

"You fancy one of these son?" Lenny asked.

"Sure do," said the lad.

"You passed your test then?" said Lenny.

"Last August, and first time," he said proudly.

"Well Laddie, next time I'm in the village, I'll let you have a go in it."

Slamming the door shut he wound down the window smiling at the boy's surprised face. He beckoned the lad over, "Here."

Lenny winked and pressed a fiver into his hand, leaving the boy looking gobsmacked at the gesture as the car zoomed off.

On his return to the house, Lenny was surprised to see the Hoover standing in the hall, the place looked so tidy, windows open, the curtains blowing gently in the breeze, fresh coffee was on the boil and the house seemed to have come alive in his absence. He nodded with acknowledgement at Tommy's efforts. He could hear Tommy using the phone in the lounge.

"Crafty sod, he's got his old patter back by the sounds of his performance," he muttered, poking his head round the door, he gestured silently to Tommy that he needed help.

Shortly afterwards Tommy came to help him unload the drinks.

"Well mate we haven't got much time," he said and smiled "I've booked two girls and they'll be down the motorway this afternoon."

Slipping a bag onto the floor, Lenny looked up grinning,

"You're bloody kidding, Christ that was quick; You

didn't say we're desperate did you?" He laughed, "And I also hope they're not fat mate, otherwise you'll be fucking knackered by the time this is over," he said, "Because you won't see my arse for dust, are you listening to me, Tommy?"

"Look this is nothing like you imagine, just wait and see, times have changed, and you're not screwing their grandmothers you know. I said we'd meet them off the motorway at four o'clock this afternoon, right, so don't worry. Come let's finish unloading."

Lenny opened the boot,

"Jesus Christ, there's enough here to get pissed on for a year."

Tommy said with a laugh. Tommy, his arms full of bottles, walked back to the house with Lenny trooping after him. On their return to the car the phone sounded, Lenny moved to answer it.

"Don't bother," said Tommy, "That will probably be for me anyway, I'll answer it, carry on."

A short time later, Lenny heard Tommy whispering down the phone, he listened, but couldn't make out all that was said. Stepping back out of view, Lenny started to think back to the earlier conversation.

"He's up to something. That crafty sod's been busy all right." He muttered. Moving away from the door, he rattled the bottles, the sound of which made Tommy lift his voice on the phone.

Later Tommy entered the Kitchen,

"This is the lot, where do you want it?"

"Leave it on the floor, I'll see to it in a minute, who was that on the phone?" asked Lenny.

"On the phone? Oh! that was Frank."

"Frank, Frank? Which Frank?"

"Our Frank, Frank Boxer from the firm."

"Ringing here? Have you gone mad, how'd he know

where to find us, where'd he get the number from?"

Tommy went very quiet for a moment,

"Tommy for Christ's sake answer me, how did he get our number, did you tell him?"

"Well, yes I've been in touch with him; He wants to visit next week. I said I'd speak to you first and then I'd let him know, apparently everyone thinks we went abroad, Lenny, what do you think of that, eh?"

Tommy cringed, expecting a broadside from his pal. Instead, Lenny said, "You are a crafty sod, Tommy, you've fixed it, and you've been and fixed it. Have you told him about the job? Bloody hell that's what this is about, ain't it? It's obvious that I can't stop you or change your mind on this one, but I'm warning you, Tommy, you'd better know what you are dealing with here. Look, in future, I want to know what's going on or I'm off, do you hear me, Tommy?"

"Yes, I hear you mate. Thanks anyway, I'd hoped you'd understand, but things have been happening rather fast, it will be all right, just wait and see."

Tommy hugged Lenny, "Anyway, let's get on shall we?" he said.

Together they continued to tidy the house and by 3.15 pm they were in the jag driving down to the village. Relief and happiness was evident on both their faces, they were nervous about meeting the two girls, but under the surface, both remained quietly confident about the coming rendezvous. The last few hours had been hectic and neither had stopped to think through the consequences of their actions. Not once did they question their attitude towards women. They expected things to happen at the flick of a finger; well after all, they were paying good money for the service.

On their journey neither had shown much excitement, the drive down was uneventful. It was typical of what they had both expected. A meeting off the motorway, where two very attractive women waited in a chauffeur-driven car for the men to arrive. Business is what the girls would call it, just a deal arranged through an agent, not even the fee was discussed when they met just a quick handshake and the girls' luggage was soon stored away.

An hour later, Lenny turned the bend out of the village leading up to the mansion. On the journey both girls had not been slow in coming forward, question followed question and the cat and mouse intrigue began to play havoc with Tommy's thoughts.

Karen, blonde with trim figure and long legs, sported a lemon two-piece outfit with matching accessories. Toni, her companion was stretched out on the rear seat beside her, dressed in a very fetching two piece tailored suit, leaving little to the imagination; her legs were bronzed and her colouring had not gone unnoticed by the two pals, in fact, Karen's skin was fairer with an exquisite complexion. Tommy was like the proverbial man of all seasons who just kept on wriggling in his seat, already realising that Toni wasn't wearing a bra, her movements had been self-propelled and designed to excite the two men. Toni's nipples were pushed hard against the material of her garment and it was clearly noticed by Tommy that they were slightly bigger than Karen's.

"My god, what a way to find out about sex," thought Tommy.

Toni lifted her sunglasses and smiled at him.

"It seems that you boys are regarded as being very special to someone," she said, Her glasses rested back on her nose as she turned away and at that moment Tommy felt the magnetism between them, although for some unexplained reason he felt uneasy. Karen then leaned forward and stroked Lenny's neck, then whispered into his ear.

Whatever patter the girls were working, it was very good. Both men felt different in the girls' presence and the choice of partners was very much desired by both of them.

Out in the countryside and turning into another sharp bend, a police car approached from the opposite direction, a woman officer was at the wheel of the vehicle as it passed. Lenny had quickly reduced his speed as both drivers exchanged glances on passing.

"My, she looks a pretty thing for Old Bill."

Toni said, "Do you fancy women in black tights then?"

Tommy said, "No luv, just something from the past."

Shortly afterwards, Lenny turned into the driveway of the house. The girls' faces were a delight, as the questions began to shoot out like stars:

"You live here, this is your place? My god, it's beautiful," said Toni.

Both men laughed as Karen also commented on the house. An atmosphere of sheer excitement had overtaken by the girls instant love affair that began as they turned into the drive for the very first time on seeing the manor house, The temperature rose as the two men wriggled in their seats, like fish taking the bait – hook, line and sinker, as they listened to the girls' excitement, exchanging smiling glances and a flash of white teeth said it all. Lenny pulled round to the side door of the house and stopped short of the garage double doors.

"Right girls, out you both get, just follow Tommy, I'll bring your things into the house shortly," said Lenny.

Once out of the car, the girls trailed Tommy towards the side door of the house. He turned the key in the lock and entered. Moving slowly in their new surroundings, the girls could not conceal their enthusiasm any longer.

"Can we?" asked Toni, gesturing about her.

"Yeah, sure girls, you carry on and browse, we won't be a minute and then we'll join you."

Karen was already ahead of her friend as she stepped from the kitchen into the large hallway.

"Goodness me, look at the size of this Toni!"

The girls just stood in silence and wonderment, lost in their own thoughts. Highly polished floors and gleaming wall panels mirrored their reflections, Their eyes followed the contours of the delicate and intricate workmanship. The oak staircase and balcony was the centrepiece, thick carpet lay across each tread that led upwards to the landing.

A change seemed to be taking place, a real feeling of femininity floated with the fragrance and aroma of perfume that scented the air as the girls continued to twist and turn, their eyes reaching to the four points of the compass in their inquisitiveness.

Glancing over her shoulder, Toni saw the two men engaged in whispers below, their luggage having been left on the kitchen floor. It was at that moment that her eyes met Tommy's her mouth slightly open as she looked down as if to utter words. Clearing his throat loudly, Tommy was the first to move, bringing the girls luggage from the kitchen. Lenny followed as they both headed towards the stairs as the girls looked down.

"Come on girls, we'll show you your rooms," said Tommy.

"It's beautiful," said Toni, as her hand reached for the bannister rail.

The two couples disappeared into the upper reaches of the house. For a time the house remained strangely quiet, the hall clock ticked and time went by, the only other noises to be heard was the sound of muffled voices and soft music.

By early evening both couples had made their introductions, each supported a drink as they sat together in the lounge. With drifting conversation and Lenny topping up their glasses, they were well on the way to being plastered before the night was out. Laughter was soon to follow as the drink began to take effect. Tommy stood suddenly, wanting to show the girls his old war wound. As he gave a cheeky smile in the girls' direction, in doing so he reached up to pull off his shirt. Having failed with his first attempt to undo his sleeve buttons, he found his head buried in the neck of the shirt, struggling and unstable on his feet, he then became frustrated by his own actions. Pulling hard, the shirt ripped exposing a very hairy armpit.

Amazed by his actions, both girls turned to each other, rolling with laughter; Lenny bemused by Tommy's behaviour. Toni was the first to move, standing; she reached out to free the material, at the same time Tommy leant forward slightly and in doing so his shirt came apart at the seams. Standing and cursing, with his shirt in tatters, he fell back into the armchair, grabbing Toni by the waist as he fell.

Now hysterical with laughter, Karen joined in the fun. Grabbing a cushion she threw it across the room, skimming over the top of Toni's head, as she lay splayed out across Tommy. Karen went to make a sudden move to retrieve the cushion and Lenny was quick to act, rushing forward as she tried to reach the cushion, laughter rang out as the breathless pair playfully fought each other. Stopping in her tracks Karen turned in Lenny's arms, his grip supported her weight as her hands cupped his cheeks, she kissed him full on the lips and the sudden surge of her passion left him gasping for air as they both slid to the floor. His hand travelled down her back and caressed her bottom, turning, she strained her eyes towards Tommy and Toni, and then she moved her face under Lenny's. Now entwined in his arms, she gently kissed him, his weight now upon her as he nibbled along the nape of her neck. The effects of the drink were now taking over as Karen lay back exhausted from their playing and blinded by the ceiling light.

"God, I can't breathe, boy oh! boy, my heads swimming," she murmured.

They both stirred and sat up, Karen's hands moved around her body as she rearranged her clothing. Lenny was all smiles as he stood and helped Karen to her feet;

she turned away from the other couple now engrossed in their own emotions.

"Boy, Oh! Boy, that was nice while it lasted," she said smiling.

Squeezing her hand, Lenny whispered,

"Come on off to bed, I'll tell the others."

Holding the nape of her neck and rubbing, Karen walked towards the hallway, stopping to remove her shoes.

Just sounds of kisses could be heard as he turned and left the room.

On reaching Karen, he slid an arm around her waist and took hold of the bannister as they both climbed the stairs. On the landing, they kissed gently, lips, ears and neck, Lenny forced back her head as his passed under her chin and still she clung to him. Without any hesitation, Lenny lifted her into his arms and swept her off to his room, and laid her down on the bed. Stumbling to one side, he fell onto the bed next to her. The room was quiet as the two lay momentarily still.

Minutes later Karen lifted and swung her legs off the bed, and then turned to view her partner sprawled out with his toes touching the floor. Going to the en-suite bathroom, Karen emerged wearing a pair of briefs and a 'T' shirt. During her absence, Lenny had attempted to remove his trousers and pants the lay twisted around his ankles, exposing a naked bottom, which stared Karen in the face. She turned and went out onto the landing. The house was now in total darkness. She couldn't call her friends for assistance and felt uncomfortable in the big rambling house. She quickly returned to the bedroom. Lenny was again fast asleep. Leaning over him, Karen slid the shirt from his body. She took off his shoes, pants and trousers. Grabbing his wrists, she tried to pull him into a vertical position.

At her touch, Lenny began to wriggle and twist in his sleep. Karen was really fed up and she sat perplexed on the bed wondering what to do next. Staring down at her naked companion, she ran her fingers down his spine and over his shoulders hoping he would wake, but Lenny remained motionless. Feeling more frustrated than angry on their first night together, Karen went to her makeup bag and returned to Lenny's side. His lily white buttocks were like the outlines of a small peach, neat, round and with a narrow crease. Choosing a maroon lipstick, she gently drew two eyes, one on each cheek of his bum, eyebrows underneath the waistline and big ears on both thighs. Finishing with a green lipstick, she signed her name across his back. Gently she manoeuvred him from the bed onto the floor, placing pillows under his head and a cover over his body before leaving his side for the comfort of the bed. She lay between the covers and dreamed of the day's events, patting the outer cover against the outline of her body.

Karen drifted off to sleep and then stirred, trying to remain awake awhile longer, but slowly sleep overcame her.

During early hours, clumsy stirring and the presence of another awakened her. The room in darkness, she listened without moving, her heart racing as she felt fumbling hands reach out and grasp her waist. Lenny had appeared from off the floor.

Half awake, she turned towards him; he struggled to come closer to her side. He continued to pull at her carelessly and Karen became annoyed with the way she was being handled. Lenny, like a mole burrowing deep, found a resting place for his head in the shape and comfort of Karen's stomach. She felt the warmth and gentle pressure upon her, his deep breaths tickled the hairs on her legs. His hand pushed and glided up her leg to her waist and his lips caressed a nipple through the material of her 'T' shirt. Now, gentle with each touch, Karen felt moisture seep through the material and dampen her skin. Karen used her fingers to touch his head. Gently she ran her fingers through his hair. Her feelings were on fire with each sucking motion upon her nipple. She felt her muscles tense from the tips of her toes and pushed back to lie fully outstretched. Lenny released one breast only to move to the other. Karen remained still, waiting in anticipation. Lenny continued to be eager, drawing on the pinnacle of Karen's femininity. She lay bewitched by his movements, his drooling lips wetting her 'T' shirt, as with each touch she drew the heel of her foot back and forth, pressing deep into the mattress. A calm feeling ran through her body, through every nerve ending as the nipples hardened. His hand continued to work around her waist and side, up to her armpit, his fingers searching and stroking over her warm flesh as he moved further up her body, Karen smelt the fragrance of 'Yves Saint Laurent', waft into her nostrils as her hand floated down his back slowly caressing his body. Her hand became greasy, and she didn't realise that with each movement she was smudging her drawing in makeup upon his back.

Lenny had slipped further down the mattress. Wiping the grease from her hands on the sheet, she moved back to her partner, but only the sounds of his sleepy contentment could be heard. She lay for a few moments wondering if he would stir once more from his overwhelming desire for sleep, his sighs and rasps became a rhythm of entrapment, her eyes fluttered to stay awake in the darkened room but slowly she lost her fight against the demands of nature and she soon drifted off to sleep.

CHAPTER FOUR
Body Talk

Waking at 8.30am the next morning, Karen, her mouth dry, gulped to moisten her throat as she stirred and pushed back against the quilted pillows. Leaning on her right elbow, Karen blinked in the darkened room and looked down at Lenny on the pillow next to her. It was then that Karen caught the short sniffs of stale alcohol seeping in bubbled bursts from between Lenny's lips. Unable to tolerate anything quite so unromantic from her partner, she quietly slipped from beneath the covers. Karen stretched, and then pulled the crusty 'T' shirt from her breasts, falling off balance as she did so. Her fingers at the time were ruffling through her hair as she jutted forwards. She fell sideways; her hands reached out and sunk deep into the mattress at the edge of the bed. She looked for any signs of life from Lenny. Her body arched forward as she rubbed her chin across her breast bone to relieve the pressure on her neck and shoulders, her head turned sideways under her long, blonde, flowing hair as her eyes sought the light through her fringe. Through the curtain faint strips of daylight reflected on the bedside table. She moved towards the light, quietly slipping behind the furthest drape, which wrapped around the contours of her body, sealing the light from entering the darkened bedroom. Karen felt the morning glow upon her body as she gazed out over the landscape of lawned gardens hedged in woodland and thicket. The sunshine swept over the rooftop like the flashing blade of a swordsman, thrusting here and there amongst the branches of nearby trees.

Already the day looked perfect, a day of dreams. She could see a rabbit, and a bird swooping low to gather lift before reaching high into a tree to perch. Fascinated by the sheer delight of the morning, Karen stood tip-toe with both hands pressed against the glass. In a contented manner, she stepped back, leaving two beautiful palm prints moistened to the glass.

She fumbled for the ensuite bathroom on the opposite side of the room and entered the spacious surroundings. A sunken bath sat just below a large window that reached down to the floor, with three steps positioned between the upper and lower floors. Wall mounted polished shelves were fitted at each end of the bath, with ornaments displayed at all levels. Fitted lemon carpet throughout colour-matched the roller blinds over the window, the bath and vanity units were feint orange ochre, with matching hand basin, bidet and toilet set in a cream surround and trimmed in varnished woodwork.

Karen's curiosity overcame her as she began to peek amongst the fitted cabinets, cupboards and drawers – was she to find the signs of another woman? The cologne and deodorants were of a man's taste, all the signs belonged to Lenny. She smiled at the result.

She then tiptoed back into the bedroom to get her things. Stripping off her 'T' shirt and briefs, she rummaged naked and gathered a few thing of her own. Before returning to the bathroom, the bath water rippled at the surface as she took hold of her long blonde tresses, clipping a rubber band around the ends to form a ponytail. Leaning back she placed the nape of her neck on the rim of the bath, wallowing in the warmth that lapped her body.

Her hands lathered her breasts and midriff as she squeezed out the soap bubbles through her fingers. Up and down her hands continued to glide over her skin, until finally, she submerged up to her neck in the water.

Sliding back over the contours of the bath, her head came to rest on the edge, looking up; the steam bloom had gone from the mirrored tiles on the ceiling. Only occasional wisps of vapour could be seen rising from the surface. Karen enjoyed the moment as her eyes closed and relaxed in the quietness and beauty of her surroundings.

Karen heard a swishing noise and suddenly Lenny appeared, crawling commando style through the open door, stark naked his backside in the air. She clasped a hand to her mouth to suppress her laughter as a pair of eyes she had drawn earlier on his backside were rather smudged, she pretended that she hadn't noticed him enter.

Lenny was unaware of Karen's artistic flair as to what she had drawn on his buttocks, the distortion of the two eyes she had drawn earlier moved more in a drunken slur with each movement of his legs as he crawled further across the floor towards the bath. Karen held her composure for as long as possible until she screamed aloud as Lenny jumped to his feet, the sudden move made Karen lose her grip and slipped down under the water line. Lenny was quick to the rescue. With both hands he plucked her from the depths of the bath, lifting her to a sitting position. Gasping for air in her excitement, she was only too pleased for the assistance.

Lenny wiped her eyes with a towel, while he supported her neck. Karen responded by taking the towel from him and wiped her face; finally, she emerged with a smile. He apologised quickly amidst her coughing and spluttering as she regained her composure. Karen had withdrawn to the end of the bath, her head rested on her knees, she turned and faced him. Lenny was standing now and she admired his nakedness. Karen moved her legs and indicated for him to join her in the bath. Sitting on the rim, he twisted and turned, Karen laughed aloud. Lenny couldn't understand the reason for her laughter until he saw her pointed finger,

"What – What's the matter?" he said.

"Look at that, what is it?" she said laughing

Lenny stood up and turned; coloured streaks were around the rim of the bath.

"It's off your bum."

"Did you do this?"

Karen nodded in response.

"Bloody hell, how'd you do it then?" he reached out towards her with a hand painted in rainbow colours, at the same time he laughed and shook his head in disbelief.

"I really don't believe this, I really don't."

"Well that will teach you to fall asleep when you're with me – it just happened on the spur of the moment, I couldn't resist the opportunity." She continued to laugh throughout.

"Well, I'm sorry for that, but how can I get this stuff off?" Lenny replied.

"With soap and flannel."

"And that's all?"

"Yes – Hurry up and get in the bath, here catch."

She threw a soapy flannel onto his buttocks and rubbed hard, at the same time he dropped over the side of the bath, splashing water everywhere. Karen let out a shriek as water spilt onto the floor.

Lenny continued to rub his buttocks, and at the same time leant forward towards her. Sitting back on his haunches, Lenny remained still as he stared into her face, as he again shook his head gently from side to side.

"You little sod," he then whispered.

Without warning, he lunged for her and she let out a scream.

"Oh! God," she cried.

Lenny laughed and said, "He won't help you mate."

Suddenly down in the water, he remained still, Karen had opened one squinting eye in his direction, Lenny remained with his head at an angle looking up into her face, he gave a crafty wink but remained staring into her face, she felt the intensity of his eyes on her, flutter's of excitement returned and stimulated her mind.

"Why is he staring like this?" she thought.

Feeling coy and embarrassed by his mannerisms and the deep stare he gave, she responded in the same way. Their eyes met, Lenny was enchanted, her beauty and exquisite complexion, but she nudged him in the chest with an elbow as his eyes continued to scrutinise her.

"Oy, what are your doing down there?" she said.

"What?"

"Stop it."

He just grinned when finally he moved and sat up.

"God you're a beautiful woman, do you know that?"

Her gaze upon him was fixed and the outlines of her face were soft but she gave no reply.

"Did you hear me?" he said

"Mmmm, I heard you, Lenny."

He placed his lips onto the lobe of her ear and sucked and nuzzled her flesh, a hand lay across her chest, and with one hand she rubbed his arm in contentment, Lenny continued on her lobe and neckline, then straining himself he reached the point of her chin, Karen moved her head towards him.

Moving further up the bath, Lenny took hold of her head and gently pulled her towards him, his tongue running over her eyelids, nose and mouth.

She pushed her lips hard against his, long and lingering the kiss remained, quivering and trembling in eagerness. Her eyes flickered open and shut as she felt the pressure and gasped for air. Pulling away, he followed as her eyes looked deep into his face, he was smooth skinned around his eyes, nose and was shaped by the crow's feet that gave him the extraordinary masculine character that she so admired.

She ruffled his wet, flattened hair. He then slipped from her grasp as his lips moved down onto her breasts. She felt his legs move and tremble as her fingers ran up and down his spine to the nape of the neck. As she slipped her palm down between his legs, laying her head flat on his pubic line, the tips of her fingers tingling.

Lenny had already placed his hand down onto her flat tummy as she arched her back. Karen without pubic hair, a practice she had long adopted as she was meticulous about her hygiene and appearance, and this was one area which remained bare for as long as she could remember. She was thinking that Lenny was certainly good for his age, tender, a good kisser; my he can really turn it on but bugger the bath, let's get out of here. Taking hold of his balls, she gingerly fondled his scrotum sack below the waterline.

Lenny continued on and on and around her body when he finally moved back a little exhausted from his efforts,

"Blimey girl, I do ache."

"I thought you were having your dinner down there."

"You did – well it tasted nice to me kid."

"God you bloody men."

"And what's that supposed to mean?"

He pushed himself into a sitting position, Karen's eyes were mesmerized.

"What's that floating down there?" she said, Laughing, her hand slowly reached out and took hold of his penis, which had burst to the surface of the bathwater like the periscope of a submarine, she took hold of his wrinkled penis.

"Hey do you mind girl – Gordon Bennett, that feels nice."

As he pushed his pelvis towards her clenched hand, Karen took the tip of the foreskin and gently pulled it from the water, then flop, she let go, repeating it twice more, watching in silence.

"Fascinating, don't you think Lenny?"

He looked down at his bobbing penis now shrunk even more and a fraction of its full manhood size.

"Do you know I've never taken much notice of it before, it's such a small thing that does a lot of damage in relationships? but small is beautiful especially when you watch it grow and harden right before your eyes, lovely ain't it, no woman would miss this for the world," he said, being somewhat serious in the beginning which widened to an eventual big grinning smile as he looked into her face.

Karen had by then turned staring at him with a frown, realising that their feelings and arousals had subsided. Lenny was the first to move,

"Come on sunshine, give me your hand."

Reaching out he gently pulled Karen from the water. Turning he was the first to step onto the floor. Still holding her hand, he watched as she followed him, he reached for the large set of towels, Karen half turned as he clutched a towel to his chest, using it with his head bent forward over his knees as he rubbed hard at the wet hair. She fumbled and rubbed her body from within the confines of the wrapped towel, then moving to Lenny's side she leant over him as he watched her approach, their lips met full on, Karen pushed down hard as he slowly fell backwards onto the carpeted floor. As they kissed their passions ignited. Lenny reached out and pulled her to the floor, at the same time, pulling the towel from her throbbing breasts, and she fell forwards on top of him, their hot naked flesh gripping together. She placed her hands on either side of his shoulders as they looked into each other's eyes. His smiling face greeted her stare as their eyes met and melted in each other's glances until their lips met once more. Then slowly he placed his tongue on the rim of one ear, tantalising her, round and in, he followed down onto her lobe. Karen twisted and turned from his grip, her taut muscles rippling. Pulling away she rolled onto her back. Lenny followed and hovered over her as his eyes reached the contours of her breasts, his legs and torso moved across her. He ran his tongue down the length of her body between her breasts, over her flat stomach and over the shaved pouting mount of her pubes. Her legs opened wide, waiting with ultimate feelings leaving him unrestricted to explore further, down and down he continued, his tongue flicking and darting into her barren moistened area that responded by relaxing the found opening for his tongue. Unable to resist she reached out to pull on his shoulders, her panting became louder and moved with greater skill. Her whole body was now moist from the perspiration that gave her flesh a glistened sheen from the sunlight that angled through the long window of the bathroom. Unable to control herself her legs spread wider as he pushed further the tip of his tongue deep into to her pulsating vagina, darting between her inflamed lips she grew wetter, hot and wet, the aroma of sex filling the room. Karen rocked and swayed her legs from side to side to encourage him to enter her as his face was touching her moistened open vagina. She couldn't control herself any longer as she trapped Lenny's head between her thighs. He moved with her as he felt the pressure upon his ears. With a sweating body and aching jaw, he used his full weight to push open and part her thighs as he climbed above her. Lenny arrived with passionate kisses to her lips; again he could hear the soft whispers and murmurs seeping from her in between the kisses. Finally, she turned panting.

"God, I can't breathe," she whispered

Suddenly she reached the point of no return. She pushed her body up, she arched her back crying out as she lost all control, her buttocks raised even higher off the floor, she bucked and bucked as Lenny thrust deep into her as his torso was humping her hard and fast as he held and pulled on her shoulders so their bodies came hard together with each pushing motion, his lips reached round to the side of her face as he whispered to her,

"Go on, let it go, darling, let it go don't wait for me, go on let it flow pleaseeeeeeeeeeee do it and I'll catch up, we will ride together you see, I am with you babe, go on it's time for a good hard fuck to remember, let the juices flow."

Their sweating bodies glued tight and rocking together both in full flights with hard animal noises pulsating from both their lips. Sweat sucked and smacked as their bodies came together and parted time and time again. He whispered encouragement as he finally spurted into her from his hooded stiff member placed deep into her pudendum as both their pubes ground together on their bones. Karen felt the deep rush of warmth from him as she felt that sudden orgasmic flutter herself at that moment that warbled her voice in absolute delight with lots of screams as she gripped him tight not wanting to let him go. She lifted her legs and wrapped them around his waist so as not to loosen his grip on her as he continued to thrust in and out moving like a steam rollers piston, as he tried to move back onto his knees straining and lifting Karen off the floor, at the same time they were both stuck together, sweating profusely by this time in what appeared to be in buckets as both their faces were like the colour of beetroot, just an incredible performance thought Lenny as he made his final thrust into her as he was done all in as they both lay together panting and gasping for air after such a sexual experience with aching muscles to remind them both of their first encounter together, with light relief they both momentarily laughed as they stared into each other's faces. Eventually now both calm from the experience, Lenny turned on his side and cuddled up as Karen threw an arm over his side to acknowledge her satisfaction as they continued to lay on the floor of the bathroom. Lenny had pushed a towel under Karen's head whilst lying on her back she had bent and drawn her legs back towards her body, both still naked and neither ready to make the first move to get up and dress. After some while, Lenny placed a hand over Karen's pubes and cupped her vagina area it was then that he slipped a finger into her deposit and felt the warmth of her silky lining as he gently stroked her inner flesh that was so moist to touch as some of her juices seeped from her. Moving, Lenny was not ready to get up and leave, as Karen began to wriggle on his touch as her mind was swimming with emotions as he turned onto his knees and leant over her as he indicated to Karen that he was ready to go again as she saw the stiff hardness appear and grow, she opened her legs as Lenny moved into between as his member was swinging about with his movement, Karen reached down and took charge and guided him towards her, she prodded her opening and widened her legs as she guided him to her. Lenny came over her and gripped one of her buttocks, gripping firmly he moved slowly as he teased her inner strength and still pulling on her buttock he began to move with a greater momentum as he gathered more rhythm to his thrusting. Karen was rather surprised that Lenny was going again, as he was pumping her and when suddenly his whole body stiffened and arched as he reached his climax for the second time that morning. Karen felt the warmth seeping into her filling, and she realised that many years had passed since she had such an experience with such intense feelings that gripped her in every way imaginable as she lay perplexed by Lenny's energy as she felt so weak and so relaxed in her demeanour. Lenny rolled over onto his back and Karen felt his weight move from hers, the sounds once again of her heart beat still pounded in her ears. Eventually, she stood up slowly, shaking her head in the process as her ponytail fell over her shoulders. Lenny remained on the floor admiring and soaking up Karen's movements, her long legs, her flat toned stomach, was the femininity that he had just fucked and fucked hard as he remained in disbelief of his own actions and the lucky man he was. Lenny eventually stood up and joined Karen as he gently rocked her backwards and forwards with his cuddles, at the same time the bath tap had been turned on to warm up the water as she took advantage of bathing alone as she broke from Lenny's clutches, he sat and waited until she had finished before he too entered the water to wipe the perspiration from his flesh.

Karen had moments earlier clambered from the bath and walked into the bedroom; she rummaged through her suitcase from which she took a red and black striped pair of lace briefs. Stepping into them, she stood flexing her legs as she pulled on the material; her fingers ran around her inner thigh as she pulled out the lace front.

Lenny finally emerged from the bathroom, she stood topless as she faced him and placed her arms around his neck.

Whispering, he said, "What can I say – fantastic, beautiful, wonderful, and I want more and more of you."

Karen listened and smiled at his every word. Lenny turned her by the waist and moved her back onto the bed, whispering again; "look I don't know what you're thinking, but it was fantastic, my mind has blown a fuse. I' knackered and my bleeding legs are like jelly, they won't stop shaking, here you feel," he laughed patting a leg. She smiled liking his sense of humour.

"Honestly, it's been a bloody long time since I've made love, and when Tommy said you were both coming down on an arrangement, I didn't know what to expect. The point is, I've had butterflies in my stomach since you arrived, right here (he touched his tummy) I don't mind admitting it, but I was bloody scared. I've never felt like this before and it's bloody stupid for a bloke of my age. You are a beautiful creature, a real cracker and well, I know you work for an escort agency, but it don't bother me that Tommy had a favour done him."

Karen said, "Lenny you don't have to say anything, we came down on business, don't worry about it, please it's just a..."

Lenny quickly interrupted her, "I know, I know, but I want you to understand that my love making was for real, it wasn't a case of a good bunk-up, I could have got that anywhere, I wouldn't have bothered with you if I didn't fancy you. Look, I wasn't making love to a robot or a cold fish, you were alive, we came together like we did, it was real. I couldn't have made a better choice. I'm not just thinking of you as a piece of meat for a good fuck. Oh! Christ I'm screwing this up, I can't get it out, you've got in there and in there do you hear me (he pointed to his head and heart) you were brilliant and like I said, I want more and more of you."

He reached out and ran his fingers through her hair and traced her facial contours as he rubbed the tips over her lips,

"What more can I say, except you were very loving to me and I want to thank you for sharing your feelings with me. I'm sorry, I don't know what to expect."

Lenny leant over and kissed her lightly on the lips, she touched his cheek as she gazed into his eyes, a faint smile as she looked on in bewilderment, lost for words.

"I don't know what to say, Lenny," she said after a long quiet moment.

He still held her tightly.

"I'm sorry, you've taken the wind out my sails, I didn't expect this, it just happened," she added. "I felt very different, strange if you like, I can't explain, but it happened it I just felt that moment of total freedom, I suppose that's how all women would like it to be. It just happened, what with the house and the quietness of our surroundings, I suppose it was the perfect setting for love making. I don't know, my escort work is mainly for dinners, I don't get laid on every date, in fact, I really don't give myself like this to anyone, it has to be right for me and it ended up being right for both of us."

Lenny again interrupted,

"Shhhh, don't say any more, let's just chill."

"Well I want you to know that our love making was good for me too, I needed that as I got something from it, well it wasn't one-sided was it, I wanted it to happen as much as you and boy what a good fuck we had," she said laughing,

"No wait, it's your life, so don't explain on my part, it's really got fuck all to do with me, I don't want you to humble yourself on my account, do you hear me, that's not what I want."

Tears ran down her cheeks as she listened to him.

"Hey, come on kid, I haven't done or said this to hurt or upset you, that's not what this is about, I am in my own way trying to say thank you. Something happened in there and the chemistry was spot on it was a beautiful experience for me and it's something that I'll never forget, do you hear me, it was a very special moment, come on let's finish up here."

"I'm sorry, I've never felt like this either, I'm confused," she sobbed, "and I don't know why and I don't normally talk about sex with any partner. It's never happened like this before, so stupid, I just do it like anybody else and then the man rolls off and goes to sleep, and that's what happens to couples. But to discuss it, never. I never thought a fella would bother, once the grunts and groans were over, but you're different Lenny and in so many ways, soft and gentle and more."

"Hold on a minute sunshine, look, it's the way you are and feel, so don't knock yourself."

"I'm not, you found a soft spot, you turned the key at the right time in my life and I can't explain it but your actions were different. Course, I've had boyfriends like any other girl, I wasn't a virgin when I came here yesterday, but like I've said you were very gentle with me, not like a bull in a China shop, you bothered and cared in the way you touched me and that showed, the way you held me, that's hard to find in a man, I've never made it like this before and twice at that (she smiled) Last night when you carried me into your room, I expected something to happen, then when you fell asleep I just couldn't believe it. I was beginning to think you didn't like me. You pushed my button, Lenny. Do you know it's funny when you think it through, but many women often talk about that personal feeling that we're supposed to feel as women, the big 'O' and yet many go lifetimes without experiencing that lovely warm heavenly feeling that you don't want to go away. It's very special to me and not to anyone else, your seed is now deep inside me and you've done something to me, I wanted it to happen, I made that choice by being here and I took it with you – look, Lenny, sex is so bloody easy with men, but loving is something else that comes with one's feelings and emotions at the time,"

Lenny nodded in agreement.

I'm happy Lenny, I really am and I'm also a quiver, my legs are shaking too, what do you make of that?"

As they laughed together, Karen reached down to touch her leg. Lenny's hand followed as he placed it over her hand and kissed her.

"And I thought it was middle age," he said.

Karen's face suddenly changed to one of surprise.

"Oh! Quick Lenny pass me a tissue,"

He stretched over to the side table nearby and pulled on the open box, Karen took hold of the tissue and pushed up her buttocks as she tucked a handful of tissue into her briefs. Lenny watched in astonishment and said,

"Goodness me, love does have its handicaps."

"What goes up must come down," she said with a coy look.

"Do you know, I've never given that a thought?"

"Why should you, most men have no idea about it?"

"No daft, it's a long time since I saw a woman do that."

"Oh! I see, you are serious then at what you've just said?" turning and flashing her bright green eyes at him.

She looked into his face and waited for him to respond.

"I am serious about what I said, it's been a long time for me, I haven't been with a woman in years and I really mean that, it's just something that's been taken for granted."

Using two fingers he gave a 'Benny Hill' boy scout salute, Karen screeched aloud and gently pushed him, "You silly sod Lenny." She said.

"God a virgin, I didn't know that such a man existed in this day and age."

"Bloody cheek, do you mind? Look, it's just that time has passed me by; mind you I've had my moments in the past you know. Yes, sure, and the heartbreaks that go with it, but no-one to settle down with. It never got really serious, that's how it was in my day."

But Karen noted a slight wobble in his voice,

"No regrets Lenny," she said quietly as she held the tissue in place, "You do surprise me, though. I would have taken you for being married or divorced – sorry I'm prying now and I shouldn't, it's none of my business – You're a nice man though, you're sensitive. God you make me feel so different, I can't believe this is happening to me," she turned and cuddled him. She felt his loneliness as she gazed up into his eyes.

"Come on kid, let's get downstairs for some breakfast."

Moving away from the bed, they dressed in silence. Lenny was unaware of hidden glances that she sneaked whilst he rummaged on the floor for his lost socks as he couldn't be bothered to find a clean pair from somewhere. Karen remained watching as she buttoned the front of her pink silk blouse, then she stretched as she ran her fingers through her hair,

"How do I look Lenny?"

He turned and looked up from his kneeling position.

"Bloody hell girl, you're everything I said you were. Christ, I could screw you till the cows come home, I really could. Hey, I'll tell you what, let's skip breakfast and stay up here.

"What about the others, there'll be waiting for us."

"Yeah, I suppose so," said Lenny.

Karen's face was radiant and unblemished; her green eyes sparkled in the morning sun. They finished dressing and together they left the room. As they descended the stairs faint sounds of music could be heard from below. Entering the kitchen in the direction of the music, they were taken by surprise when shouts and applause from Toni and Tommy echoed out.

"Christ, at long last, we thought we'd lost you both."

"Why what's the matter with you?" said Lenny

"Time, the clock," said Tommy.

"Yeah so what?" said Lenny laughing.

"It's half eleven that's all."

"Christ it's not. Is it really? Bloody hell,"

Lenny turned and grinned at Karen. Toni had taken the coffee pot and stood pouring into the mugs now ready on the kitchen table.

"Sleep well?"

She directed her words to Karen.

"Mmmm lovely, it's so quiet here," she gestured with a shrug as she looked around her and gave Toni an 'O' signal (thumb & finger) with her hand.

CHAPTER FIVE
Birds And Bees

During the early afternoon, both couples walked in the grounds, taking the path which led from the rear porch to the copse and the spinney beyond. Lenny carried a bag containing wine and glasses as surprise refreshment for the afternoon's break. Reaching the boundary fence, they each pressed against it, looking out over the valley below.

Since leaving the house neither girl had spoken, Suddenly Karen twisted around and faced the way they had come, it was as if she were mesmerised and was waiting to be pinched and woken from a dream. She could see the mansion rooftop through the trees and turned to glance once more at the tall lean man beside her those tender moments with Lenny engraved on her memory. It seemed too good to be true, and she reached out and took Lenny's waist tightly, laying her cheek on his chest. Lenny reacted with a smile as he looked down at her.

Gradually, Tommy and Toni became untangled from each other's arms, as the group moved down to the wooden stile. Lenny was the first to point the way and said,

"No, this way, let's go down by the river."

Ambling down across the meadow, each couple entwined as they continued to cuddle and whisper. They reached the river bank at the bottom of the valley. Birds dived around the water's edge, a pair of moorhens flashed over the rippling surface and vanished into the safety of the water reeds.

Karen and Lenny remained by the old water trough perched on the rim, with legs outstretched. Tommy and Toni strolled down to the riverbank and were soon out of sight.

Basking in the hot afternoon sunshine, Karen pouted

and blew cool air up over her face; wisps of hair danced and flickered from the uplift that caught her fringe. Her eyes remained closed as she rolled her head from side to side.

Lenny remained close from where he sat he stared towards the flowing water and felt unusually at peace in the tranquil setting. Lenny whispered to Karen, and she turned to cup his face. For a man of his age, she found him to be very handsome, with light brown hair to his shoulders, the hairline receding just slightly at the temples and sweeping back at the front with a soft curve. Karen manoeuvred herself onto the side of the trough, Lenny took this opportunity to move closer, his feet raised dust from the ground as he stood and moved up against her, his body nudging her legs apart as he moved between her thighs. Placing his hand around her back in support, he stroked her thigh through her jeans. Wriggling provocatively, she pressed her weight against him, looping her arm around his neck with her fingers locked. Lenny moved from her thigh to her waist line and slipped his hand inside her jeans. He pulled out her silk blouse and caressed the nubs of her spine. Her skin warm and soft to his touch. He undid the buttons of her blouse and took the pink buds of her nipples one after the other into his mouth. She trembled from the sensation and pulled him tight towards her. Lenny was already sweating and panting in the warm sun. Her full breasts were round and petite, the nipples standing out firm and erect. She gripped hard at his shirt and dug deep into his flesh as he repeated the action. The smell of arousal was wafting from her exposed flesh and Karen took control, stopping Lenny in his tracks by crushing him against her body. The pressure stifled Lenny; her hands were everywhere as her fingers pummelled his flesh through his clothing.

Without warning, Lenny gave a loud gurgling scream, pulling away quickly as he slipped to the ground in pain. Karen watched, open-mouthed as he slipped from her grasp,

"God, what's wrong Lenny?" she cried in panic, clutching at her open blouse.

Lenny lay on his back in agony, and reached for his right leg, rubbing frantically,

"Oh! Christ, my bloody leg, Jesus Christ I've got bloody cramp."

He struggled to stand as Karen moved to help him. She vigorously rubbed life back into his leg. Lenny was still cursing and shouting the heavens.

"Karen, what are you doing?"

"Helping you," she said.

"Karen, it's the wrong bloody leg, it's the other, Jesus Christ!"

Karen let go as Lenny slipped back onto the ground with his leg waving in the air. Karen saw the funny side of her actions, bending forwards clutching her face; she stepped backwards out of his way.

"Oh! Bloody hell it hurts." Lenny was gritting his teeth in agony.

Dropping onto her knees, Karen looked on as Lenny continued to massage the leg. On both knees, Karen hesitantly edged towards him. He reached out and placed an arm around her back to reassure her. She remained on her knees, close by him. Finally, Lenny again tried to stand; Karen moved to support him, Lenny planted a kiss on top of her head and gave her a pat on the backside at the same time,

"Come on, let's have a drink shall we, pass me the carrier bag from the trough." He produced a bottle of wine wrapped in a sodden towel.

"I wondered why you were so secretive about the bag, " Karen said jokingly.

"Well now you know mate, this was supposed to be a surprise," said Lenny. Karen held out the two glasses whilst Lenny poured, taking their first sips together, they toasted each other.

"Well it looks like the other two have missed out," said Lenny.

"Give them a shout, they can't be far away," said Karen.

Lenny's voice echoed through the valley with no response. He repeated the call as they both looked along the riverbank. The only movement Lenny saw was the reeds swaying nearby as water rippled with the occasional dart of a bird.

"How far could they have gone?" asked Karen.

"About a quarter of a mile, that's if they walked to the boundary fence in the distance – you see where those two big trees are?" Lenny pointed. Karen nodded,

"Well that's the limit, shall we try and find them?"

"We can, they may not want us to find them though, have you thought of that?"

"Well we can't stay out here all afternoon, it's too hot, we need to find some shade," said Karen.

They strolled arm in arm together along the river bank, the air remained hot and humid, even with the clouds that cast fast moving shadows against the hillside. The sun beat down on the rapeseed growing in the opposite field, reflecting a carpet of bright yellow. With no sign of Tommy and Toni, they continued along the bank, when suddenly Karen's eye caught sight of a water rat swimming in the water, a trail of ripples followed as the creature headed for the bank. She held onto Lenny as the animal came closer. Lenny realised that her blouse remained open, bringing Karen back to the water's edge; his eyes fell on her nakedness as he turned to face her. With slow deliberate actions, he lowered his head towards her. Gently kissing her lightly on the lips, as unexpectedly Karen let out a little scream of delight, then a stifled murmur as his, strong arms grasped around her body as the kiss became more passionate. Then Lenny's mouth moved onto her cheek, ear lobe, and neckline and slowly continued down onto her right breasts. Karen remained still as she felt his lips caress the nipple. Biting her bottom lip, she looked up into the sky as Lenny tantalised her flesh. She wanted him to take her again and was relieved when they toppled slowly to the ground. Sitting astride Lenny, Karen reached behind and caressed between his legs. Her breasts were pushed outwards with her back arched. Slowly, her caresses forced from under his trousers a hardness of some quality.

Lenny was greatly aroused and cupped her breasts squeezing the firmness of flesh. They gradually rolled over and changed places on the ground, without hindering their erotic feelings. Kneeling over her, Lenny buried his lips into the left side of her neck.

Karen awkwardly unbuckled his belt, unzipped his jeans and drew his throbbing cock into her sweaty palm, her movements so erratic her nails caught against his skin.

"Christ!"

Lenny moaned out loud; she quickly apologised, showering him with kisses. But still she held him, his cock growing bigger by the moment. Lenny sensed that he ought to be doing more as he struggled to remove his jeans. Part of the passion was remaining together; Lenny was somewhat uneasy, uncomfortable and fretful as he continued to struggle in the confusion of tangled bodies.

Karen had become single-minded in her quest as she also attacked his jeans by pushing down hard with her left hand, the garment eventually reached his knees, then quickly she attacked his under pants with the same ferocity. Pulling on the elastic she exposed his manhood.

Lenny felt the elastic dig into him as he reached down and wrenched the garment from his body in haste. Sliding back onto his left shoulder, Lenny moved his right hand down to her waist, gently pulling on the zip, which slowly exposed the top of her black and red striped briefs, prising the garment away from her body. At the same time, Karen lifted her buttocks off the ground, using her right hand in conjunction with Lenny's they together slipped her jeans down from under her legs, her backside came to rest on the dusty ground. Now free, Karen felt the rush of air against her thighs and legs.

Lenny moved his right hand underneath the top of her briefs, sliding down, he tempted her feelings with dryness of his fingers, easing around her vaginal lips with extreme sensitivity, Karen's passions were more in earnest as she felt his fingers grope persistently then slowly, he pushed deeper with one finger on her clitoris, with a deliberate rhythm he felt the moistness from her inner spring lubricate his touch. Lenny was encouraged by her excitement, as her legs slowly parted. Lenny became mindful of his aching wrist and fingers from working down below when he felt Karen tug and pull at his torso. Realising that her passion would overflow without him, he edged over his lower frame between her parted thighs, pulling her briefs to one side, he pushed and entered her immediately and Karen felt his sudden hardness enter her as she let out a whimper as he prodded at her until a rhythm was acquired in tempo to the movement of their bodies.

It was Karen who had taken the initiative; she was very much a force to be reckoned with, as her loving tenderness focused on an overwhelming urge to be fulfilled by her partners. Lenny was struggling in the heat of the afternoon, when Karen, holding him tightly, whispered:

"Slowly, ahh, that's nice, gently now, darling, move slowly with me please, Oh! God that feels good yes, yes, yes keep it going please Lenny, hold me, yes hold me. Oh! God that's so nice. Roll onto your back, roll over and don't let's part Lenny, please don't."

Lenny was grunting in pleasure. Finally, from a change of position, Karen remained above as she leaned back on her loins and discarded her blouse to get totally naked. With Lenny's penetration, Karen brought her legs closer together, her muscles stretched hard against the ground, her inner contractions ran deep as she grasped Lenny's penis within her. Then, suddenly, she flung herself forwards as she reached a pulsating orgasm that oozed from her body. Lenny followed with hard bucks as he tried to stay the distance, for Karen was bent over riding furiously like a jockey as she was floating and gliding on a beautiful wave of warm passionate emotions . She thrashed and squealed out with loud cries of delight. Their lips came together in a long series of lingering kisses, which brought a final calm as the lay embracing on the dusty ground.

Exhausted, Karen moved off her partners and sat nearby with her legs drawn up, laying her head sideways as she looked down at Lenny's body, just silent he remained with closed eyes and open mouth as his chest heaved from his slow steady breathing. Karen wiped her lips back and forth across her knees, and then stood, her silhouette cut out the dark against the sunny sky as Lenny glanced up.

"I'm going for a paddle."

Lenny turned onto his side and watched the naked figure enter the water. Her voice trembled as she called out to Lenny, and the coldness of the water was a welcome relief from the hot sun. Karen allowed the ripples to glide over her shoulders as she lay and bathed alone.

Raising himself off the ground, Lenny pulled on his jeans with the legs rolled up to his knees. Moving down towards the water's edge, he stopped and watched Karen submerged in the water. She was smiling, then moving to stand waist high in the water. She beckoned him to join her, scooping water up with her hands and throwing it at him. He tried to do the same with a flick of his foot, skimming the surface; instead, he overbalanced and slipped to the ground with a thud.

Lenny was lucky not to have fallen in. With laughter,

Karen moved towards him. Stuck half on the bank, Lenny stared at Karen's incredible body, her open nakedness was a glorious site befitting any man's eyes. She was indeed a beautiful woman and he couldn't remember another time in his life when he had been so happy. Lenny continued to look on in wonderment capturing her every graceful movement as she edged towards him. It was as if he was afraid that she might disappear with a blink of the eye, to wake from some kind of dream, everything was surreal to him.

Her lithe figure drifting through the torrents of splashing water, her legs raised and descended with arms outstretched as she bounded in leaping strides towards him. Droplets of water fell from her body, her hair swinging with each toss of her head as if in slow motion as with each of her movements Lenny didn't want her to stop. His eyes rested on her generous breasts bounding as each muscle rippled across her body.

At the river's edge, Lenny held out his hand to help Karen from the water. Their eyes came together in a long stare, as he looked into her green eyes. He pulled her towards him and hugged her close, kissing her forehead. He said quietly and with a lump in his throat.

"MY god woman you are just unbelievable, I'm fucking knocked out, I'm lost for words, in less than twenty-four hours we have fucked ourselves silly, we can only be a rutting pair of Deer or some randy old Rabbit that does a do-si-do in the corner somewhere," as he quipped and laughed out loud.

Karen lowered her eyes with embarrassment and then they parted as Lenny stood back with his hands on her shoulders. He wanted to see her looks, but his eyes strayed once again over her nakedness, her skin goose fleshed from the chill of the water.

With an arm now around her shoulder, Lenny turned and walked Karen towards where her clothes lay. Gathering them up, Lenny used his shirt to dry her; he remained lost for words. She was quickly stepping into her briefs as Lenny held open her jeans at the waist, next he helped her on with her blouse, and taking hold of the opening he tied a knot underneath her breasts leaving a bare midriff. Karen enjoyed the attention, still hanging onto the knot he tied, they kissed and he asked if she were comfortable. Returning the kiss she again hugged him. He moved and bent down to slip on her trainers, her fingertips rested gently on his broad back for support. Sitting down he pushed on his shoes, then picking up the carrier bag, they walked back onto the pathway and continued their search for Tommy and Toni. Lenny heard muffled voices ahead of them.

"Is that you Tommy?" Lenny called out.

"You bloody know it's us," came Tommy's curt reply.

Karen frowned as she looked at Lenny. He grinned.

"Christ I might have known," said Lenny as they continued to walk in the direction of Tommy's voice. It was then that the couple caught sight of Toni pulling on her 'T' shirt. She was blushing and alone. Tommy was standing behind a tree, urinating. He next appeared, zipping up his flies,

"That's better, I needed that. I could just do with a drink right now, it's been thirsty work."

Toni looked away and plucked the grass from off the ground from where she was sitting. Karen and Lenny grinned at each other, as he held aloft the bag.

"You're too late mate, we've drunk it."

"What, you're telling me that you had a bottle, Cor bloody hell, we could just do with that."

"Sorry mate you weren't around," said Lenny.

"Great girl this one, bloody marvellous she is, we've had a bloody good laugh," said Tommy

"Christ doesn't he go on?" she said, smiling cheekily

From a distance, the ambling quartet climbed the slope and crossed the meadow back to the house. At the river's edge a lone figure, drawing on his pipe, watched them intently climb the slope to the house and saw them disappear into the gardens beyond. From a crouched position the gypsy dribbled tobacco-stained spittle from his pipe onto the ground as he continued to watch from afar for any signs of further movement from the mansion house. The distant voices faded as the quartet was finally out of his view. He remained staring towards the house when several gypsy boys came to join him; not knowing what it was that had held his attention.

Tommy was first through the side door of the house. As Toni passed him in the kitchen Tommy couldn't resist a playful slap on her bottom as she went by.

"Come on let's get our drinks before anything else," said Tommy

He poured a whiskey and downed it in one gulp and smiled saying,

"God, I needed that, now what are you all having,"

Handing Lenny a whiskey, the girls remained undecided, whilst Lenny settled comfortably on the sofa with Karen.

"We'll have a white wine please," said Karen

It wasn't long before Lenny found his eyelids heavy, fidgeting every few seconds to stay awake, conversation was nothing more than idle chat between them. Just after half-past six, Toni decided to make a move as she was bored. Standing, she left a magazine on the small table beside her and moved over to the bay window of the lounge and looked out and stretched her arms as she turned and walked towards the door of the lounge, only turning back to look at Tommy.

"I need to have a shower, are you sure you don't want help with dinner,"

"Brown eyes, you go and have your shower," said Tommy

"If you are sure," turning to Karen, she said, "Are you coming up?"

"You go ahead, I'll be up in a minute, I'm really going to enjoy my bath, my legs ache with all that walking," said Karen.

Laughing out loud Tommy said, "Yeah and the rest girl, go on with you, pull the other one, it's got bells on."

Karen was on the stairs when Tommy had stopped talking. The noise had made Lenny stirred, sitting on the edge of the sofa with an aching back and knackered body, he reached out for his drink on the coffee table. For a moment his mind numbed from the slumber. However, with the girls out of the way, he said to Tommy,

"Don't forget to bell Frank about tomorrow,"

"Thanks for that Lenny, I needed a reminder."

Getting quickly to his feet,

"I'll do it now, while the girls are out of the way."

Reaching the desk over the cocktail bar, he fumbled for his diary, thumbing through the pages; he muttered to himself and said

"Here it is," he said, finding Frank's phone number he dialled it.

With his back towards Tommy, Lenny closed his eyes and gave a crafty grin to himself, as he listened to Tommy's conversation, hooked on every word as he mimicked Tommy's voice over. Lenny couldn't believe that his old mate Tommy was acting like some old tosser on the phone,

"Talk about bullshit and sucking up, blimey," he thought, "This is enough for me, I off to the bloody kitchen," he mumbled to himself.

He was soon occupied with a variety of foods laid out on the table. He flitted from one cupboard to next, choosing the utensils. Unperturbed by the others, Lenny was now preparing the main meal for the evening. In the top over he placed for plates for warming, then his speciality – Chicken breasts with King prawns in a tomato sauce, mixed with red wine, mushrooms and herbs. Fussing over his selection of new potatoes, he stood at the sink removing the peel. From the freezer, he took out some peas, carrots and other vegetables and also Yorkshire puddings. With a crash, bang wallop and a slow pirouette around the kitchen furniture, Lenny placed each of the saucepans onto the stove. Then several knows of butter were placed into the multi-cooker. Having lightly rubbed garlic into the breasts of Chicken, Lenny next placed the four portions into the heated dish and replaced the lid to simmer and brown in its own juices. With an eye on the clock, he pondered for a moment,

"Yes," he thought, staring at a very large swede, and decided to introduce at the last minute his favourite dish for dinner. He hastily peeled and diced the vegetable, adding a large chopped onion, then emptied the contents into a saucepan half filled with boiling water. Lenny kept a watchful eye as he slowly reduced the fluid from the saucepan. With extreme care, Lenny now had a fine mushy mixture. Placing the mix into a electric blender, adding grated cheese, double cream and a tot of sweet sherry for a rich flavour, he watched as the machine whisked up the ingredients into a nice pinkie colour. Finally, Lenny placed the mix into an open flan dish with a layer of grated cheese over the top, adding sliced tomatoes and mushrooms in a pattern over the layered cheese, and then popping the dish under the grill to brown off and seal the flavour. Lenny left the kitchen, shoving a slice of tomato into his mouth, and returned to the lounge. Tommy had just finished, when Lenny popped his head round the open door as Tommy put down the phone.

"Is it done? Is he coming down tomorrow?" Lenny asked him.

Tommy nodded in reply.

"It's done; we'll meet as arranged at three o'clock,"

"Well that's that then mate, so let's party, dinner's nearly ready, so what are we waiting for – I'm going up for a shower," said Lenny.

"Okay – you go up, I'll be there in a minute," said Tommy

As Lenny entered the bedroom, Karen stood sideways in front of the dressing table, her left foot rested on the edge of the chair, as she slowly pulled on a black silk stocking, emphasising her movements when Lenny entered. She drew back the dress, revealing her thigh, reached under the hem and pulled on her matching black suspenders, She leant forward, straightened her dress and did a twirl,

"Well I'm ready,"

"Beautiful sunshine, black's my colour,"

Moving towards him, Karen cupped her hands to his face and kissed him full on the lips. "Is there anything I can do for you kind sir," she said.

"Yes, sit and talk to me while I get showered and changed."

Tommy and Toni were waiting on the landing for Lenny and Karen to join them as all four went downstairs together. Lenny said, turning back to Toni:

"My! My girl! You look bloody handsome in that Blue dress,"

Tommy smiled with approval at Lenny's comments.

With the sound of soft instrumental music in the background to give that good factor feeling as they prepared to sit down for dinner, the setting was set for a relaxing evening. The lit candles cast shadows around the curtained room, flickering from wall to ceiling a cosy atmosphere; catching the girl's eyes and making them sparkle as they picked their way through dinner. Conversation was light-hearted with many entraining tales told by the boys. The evening was full of laughter, as hour by hour their personalities became more open and bonding. Long into the night they remained seated at the table. It was around one o'clock when Tommy said,

"Well – what an evening, let's do what the French do, go to bed and clean up in the morning, I'm truly knackered," as he stood and pushed back the chair,

"Fucked is the right word and in more ways than I can describe, ladies," he added glancing at Toni as he spoke. Within minutes of them entering their bedrooms for the night, the house fell silent.

Outside in the grounds gypsies had entered the rear of the property via the meadow, just wandering shadows moving among the shrubs and bushes. The group of six men remained seated in a circle; one scratched the ground with a stick whilst another passed cigarettes round. The only trace by daybreak was a small pile of discarded fag ends tucked alongside one of the protruding roots of a tree.

CHAPTER SIX
Frank's Arrival

Nine o'clock next morning (Thursday), Toni was first in the kitchen, filling the kettle, then off to the lounge to draw back the curtains as sunshine burst into the room. Karen entered the room with a mug of tea and an envelope,

"Here catch Toni," she tossed the envelope towards her.

"Get a load of this, we've been treated by the boys and loaned the Jag for the day, How about that,"

Toni opened the contents of the envelope onto the sofa,

"Bloody hell, what's all this for," she said

With a flick of the wrist, Toni tossed a wad of tenners into the air,

"There's a note inside – read it," said Karen,

"To be spent in any way you girls wish, take the Jag and drive carefully, no rush to get back, enjoy yourselves girls and see you later, as me and Tommy have some urgent business to attend to, signed Lenny," said Toni.

"That's turn up for the books, wonder what their business is that's so urgent, What's going on, did you know about this," Toni said to Karen.

"Only vaguely, Lenny mentioned something last night about business and they wouldn't have time today, money wasn't mentioned and I didn't think any more about it until I woke up this morning and saw the envelope Lenny had left me," said Karen.

"Have they left the house then," said Toni.

"Well no, Lenny was still in bed when I came down," said Karen

"Bloody hell I don't believe this, have you counted it," said Toni

"No, not really, it's a lot of notes, gotta be a grand, let's do what our masters command and fly, come let's get ready and go," said Toni.

Ten o'clock the girls had left the house and were driving through the village.

By eleven o'clock Tommy had arrived in the kitchen, missing the girls note left on the table. Shortly Lenny appeared in the kitchen and joined him at the table, pulling out a chair he sat. Tommy stood up and moved leaning with his back against the sink, then looking down at Lenny, Tommy said,

"Christ old boy, you look bloody rough, (laughing) you both been at it again last night, you randy sod,"

"Leave off Tommy, that fucking wine I bought it's screwed my guts, I" be alright when I've had a coffee," said Lenny.

"I bloody hope so my shiner, we've a lot to do today, remember," said Tommy.

Lenny reached for the note, "What's this Tommy?"

"I don't know mate, I didn't see when I came in," said Tommy.

Lenny read the note,

"That's nice it's a 'thank you' from the girls, I forgot to mention last night I left the girls some cash this morning and sent them shopping and loaned the Jag for the day," said Lenny

"What you do that for Lenny," said Tommy grumbling,

"Frank, remember he's coming down today or have you forgotten, you don't want him around with the girls here do you, Hello do you hear me, Tommy,"

"Oh! bollocks, yes you are right, I just haven't switched on yet, the Jag, the Jag we need transport to pick him up," said Tommy.

"That's alright use yours, it needs an airing," said Lenny grinning.

Tommy went to the back door of the kitchen and looked out towards the garage,

"Doors are open, they must have gone," said Tommy.

"By the way, you are a crafty sod, I've got a bone to pick with you, you told me on Tuesday that Frank was coming next week and it didn't dawn on me until last night that he was coming in a few hours time, so I left the girls a grand to get them out of the way," said Lenny.

"Yeah, I fucked up; I thought it best to get him down ASP so that I can get matters sorted with him, forgot to mention it with the girls at the house, I got carried away, (giggling to himself) I dropped a bollock there their mate, sorry, Yeah that was good thinking, getting the girls out of the way," said Tommy

"I hope you know what you are doing Tommy," Lenny said as he reached for the coffee mug. Tommy remained standing and thinking.

"How you feeling now," said Tommy.

"Fucked, I am well and truly fucked, I have no energy left in me, do you know I have used up five years of sperm in the last twenty-four hours and Karen is walking around with it, she has one hot tummy," said Lenny.

Tommy spat coffee from his mouth on hearing Lenny's words; he couldn't contain himself as he belly laughed in hysterics.

"More than five years, I thought it was longer than that mate," said Tommy.

"Brenda, Brenda do you remember her, she use to be a visitor at the nick, well she use to give me a hand job on visits, under the table and all that," said Lenny grinning, "See you don't know everything Tommy, there are some secrets left,"

"Bloody hell you old dog, have you got any more surprises this morning," as he curled up laughing as he hung onto the sink, muttering, "Hand job, finger licking times I bet, so you never got your leg over with her then Lenny," said Tommy.

"Yes I did, when we came out, we met up in a hotel and done the deed, she hadn't been serviced by her hubby for some time, so I obliged her for a one nighters, fucked on and off all night, she was getting a bit sore towards morning so we just cuddled up until we left the next morning," said Lenny thinking back to the past, "I wonder where she is today," he muttered, " I hope Karen doesn't want poking again tonight, I ain't got any more energy left Tommy, my leg muscles ache and my balls don't know what day it is, been in the dark for much of the last forty-eight hours with very sticky moments, I keep getting a hard on and it is beginning to hurt with the rubbing against my pants, I am drained," as he spluttered and gave out one big belly infectious belly laugh that gathered momentum, "No one would believe this at my age," said Lenny, as Tommy joined in the laughter, coughing and spluttering on Lenny's words, Tommy's laughter brought real tears to his eyes, "Oh! Lenny, you are bloody funny,"

"Well I mean it mate, these girls are serious business, I'll end up pegging out at this rate, God they are both stunning though, you did well there Tommy, good contact you have,"

"You are bloody funny at times, Lenny, you say some strange bloody things, is Karen able to walk without crutches Lenny," said Tommy grinning.

"Anyway Lenny, listen up I need to make a move and organise the Range Rover for the pickup, I'll put the private hire signs on the doors to make us look legit, seeing as you let the Jag go," said Tommy and followed up with a final comment, "We need to be gone by twelve-thirty,"

"If I can make it back up stairs Tommy, I'll get a shave and get ready," said Lenny.

He was still smiling to himself when he left the table,

Tommy shook his head as Lenny left the kitchen. Soon after Tommy had left those for the hideout of the Range Rover, when he was attracted to something he had noticed something on the boundary fence, his eyes caught sight of flapping material and went to investigate. He untangled the material clearly torn from a garment of some kind, possibly a 'T' shirt. Tommy was alarmed as this material was new and not from the girls clothing, it wasn't there when they returned from the meadow yesterday. He stood momentarily in deep thought as his eyes scanned the area around him looking for other signs,

"Fucking hell this is all I need at this time, I wonder who has been wandering around the grounds," he thought to himself.

Tracing the worn out ground back to the adjacent woodland, he followed a small trail for some yards then walked across a carpet of rotting leaves to the 'Oak' tree. It was whilst down on his haunches surveying the ground that he noticed a partially hidden cigarette packet tucked into the crevice of the tree and a pile of discarded fag ends by the roots.

"Christ, gypsies, fucking gypsies I bet the bastards have been up here all fucking night," Tommy muttered to himself, On standing Tommy looked back to see what could be seen of the house, " I wonder what they are after," he thought, as little could be seen of the house from where he stood, "I am not having this shit off them, no bloody way am I going to put up with their fucking nonsense," mumbled Tommy, "No bloody way, I'll fuck them up alright," as he repeated himself and feeling angry at the same time.

Back in the house Tommy was quick to climb the stairs and went to a panelled hidden door off the landing which he opened, the second door beyond was a heavy steel construction which led into his secreted office. Tommy was quick to examine the video tape from the previous night, he had installed a twenty-four-hour

71

monitoring security system during their first year at the house. Screening back the tape Tommy soon realised that the system didn't quite capture the area he wanted to see, the system was not as foolproof as he believed, it needed to be adjusted.

"Damn the fucking thing, after all these years I now find a problem with it, Mmmm, this could be a blessing in disguise, I wonder how long those bastards have been using the grounds," as he banged his fist hard on the desk in frustration as he turned to leave the room and headed for his bedroom further down the landing. Lenny had already made his move downstairs and started to collect the crockery from the night before and filled up the dish washer, eventually, he had tidied up the lounge, at the same time he was clocking watching and shouted up the stairs to Tommy to hurry.

"Times getting on, we've got to be at the station by two o'clock, remember,"

"Alright I am coming," came the shouted reply from Tommy.

"I am just finishing up," he said.

As good as his word Tommy appeared.

"Right let's get moving, I'll lock up and put the alarm on," said Tommy.

"Why are you so agitated mate, putting the alarm on, when did we ever," said Lenny.

"I'll tell you later mate, I tell you in the car," said Tommy in haste of leaving the house and closing the garage doors.

Lenny frowned to himself as he realised from Tommy's flusters that something was worrying him as they went over to the woodland. Soon Tommy was focused on his driving through the countryside as they made their way towards the Motorway, during the drive Tommy told Lenny about finding the material, cigarette packet and discarded fag ends he found in the copse above from where he housed the Range Rover in a secret underground menagerie below. Lenny listened intently on Tommy's every word,

"So what are we going to do about it, Tommy,"

"I don't know mate," said Tommy, "I am still working on it,"

"I know, the dogs, we ought to get the dogs back from the kennels, we need them in the house quick," said Lenny trying to be helpful, "Do you think they might have seen us leave the house today Tommy,"

"I don't know mate but we can't take any chances, ring and arrange for the dogs to come back ASAP," said Tommy.

"No give them a call now and see if they can drop them off after we get back with Frank," said Tommy urging Lenny to take note of the urgency and make that call.

Tommy realised that he must stay calm about the situation and not over emphasise and panic otherwise his planning and arrangements will be right out of the window and bad for business with so much at stake regarding both their futures at the house.

Arriving at the Railway Station Lenny was given the task of waiting on the platform, the train pulled away as Frank's large figure could not be mistaken as he ambled towards the exit gate. Frank Boxer, a large framed man and well over six feet, he was a man who always wore red braces as his trademark, he didn't give a damn what others might have thought, he loved his braces, a man with big hands and a big punch to go with them. Frank's jovial smiling face was the real signature of the man, a character larger than life and a career East End criminal, a real Londoner through and through. Lenny stood grinning as Frank came closer, and then locked in a big bear hug of a greeting from Frank, with a few vocal quips between them as Frank dragged his case towards the waiting vehicle and Tommy outside.

"Bloody hell, just look at the man, he hasn't changed,

just a little older, but still the old Frank he remembers," said Lenny in whispers to himself.

Frank was more barrel size around the chest, with a waist that was squared and thick to his thighs, which in turn made him sway and wobble as he walked, but for his size always well dressed, wearing dapper suits, and shirts and all hand made with cufflinks worn like diamonds on the sleeves of shirts. Lenny rooted to the spot and nodded with both hands in his pockets as they stood waiting for Tommy to pull up as he said, "Frankie, you look bloody well on it, whatever it is mate,"

"Well that's what a good woman does for you Lenny, my Prim looks after me, she doesn't miss a bleeding trick mate, and she's a good'en alright,"

Lenny couldn't stop laughing, as Frank stood out like a dog's dinner on a monkey's veranda, he didn't need to advertise the old Frank as he played the part very well as he hadn't changed in all those years.

"Christ, Tommy will have kitten's when he sees him dressed to the nines," thinking quietly to himself.

"You still patronise Saville Row then mate," said Lenny.

"Never miss an opportunity me old mate, you should know that," said Frank chortling to himself.

"You on your own Lenny," said Frank.

"No Tommy's somewhere waiting in the care, Traffic wardens Frank gotta be bloody careful we abide by the law and no distractions," said Lenny

"No I meant on your own, not a woman in your life," said Frank being nosey.

"Oh! Yes me and Tommy have a couple of girls you're meet them later tonight," said Lenny

"On your wave length Lenny, so what are we waiting for - let's go," said Frank in typical touché banter.

Tommy appeared in the Range Rover, Frank noticed the hire notice on the door, "Still using that same old dodge then, Lenny," said Frank.

Tommy parked up and alighted from the vehicle to greet Frank, "Fucking hell Frankie, you look like Robin Hood in Piccadilly Circus," said Tommy muttering to him as he hugged Frank for the first time in years. Frank soon had the front passenger door open as he leaned into the vehicle and sniffed the air.

"What you doing Frank," said Lenny

"Sniffing can't smell any fanny," as he stood and goaded Tommy and Lenny with his open banter, "Bloody hell he hasn't changed Lenny," said Tommy.

"Tommeeeeeee, How the devil are you old mate," Frank roared out loud for the entire world to hear.

"Come on saddle up and let's get out of here," Tommy said as he got back into the driver's seat.

"Nice motor Tommy, nice," said Frank looking around the interior, "Lenny's been telling me about your apples and pears and your bits of fluff," said Frank turning round to wink at Lenny in the back seat.

"Yeah, we got visitors and some unwelcome at that," said Tommy, "You will meet the girl's tonight mate at dinner,"

"And what's the unwelcome bit you mentioned," said Frank.

"Gypsies mate, been in the grounds of the house last night," said Tommy.

Both Frank and Lenny remained silent on Tommy's answer for much of the journey back.

"I see you are still wearing braces, Frank, I thought you would have worn casuals to come down it," said Tommy.

"Casuals, What are they, give me suits any day mate, the old braces do me proud, gives me a lot of air and movement in the crutch, I don't like my balls being squeezed, that's Prim's job," said Frank croaking out loud his reply.

Both Lenny and Tommy laughed aloud at Frank's comments, transfixed on his hilarious statement,

"This is going to be a night and a half with Frank's version of events, Christ wait until he sees the girls," thought Lenny as he quietly giggled to himself.

"No I thought perhaps you would have worn jeans and 'T' shirt," said Tommy

"Tommy what's a matter with you, where am I going to find a forty inside leg and fifty-six-inch waist," said Frank

"Christ is that what you are," said Tommy.

"Too right I am mate, Primmy looks after me well," said Frank obligingly.

"I would have thought Primmy would have got you moving to Essex from the old place by now," said Tommy as he concentrated on the road ahead.

"Essex, me in Essex, there a load of fucking gypo's up there, there as mad as hatters, there gun fucking crazy mate, I don't need aggro like that do I, me and Prim are better off in our little place and take bloody good holidays abroad in the sunshine in our place in Spain, that does us plenty," said Frank proudly pointing out his point of view and being right for him.

"No I understand how you feel mate, many have left the East End over the years and gone to Canvey Island or like you say Spain, get out of the way of Old Bill," said Tommy.

On the remainder of the drive home, all three friends continued to reminiscence about their former lives together in the East End of London. When just a mile from home, Tommy pulled into an open gate to a Christmas tree plantation, stopping and turning off the engine he suggested that the three of them should take a walk in the country air and stretch their legs awhile. Frank was quite nimble for a big man, as he alighted from the vehicle, standing he outstretched his arms like the jib of a crane.

"It's best this way Frank, gives us a few minutes to check the road out, we are only down the road a bit, we just need to be sure," said Tommy.

"My, My you haven't lost your touch, I didn't think us villains did that anymore (laughing out loud) I mean there's none of the yard boys down here surely, the country boys in blue are fucked and the world is our oyster, ain't that right boys," said Frank.

Strolling towards a nearby gate Frank removed his jacket in the warm breeze of the sunny afternoon.

"So what's all this about the boys, who owns all this lot, there's a fair bit of bread (money) here, you'll make a fortune in London with this lot," said Frank.

"These estates are managed Frank, all spoken for and probably sold in London at those big auctions, business is business in any language even in the sticks," said Lenny

Frank chortles to himself and pulls out a packet of cigarettes and lights up, tucking his jacket under one arm, he ambles off for a pee behind a tree.

"Bloody handsome day, it's quieter than a bleeding cemetery," roaring out loud as his head appeared from behind a tree as he said it, then the sounds of breaking wind could be heard.

"Bloody hell Frank you are giving it the works," said Tommy, as he scratched his head in bewilderment.

Lenny had turned his back and looked upwards as he smiled to himself, he was quietly giggling at Frank's remarks.

Frank soon emerged from behind the tree with a burning cigarette hanging from his lips, shaking one leg as he walked back leaving a stream of steaming urine running across the ground behind him as he pulled up his trouser zipper.

"Regretting this Tommy, said Lenny whispering in Tommy's direction.

"Don't say it please, we'll be alright when we get back to the house, give him a couple of good stiffeners and he will soon be on his way, said Tommy in a low voice to Lenny, "Do you still drink whisky Frank," shouted Tommy.

"Do I still drink whisky, what's the matter with you boys, it's like asking a blind if he can see, course I do," said Frank

"Rights lets be having you and we'll be on our way," said Tommy with some authority,

As Frank already appeared to be on a jolly, perhaps even beginning to forget what he had come for. Frank grinned and frowned as he looked at Lenny, but also pointing in Tommy's direction.

Within minutes Tommy slowed as he approached the entry gate near the mansion, he touched a switch that went unnoticed by Frank, meanwhile, he has sat leaning his larger frame against the passenger door as he faced and chatted to Lenny behind him. Tommy had driven slowly across the open meadow onto the dried river riverbed, before stopping at a small gate adjacent the garden at the side of the house.

"Right we'll here Frank, this is it," said Tommy

"Where's the house then, Tommy," said Frank.

"Up behind those trees, all this here is ours; we'll go through the side gate and I'll show you the grounds Frank, said Lenny, "Whilst Tommy puts the motor away," as Lenny winked to Tommy as he and Frank walked away from the vehicle.

Reaching the house by the side door, Frank laboured through the open door in the kitchen, whilst steadying, his hands held onto the door frame as his eyes raced everywhere.

"Bloody hell this is as big as my living room," scratching his head, Frank was bemused as he propelled himself through the door, "Do they still call this a house," said Frank.

"Come on Frank follow me and let's get you that drink," said Lenny.

Frank lumbered forward with his hands in his pockets as he trailed after Lenny; meanwhile, Tommy had returned to the vehicle having removed Franks suitcase before he tucked the Range Rover away and out of any prying eyes that may be watching, from somewhere close.

Frank was soon fiddling with trinkets he had eyed on his way through the hallway when Lenny shouted out as to where he was,

"These all legit Lenny,"

"What's that," said Lenny

"The trinkets in the hall," said Frank, he could hear Lenny laughing in the lounge, entering Lenny was grinning ear to ear at Frank's comments,

"Come on make yourself comfortable," as Frank aimed his large frame towards the most comfortable armchair he could find in the lounge.

"This old wing back will do me, old mate," as Frank sat deep into the armchair, as Lenny brought over his whisky. Frank really looked the part, whilst drawing on a lighted cigarette.

"I can't get over the size of this place, just the thought of walking about knackers me, Prim would be shocked if she saw it, Lenny,"

"I'll leave you for a few minutes, you get on with your drink, here I'll leave the bottle on the side," Lenny placed the bottle down alongside the chair as he told Frank to help himself.

"Listen, listen to that noise, he's fucking asleep already, that's him snoring and away with the fairies (laughing) Oh! Fucking hell Lenny," said Tommy.

"Leave him, Tommy, let him sleep, keeps him out of our way for the time being," said Lenny pleading with Tommy to leave him alone.

"I'm going up stairs to check up on the kennels and let them know we are home for the dogs," said Lenny in a hurry, "Then I need to check out the back and make sure their kennels are okay," bounding off taking two steps at a time as Lenny raced up the stairs.

By five-thirty the girls hadn't returned as Lenny finally joined Tommy at the open kitchen door.

"Yeah the dogs will be back soon," said Lenny.

"Right, come with me and I'll show you where I found the fag packet and dog ends," looking back into the kitchen before moving off,

"I'll leave the door open, we will only be a minute, you can come back later and take the dogs for a walk up here, you might find something else that I missed," said Tommy feeling anxious again and frustrated more than ever knowing who it was, just shadows in the night.

"Mmmm," murmured Lenny.

Without leaving the pathway which led from the house, Tommy first pointed in one direction to where he found the material and then turning in another direction to where Lenny was clearly able to see the big 'Oak' tree from where they stood.

"You see mate someone has made a run through here, this is not made by an animal, I bet those bastards have been coming here for days or weeks without us knowing," said Tommy.

"Do you think they are casing the house?" asked Lenny.

"I just don't know mate, but I ain't taking any chances on that," said Tommy, "Look, We can't call Old Bill out can we, we don't want them nosing around as well, we are fucked at the moment, got to deal with this ourselves mate I'm afraid," said Tommy.

"Yeah, you are right mate, I appreciate what we got to do," said Lenny in a concerned voice, "Let's wait for the dogs."

"We need to nip this in the bud mate and quick, if it's grief they want then grief they shall have, I am not pissing around with amateurs," said Tommy in a more heated and strained voice.

"Well whatever we do, we need to get it right, there be no second chances on this, there be like ants round a honey pot, you know what gypo's are like if you upset them, they're like a fucking rubber ball, always bounding back for more and more," said Lenny seeking answers to his words.

"I know, I know, I know that's what worries me, I wonder if the old man knows anything, I could try him away from the camp, might bung him a few quid to keep an eye out," said Tommy

"Well, try him if you think it might make a difference to our situation, can you trust him though, he's not likely to drop us in it is he," said Lenny.

"Anyway, keep it to ourselves, I am not wanting to say anything to Frank and the girls, I wanna play it by ear and suss it out first, right let's get back to the house," said Tommy.

Returning to the house, Frank was still fast asleep in the chair, back in the kitchen they both sat at the table waiting on the girls return.

"They are late coming home, give them a call," said Lenny

"I ain't got a mobile for them, we're stuck until they arrive," said Tommy.

"Thought I might find you two in here, I'm getting cold, Christ I needed that nap, I'm buggered, I need a wash and brush up boys, where am I billeted, who is going to show me," said Frank, " Have your lady friends returned yet, are they here,"

"No the girls are not here yet, come on Frank I'll show you your room," said Lenny.

Near to seven o'clock, the boys heard the sounds of a

vehicle approaching the side of the house,

"The girls," said Lenny, "They are back."

Tommy was up at the window craning his neck,

"Yeah, that's them," said Tommy.

"Right, let's see, it's not bad timing with Frankie out of the way," said Tommy glancing towards the open doorway to the hall.

"Hi, we are back," came a shout from Toni, as she saw the boys appear from the kitchen. Both Tommy and Lenny approached the girls with grinning faces.

"Had a good day," said Tommy.

"Marvellous, just marvellous," as Toni greeted Tommy with a kiss on the cheek, and then taking his arm as she pulled him to the rear of the vehicle, whispering as she opened the boot, "I bought underwear, Lemon silk, just wait till you see it."

Tommy remained silent on her whispers sporting only a big happy smile as his eyes saw the array of neatly stacked shopping in the boot. Tommy looking up for Lenny to help saw he and Karen locked in a jovial smooching embrace by the passenger door, his gaze seemed to linger on the couple, thinking to himself, he couldn't help but notice how genuine the couple had become towards each other in such a short time. Then the silence was broken by the appearance of Frank's lumbering frame moving across the gravel drive. With both hands reaching deep into his pockets and red braces straining at the waistline he continued to amble up to the two couples. Karen saw him first and whispered to Lenny, the couple untwined themselves from each other's grasp as Karen was introduced to Frank; Toni also approached and introduced herself.

Looking down at Frank's feet.

"What the fucking hell are those," said Lenny out loud, "Tommy have you seen anything like this before," as he turned and beckoned him. Tommy walked from the rear of the vehicle, as Toni shook her head as her eyes followed Tommy's movements as she stood with Lenny and Karen,

"Jesus Christ, Frankie, what bloody hell are those," said Lenny, as they all looked down at Frank's feet and laughed as they saw him wearing a large colourful pair 'Mickey Mouse' slippers,"

"I don't fucking believe it, Frankie, You get worse as you get older mate, where on earth did you get them from," said Tommy with eyes popping out on storks.

"Primmy, my old lady," said Frank.

Without serious concerns for the piss takers around him, Frank finally saw the funny side of his actions and laughed with them. As with both hands he gripped his braces and leaned back as he pushed out his barrel chest as he rocked on his haunches, which in turn brought the features of his slippers to life. It was obvious to them all that further introductions would not be necessary as the group helped form a line to remove the shopping from the vehicle.

"With all this laughter Tommy, I had forgotten the takeaway we brought back, it's on the floor in the back, will you bring it in for me," said Toni still giggling at Frankie's turn of events.

It wasn't long before the vehicle was emptied and Tommy had driven the Jag into the garage and closed the doors then returned to the house.

At eight-thirty came the sounds of the doorbell, "Who's that calling," said Lenny as he went to open the door when suddenly he was confronted by four bounding and leaping dogs running into the house and barking loudly, "Oh! Bloody hell, Tommy the dogs are loose," too late, you could hear all hell had broken out in the kitchen, with the girls shrieking and Tommy's loud voice trying to command the situation.

Closing the front door Lenny was soon in the kitchen to bring the dogs under control, one by one each sat and responded to his command to sit and stay.

"Beautiful looking animals Lenny, what sort are they," said Karen.

"Weimaraners, known as the silver ghosts," said Lenny, "right I need to get two of them into the kennels outside, the other two stay in the house so I'll get them sorted and we can have our takeaway, if one of you can sort that out while I've gone," said Lenny now rather excited that his dogs were back at the house, happy was the right word to describe his feelings.

"I have never heard of the breed before tonight," said Toni.

"They are German hunting dogs officially," said Lenny, "Anyway let's get these two outside and bedded down for the night."

By ten o'clock Frank was again well out of it from the evening's events, the girls loved his funny sense of humour and the many stories told about their boyhood years. What the girls found most hilarious about Frank was that he tended to stand up and act out some of the incidents he described in detail. Again with each passing drink down the gullet he became funnier and at one time Lenny stood to assist him, only for the pair to fall on the floor. Tommy got up to help them both, bending, he pulled Frank's arm.

"Christ he's a ton weight," he blurted out laughing. Letting go Frank flopped back onto the floor like a beached whale.

"Bloody hell, I can't move him, Frank can you hear me old mate, let's get you up off the floor," said Tommy shaking his head, "I don't know how we are going to move him, he's right out of it."

Meanwhile, Lenny had struggled to his feet, having felt his own strength ebb and flow from his body due to the hilarity, although trying to remain serious he ignored the ongoing laughter from the girls.

"Come on Tommy let's have another go, you get under

one arm and pull," said Lenny, "Bloody hell Frank you can't lay here all night, move your feet," said Lenny directing his whispers at Frank.

"I don't know how the fuck we are going to get him upstairs to bed, do you," said Tommy in a more concerning voice, "We can't leave him down here because of the dogs."

Increasingly concerned by the thought of getting him upstairs to bed. By now the girls came to the rescue realising that more help was needed to move Frank off the floor. When finally all four struggled and lifted Frank off the floor, when another hilarious moment of the night, Frank's slippers came alive as they moved and dragged him to an armchair, also the girls noticed his trousers were coming adrift, when finally Frank began to respond to his situation and with further help the boys managed to get him out of the lounge for the stairs, with slow positive steps they began to climb the stairs with the girls following up the rear, finally getting him into his bedroom the boys laid him clothed on the bed as the girls placed blankets over him. Leaving Frank to sleep the four stood out on the landing, when Tommy decided he was staying up and going to bed, "I've had enough, I am knackered," winking at Toni to encourage her to turn in for bed, Toni said, " Me too Tommy, I'm coming with you."

Lenny got Karen to turn in whilst he went back downstairs and got the two dogs organised for the night and making sure the house was locked up and curtains fully closed with all the night's fracas.

Tommy left Toni to get ready for bed as he made one last visit to check on Frank, he was well settled for the night with deep sounding snores echoing the bedroom, closing the bedroom door, Tommy wandered along the corridor taking notice of the moonlight which had cast long shadows on the landing floor, the light and dark effect reminded him of a Zebra crossing. With this in mind, he stepped to one side of the oval landing window and peered out and saw how illuminated the grounds of house were. With blank thoughts he remained staring out of the window, believing that he observed an elongated shadow appear and quickly disappear into the thicket by the adjacent the wooded dell.

"What was that," thought Tommy, "I'm sure something was moving then."

Seeking further answers, Tommy side stepped along the landing whilst still looking out of the window, realising he could go no further. He turned suddenly, while still pondering on his thoughts. When out of the darkness Toni appeared on the landing walking towards him. She moved between the light and the dark of his imaginary crossing without stopping. She appeared to be stark naked, although Tommy couldn't see any movement from her breasts as she came closer, nor could he see her darkened pubic line in the ever changing light of the landing. Before you say a word, Toni raised a finger to her lips, saying, "Shhhhhh," as she cuddled up tight against his body.

"I'm waiting for you to come to bed," said Toni as she nibbled gently under his chin with her teeth.

He placed his arms over her shoulders, with his hands clasped in the middle of her back. The couple remained motionless in the shadows of the moonlight, as at the same time Tommy had turned Toni slightly so that he could continue gazing out of the window. Without making further comments about the night's events, Toni sensed and felt that Tommy lacked feeling, even with such an up lifting cuddle it seems that Tommy was preoccupied and hadn't noticed what she was wearing. Impatient with him Toni wriggled from his grasp, her movement disturbed his thinking, and he let go of his grasp. Toni fumbled for his hands and placed them on her breasts as encouragement, she felt the sudden warmth of his hands through her silky garment she wore, and covered all of her assets and more exposed the real contours of her body. Tommy felt the smoothness of the silk as his hands glided over the material. Then Tommy whispered to Toni,

"Sorry darling I was miles away in thought, it's so peaceful up here and what with the moonlight coming through the window, has just added to my thoughts and the romance it brings me with you."

"Yes it is a beautiful night," she whispered.

Tommy leant forward and kissed her cheek, Toni took hold of one hand and enticed him towards her as she pulled on his arm moving away from the window heading towards the bedroom. Although, and before she knew it, Tommy had quickly whisked her off her feet as he carried her to the bedroom, Toni squealed with the sudden movement. Placing Toni gently down on the bed, Tommy started to undress as he gazed down at Toni, leaving his trousers and underwear on the floor, as Toni's eyes were feasting on what Tommy had exposed just inches from her face. He was stretching upwards as he removed and tossed his jumper to the floor, in doing so Toni saw the his wobbling penis rise up and harden stork like as Tommy turned off the main light of the bedroom, as Toni turned on the sidelight by the bed, when she turned back Tommy was pissed proud and needed the loo and not what she had thought, when Tommy returned from the bathroom and said to Toni,

"Jesus I knew there was something different about you, it's bloody gorgeous darling," he paced over to the bed and realised that Toni's rising agenda was unstoppable now with a full hard on as he admired her new underwear that she displayed for him.

"You look very happy," said Tommy smiling down at her.

"I am Tommy," Toni replied as she moved across the bed towards him, she slid off the bed and rummaged through the shopping she had brought.

"Are you ready for this Tommy and put that thing away, it's not needed at the moment, perhaps later," she said jokingly.

"Put a sock in it and get on with it girl," said Tommy in jest.

"Sit down and watch my treat Tommy," as she appeared from the open doorway of the bathroom in a lemon cameo knickers set.

With lace edging and a plunging neck line, with a high cut on the thighs, revealing her slender figure as she teased him in her walk about across the floor.

"Wait a minute we need some music for this," said Tommy, let's do it proper if you must, "Come on girl, flaunt it for me," Tommy said laughing at the same time his penis was up and down like a yo-yo as his mind turned to fucking,

He wanted to fuck her hard and fast as his eyes cast over more garments that she had bought earlier in the day. Tommy pulled himself back onto the bed in a prone position as Toni could see all of his five or could it be six inches of hard cock that waved every time she came close to the bed. Tommy's torso was becoming more tempting than continuing with her fashion parade, she too was beginning to concentrate on his penis more as she felt right horny herself, she had whipped up her own frenzy of delight as Tommy witnessed her class of femininity as she finally walked slowly to the bed and removing what little she had worn. Naked Toni climbed onto the bed and crawled up Tommy's torso, leaning forward they kissed long and hard as she took hold and fiddled with Tommy's hardness as Toni pushed his penis into her vagina, it was that moment of deep breaths as she felt him inside of her, as she began to wriggle her buttocks slowly and with ease as she took charge, it was her time to thrill Tommy in ways that men often dream of. Tommy reached up to hold her breasts as Toni's hands were pressing down on either side of his shoulders as she got into her stride of riding Tommy, as he started to move and buck with her as she was the 'Cowgirl' riding a 'Bronco' stallion as the bed was creaking and the mattress bounced up and down as their togetherness was now on fire as their bodies became one in rhythm, Toni was really going it in haste her buttocks moved back and forth at a fast rate of knots, incredible as Tommy hung on for dear life, trying to keep up with her pace when finally they both came together, Toni laid her head on his chest panting large gasps as her breathing was erratic and then finally she rolled off him onto her back exhausted. Both laid still just staring up at the ceiling, as Tommy watched the fullness of her breasts heave and rise time and again until her breathing became more normal, when she turned on her side and cuddled up to Tommy who remained on his back as he placed an arm over Toni to respond to her cuddling him. It was some minutes later, in fact, a good while later Toni moved and got off the bed, she stood and parted her legs in front of Tommy as she cupped her vagina and said, "Boy that was some ride Tommy, my pubic bone aches and is sore," as she turned and walked to the ensuite bathroom. When she emerged minutes later Tommy was fast asleep he remained in the same position she had left him, naked on top of the duvet, whilst she managed to partly slip underneath the cover and fell asleep.

Later, however, Tommy's sleep was disturbed by his tossing and turning awake he just lay in the darkened room, his thoughts troubled him by the gypsies and the moving shadow he saw earlier. Slipping off the bed Tommy went over to the window and peered from behind the curtain, the grounds appeared serene and quiet as the moon had moved further round the house as he returned to bed. Toni remained under the duvet in a deep sleep as Tommy crawled back under the cover, and fortunate not to have woken her with his restlessness as he tried to settle down again.

CHAPTER SEVEN
Night Assailants

Around five o'clock the next morning (Friday) Tommy stirred again with broken sleep, he lay restless and dripping in sweat, as the beads of perspiration ran down his naked flesh, as he felt the wet coldness of the damp sheet underneath him. Again slipping from under the cover with his fingers scratching his head in despair at the frustration he felt.

"Christ, I'm bloody knackered," he whispered to himself, he looked back at Toni she slept on, cocoon-like, the weight of her head on the pillow, her face hidden from his view.

Quietly Tommy made his way in the half-light to the adjoining bathroom, his flesh felt clammy and unpleasant as he closed the door behind him as he stepped into the shower to clean up. Minutes later he had gathered up his clothes and headed for the bedroom door, once out on the landing he dressed himself, feeling more comfortable after the shower as he made his way slowly down the stairs in the half light, step-by-step he descended down. At the bottom of the stairs, he saw the two dogs excited as they twisted and turned as they watched him, ready to greet him with wagging tails and whimpers, wanting to be fussed by him. The downstairs was full of changing colours as he reached the hallway, edging closer to the kitchen with both dogs under his feet, he remained alert listening for the slightest noise that would draw his attention. Tommy was not at ease; his mental intuition and instincts were telling him that all was not right. He returned the dogs to their beds and got them to settle down as he went back into the hallway, when he saw from the darkness of where he stood a moving silhouette outlined through the frosted front porch window, someone there, but whom?, he remained in the shadows of the hall and patiently watched to see what would happen next. It was clear from the shape of the head that it was a male person in the porch. Tommy went back into the kitchen and peeked out from the kitchen window, it was then he saw a moving shape of a person moving underneath the window going in the direction of the front porch, Tommy thought, "At least two in the grounds, mmmm, fuck it I am not having this every bloody night," back to the hallway he saw two figures outlined and appeared to be in conversation from their body language. Tommy slipped across the hall into lounge, from the side of a curtain he definitely saw and realised that there were two males, although he couldn't guess their ages from where he looked, then the figures moved and crept past the bay window heading round to the east side of the house, a sudden flutter of nerves was caused by the chimes of the hall clock, swearing to himself, he continued to edge closer to the glass of the window and angled his head to watch the two figures, without warning a face appeared at the opposite end of the bay window with cupped hands pressed against the glass.

"Oh! Shit, bollocks," alarmed at his near miss of being seen, Tommy quickly slipped down onto the floor under the window sill and waited in panic giving the figure a few minutes to move on. By this time Tommy had worked himself into a stupor and had enough of this nonsense, believing the time was right to make a move back into the kitchen. At the back door of the kitchen he turned silently the key and then with two hands controlled the silent opening of the door, once slightly ajar, he eased himself through the opening, leaving the dogs in the kitchen, he decided that it be best and see for himself without raising and creating a scene. Leaving the darkened lobby of the back door, he stood on the gravel pathway, his ear half-cocked for the slightest noise. Peering over the low wall opposite and adjacent the pathway, he saw no signs of activity. When without warning Tommy dropped to the floor and hugged the wall in the darkness with a seething pain to his back he fell forwards kneeling on the ground, when he received more blows to his head and back. Tommy was beginning to hurt; he felt anger rising in him as he wasn't able to get to his feet from the blows he received. It was then that Tommy saw a running figure approaching from the front, the figure came from nowhere. He saw the figure kick out as on instinct he parried the blow with a good thump of his own to the bollocks of his frontal assailant. Now on his haunches Tommy lunged forwards and reached out and connected with the figure as he grabbed the genitals of his assailant, this time Tommy held fast as the figure squirmed and squealed as he tried to escape Tommy's grasp, it was hurting the assailant he was in pain and Tommy needed to see the face. It was then he felt a shove from behind as he fell forward he released his grip on the other attacker, he knew he had to get back on his feet otherwise he was going to get a good kicking and that could have greater percussions on protecting his body from such action. But then Tommy heard running footsteps on the gravel, not knowing if others had arrived and knowing the kitchen door remained unlocked concerned him greatly as he laid down and crawled into a ball foetus like and waited for the attack which never came as he lay for some minutes before he decided to make a move as he used the low wall to stand as he fumbled and stumbled as he pressed his back against the brickwork for support.

"God I fucking ache the bastards next time there be no next time, this is war for me, the fuckers are not going to win," as he murmured to himself as he wiped his mouth clean from the dirt.

Tommy remained outside for many more minutes to recover and to wait should the figures return as he staggered back to the lobby of the back door, shocked and bruised as he his ego was well and truly dented by this incident, blowing hot and cold by the time he entered the kitchen and pulled out a chair. Motionless, he lay with his head resting on his folded arms pressed to the table, here he remained for a good half hour, eventually moving he entered the downstairs closet to clean up as he felt the soreness of his face and was becoming painful to touch, also his vanity of wondering what damage had been done to his looks.

"How can I keep this from the others, it's become a fucking nightmare, it's beginning to do my head in," said Tommy as he continued to mutter to himself about the events, he was now a victim.

Applying cold water flannels one after the other made a real difference, he felt the effects immediately as his senses came alive, he was more angry than sorry for having been caught out and should have allowed the dogs out, he had learnt a hard terrifying lesson from this attack and he knew ten years ago he would not have been caught out like this. As he continued to bathe his face, Tommy heard noises from outside,

"What the bloody hell is going on,"

Lifting his face to see out of the window, he saw six figures running through the grounds along the grass edge heading towards the entrance to the house and the lane beyond.

"Fuck me there like bloody ants, they're everywhere, the bastards," said Tommy as he made himself angrier by the minute, he remained watchful until he saw the last of the figures disappear out of sight.

Now near to six o'clock (Saturday morning), he decided to go back upstairs to bed. On the landing he undressed and stashed his clothes away, naked he crept back into the bedroom and slipped under the duvet cover, Toni was still fast asleep, she never stirred from his movements. He did his utmost to move as little as possible in his quest for comfort and sleep, it seemed ages before he finally fell asleep.

It was near to ten o'clock when Tommy finally roused, he could hear the chink of china. Toni had entered the bedroom with an aroma of fresh coffee which she carried on a tray. Next Toni put down the tray and went and drew back the curtains letting in the morning brightness as she brought the tray to Tommy, he lay on his side with flickering eyes as he could not adjust to the daylight, he felt sore all over and hoped that it would not be noticed by anyone, especially Toni.

"I'll leave the tray on the side, I'm going for a shower," said Toni in a happy mood of morning contact.

"Okay love, you get on, I'll drink my coffee in a minute," said Tommy in a croaky dry voice.

"Are you alright, your voice sounds a bit horse," said Toni as she was undressing.

"No I'm alright, just a dry throat," said Tommy disconcerted by Toni's comment.

Twice Toni appeared naked from the bathroom to rummaged through her things, including the previous days shopping bags still unpacked on the floor.

"What you forgotten, sunshine, need any help?" said Tommy jokingly.

"No I am sore from last night's performance, I need some cream – You had your coffee yet, drink it before it gets cold."

"Alright, alright, I'm just watching you, God you do have a bloody good body on you and legs right up to your arse," he said with hilarious laughter as Tommy was peeking over the duvet.

"Never mind me, drink your coffee," said Toni also smiling to herself.

When Toni closed went back into the bathroom, Tommy reached out and slid the tray towards him across the bed cover, sitting up, he finally gulped down the coffee before Toni reappeared.

By the time Toni left the bathroom, Tommy had decided to quickly dress and leave the bedroom for the downstairs, when he heard Toni call out.

"Tommy, have you finished up here?" said Toni as she surmised that he had gone down before her as the bed was empty, leaving a crumpled duvet behind.

"Yes love, sorry I forgot the tray – Do you want me to fetch it," said Tommy replying.

"No I'll bring it down in a minute, I was about to say the showers empty if you want it," said Toni.

"Christ I must keep this simple, I must," thought Tommy to himself, this is getting complicated with all this chatting.

At the first opportunity, Tommy went into the downstairs closet and looked in the mirror for any visual signs of the attack, his face rather puffy around the right eye and abrasions down his neck and arms. He began to work out a game plan should anyone make comment about his face. Minutes later he was filling the kettle when Karen and Lenny appeared in the kitchen.

"I've been looking in the mirror at my swollen face, I reckon Toni attacked me last night," he said jokingly and rather casually he soon changed the subject.

"How'd you do that Tommy," said Lenny concerned at what he had seen.

"I came downstairs in the night and tripped, the dogs thought I was playing as the rushed to lick me," said Tommy

"You could have broken your bloody neck, didn't you put the lights on?" said Lenny.

"No, I didn't, said Tommy

"More bloody fool you," said Lenny

"Who could have broken their neck, said Toni entering and carrying the coffee tray.

"Tommy could have done, Look at the state of his face," said Lenny shaking his head, "You are a bloody fool."

"Let's have a look at your face Tommy," said Toni in a concerned voice, "I never saw this when I brought up the coffee earlier," said Toni, "Why didn't you say something then."

"Didn't know did I until I looked in the mirror," said Tommy "It's a bit sore but I'll be alright with a cold flannel." Tommy sidled up to Toni for a cuddle, hoping this would end matters and to focus on other things. However, Toni wouldn't let go of the situation,

"What time did you come down then," she said.

"About five o'clock," said Tommy, "You were fast asleep and all snug when I left the bedroom."

"It looks lovely outside this morning, is it chilly out," said Karen.

"No one has been out yet mate," said Tommy, "It's time to let the dogs out for some exercise Lenny; they have been as good as gold."

"Has the paperboy been yet, I don't want the dogs to scare him, do I," said Lenny poor excuse for not going out, "I need a drink first to get myself going."

"Has anyone seen Frank this morning, I haven't heard a peek out of him," said Tommy, both the girls shrugged their shoulders in answer.

"Well speak of the devil that sounds like him now," said Tommy, as the dogs with pricked ears and a short woof, woof sounded an alert to his movements.

With idle chat continuing among the group, Tommy ambled to the back door and disappeared outside, he continued to hear the voices behind him as he stood and looked around from where he was attacked and fallen. After a few minutes Tommy returned, the others were eating toast, as Toni beckoned him to come and sit down, as he pushed the toast rack in his direction across the table.

Chewing on a piece of toast, Karen said,

"Lenny we'll need to be down at the pickup point by one o'clock, what time do you want us ready bye."

She turned to Toni and said,

"What do you think Toni?"

"What's the time now, "said Toni.

Lenny quietly looked down at his watch and replied.

"Just after eleven,"

"Well you all have a busy hour ahead of you – You carry on and I'll deal with the washing up," said Frank, rather business like.

Frank carried on regardless whilst the others removed themselves from the kitchen, the girls went back upstairs, Lenny took the dogs out and Tommy had already for the second time that morning disappeared. It was left to Lenny on his return to get the Jag out of the garage and ready to drive the girls back to the pickup point, leaving open the front door as he loaded up their luggage.

Lenny was fidgeting, he knew that such a moment would come for the girls to leave, he hoped and prayed this was a beginning and not an end to a beautiful time together, in four days at the house, the stillness and the calm had been broken in the most unexpected way and more extraordinary was the way that he and Tommy took to the girls and vice versa in such a romantic setting and how their personalities so gelled together and so worn out physically by the fucking that went on between them, impressed that he could keep up, not sure about Tommy but he seemed really taken with Toni, "So fingers crossed," he thought as he remained quiet and pondering on what their answers might be for the future of their friendships. Although, Lenny knew he was more sensitive than Tommy when it came to girls, as he really cared and wanted a relationship, but their careers as criminals always took precedence over everything they did together. Now they both feel the loneliness in middle age.

What began as a working arrangement for the girls, and now they each bonded and developed over the four days, was one of clear affection for each other. Yes, Lenny had accepted the girls were working girls, but then he also felt a deep sense of satisfaction that they as two couples, created something special between them forever more, and that's something that money can't buy. Lenny also realised that he needed more in his life than he had at the present, since Karen's arrival, Lenny also acknowledged to himself that he had stayed off the booze and no longer binging, he knew that boredom in the extreme was an enemy in disguise and had to be defeated if he was going to survive into old age, rather buried by drink alone.

Whilst thinking quietly to himself, Lenny had paced umpteen times from the stairs to the front door; he was edgy and impatient as he waited for the girls to appear on the stairs. Again many questions went through his mind, and again it came back to the same question as to whether they would see the girls again and soon.

Frank not wanting to play gooseberry kept tucked out of the way, although, he remained with a cocked ear for when they were ready to leave. Tommy appeared through the back door, he had been on a scouting trip in the woodland, not letting on to the others; he was soon in Lenny's company waiting on the girls.

"Jag's packed, girls will be down in a minute, Tommy," said Lenny quietly.

"Sure Lenny, sure, I'll wait here for them – Jag okay?" said Tommy.

"Yeah, I've checked it over," said Lenny nodding.

"What do you think then Tommy – About the girls going," said Lenny enquiringly.

Tommy shrugged his shoulders and didn't reply, as he turned away and looked out of the open front door.

"Well, what do you think – Will we see them again he asked," said Lenny anxiously.

"It's up to them Lenny, if they want to come again, there welcome you know that mate, anytime they chose, said Tommy without blinking an eyelid.

On the stairs the girls appeared together, Lenny felt awkward, as this was truly not the moment he had been looking for as he watched them both descend the stairs, Tommy stood more towards the front door than the stairs, he remained rigid with both arms folded across his chest, as he watched the girls appear. Karen approached Lenny and led him off into the lounge.

"Well, love this is it," said Lenny as he held her hand, "What do we do now – Karen,"

Lenny just remained staring into his eyes, his hand gently caressed her cheek, as she felt the warmth of his palm, and she leaned and pressed her cheek deeper into his palm as she moved her head back and forth with his touch. He twiddled and fumbled her fingers, as he didn't know what to say to her.

"Oh! Christ Karen, I don't want you to go – I'm going to miss you and Toni," said Lenny whispering.

"Are we going to stay in touch Lenny," said Karen.

"I want you too, I really do – I mean that, you can come anytime you wish, just ring me, just ring, even if it's only for a welfare chat," said Lenny emotionally.

"Look Toni and I have discussed it between us, we both want to stay in touch, we have loved every minute of these four days between us, and I can tell you this is not what we expected by any stretch of the imagination, honestly, this is truly not what we expected at all," said Karen being very convincing with Lenny.

Lenny couldn't stand back anymore as he gently took Karen into his arms and kissed her passionately on the lips, Karen responded just as passionately as they were now locked in a tight embrace, as Lenny's right hand clasped her breast through her clothing, Karen pushed herself even harder against Lenny's caressing hand. Gasps of sighs and pants were beginning to echo in the lounge and hallway as they continued to twist and turn each other in a more sexual way, as Lenny's left hand pulled her buttocks towards him as they began to gyrate together, as their feelings were intense and eager for more and more of their touches upon each other. As they parted Karen was breathless from their encounter, her thoughts and mind swooned as she just stared wide-eyed at Lenny's gracing smile. Then with one last movement she gripped his mouth with her hand as she stood on tiptoe to kiss him with one last lingering kiss, tears were beginning to swell in their eyes as they both began to snivel from the intensity of their passion for each other, the room was electrifying as they finally parted and joined Tommy and Toni at the front door.

"Toni, Frank, don't forget to say goodbye to him," said Karen calling out.

Both girls met Frank at the kitchen door and kissed, hugged and thanked him, for all the funny stories he had told in making it such a memorable occasion, and for them to remember his stories long after they had gone. Their leaving the house was a tearful moment for them all, Frank acted like a big bear with an apron round his waist, Lenny was just as weepy as the girls, and Tommy remained somewhere in between the highly emotional atmosphere and his feet set in concrete. Although Tommy really did care and he responded admirably to Toni in the quietness of their time together, without disclosing too much of each other's past relationships. Tommy hoped it would blossom in the future, as he planned to see Toni again and she was just as keen to see him, without making a commitment on how their friendship, their adventure, their relationship would develop together.

Within minutes of their goodbyes to Frank, both the boys and girls were heading out of the driveway in the Jag. After an hours journey, the group reached their rendezvous point in good time for them to continue their goodbyes with each other.

"I'm sorry you two that I'm such a pain, I suppose my crying was expected," said Karen as she forced a smile from her tearful face, Toni had reached out and taken hold of her trembling hands for comfort.

"Don't worry green eyes, I want you to ring me, when

you get home, so I know that we know you got home safely," said Lenny somewhat concerned by the events of the moment.

Tommy and Toni seemed to have matters more under control as their conversation appeared more conventional, as if their parting had been arranged differently between them and at some previous time, but then this was always the way Tommy worked his affairs, he never left anything to chance at the last minute.

Within minutes of their arrival, the chauffeur driven car arrived for the girl's journey home, again suddenly as it began four days earlier it is now all over, the girls waving from the backseat as it sped off from the slip-road into the mainstream of vehicle traffic.

For the boys, their return journey home was uneventful, as they both remained relatively quiet, with hardly a peek out of either. Clearly, the last four days had not been quite what they expected from the girls visit, from a full on sexual experience that was long overdue for both of them, to a soul searching period where they both got to know intimately their respective partners. Who also came for a more mundane visit and the friendship that clearly developed between them and at such a fast rate of knots? That had left all four rather bewildered and emotionally affected by the bond-ship and how each other's personalities dovetailed over those passing days, that clearly indicates a potential for more of the same contact between them with the trust and confidence they achieved throughout their togetherness with each other.

CHAPTER EIGHT
Forward Planning

By three-thirty that afternoon the boys had been home an hour when Tommy made the decision that Frank and Lenny had long been waiting to hear.

"Right boys, before we get down to business, I have something else to tell you first," said Tommy in rather an authoritative manner.

Lenny gawped bewildered at Frank, and Frank was just as bemused at Tommy's words and the tone in which he spoke.

"Look, I want to get something off my chest first," Frank jovially interrupted Tommy speaking.

"She's gone home Tommy – I hope you are not hallucinating my son,"

Lenny burst out laughing; he of all people saw the funny side of Frank's comments, whilst Tommy looked at the ceiling and all four walls of the lounge before he came back down to earth with a grinning face.

"Oh! Bollocks, let's have another drink, whisky, speak up boys, be quick my darlings – Who wants what," said Tommy, prancing around like some pregnant bloody gnat.

Lenny looked on astonished; he was taken aback by Tommy's sudden change of attitude and personality. Frank, well Frank was good old Frank, it didn't matter either way to him what Tommy was up too, he was enjoying himself with the boys, and the free drinks, of course, especially away from his wife Primmy.

"Right, listen up, last night and about my injuries, well it wasn't any accident, I got caught with my trousers down and got a good hiding for my troubles," said Tommy in a blurted fashion of annoyance.

Lenny and Frank sat dumb struck at hearing Tommy's statement.

"What do you mean no accident, done over by Toni," said Frank in jest.

"No you silly sod," said Tommy quickly.

"Gypsies, not the fucking gypsies Tommy, don't tell me they came back last night," said Lenny holding his head in his hands.

"Gypsies, spot on Lenny, I saw some movement outside, this was about five o'clock this morning, so I watched and waited – saw one standing in the fucking front porch, then later I had to lay on the floor in the lounge, as one came up and looked in the window and tried to look in (pointing to the bay window) he couldn't see in because the curtains were pulled, anyway, I waited awhile then went to the back door to have a look around and I got jumped for my troubles," said Tommy quietly, "But me hearties, I got one of the bastards, I grabbed hold of his balls and by fuck he squealed like a stuck pig," said Tommy in a robust manner as he gestured a hand movement.

"Cor, I bet that bloody hurt him – Tommy, I wouldn't want you grabbing my balls like that, Cor it brings tears to my eyes just thinking about it, I'll have to keep my legs crossed around you, Tommy," said Frank in raucous laughter, "Can you imagine his squeezing your balls Lenny – especially after four days on the nest like you two have had," said Frank.

As their conversation became more comical in the verbal's of hilarity in every which way their quips could be delivered, yet they realised deep down how serious the situation was. Lenny was probably more worried than he let on; it was an escalation from gypsies using the grounds as a meeting place for a pow-wow to being attacked in the grounds of your own home.

"This is not good Tommy – This could be deep shit all round if we're not careful, especially at this time," said Lenny concerned, "Look why didn't you let the dogs out, let the dogs have a taste of flesh, the bastards won't want to come a second time," said Lenny in an aggressive tone.

Frank was twisting his head first one way then the other, as he was gripped by the excitement, one minute Frank wanted to chip in and say something, then he didn't as he hesitated, in between taking sips from his glass, he was enthralled by what Tommy had said. Then before the boys knew it, Frank was up on his feet shadow boxing, his old legs were trading off, one way, and then another. It was at this point Tommy and Lenny took a dive across the floor. Frank's swinging right fist came out of nowhere, the boy's realised (belly laughing out loud and calling Frank's name as they dived) Frank packs a mighty punch for a big man. On their sides and propped up on their elbows the boys watched Frank as he continued his 'Muhammad Ali' foot routine, then right, right, left went his arms, now redden in the face and snorting like a bull, Frank was moving like a one legged ballerina, with pendulum bulbous eyes hanging out of their sockets, Frank looked ferocious. The boys couldn't stop laughing, both near to tears as they tried to communicate, Frank was well and truly on another planet and away with the fairies.

"Just like the old day this is boys, I say give them a bunch of fives (holding up his fist) What'dya say boys?" said Frank growling as he suddenly stopped in his tracks and stood erect laughing and aching from his exercise.

"You finished," said Tommy tearfully laughing.

"Yes boys carry on, "said Frank chuckling to himself.

"Bloody hell – Frank, you're pretty nifty on those pins of yours old mate," said Lenny making light of Frank's sudden outburst.

Frank was about to crawl on the sofa, knees first, when a noise could be heard in the hallway, at the same time a knock at the door sounded, which brought silence from the boys as they listened.

"Who's that then, Tommy?" said Lenny somewhat

surprised by the intrusion.

"I've got no idea mate," said Tommy

Frank was hanging onto the sofa for dear life with both knees wedged down in the cushions with his hands gripping the back of the sofa ready to push himself off.

"Might be the gypo's inviting us to tea boys," said Frank giggling at the same time, taking the piss.

"Come on Lenny, let's have a look, you stay here Frank, we might need you in a minute," said Tommy.

"Hey Tommy, look at Frank, he's got a right arse on him," said Lenny whispering to Tommy as they left to answer the front door.

"Shhhh, don't let him hear you say that, he knows he's put weight on, that's a sore point right now, just humour him," said Tommy as they walked down the hallway.

Leaflets had been dropped through the letter box and scattered over the floor as the sound had alerted the dogs, rushing and barking on hearing Lenny's voice. Lenny felt the full impact as they collided with him.

"Easy boys, come on settle down, Taz sit, sit," said Lenny with a commanding voice.

The dogs ignored his command as they became more excited as they turned and went off and found Frank in the lounge, still kneeling on the sofa when Lenny reached the lounge door both dogs had ignored Frank but their hackles were still raised as they continued to bark.

"Hold on a minute Frank, let me get the bloody dogs quite, I can't hear myself think," said Lenny rather amused at the way the dogs were acting.

"Hurry up Lenny, I'll piss myself if I have to stay like this any longer," said Frank as he pressed a cushion to his backside.

"Lenny this is a fucking nightmare, where's Tommy," said Frank.

"He's at the front door," said Lenny as he brought the dogs under control and returned them to the kitchen, closing the door he went to rejoin Tommy at the front door.

"No one there, I think they left the knocker up and it fell down and that's what we heard as the second sound, I've been out and looked around, can't see anyone mate," said Tommy.

Returning to the lounge, Frank appeared in the hallway,

"I must have a pee," he said, "I was more worried about my arse than anything," said Frank as he chortled and shuffled off to the loo closet.

"Frank had a cushion pressed to his arse to protect himself from the dogs," Lenny said laughing to Tommy.

Tommy remained standing and decided to go back upstairs for awhile.

"Do some sandwiches for us, Lenny, when I come back we need to get down to business old mate, I need to check on the office, okay," said Tommy as he disappeared up the stairs.

Tommy spent some minutes checking the video cameras in the office before returning downstairs and putting Lenny at ease at the same time. Having appraised and checked e-mails and other matters that needed his attention, he also handled a number of mobile phones for messages. The array of IT equipment at his disposal was impressive, to say the least; the office was really designed with hi-tech communications and had been well rehearsed by Tommy over many months by organising his foreign contacts. He was very much in control and obviously had been well organised behind Lenny's back he placed much priority on his forward planning, he now needed to bring Lenny and Frank into the fold and on his side for the big caper he had long planned. Tommy's present market was all cash and nothing doing on credit cards it had to be untraceable transactions and his word against another's. It showed on his smiling face, as he moved around the office. One could feel his intensity at what he had and what he hoped to achieve with his team he hoped to recruit to pull off the biggest job of his lifetime.

The room was purpose built like he had secreted in the copse for self-survival and self-preservation, it was about hard cash to replenish their twiddling bank balances.

The ventilation system in the room had been devised through an air intake shaft that was hidden in the roof of the building and was able to accommodate weather changes throughout the year. But above all somewhere in the large office was an escape hatch linked to another room in the house. Not even Lenny was aware of the extra services Tommy had designed and added to the office for their safety, should they ever need such an escape plan in the future.

So it seems that on their release from prison Tommy had not really left his old life of crime behind him or was it more of a pretence on his part. Considering the workmanship and the skills he had manufactured and developed over the years. But what of Lenny, had he been ignored in Tommy's plans, they do own and live together in the mansion. It was during their first year at the house that Lenny followed other past-times in the fields around the house, running the dogs and a great interest in nature. Lenny would be the first to acknowledge the happy times and clearly by his general attitude overall he would want never to return to the hustle and bustle of London life, as he had found contentment.

On the intercom Tommy could hear the feint voices of Lenny and Frank, as the dogs could clearly be heard scurrying around downstairs and drowned out their words, so downstairs he went rather than wait for him to be called.

"Are we going to settle in the lounge or the kitchen,"

said Tommy.

"Lounge," said Lenny, "we've plated up the sandwiches, just the coffee to come and we are ready."

Again settling down in the lounge Tommy was ready to explain his plans and the reasons as to why Frank was brought down to the house in partnering Tommy's ideas for a big crime caper.

"Now I have been planning a big job and decided that a place like Bristol offers us a great deal in terms of merchandise, with many industrial estates in the suburbs and the accessibility is good, with plenty of motorway access which includes airports, trains and the sea. London is a knackered place; it's tired and fucked, because of all the foreigners and the terrorist threats, it's not worth considering as everybody appears pissed off and the Police don't seem very bright these days, there only interested in social work and traffic offences and that said, as Lenny knows the Police are having trouble with their phone lines," as Tommy said as he handed Frank the local newspaper and showed him the headlines, "Read this Frank."

"London is aggro with heavy traffic and that's what we can't afford to be caught in traffic, I need everybody involved to be away in minutes after each caper, no hanging around, I want transport well organised especially for those from Europe so they can get early morning planes and boats and be gone before the ports are closed down, even so that is a can of worms as the borders is an open sieve, but we need to be sure, we cannot leave anyone behind, caput," said Tommy.

"What's this about Europe Tommy," said Lenny as Frank acknowledged the question.

"I am going to bring a number of skills from Europe and on a need to know basis, none will be aware of each other unless they work on the same caper, but no personal details to be spoken or revealed by anyone for obvious reasons of personal safety in case it goes belly up," said Tommy waiting on their answer, Lenny and Frank just nodded, "So if you can get your heads around that, I bring them over as and when required, most of them are clean and no real form in the kind of capers I've got planned, see my point of view, got any comments about it," said Tommy, both Frank and Lenny said, " No comment, carry on we're listening to you, Tommy."

"What I am proposing is a number of capers's going off at one time, so the Police, should they get wind of it, will be run off their feet, they won't know which way to turn," said Tommy, "You see, we fox them so we can clear up some good jobs, that has a lot of rewards in more ways than one," he said with bouncing enthusiasm that really grabbed the boy's attention.

"I am going to run an operations room with communications, monitors, screens, mobiles so we remain ahead of the game at all times, we need fresh blood, no silly sods or chancer's otherwise we will be screwed with cowboys around us and we will come unstuck, that is why I am bringing some in from Europe to keep a level on the situation, all well recommended good CV's for us to judge and work with. So I will need to be selective of our targets, what are the values to be had, can we achieve our aims in the allotted time on the night we go, go, go," said Tommy punching the air with delight.

It was a good couple of hours by the time the boys had finished and of course, Tommy was well pleased as Lenny and Frank realised the importance of being selective and denying anyone who speaks out of turn as being a possible trouble maker who won't adhere to orders.

Tommy had arranged for Lenny to go down to Bristol on Monday and do some filming of possible targets.

It was late by the time Lenny heard from Karen, she called him on his mobile, so he felt good that she had been in touch and they both got home safely.

Frank remained fixed and comfortable in his armchair, sipping and thinking on his whisky and chewing a stale sandwich that had been left on the plate, he felt good at Tommy's proposals, all sounded very legit and very interesting to go overseas for the teams. He was pleased at their first meeting it made more sense to him now and why the Gypsies need to be sorted out.

CHAPTER NINE
Found Property

Just after eight o'clock the next morning (Saturday) Tommy's hand touched the warmth of the kettle. Lenny had in the meantime taken the dogs for a run. It was Lenny's absence that Tommy began to ponder about a number of things, and how in little more than a week the house had taken on a different meaning, it was more than just living in isolation. It was about the living, it was about the vibrancy and the adrenalin that flowed in their veins, he began to feel their lives had more meaning and purpose today than since leaving prison as dejected men five years earlier.

Frank had been up before six, washed, shaved and sitting on his bed just thinking and churning over the events to himself. Meanwhile, Tommy on hearing the baying sounds of the dogs (deep and throaty would make anyone go weak at the knees) knew that Lenny was around and nearby, when he suddenly poked his head round the kitchen door, his body stopped the dogs from charging in.

"Come and see what I've found Tommy," said Lenny eagerly.

"Hold on a moment let me put the milk in my tea and I'll be right with you," said Tommy seeming puzzled by Lenny's request.

Outside on the garden wall, Lenny had laid out a number of small pieces of cloth he had removed from a plastic shopping bag. Each piece had been deliberately wrapped in such a way so as to conceal its hidden content which Lenny was about to expose. Sipping his tea as he slowly walked the few yards to join Lenny. Tommy saw the neat row of pebble like parcels.

"What have you got there," said Tommy with an inquisitive voice.

Lenny was still retrieving from the plastic bag as he

continued to place the little parcels on the wall.

"Well the dogs have turned up this bag; it was buried down by the boundary fence by the lavender bush. It's clear that someone has deliberately hidden the bag, these are sparklers, Tommy, bleeding bling mate and lots of it, take a look for yourself," said Lenny calmly handing Tommy one of the parcels, then closed the bag.

"How many are there," said Tommy

"Thirty-seven in all," said Lenny

"And how many items are there," said Tommy

"I don't know yet I haven't had time to count them all, but a good few by the weight of the bag," said Lenny.

"Let's have a bloody gander then mate, let's get them in house and on the table for a proper look," said Tommy.

Once in the kitchen it was like Christmas morning unwrapping the parcels one after another, jewellery everywhere as each parcel revealed something different.

"Looks nice pieces," said Lenny

"That's what I am afraid of mate," said Tommy

"We are going to be fucking dropped right in the shit with this lot buried in our garden, just think about it for a moment," said Tommy.

"What do you mean Tommy, I don't follow you," said Lenny.

"This is nicked gear and I bet it's the fucking travellers who've buried this for safe keeping, this is why they have been hanging around the house, this is what they're up to, using our place for their runs back to their camp, if they got turned over nothing would be found and we are fucked as it's on our ground and if Old Bill gets wind, then they are sure to visit and questions will be asked about who, what and when, they have some fucking gall those gypos, they really do," said Tommy searching and thinking for answers,

Tommy emphasised the bigger problem to Lenny, Handling piece-by-piece Tommy's eyes examined each item.

"Call Frank down and let's see what he thinks," said Tommy.

Frank was elsewhere drinking tea and eating his morning toast unaware of the find.

The kitchen door had been left open as the dogs were still roaming around in the garden; Lenny went to bring them in and noticed they were up by the front gate.

"Tommy come here a moment, look at the dogs, there picked up a scent of sorts, look at them," said Lenny

Tommy joined Lenny outside and watched the dogs with noses sniffing the air, they have picked up something mate, look they are rooted to the spot.

"Keep your eye on them, Lenny, I'll go and fetch Frank," said Tommy.

Moments later all three men were stood on the gravel drive just watching the dogs react to something they are sniffing in the air.

"Here have a look at this, the dogs found a hidden bag with these little cloth parcels inside, see what's wrapped inside," said Tommy as he chuckled to himself.

"Fuck me, you struck gold here Tommy, this is the real McCoy, bloody expensive stuff, is it all like this," said Frank.

"Don't know, we've just been unwrapping it - it's all on the kitchen table," said Tommy.

"I saw stuff on the table when I came out, that's it is it," said Frank, as he continued fondling the piece of jewellery Tommy gave him, "Expensive this mate, it's got to be knocked off," said Frank., "This piece is marked," as he handed it back to Tommy.

Lenny was still eyeful of the dog's behaviour up at the gate; he went off and fetched an empty bucket which he filled with water from the outside tap, calling down the dogs as he filled their bowls.

It was whilst doing his chore that he noticed

movement up on the ridge in the woods opposite, he could see figures moving, Lenny didn't react as if he hadn't seen them, probably walking in the field, but who are they? Were they watching us and the house? Do they know what we have found? Lenny's mind raced ahead of his answers realising that if they were gipsies then they have been rumbled and not over exaggerating the possibilities of them having real trouble and the possible repercussions coming their way for removing the plastic bag.

Back in the kitchen Frank went through the jewellery piece-by-piece and guarded his mutterings to himself until he was sure that the pieces had been examined before he gave his opinions.

"You have hit the jacket pot, this is very expensive stuff, some of it appears to be Russian, but even so this is high-quality stuff mate," said Frank.

"Fucking hell, what do we do now, either way we are going to get trouble coming our way, so what is the lesser of the two evils, keep it or hand to the Police, then they will check us out and so and so on, we won't get no bloody peace once the cat's out of the bag," said Tommy more angry and frustrated at the way they have been used innocently and no one would believe them because of their backgrounds.

"Well boys, whether you like it or not, you are well and truly fucked over this lot," said Frank, "So how to control this, make it work for you, don't put it back just hide it and hide it good," said Frank

"How'd mean," said Tommy frowning, not understanding how they can make it work for them.

"Look what did our old grandfathers do back in their time, when they got their hands on stuff like this," said Frank, "They hid it in the plaster, you do the same, do some decorating, wrap each piece in cling film and dig out little holes in the plaster, just big enough to pop each piece into, then make good, then paper over it and just leave it," said Frank in a serious tone of management, "Who is going to prove otherwise if you are turned over, gypsies or Old Bill will not find the stuff will they, who thinks of holes in plaster, the young coppers today wouldn't have a clue like the old masters of the footpads, they sniffed it out of you, just like the dogs," said Frank.

Lenny having sorted out the dogs, he brought the usual two back into the house and the other pair he put in the kennels, as he returned to the kitchen, Tommy turned with a hand rubbing his face as he looked concerned.

"Frank says it's all coshed mate, expensive stuff all of it, Frank suggests we keep it as either way we are going to get some shit, so we go for the short straw Lenny," said Tommy, "Some Russian bits in there as well, Frank suggest we keep it and hide in the plaster work of the house, wrap all the pieces in cling film and dig holes in the plaster like our old granddads did and then make good the plaster, paper over it and just leave it," said Tommy.

Lenny's face was a picture of confusion as the situation gets worse by the minute, although realising that that was a good suggestion of Franks to hide all the items. "Who would find it, no one not even Old Bill unless they came with a metal detector and that isn't going to happen, is it," said Lenny.

"The only real option left is to keep our mouths shut and deny all knowledge, not even to mention the gypsies in the garden, as they are not going to Old Bill and complain about their missing jewellery and we certainly can't take this anywhere to be checked out, even for the values of the pieces. We just don't know where it has come from and what trouble that could bring us," said Tommy.

"The travellers are going to come looking, you two just need to be on your toes, that's all, are your outside lights working, check," said Frank.

"I have no idea we have never used them," said Tommy.

"Look I could arrange a couple of boys to come down to take the sting out of the situation, but again that could be a bit dodgy with too many men around the place it will only draw someone's suspicion and then rumours start and then Old Bill's on your doorstep," said Frank, "Look there is one way if things got out of hand, sort them out on their own doorstep, where are they living Tommy," said Frank.

"Up the lane a bit, they camp on the side of the road, it's not a proper camp site," said Tommy.

"Well that's ideal then, a fast drive through the lane, bang, bang and off, pepper the side of the caravans, that will soon shift them mate, cause panic," said Frank in a serious mode of words, you could sense Frank was really truly living the drama.

"Right then Lenny would you fetch the digital, we might as well film this stuff whilst it's sat here," said Tommy.

Lenny went upstairs to fetch the camera, the dogs had retreated earlier to their baskets and were catnapping and eyebrows tweaking from side to side as they observed the boys movements.

"I think this changes everything at the moment and requires all hands on board, I'll give Prim a ring and see if I can stretch this out till Tuesday, what do you think? You need extra hands over the weekend and without going overboard with manpower," said Frank, "At least I can do that for you, Lenny can still do his run on Monday as planned, and I'm here to cover for him and I'll go back to smokey on the afternoon train on the Tuesday," said Frank.

"Well you better bell home Frank and see if Prim will wear it – You see the other thing that bugs me, we don't know how long that's been buried in the garden and where it has come from, whether local or miles away, It's obvious that it's from several places," said Tommy feeling more comfortable with Frank offering to stay over and help.

"The point is Tommy, Listen up Lenny, we've all assumed it's nicked stuff and been hidden by travellers, now that's all you need to be concerned with – If it's not travellers, then who did put it there? – If it's not travellers then you are off the bloody hook, because there the one's who's been pushing their luck and you think they're the same ones who attacked you," said Frank metaphorically.

Meanwhile and during the conversation Lenny returned with the camera, leaving it on the table for Tommy,

"Listen up before I forget, when I was watering the dogs and before I came in we were being watched from the woodland on the opposite side of the lane, I didn't react just carried on and saw the figures move off into the field, it could be gypsies or walkers, but whoever they were they stood watching me, so perhaps there is a story in this," said Lenny.

Tommy filmed the haul of jewellery and decided to remove every little trace of their find to the safe upstairs in the office until they are able to do what Frank suggested.

"We are now in a waiting game, boys, see what happens to night," said Frank.

With the excitement now over and the boys having made a decision on the find by mid-afternoon Tommy went over to his workshop in the copse.

(It made him very proud of his man made achievements so far, the remains of four lorry containers buried under tons of earth to create the copse, it was a reflection of their hard work in their early years in forming a hidden base underground, the steel containers laid side by side like the advents of a cemetery, their headstones were the flowers and shrubs which covered and sprouted over the formed landscape which camouflaged the dell area above. It was a dream of fantasy, a place to be away from the outside world, in tranquillity and reality of their own enterprise, although it had been nearly two years since Lenny visited or used the site, it still offered him an interlude and a hobby of developing new skills when alone)

Deep in the bowels of the complex, Tommy had been instrumental in making many set pieces of equipment to be included in his planned crime operation, although, there were other ideas and components to be designed and considered, some was clearly dangerous work when working on some large structures alone. Tommy at times could really do with another pair of hands for some of the heavy lifting, he had improvised in lifting dead weights by devising new equipment to operate safely, but nevertheless, still dangerous work at such depths should he have an accident.

Contained in the steel tomb below ground was an array of sophisticated components ranging from a range of personal radios with charged batteries topped up, pulleys, ropes of all sizes, collapsible ladders, a selection of hooks and grabs for anchoring to buildings or objects. Tommy recently completed a section of tiled roofing with a detached chimney, the design of which was light weight and was to be used to cover an entry point on one of their capers. It would mean that the section itself could easily be carried or moved by one person, where a section of the roof would be removed and the new section overlaid and inserted to be authentic and camouflaged to prying eyes from the ground, no one would recognise the changes at night time. The inserted section operates like a trap door allowing access and entry at one location with sufficient space to take or remove large interior objects from a building. In fact, Tommy had even designed the hangers for the relevant roofing rafters to sit on, and support the main roofing structure.

The infrared communications system designed by

Tommy, was a portable apparatus that required to be linked to routers to provide a silent messaging carrier with use of a laser beam acting as the main source, Tommy hoped this would be one of his wonder tools but needed time to experiment further as he again needed another pair of hands to operate the system. Tommy was no last minute chancer his attention to detail was more exacting on him mentally than he realised at times, due to his often bouts of tiredness, he was clearly over doing it.

During Tommy's absence, Frank had remained in the lounge and long been engrossed in the contents of a folder Tommy had left him. Reading through the details it was obvious to Frank he had deliberately left out large chunks of information, it was not Tommy being bloody-minded but cautious and a little bit too cautious and over the top for his liking as he was not a mind reader as he muttered to himself as Frank was desperate to assume Tommy's thinking for him to be on the same page as him. Tommy had been forthright from the start that his planning was the beginning that was like no other in the history of crime, and trust and confidentiality was of prime importance in protecting them and all who took part and why he had to be so meticulous in choosing his teams.

It was important and essential that much of the detail was divulged only on a need to know basis and not committed to paper, which could identify the relevant sources of targets and people. Tommy had emphasised some of the main issues confronting him and the challenges ahead as coloured pointers left in Frank's folder.

But when was that day to come?

How would this all be apparent and come together on the day?

How would Tommy control so many foreign operatives?

What contingency plans had he in place in case of a fuck up

Frank's mind boggled at the sheer scale and Tommy's audacity to think he could pull off such a large crime caper without being caught, questions, questions, questions raged in Frank's thoughts. But he also knew that Tommy had been one of the best planners in the business; he had been a legend in his day he and Lenny only got caught for being grassed up by an insider and can understand why he is so cautious. Yet over the years, the identity had long been known of the informant and not once had Frank heard on the grapevine that Tommy or Lenny was out for revenge, instead they slipped quietly away without any fuss being made and ripples of animosity being left behind by both.

Tommy was now in his element he embraced new technology to further his aims of success and rich pickings by making it all work for his planned crime spree. He was good at reading the trends of the future knowing how to capitalise on the real benefits to be had. Tommy was his own man and he had looked after Lenny as the years have told their own story about their bonding and lifetime friendship as both being joined at the hip.

By the time Tommy returned Frank had nodded off clutching the folder to his chest and the two dogs had sprawled out alongside Frank's sofa, the dogs' eyes blinked as neither took much notice of Tommy's presence, it was rather a serene moment he witnessed as he turned and left the room.

It was hours since he last saw Lenny, he had gone off to do some chores, it had been days since washing was seen on the line and needed to be to show that the house was occupied and the Hoover hadn't been touched in days, now it's evening and coming on dark it was climbing the stairs and off to bed.

He left his bedroom door slightly ajar on his

retirement for the night, still very uneasy about the day's events and the problem with the jewellery which was more than troubling. Before climbing into bed he had wrapped the curtain around him as he stood at the window surveying the grounds for any signs of movement, his leg muscles still gave him gyp and clearly needed to lay down and get off his feet as he finally climbed into bed.

It hadn't appeared long when Tommy was disturbed by the sounds of whimpers and scurrying around, he was exhausted as he strained his ears to the noise and movement of the dogs. "What had they heard, what's disturbed them," he thought, he didn't know what to make of it as he was still half awake as he continued to listen from his bed.

It was around three o'clock in the morning (Sunday) when he felt prodding on his back, turning over he realised that one of the dogs had entered the bedroom, he also realised that he had gone back to sleep earlier when he heard the whimpers and not responded to the sounds.

"Christ what is going on," as he spoke to one of the dogs who were both pacing around the room, "What is it boys," Tommy whispered to the dogs. Tommy was sensing something was wrong for the dogs to be acting up like this.

He listened, the dogs remained close by as he saw their eyes watching his every move, as he slowly slipped off the bed and moved towards the open door and the landing, the dogs remained quiet by his side. Reaching the bottom of the stairs without incident he left the dogs in the hallway whilst he slipped into the lounge first and then the kitchen, groping in the darkness it appeared to be in order, finally creeping up to the front door he pushed out the flap of the letterbox and listened for the slightest sound, nothing could be heard, perhaps a false alarm he thought. However, he decided to spend the rest of the night on the sofa, daybreak saw a turn of events that brought shock waves to Tommy's aching body. The dogs had reacted to further noises and both had rushed towards the kitchen, he followed as both animals were flapping about wanting to go outside as they stood waiting at the rear door. Gathering his senses he let both dogs out of the house, it wasn't long before the dogs hit base, hearing deafening squeals and sounds of running footsteps on the drive as he listened from the rear porch. Moving out of the porch he could hear crashing and thrashing noises coming from the undergrowth and by the very tone of the dogs baying sounds that made it evident that they were in hot pursuit of what? – Tommy decided to get the key and go round to the kennels for the other two dogs, this time he decided to place collars and leads on both and kept them close to him, as he waited on the return of the two dogs in hot pursuit, when both eventually returned exhausted as they both literally collapsed and laid on the ground tongues out and panting heavily. He brought all four dogs into the house and plied them with cold water with ice cubes, at the same time did they catch their quarry and did they draw first blood was the question most uppermost in his mind as he grinned to himself, would daylight provide the answers he sought he could only wait for the time to pass to find out.

Tommy finally awoke from his unscheduled sleep at the kitchen table, he sat back with both palms flat on the surface as he gathered his senses,

"Christ how long have I been here," he muttered as he looked around saw all four dogs sprawled out asleep.

Tommy's physical strength had taken quite a knock and it was beginning to show, bruising to his face was evident and his knees were playing him up with his persistent bending and kneeling. He was far from squeamish about his injuries, although, silly because he hadn't bothered to seek medical treatment, but then as he thought would it have made a difference other than resting up and that he couldn't do at this time, but he was still paying a price for his actions and stubbornness. Standing away from the table and feeling rather light headed he was still eager to get outside and check on the earlier events that upset the dogs, he was only interested in seeing daylight and there was plenty of it now this Sunday morning as the time was much later in the morning and good enough for him to whistle the dogs as he left by the kitchen back door. The dogs were soon racing off in one direction as one by one they followed each other into the shrubs and bushes along by the boundary fence.

Very early next morning Lenny had roused Frank, realising as he passed Tommy's open door that he was already downstairs, and soon he followed down to the kitchen where he saw the back door had been left open. Minutes later Frank had joined Lenny and they both left the house puzzled as they stood outside listening for any sounds, when 'Raz' & 'Taz' appeared from the bushes ignoring them, as both dogs ran straight across in front of them to the opposite side of the grounds and disappeared up into the wooded copse.

Frank and Lenny went to where the dogs first appeared from,

"Fucking hell it looks like a bomb has been dropped, look at the bloody mess over there Frank," said Lenny in an astonished fashion of disbelief.

Both began calling Tommy, remaining where they found the mess both searched high and low for some evidence, what caused this mess and what part did the dogs play in all of this, when Tommy appeared from somewhere.

"What the fuck has been happening Tommy, look at the bloody mess," said Lenny shouting.

"Those bastards gave us another visit, they came back in the night and I let the dogs out," said Tommy.

"How'd you know they came back," said Lenny.

"Dogs came into bedroom and woke me up, came

downstairs and looked out, nothing was amiss at the time, so I camped out on the sofa, then I saw movement, shadows across at the window, so I put the dogs out and all hell broke loose and this I suppose is the results as I didn't see anybody after that, only the dogs baying and sounding off, nothing, I have found nothing, I've been down to the boundary fence and checked where the jewellery had been left," said Tommy in a right foul mood as you could cut a knife through his simmering anger at the nights events.

"Look me and Frank is going down there to have a look around," said Lenny now more anxious than ever to get this put to bed.

It didn't take long for the pals to confirm that someone had been digging by the Lavender bush, returning to Tommy seated on the ground and looking really worse for wear at this time of a morning.

"Well that confirms your worst fears Tommy, Someone's been turning over the ground, there obviously looking for something, could be the plastic bag mate," said Frank

This was the news that Tommy didn't want to hear, he hunched his knees to his chest and just continually rubbed his shins as he stared out over the landscape below. Tommy didn't utter a word, as Frank and Lenny stood wondering what to do next urging Tommy to go and get his head down and rest.

It was then, that Frank turned back to face the house when he noticed a figure squatting among the bushes in the copse, the figure was puffing on a pipe and casually appeared relaxed and not hiding from their view. Frank told Tommy that they were being watched.

"That's the old man, he's got something for us I bet, thank fuck for that," said Tommy, "That's him, have you got any dosh on you, Frank," said Tommy bouncing back to life with an urgency.

"No it's back in the house, how much do you want

Tommy," said Frank.

"Five tens will do me, keep him sweet for more next time," said Tommy.

Frank and Lenny both helped Tommy off the ground,

"I'll go and have words with him if someone would go back and get some cash for me," said Tommy as he leant forward and brushed himself down, "Take the dogs back, I don't want them chasing the old fellow off," said Tommy to Lenny.

Tommy walked off in the direction of the gypsy, as he climbed the bank of the copse he was alone. The old traveller had remained hidden in the undergrowth, although, very watchful, it had more to do with the adjacent lane behind him and whether any of the younger members of the fraternity would come down and be nosey and catch him out. Tommy finally came into the presence of the old man, who said his name was Ben Witney from Oxfordshire.

"Tommy's not looking too bright he looks bloody rough at the moment, he ought to go back to bed and rest up when he's finished with the old man and get some sleep," said Frank to Lenny as they both walked back to the house.

"You tell him, Frank, you suggest he gets his head down and rest up," said Lenny, "Look fetch the cash and leave it by the bottom of the fence up at the gate, the old man will know where to pick it up from where he can see you put it, it's safer for him to be on the outside of the fence than in the grounds," said Lenny.

Frank minutes later appeared and waved the money in his hands as he went and placed it in the grass by the front gate then he returned back to the house and waited on Tommy's return.

Lenny was already speaking to Frank in the kitchen, "I ain't fucking going back out there again to clean the mess up that can wait another day.

"That reminds me, Tommy was on about popping

down to the local boozer and see if he can ear-hole gossip about the gypsies," said Lenny.

"Well he still can but he needs to get his head down before he falls down, he is a stupid sod," said Frank.

"No I suppose you are right, only I am going to have an early night so I can leave early in the morning," said Lenny.

"Of course Bristol tomorrow," said Frank, " Well that's not a problem as I am staying over and I can watch a bit of telly while you have gone, take my mind of all the excitement," said Frank laughing.

Both pals waited on Tommy's return and rather shocked to learn that it was nearing nine o'clock and not later as they both thought, when Tommy finally appeared with the old man having slipped away from the grounds.

"What you carrying there Tommy," said Lenny.

"Mushrooms, mushrooms, he's got a bloody great bag full of them, so we can have a good breakfast and the old man has got his alibi and the fifty quid so he's sorted," said Tommy.

"What's chirped you up mate, got some news then," said Lenny.

"Well the old man has really done us proud, the young'uns have been choring (stealing) up in the Midlands, apparently the stuff we found in the garden has come from a number of burglaries (dwellings) they are hoping to sell the lot for a couple of grand (pause) that's their opinion, we know the jewellery is worth a lot more (nodding at Frank and Lenny) Right what's happened is the young gypos down here who nicked the stuff, have had a run in with some other group of travellers up there, apparently this fucking group down here are like a load of bunnies rabbits, I don't know how many were involved, but they gang banged three of the other gypsy girls who were up for it but things got out of hand and they all got caught. Only the old man was saying that the girls agreed the leg over's, but only one at a time (pause) Anyway, they had been drinking cider and something else and it got ugly and were chased back to their own patch. Now this is where we come into it, the locals think they were followed and that the other lot nicked the plastic bag with the jewellery. That is when I saw movement outside and let the fucking dogs out, that's when things started to liven up in the garden – The dogs did attack and nipped a few, but we don't know how many there were in total, but the dogs surprised them and they all shit themselves, the bites ain't done too much damage, it's more of their pride hurting for now," said Tommy with a big happy smile on his face and a man who had the world lifted off his shoulders.

"Well that fifty quid is well spent, that's worth waiting for – How long having you known the old geezer Tommy," said Frank.

"Since we came here really he's always been about and we have acknowledged each other from time to time, I have helped him out with a few bob now again for doing some of the small jobs I've got him to do, although, mainly keeping an eye on the house mainly, he loves a good yarn, he tells great tales believe me, some are really funny, I only knew his first name didn't know where he came from," said Tommy now more relieved than ever.

"I am fucking amazed that it's turned out like this," said Lenny, "I just can't believe it."

"The old man did say that some of the houses burgled belonged to foreigners, but he didn't know who they were," said Tommy, "Well we know there is Russian jewellery among the pieces, so say no more, we can only wait on the next chapter and for the moment we are off the hook," said Tommy rubbing his hands together saying he needed a coffee.

"He also said it could be a week or more for the young ones to make up because of the gypsy girls involved, they have got the taste for more and likely to go back as the boys have been knocking off the girls for some time, swapping partners at the same time, so we need to be on our toes in the weeks ahead," said Tommy.

"Right first things first Tommy, you look fucking knackered mate and Lenny and I think you ought to get your head down, Lenny's already said he is going to have an early night because of tomorrow and I have the telly to watch later, so have your coffee and fuck off to bed," said Frank gesturing the open down of the kitchen and upstairs you go, mate.

"Point taken, coffee, shower and bed in that order right," said Tommy, "And the old man was happy with the fifty."

CHAPTER TEN
Bull & Butcher Public House

Sunday evening Tommy eventually arrived at the local pub for his first taste of real ale served up in the Bull and Butcher the villages only public house, situated on the outskirts of the village and two miles from the mansion house.

Pub life had been Tommy's home for many years back in the days of the East End of London; it felt strange as the interior was very countrified and different to the places he once frequented. He soon had his backside seated on a bar stool with his legs straddling the lower rungs, with an elbow resting on the edge of the bar, he felt relaxed and comfortable. The licensee's wife Judy Stoles had just placed Tommy's change on the bar, when she acknowledge another customer arriving in the pub.

"Hello Bob how's my favourite copper tonight," said Judy.

"Fine, just fine, how's yourself sunshine?" asked Bob.

"Usual Bob," said Judy.

"Please," came his reply.

Tommy just supped the frothing head of the beer, the coldness hit the back of his throat as he smacked his lips in the delight.

"God, that tastes nice, that's what I call a real beer," said Tommy muttering to himself.

He knew without turning around the local was very popular for the sounds of the door opening and closing as people certainly arriving in their numbers, of course, the priority by some was to claim their favourite seats for the night. Tommy grinned as he had already worked out the locals who were jockeying for their positions before ordering at the bar.

"Should be an interesting night," he murmured into the froth of the beer.

Bob, the policeman had remained standing alongside Tommy. Tommy listened to the idle chat from various conversations that crisscrossed around the pub, Judy Stokes was calling out some orders even without some being customers at the bar, she was good at her job, thought Tommy, she certainly appeared efficient on face value of his observations, as he hadn't long been in the pub himself and she certainly was a friendly lithe looking forty-something year-old woman. Sporting a beautiful ponytail, which was tied neatly by a small ribbon, yes she was a very attractive woman who held one's attention as she moved back and forth along the bar.

Tommy remained silent as his eyes darted at every opportunity to look around at the locals without being too suspicious himself.

"I didn't expect you in here tonight Bob – I thought you were going away on a course," said Judy Stokes.

"No I've just finished work, I stayed over to sort my paperwork out, I'm off tomorrow first thing for a month," said Bob, lifting his glass to his lips.

"So who's holding the fort while you're away?" she said.

"John will cover for me while I'm away, Yeah it's going to be funny going back to school at my age love," he said grinning.

"How're the kids, has she let you see them'" said Judy.

"Yeah, I had them yesterday for a few hours, it's still the bloody same, nothing's changed with her attitude, she still sounds like world war three," said Bob.

Judy and Tommy burst out laughing at his comment, Bob acknowledged Tommy's interest and focused his next sentence at him.

"I'm in a bloody separation at the moment, especially as I'm on a month's course (pausing and faced Judy) The worst thing is – she won't bloody speak to me after all these years, she has totally blanked me off and threatened me with divorce," said Bob

"It's a shame that she's acted like that Bob – Perhaps being away for a month might make her see sense, she might come round you never know it could be a blessing in disguise," said Judy.

"Yeah I bloody hope so, it's doing my head in at the moment (pause) not knowing what ails her and what with the bloody travellers who needs enemies," said Bob as he downed the remains of his pint.

"Please, I'll have another love," said Bob

"Here let me get that for you, I'm about to have another and that is my lot I am driving," said Tommy.

"Bob's our expert on the gypsies and the travellers that are around here," said Judy.

"Talking of gypsies Judy, remember what I told Dan awhile back, those up on the ridge are real trouble at the moment, many of the elderly round here have had visits from them lately, So remind your husband to make sure he locks everything up at night, I mean that otherwise they will clean you out if you give them a chance," said Bob, "Remember you're the last place on the way out of the village."

"I'll remind him about what you said, he's out the back somewhere, he is around, unless he's crept upstairs to watch telly," said Judy laughing.

Tommy placed a fiver on the bar for the two beers; Bob raised his glass and thanked him for the drink.

"I couldn't help overhearing, but are you in the local force," said Tommy.

"Judy loves everybody to know I'm a copper (pause – as he nodded in her direction) she's lovely, good landlady – Yes sorry, yes I'm in the local force, I'm stationed in the village, but my work with the gypsies take me all over my force area, bloody early starts and long hours, that's part of my marriage problems," said Bob phasing his conversation as he seems to go off in a trance like state of concentration, then suddenly said, "God bloody women, why do they have to be so unreasonable?"

"I'm afraid I don't have an answer on that one mate – All women seem to be a bloody mystery, I steer clear of them most of the time, it's only when nature calls do I take an interest," said Tommy.

"I take it you are not married either – I see what you mean about the urge of nature calling, the trouble is when you've got kids, that's when it hurts," said Bob rather quietly.

Tommy slowly and skilfully manipulated the conversation more towards the subject of gypsies. Bob the copper was more than reciprocal about his work and so Tommy continued to work this to his own ends. It was clear from the conversation that gypsy crime was a political football among senior officers and politicians alike and pressures had been brought to bear on the lower ranks of the police service, in fact the gypsy has become the untouchables with many pressure groups in support and the old political correctness that is ear marked by a load of farts who spend much of their working days watching their backs and have ears of brick dust, they are only in it for their own sad agendas as if representing the whole of society, hear no evil, speak no evil is more their motto.

"It's scandalous in the way these people are allowed to get away with it, I have met some lovely people in the fraternities, the real old Romany families who just want to earn a crust and be left alone, but there are other breeds who have tagged onto the gypsy name who are professional criminals twenty-four seven, and as you can appreciate they all get tarred with the same brush – The fraternities have their own pecking order, some have done well, some own land, some have their own legit businesses, there are many Romany travellers who live comfortable ordinary lives in houses, they too know when to change direction, they know that scrap metal and old cars can no longer give them a living like the old days, so diversify, the same as our society does, markets change and so do trends – But the lot we have on us at the moment are all over the bloody place committing crime and of course the name of the game today is softly, softly, governor's are scared of them, governor's have spent much of their service with their heads down climbing the promotion ladder and have very few practical skills and knowledge, certainly not streetwise many of them, the public see a uniform, there've got no idea what's under the helmet and the mind of the officer, the public would be shocked – Still what's the time, I must be on my way, get organised for the morning," placing down the empty glass,

Bob called out to Judy that he was going and then turned to Tommy and said his goodbyes. When Bob had left the pub, Tommy said to Judy.

"Very interesting bloke, your Bob," said Tommy still fishing for knowledge.

"Bob, he's a lovely fellow, I wish there more like him, he's very popular around here, so easy to get on with and he listened, he makes time for people," said Judy.

"He was telling me about his separation," said Tommy

"That's been a terrible time for him, she couldn't stand the long hours on her own, she didn't understand his work, he deals a lot with the gypsies, sometimes he would have to go away for days on end with his work," said Judy.

"Yeah, he was talking about the gypsies before he left, he doesn't think much of his governors, I get the impression they're all frightened of officers like Bob, he knows too much and obviously has done plenty, so his knowledge and skills are greater on the ground than theirs – Policing is about politics today sunshine, but then what do ordinary folks do, we moan and whinge and go back to sleep until it's on our doorstep, then we start moaning and whinging all over again because no one wants to help or get involved, it's far easier for us to give money to bloody charity, it ease's our conscience and that make us feel good, so sod the old folk on the way, there've had their time on earth, it's about keeping your nose out of what doesn't concern you, don't take things too seriously – The English have lost the plot, we're pawns, we're a bloody sponge for all in sundry to squeeze us dry and we don't bother to stop it, so I can understand a bloke like him trying to do something about it, but his hands are tied, he's only going through the motions of doing his job, I feel bloody sorry for him, I really do, I know how he must feel inside and that's bloody awful," said Tommy.

"You are not a politician are you, that was a good speech of yours plain and simple, you and Bob would get on fine, he has had it rough lately, he is a good copper and very fair with people, he helps the elderly in the village a lot, they've been plagued for months by those bloody pests, door knocking and harassing them for work and drinks of water, it's terrible for them, so frightening at their age," said Judy as she continued to rub the bar with her hand.

"What do you mean," said Tommy, "About the elderly, I mean."

"Some of my customers have been on about the treatment of the elderly, apparently there manner at times has been quite threatening, I mean the other night a customer was telling us about a pensioner, who wanted a roof repaired, anyway he was conned out of two thousand pounds by those bastards – They even had the cheek to take the old man down to the bank and wait for him to draw his cash, then they dumped on the edge of the village and made off, he was so upset and confused when he was eventually found – Poor dear," said Judy with a concerned and somewhat angry voice.

"Bloody hell just like that," said Tommy somewhat astonished.

"That's right, I mean my Dan was listening and he thought it shocking that they can get away with it – Anyway it was Bob who caught them in the end and got some money back for the old man, next time you see Bob you ought to ask him," said Judy.

"It's funny you should say that, he did mention the gypsies just before he left," Judy interrupted.

"Well Bob's the one to put you right about those bastards," said Judy.

"From his conversation, I got the impression that he didn't always get the backing from senior officers, It sounds to me as though senior officers don't think these people are capable of such crimes, especially on a large scale, I' surprised that he doesn't get the support and the equipment he needs to do his job to trap the bastards, the way I see it, is if you are of no fixed abode and live like they do, you can do anything, the ones who are penalised are the likes of me and you because we live in houses, it's easy to find us at home (pause – laughing together) Can you imagine one morning waking up to thousands upon thousands of people leaving their homes to live like gypsies, you think of the panic politicians will be running around like red arsed headless chickens, - No they should allow the , 'Bobbyjacs' time to do their jobs properly, they should let those with the knowledge and the experience do their work and do their jobs for much longer than they do, they are after all public servants we are paying them, they work for us as a whole and not their bloody management, - Mind you I've also met some lovely travelling people over the years, there not all trouble makers but sadly that's often the picture that's painted of them, people are frightened by the very word gypsy, but I can assure you they are not all bad," said Tommy spoken as if he was an authority on them.

Judy moved away for a moment to serve a customer, Tommy sat and continued to drink from his glass and watchful of those in the bar, he was very observant even right down to the smallest detail, his eyes focused and panned like a zoom camera, recording and noting all that happens around him, people's mannerisms, he was very astute and very mindful of how suspicious people can be at the slightest moment, especially of strangers coming in their midst the same in any community always very wary as he sat straddled on the stool. Judy returned as Tommy said,

"Have you had travellers in here? Have you had any trouble with them?"

"Yes we did have some bother a few years back, we won't serve them if there are too many, we don't encourage them in here. My Dan was in here the last we had aggravation, it was a load of Irish travellers, it was a bloody nightmare, Dan turned the hosepipe on them, women and kids the lost scurried away dripping wet by the time Dan had finished with them," said Judy. Tommy was laughing out loud, "I would love to have seen that, I can just picture them all running off," said Tommy as he continued to laugh, when Judy said, "The funny part was Dan had flooded the bloody bar area that night he had made a right mess in here, he won't have any truck with them and they have never been back to this day, even if he sees a traveller pull outside he is out there chasing them off, my Dan is not scared of them, he's ex-military knows how to look after himself, even Bob has told us about the bad blood among themselves," said Judy grinning and laughing as she demonstrated Dan's actions with the hosepipe, sheer mayhem.

Tommy was hysterical so were some of her customers, she even made the swishing noise like gushing water.

"Look up there on the ceiling there still are stains from that day, the place should been painted after the mess, but Dan is Dan and said leave it up there to be seen by all as a reminder, he will eventually do it, when he's fed up looking at it," said Judy still grinning.

"Did you wet any of your locals that night," said Tommy chuckling.

"No but that was a night to remember, I was scared at the time wondering how it was all going to end, I expected them to come back and do some damage, but it didn't happen, thank god," said Judy.

"That is one of the funniest stories I have heard in a long time, using a hosepipe, I wonder how many have thought of doing that over the years," said Tommy, good comedy he thought.

"Like you said earlier, not all travellers are bad, Dan uses a couple in the garden to cut the grass, funny that one of them is an old fellow called Ben, the younger one can't sound his 'H's properly and of course you can't help him, as he can't read and write, he hasn't got a clue, is a worker and so funny when he tells a story, keeps us in fits sometimes he loves his cider concoctions though," said Judy smiling to herself.

Tommy decided to drink up and make his way home, saying his goodbyes and a friendly wave to the other customers he left the pub, before leaving, Tommy turned and said, "Bob's surname, do you know it,"

"Yes it's Bob Benyon, said Judy as she waved him out the door, "See you again," she called out.

On his way home, Tommy saw a couple of youths struggling to push a car up the lane, a mile from the pub, Tommy slowed and drew alongside them and called out.

"You alright - Far to go," shouted Tommy from the open passenger window.

On hearing Tommy's shout, the youths left the vehicle and ran off into the nearby field, leaving the vehicle abandoned and without lights, but the biggest danger was when the vehicle started to roll backwards on the incline, he soon realised that the handbrake wasn't set, as he pulled to the offside to avoid a collision, a few yards backwards and the rear wedged into the grass verge and stopped.

"Jesus Christ, those were young gypsies, I should have known, I bet the fucking vehicle is a nicked motor," said Tommy reasoning out his thoughts to what he had seen, as he accelerated away at high speed, a mile further and he was home and tucked out of the way.

Tommy quickly entered the house, passing through the kitchen to the lounge, Frank was sprawled out on the sofa with his eyes glued to the television, and Tommy was the first to speak.

"Do you want a tea or coffee mate?"

"I'll have tea mate, how'd you get on down the road, any good," said Frank listening for an answer as Tommy moved back to the kitchen.

"I'll tell you in a minute, it's been a funny old night," he called out answering Frank question.

Minutes later he returned with their hot drinks.

"Lenny turned in," said Tommy

"Yes mate, he went off early," said Frank.

"Do you know if he gave the dogs a run," said Tommy

"Yes mate, he's seen to them, I think one or other has followed up the stairs," said Frank

"Yeah you are right their baskets are empty, that's probably where they are upstairs,"

Frank sat up as Tommy passed the tea to him, he plonked himself down on a nearby chair, slurping tea at the same time.

"So what happened then mate, was it good," said Frank eager to know more.

"Well yes, I met the local copper who's an expert on the gypsies, but he's got some aggro with his wife and he's away for a month on some course tomorrow, so it was a quick drink with him, but I managed to have a chat, he's a nice bloke, down to earth – Anyway I spent more time chatting to the landlady and she told me about the problems the old folk are having with the travellers in the village, it seems our friends up on the ridge are out and about and are very busy boys in crime," said Tommy.

"Get any names Tommy, does she know any of them," said Frank.

"No, she didn't mention names, other than the copper's, his name is Bob Benyon, so remember that, it might come in handy, you never know?"

"So what do you reckon on tonight then Tommy, was it worthwhile in the long run," said Frank rather inquisitive.

"Christ yes, the landlady, she's called Judy, she told me about the time when her old man used a hosepipe on some Irish travellers causing trouble in the bar, he got rid of them and flooded the floor area of the pub at the same time, it's how she told it, it's a bloody funny story, I can just picture those bastards running out the door and wet through," said Tommy laughing along with Frank's giggling.

"The copper sounds interesting, at least you've got his name and knows what he looks like and he won't be around for a month, that helps us mate surely, a gift from the heavens you might say," said Frank sitting more alert to Tommy's conversation.

"It was a stroke of luck meeting like that, in fact, I would not have known he was a copper, it was the landlady who shouted that out in the pub, so we all knew then," said Tommy he was surprised at the way the landlady introduced him and then said.

"Well it's the first time out of the traps for me, I've never been in there before tonight, neither of us visits pub's locally, we just haven't done it and tonight it pays off," said Tommy thinking on his own words of encouragement.

"Well at least you got something out of it mate," said Frank reassuringly.

"You see Frank, I have this ardent feeling and sense a tremendous expectancy of winning hands down on one of the biggest Crime capers of all times in Britain – You know about five years requisite and spent convictions, well think of it another way, Lenny and I have not been turned over or been in the limelight or got a parking ticket in five years, right, so let's take this a stage further – When did we get sentenced for our last job, now think about it, now how many of those coppers do you think are still serving today, those who did us were experienced twenty plus men and I bet many on their last legs to the point of them retiring, you see where I am coming from Frank – We are looking at Bristol and not London, so the coppers are going to be a lot younger in service and wet behind the years, they have no real experienced officers to teach them, they're only dealing with parking and traffic offences, juveniles and cautions, they don't investigate anymore, the public are doing it themselves – look at the laughs we had in the joint we all mucked in together, now you got all these different gangs and all out for a fight and easy to get into trouble in there today. When they brought in the cautioning system it was lazy Policing at its best, kept the old Politicians happy especially the stooge who created it, dead brain, but nevertheless, cautions are a licence to commit crime in a big way and really in big time and it pays to put your hands up to what you have been caught with and you are soon out the door of the nick, so I say it's god save the criminal, did you like that Frank," said Tommy as Frank was already bursting with laughter as it all made sense to him, switching his voice to the comedian.

It was Frank who was about to interrupt Tommy.

"Fucking hell Tommy a blue light flashing, you've got a blue light flashing in the hall," said Frank as Tommy turned towards the open door of the lounge.

Frank laughing moved off the sofa, he thought it hilarious that this should be happening of all nights. Tommy looked shaken and shocked at what he was seeing.

"Bloody hell," said Tommy.

Tommy jumped off the chair and looked into the

hallway; Frank was already following him to investigate.

"I don't fucking believe it," said Tommy.

"What don't you believe," said Frank found this rather funny.

"The blue lights are coming from outside the front porch," said Tommy, staying close together they crossed the hallway into the kitchen, "Come on Frank the back door."

Looking out the blue lights were in the lane at the top of the drive, Tommy was cursing to himself, "Coppers are up there, can't be coming in here Tommy surely," said Frank trying not to alarm Tommy any further at the unfolding drama.

"I wonder if they have had a chase on, I saw a couple of young ones on the way home earlier, they dumped a vehicle they were pushing and ran off the fuckers," said Tommy rather hoping that was the answer as to why the lights were flashing.

From the back door in the shelter of the porch, the boys saw an orange glow appear lighting up the night sky in the direction of the village.

"Smell it, that's rubber burning, I wouldn't be surprised if those travellers I saw earlier, hadn't returned and torched that fucking vehicle. I bet that's what's happened and the coppers are searching for them, I say looking from here and follow the hedge line down, it's about the right place where they left that vehicle," said Tommy, who was really anxious and clutching at straws hoping whatever the problem was, the police would soon quickly go away, as they both remained watching and secreted in the shadows of the porch.

"That is rubber burning it's irritating my nose," said Frank as he turned and went back into the kitchen and closed the door.

"That's a fire engine just passing the gate heading down the lane, I bet it's that fucking vehicle mate, I bet anything on that," said Tommy realising that he was talking to himself as Frank had returned to the kitchen and closed the door.

As Tommy entered the kitchen, Frank said.

"Your dogs certainly take things in their stride, they haven't put in an appearance with that excitement outside," as Tommy closed the door behind him.

"I need a night cap do you want one Frank," said Tommy.

Again both pals returned to the lounge and poured out their drinks,

"I am going to have a word with old Ben the gypsy and see if he can throw any light on tonight's events, might get some names from him, then I'll send an anon note to the local nick – do you know those fuckers up there need a few broken bones to stop the bastards wrecking and running around like they are doing, all this is beginning to do my head in, after all these bloody years have been trouble free and now we got it all on our own doorstep – I ain't going to put up with this much longer Frank, I'll sort them out proper like and they won't know what's fucking hit them when I do," said Tommy somewhat angry and frustrated at the inconvenience the travellers were causing at this time in the neighbourhood.

"Anyway Tommy don't let it get to you like this, we are the watchers and not the problem, remember mate," said Frank now concerned at Tommy's change of attitude.

"Sorry mate, there I go shooting my mouth off, here's your drink," said Tommy handing him the whisky glass, Frank looked up at Tommy's face and saw the real stress it was causing him,

Although, not concerned by the night's events. Frank acknowledged to himself that perhaps this was an area of his expertise, (Frank had already toyed with the idea of calling in a favour he was owed, perhaps he could arrange a private visit to the travellers site with no come backs to us, just this once and the travellers might get the message to move on he thought)

Frank had no intentions of telling or letting on to Tommy and Lenny but he already was considering a little secret of his own and something to think about when he gets home on Tuesday.

Tommy had put on some easy listening music, more instrumental than singing, as they both sat drinking whisky. Frank was already humming to the music as he tapped his fingers on the arm of the sofa. Tommy was more rigid on the chair sitting more like in a trance of despair as he appeared to be elsewhere in his thoughts, Frank was unaware that Tommy's thoughts were taken up by Toni's face glowing in Tommy's mind and wishing the girls were back at the house.

The music had obviously had some effect on Tommy as he took hold of his mobile and began to text a message with one hand, real dapper like. Frank watched him fiddle with the buttons as he sat with a grinning smirk, knowing that he could read Tommy like an open book at this time, it had to be Toni he was texting at this late hour. Frank continued to look and smile in Tommy's direction knowing as an old married man and one who was content with married life had no regrets he had made the right choice when he married Prim as his wife of forty years.

CHAPTER ELEVEN
Lenny's Accident

It was after six o'clock Monday morning when Lenny left for Bristol, heading towards the motorway intersection. His two pals remained in the house and sound asleep on leaving. Lenny had exercised the dog's earlier around five o'clock realising they were not likely to get an early run out after yesterday's fracas, outside he was met by an overcast damp morning at first light as he went and opened up the garage to get the Jag out.

Lenny's drive to Bristol was going to be a long one, with several stops planned enroute; time was his no rush and much to think about, especially of Karen. She had never been far from his thoughts since she left on Friday last with Toni, for him he found their parting more emotional and difficult than Tommy's, although, he never really spoke of his feelings towards Toni, he just didn't.

It was all the niceties of having Karen around, that made life more interesting, it wasn't the sex or seeing her naked, it was her personality and her femininity that he missed and enjoyed that he found most special. Knowing so little about her background made no difference to how he perceived her as a woman of modern means. He knew much of her sexual preferences and desired tastes, her hygienic ways, her choice of clothes, and her style of fashion as he saw from the girls shopping spree. Lots of questions milled in his head as he realised how lax and juvenile he had been in not taking a greater interest in her and whether she had siblings and parents alive, pointed questions and hoped for direct answers. So from Lenny's perspective so many underlying questions remained uppermost in his mind, who is Karen? And where does she come from?

Three hours later Lenny was on the ground in Bristol, eager to get started and near to surveying one of the chosen locations off the list Tommy had provided. He had made good time coming up as he managed without stopping for breaks.

By eleven o'clock Tommy had stirred on hearing the bleeping signal of his mobile, blearily eyed and half asleep he made a grab for it off the bedside cabinet, twiddling, fumbling and useless in answering, he just hated the bloody thing at times he was so impatient he wanted to throw the thing away. Knowing he was none the wiser to the caller, "Could it be Toni, he just didn't know it could be anybody," he muttered to himself.

"Damn and sod the bloody thing," he griped having missed the call.

He moved off the bed for the bathroom, needing a pee and was beginning to offer up a proud looking specimen that urgently needed the loo. By the time he stood naked at the toilet, he had to sit down and press on his hardness and not let it rise and urinate all over the place. As he was desperate to find out who called on the mobile, so with one hand still occupied, he used the other to flick through the messages. He realised that he had been left two messages by Toni. Later he established that Toni was the earlier caller, hence the two messages left. Showering and dressing he was soon quickly on his way down stairs having decided to use the house phone instead, more comfortable for him to speak at length. Refreshed he felt more alert and ready to make his long awaited call to Toni, she was that gorgeous woman, and gorgeous was the only word to describe her. As she was beginning to fill up most of the days hours just thinking of her, she brought real calm to his day.

Telephoning it was nearly the best part of an hour when his call ended with Toni; talk about mood swings Tommy was spontaneous being very overjoyed one minute and in a planning mode the next, blowing hot and cold, but excited at the news that Toni relayed to him.

During the duration of his call, Frank had put in an

appearance without disturbing him. He let the dogs out of the kitchen and smoked a cigarette as he waited for the kettle to boil. He kept an eye on the dogs as both with heads down scurried around sniffing acting like a Hoover across the ground and fascinating to watch as they moved together, real hunting dogs Frank thought, "Lovely looking, Lenny described them as 'Ghost dogs', bloody hell Ghost dogs, that brought a gruff throaty cough, that is all we need is a bloody house that's haunted," as he laughed with a somewhat dry throat that would just about top it for all of us, he ambled back into the kitchen organising two coffees and topping up the dogs water bowls as they finally returned to the house tongues dripping and panting hard.

Time was pressing as it had gone midday and neither the two pals had eaten breakfast due to their long sleep this morning, coffee was the drug they both needed most to get their late day moving.

"I can't be bothered to cook anything now, I've lost my appetite Frank, are you hungry mate, do you want something cooked," said Tommy.

"No I am okay, fags, tea and coffee, Oh! A little snifter (Whisky) does me, until I get bollocked by Prim for being lazy," said Frank answering with one of his deep throaty laughs.

By early afternoon both pals had moved to the rear patio which overlooked the valley below, as they sat in the shade feeling the warmth of a gentle breeze. Tommy had gone much further with Frank in describing the routines he had planned, outlining the proposed arrangements for their forthcoming crime spree. Piece-by-piece Frank was able to put more of the puzzle together in understanding his thinking behind some of the reasons for Tommy's decisions. Not all matters were as clear as they could be in the circumstances, but there was a lot of information to digest at this time and he still hadn't grasped the enormity of the operation and how Tommy proposed to use such a large team of players.

"These foreigners Tommy, what made you choose them rather than our home grown – I can see to some degree your reasoning for wanting new blood," said Frank fishing for more answers.

"Well think about it, like I said before, it's for our own security and safety – Look once this hits the headlines and believe me it will be world news (laughing) It will bigger than anything this country's seen, right – So first off in order that I can achieve this and remember this is where the weakness always lies mate, people talk, people drink and sound off, get excited for whatever reason they end up being fucking stupid, my way is safer because it's on a need to know basis, (Frank interrupted).

"Yeah I can understand your caution on that Tommy, but what made you go to Europe, why not Ireland, there got some pretty good players, especially with all their years of trouble, got some good heavies," said Frank reasoning his case even more.

"You have hit it right on the head, It's not heavies I need Frank it's about other things, skills and qualities not brawn and quantity. Think about this, when this hits the fan Old Bill is going to have everybody on their toes and the Home office will be up their arses, politicians will be spending more time playing with their tea cakes than providing anything sensible in their meetings, they will be fucked and why, the answer is not in Britain but Europe. The Old Bill will be doing lots of early morning turnovers and for once all the London boys will be telling the truth, (they are all innocent) none or very few will be involved, the establishment will spend weeks scratching their arses, London is virgin territory they will find nothing of interest that they can pin on anybody and plenty of time for us to organise our own safe refuges and in a more dignified way than rushing and making mistakes mate," said Tommy in an organised voice,

"Now you said Ireland, everyone that can walk and talk will be on Old Bills records, they have had years of practice in knowing who has done what, and when," said

Tommy.

"Look Frank you read the papers and watch the news (Frank nodded in agreement) every day we are reading about 'Asylum Seekers' trying to get into Britain, well we know from our own experience in the East End mate that this has been going on since the war and the politicians turn a blind eye or more so the fucking government of the day, politicians have screwed this country rotten (pause) – Look, you know as well as I, from our old stomping grounds our old contacts in the met have always said there are fucking thousands of illegal's who just disappear into the old black economy and that's not those fucking looking for asylum, this country is up the spout so why keep tabs on everybody, England has been a soft touch for donkey years – So I am going to use that for my own ends, we can get who we want into the country with very little effort, they come as tourists or just on a business trip. It's water off a duck's back, for us I want it to be on the night a walk in the park and no fuck-ups. I can get those I need over in twenty-four hours no problem and use them within hours of arriving, do their jobs and fuck off home, foot passengers on a ferry or a flight from one of those airports who do short destinations to Europe, even a short boat trip like they did at Dunkirk the shortest route across the channel to get them away and off home abroad. So Old Bill will be looking for 'Pie in the Sky' they will find nothing incriminating as my team of girls will radiate on the night with a job well done," said Tommy as he watched Franks face for a sign of life as he looked more than enthused by Tommy's conversation especially mentioning the involvement of women taking part."

"All the girls will be different on the night, to what's shown on their passports, they will not be recognised as foreigners, in any way shape or form," said Tommy underlying and emphasising to Frank just to what lengths he had gone to get it right.

"Yes, I can see what you're up to Tommy and I can also see that it's a numbers game at the end of the day for us – Accommodation is that needed for anybody, where are you going to keep them all? Are you going to hide them anywhere special? – Who's going to be responsible for them? – How are you going to keep in touch with them? And transport, what about the transport?" said Frank rattling off his thoughts in one go trying to digest Tommy's conversation.

"Right, listen Frank – All the foreigners will be staying in hotels on the day they arrive, they stay one night only and leave, each team will be staying together and we will provide a chaperone who has contact with us at all times – When each team leaves their hotels they will be transported together as a group and they will be taken to a safe place and will be briefed for their respective jobs – At all times after that, they will be our responsibility to feed them and generally look after them, until they are taken to their targets – none of the teams will meet at any time of the operation, they remain apart at all times and will have nominated drivers and vehicles for each team, the drivers will be briefed beforehand (Tommy empathised and gestured this fact to Frank) and will be provided with the exact routes from their hotels to the safe places, then the drivers will have routes and target details, drivers to be well briefed and a number of paid dummy runs need to be made by all drivers, but we do not reveal targets, that remains secret for now. So we need to be aware nearer the time of any possible hold ups, accidents on the night, road works and diversions we need to be sure we have that information at all times, I will add twenty minutes to each journey to cover and plenty of warning for us to decide on a change of plan, the beauty is that we are not in a rush to get them to their targets, what's important is their time on the ground, how long to complete their tasks and then off site," said Tommy as he sat back and sipped his drink waiting for Frank's reaction, seconds past and went as Frank just sat staring into space.

"Fucking hell Tommy, how the hell have you managed to put this together – I am bloody staggered by it, Yes I can understand how this would work, I can visualise the bigger picture, (laughing) it's fucking brilliant mate, fucking brilliant," said Frank ecstatic the mind boggled as to what he had listened to, he just sat nodding at Tommy grinning in his direction. Tommy was laid back sipping his drink as he watched Frank's mannerisms and behaviour. Unbelievable you are Tommy, we always said you were good in the business but this is being a genius, Christ I can just imagine the headlines in the papers, fucking hell, there be kittens on this number," said Frank finally finishing his conversation.

"Changing the subject, Lenny hasn't been in touch has he, I wonder if he has managed to get round the targets, I would hope he will give it until three o'clock and start making his way back before hitting the traffic," said Tommy quietly, (pausing) "Yes there is something else, bloody hell my head, the girls are coming back down on Thursday midday and staying the weekend, caught me on the hop when I rang Toni back on her call, I didn't expect that one minute, anyway, it will be great to have them down here and makes life more normal, Lenny, Oh! dear you wait and see his face when I tell him," said Tommy, "Thursday was going to be a very busy day for us and well if I put them off it might screw things between us, so we need to play things by ear when they are down, keep them occupied," said Tommy giving out one of his belly laughs, "Because you will be coming back as planned won't you Frank, you're coming down with Tim Boyce (the Silk) (Barrister) as arranged I hope on the morning train or will you come down by the car," said Tommy.

"By train makes life a lot easier, missing all that traffic, does my head in at times why do people live on motorway's – Good old Ernest Marples, he was the man who started it all, remember Tommy, all the bollocks about fast journeys and saving time," said Frank.

"Well I need to negotiate Tim's retainer, same old arrangement I suppose cash only, I am sure he won't take a cheque," said Tommy laughing.

Tim Boyce (Barrister) will be their legal brief and Tommy knew that it would be a diabolical situation to compromise their relationship with him at this time; he was going to be a very important player in this operation if the wheels were to come off for any reason. It was essential that third parties should not know Tim's professional identity no matter how close they were to him. Tommy puffed and sighed as he began to juggle the events in his mind, realising how useless it would be to make immediate plans about Thursday and the girl's arrival.

"The best way would be to let Lenny look after the girls, why we get down to business, just relax, you are winding yourself up for no fucking reason," said Frank in a fatherly manner.

Tommy acknowledges the advice given and remained silent.

"Listen do you still listen in to Old Bills radio chats," said Frank.

"To be honest I have never given that a thought," said Tommy frowning and staring at Frank's question.

"Perhaps you should consider it mate with everything going on around you might be something to think about, especially now," said Frank.

"Yeah, that's an idea never gave that a thought, good thinking mate," said Tommy, "You are right on the button there."

"Just changing the subject a minute, how are you going to link up with Tim, he lives in Cambridgeshire, will you hook up in London or what," said Tommy.

"We will hook up in London, it's a lot easier to get a straight run down and not chop and change trains," said

Frank.

"It's some years since we last met up with him, same with Lenny, I hope Tim knows what we look like," said Tommy lifting his shoulders at his comment.

"I am off to do a sandwich mate, do you want anything, it will about half six I reckon by the time Lenny gets back then we can eat together," said Tommy as Frank nodded and acknowledged his offer.

Frank remained seated as Tommy left, he was too comfortable as the weather remained very generous with sunshine and a warm breeze making Frank feel rather tranquil and lazy by late afternoon and being entertained by the passing flights and whistling birds of various species that came and went around him.

On Tommy's return and halfway through an eaten sandwich, his mobile sounded, he had left it on the stone patio as he reached down the bloody thing was bouncing around as he retrieved it, glancing down at the screen, "It's Lenny calling," said Tommy's inquisitive voice. Tommy's face suddenly became distorted and concerned as he stood up and paced around, Frank sat up and listened to Tommy's voice.

"Tommy, help me! Tommy help me!" Lenny said in a whispering voice, "I'm hurt! Tommy – I'm fucking hurting - Help me! – Pleaseee Tommy," as Tommy listened intently to Lenny's haunting and pleading words that reached his ears and his own face turned ashen at the unfolding drama.

"What' happened? – Where are you? – Lenny where are you for fuck's sake tell me," Tommy was screaming into the phone and panicking at Lenny's pleading words for help.

"Accident Tommy – I'm hurting my legs are trapped – come and get me Tommy, pleaseeee," said Lenny sounding in dreadful pain as the call went dead, it was that eerie feeling of not knowing where he was and what was the accident as Lenny's voice stopped in mid-conversation, Tommy felt an intense pressure on his chest and was beginning to feel short of breath as he kept a silent mobile to his ear

"Lenny – Tell me more – Where are you? Said Tommy shouting into the mobile.

"Intersection – Intersection," came a feint blurted reply from Lenny.

"What intersection Lenny tell me mate, we'll come and get you, me and Frank will come and get you, just tell me where," said Tommy in blind panic as he turned and faced Frank, who was sat perched on the edge of his chair twitching at the way Tommy was speaking with real fear in his voice.

"Intersection down the road – I'm trapped," he screamed out, "Fire, there is fire, Oh! fucking hell, I can't get out my legs are trapped," Lenny's voice faded and then went quiet as Tommy could hear background sounds and screams on the open mobile channel, "I've got blood on me, blood," cried out Lenny as Tommy heard his cries and sounds of vomiting over the open channel.

"It sounds bad Frank, Lenny's in an accident and he says he's trapped and there's fire as well, he's rambling," said Tommy gasping for air as he dropped the mobile as he again clutched his chest and dropped to his knees on the patio. Frank reacted quickly in retrieving the mobile off the floor, realising the channel was still open as the sounds and voices could be heard.

"Lenny (no answer) Lenny can you hear me it's Frank, if you can hear me mate leave the channel open, leave it open, stay on the line my old china," said Frank's commanding voice, at the same time he heard a gurgle as if Lenny was trying to say something. Tommy was at the same time being violently sick on the patio, his whole body trembled as his stomach heaved and reached as he felt the shock and pain at his hurting, then one of the dogs came to sniff the vomit.

"Oh! Fuck, piss off, leave it alone," as Frank chased

the dog off.

Both pals recognised the dogs' concerns as they stood watching the pals every move, they knew something was wrong, in the way animals do, by their senses and their behaviour towards them. Frank ushered the dogs back into the house and collected Tommy's car keys, he locked the kitchen door behind and hobbled off in the direction of the copse, Tommy soon overtook him in the rush to get to the copse first.

"Take it easy mate, we've got to get there in one piece, otherwise we'll be having a fucking accident, Tommy, then we will be truly fucked," said Frank.

Tommy was beginning to feel uncomfortable after rushing like he did, gasping for breath and full of panic, those few terrifying minutes have passed and now register deep in Tommy's thoughts as to the implications this is going to have. As Tommy's conversation was registering a real bolt out of the blue that shook him to the core, both felt the rush of adrenaline in their veins. As by which time Tommy had revealed the concealed entrance as the door raised to expose a Black shiny Range Rover, Frank joined him with the vehicle keys as he looked into the bowels and depths of the blackness that loomed, as the bright sunshine and half-light from the trees made it a shadowy and somewhat a creepy place. Tommy was soon in the vehicle with engine roaring, Frank stood to one side as he heard the engine revs and then saw the vehicle shape appear from the darkness, and finally reaching out and opened the door to clamber in.

"Fuck me, Tommy, I'm bloody knackered for that," said Frank trying to take the sting out of the panic and urgency of lay ahead of them.

It's said that silence is golden but at this very moment, silence was an enemy in not knowing Lenny's sudden fate, both inwardly feared the worst possible scenario as Tommy drove and stopped a short distance from the entrance and watched the door close behind him. Finally moving slowly and stopping at the gate leading to the lane before speeding off towards the village. Frank was pleased they were at last moving, he held onto the interior rail above his head as he swayed side to side by Tommy's fast driving.

(It was also interesting to note that in their haste to leave the grounds of the house, Tommy had seen the shape of Ben Witney, (gypsy) appearing in the rear view mirror crossing the lane behind them, Ben obviously was going to the copse for some reason)

Plumes of smoke could be seen on the skyline as the pals approached the village.

"Fucking hell, I don't like the look of that – A car wouldn't be that bad Frank, there's much more to this than just a fucking accident," said Tommy raising anger in his voice and now much calmer.

"We should be coming to the bridge in a moment and that should give us an idea of where this accident is," said Tommy hopefully.

Frank remained in silence just thinking, as his big hand gripped once again the passenger handle above his head to stop himself swaying. Reaching the bridge only a handful of vehicles had stopped as people gathered standing and looking out over the railings down to the motorway. Tommy decided to park up somewhere quiet, especially with a helicopter hovering above them,

"Just our luck to end up on News at Ten mate," said Frank.

"That's what I was thinking," said Tommy.

It was obvious that when Lenny had first called the accident it had just happened and of course, the media drama begins and journalists are everywhere for a story. At the same time Tommy decided on a change of plan, he drove back the way they had come to a gated field and decided to act by getting Frank to hold back the gate as he drove into field and found an ideal spot underneath a hedgerow with thick foliage and a canopy overhang to

BOBBYJAC

hide the vehicle from all in sundry, in fact, he left the vehicle in a dip out of harm's way which gave even better coverage on tilted ground.

"I'll stay here you go and have a look first old mate, my legs are playing up at the moment, they keep twitching and jumping," said Frank concerned at his plight.

"I was going to suggest that mate, to be honest, you look fucked.

"I'll see if I can get a quick gander and then I'll come back and decide on what to do next, I am worried about Lenny's digital camera and stuff he's got with him, I don't want that going on a bloody walkabout," said Tommy.

Plume of black smoke continued to rise up into the sky and would be seen for miles as the swirling mass would open up its belly from ground level and from the seat of the fire orange flames shot up the middle of the churning smoke right at its core it looked frightening from their position in the adjacent field.

"Fucking hell, look at it – This don't look good Frank, look at the orange glow in the middle of that smoke, when that smoke's burnt off the fire will bloody roar up mate," said Tommy deciding on which way to go.

Meanwhile Frank continued to listen on the open channel of the mobile, still no word from Lenny, only the sounds of metal tearing and crunching with vague sounds of voices somewhere in the midst. Tommy hadn't been long when an explosion ripped and sounded in the atmosphere. Smoke continued to billow and swirl around with the wind, you could feel the intensity of the obvious dangers as the devouring elements reached up in the sky as black smoking bits fell to the ground. From the rising plume came a sudden burst of raging energy as orange flames lit up the area. The ignition was to be the final transmission of burning, melting, combustion of heat that pumped and pushed flames up into the evening sky like a spouting whale. The effects were most shocking to be so close and in the vicinity as Frank was from his position and seeing how ferocious and frightening it must be for those much closer, the emergency services were full in attendance as blue lights were flashing from all directions and the reflection bounced off the tree line as sirens sounded as vehicles came and went from the scene.

You could hear people running on the bridge, presumably when the explosion occurred; it was clear from the noise and chaos that the situation was not yet under control. But what of Lenny his voice not been heard from and time was of the essence to find him.

Tommy had made it unhindered to the first parapet under the bridge, he had taken binoculars with him, Tommy was a quarter of a mile from the scene, although columns of parked vehicles remained on either side of the carriageways as it was obvious that there were fears of explosions as you could hear from his position popping sounds, like mini explosions. Due to his deceptiveness of his own imagination, Tommy couldn't describe the awful fear and sickness he felt in the pit of his stomach. It got so bad he slipped down the bank unnoticed and took shelter in the bushes, dropping his trousers as nature unleashed a flowing torrent of diarrhoea.

A sudden panic attack and the stress left no answer to his questions that churned over and over in his mind. He began to hyperventilate and became more concerned about his own welfare never having experienced such emotion and mental torment before with no control over the events occurring.

Tommy returned to the vehicle, opening the driver's door he explained rather hurriedly the pungent smell that followed him into the vehicle.

"God what a fucking day this is turning out to be," said Tommy angrily, "I've ended up with the fucking runs, I been squatting down in the bushes it feels as if the whole of my insides have fallen away," said Tommy

as his sweats and perspiration were clear to be seen, he
started the engine and moved off veering away from the
hedge.

Instead, he went back in the opposite direction and
away from the billowing smoke that smothered the field.
Driving to the opposite side of the field and out of view of
the adjoining lane, he again parked away from any
prying eyes that may be watching. Now well hidden and
off the beaten track he could sit awhile and gather
himself in the circumstances, it was clear also that time
had played a big part in the fact that there was little
they could have done in helping Lenny and more
worrying for them both was Lenny's immediate
whereabouts, was he still trapped, alive or dead or in
hospital.

Tommy went to the rear of his vehicle and rummaged
before placing a press card on the front windscreen,
gathering the first aid box, a small fire extinguisher and
unwinding the power winch on the front of the vehicle.
Both pals took refuge in the hollow of the hedge that
overlooked onto the motorway and near the scene of the
accident, realising they had entered a dried gulley of a
drainage pit that was to remove surface water from the
adjacent fields in other times.

"Hold it, I can hear voices on the mobile channel, it
was still open it must be Lenny they are talking about,
he's probably still trapped that seemed the gist of the
conversation he heard," said Frank with the mobile
stuck to his ear.

"Keep listening Frank, I want to play back my
pictures I managed to take earlier with my mobile," said
Tommy as he grovelled on the ground for a more
comfortable position.

Looking down from the hedgerow he had a much
clearer view of the carnage below. It seemed from his
playback video on the mobile that a huge number of
vehicles were involved and fires appeared to be coming
from two tanker lorries being the main source of the fires

and black smoke that was having such a devastating effect on the surroundings, both vehicles laid on their sides and looked gutted from the video, abandoned vehicles could be seen burnt out although, it wasn't possible to determine the position of Lenny and the Jag at the time of this accident, Tommy was not able to locate them whilst filming earlier.

From the gulley the pals managed to get closer for Tommy to resuming scanning the scene, flames could be seen in sporadic places, jumping and licking as firemen were quick to tackle, People must have perished in this mess, tangled metal everywhere, peoples belongings and first aid equipment all over the ground. Rescuers could be seen going from vehicle to vehicle, it was probably no more than forty minutes since Tommy took the initial call from Lenny, so where was he? Where was the Jag?

Tommy unfolded a high yellow viz jacket and decided to look for the Lenny and vehicle as the emergency services were clearly not fully in control of assisting everybody on the ground, Police officers were doing their utmost to gain some order of merit to those who needed help and doing their best to preserve the scene. It was nigh impossible to believe that people had not perished; debris littered both carriageways of the motorway as workers could be seen sweeping the opposite carriageway, clearly wanting to get traffic moving again.

Tommy decided to slip down the embankment and wander about the scene in the hope of finding the Jag, in his rush to get down he ended up with some cuts and abrasions and gave the impression that he was a walking casualty, he manoeuvred among the crumpled mess of crushed steel and a strong smell of petroleum stuck in his nostrils, as pockets of the liquid still lay on the surface in some cases dripping from overturned vehicles. It was then Tommy realised the imminent danger he was in as a spark could ignite and burst into flame. He could hear instructions being shouted out about the need for safety and not create the dragging of vehicles as some motorists had been doing in trying to help and not realising the obvious dangers they faced.

Finally, Tommy had been on the ground for a good ten minutes when he found members of the emergency services appear between two crushed and overturned box vans. It was then Tommy saw the Lenny's Jaguar on its side, sandwiched between the two vehicles. A small working group of emergency responders were in attendance trying to extricate a person from the vehicle. Closer Tommy saw that Lenny had been found and was being removed from the wreckage onto a waiting stretcher, observing the driver's position Tommy realised how lucky Lenny had been as both box vans were soft skinned vehicles so the impact was not as destructive as it would have been against the tankers and while the vehicle had taken the impact on the passenger side and rolled the Jaguar over onto the driver's side trapping Lenny in his seat, scrapping on the ground indicated that the vehicle had been dragged and spun for some yards before coming to rest. From the comments he had overheard it appears that Lenny had fainted from the pain to his legs, he stood back as he saw the stretcher and Lenny lifted into a waiting ambulance. All the while Tommy had discreetly filmed Lenny's extraction from the car including the medical staff who provided the support to his legs and placed a brace supporting his neck with a final check by the doctor in attendance before he was removed from the scene to Tommy's relief in seeing rather than making himself known at the time. Again Tommy looked closer at the interior of the vehicle for any of his belonging's then finding Lenny's mobile stuck in the damaged roof lining of the Jag. It was a quick trick of the hand and unnoticed by others standing around that he was able to retrieve the mobile and behind one of the overturned vehicles whispered into the mobile as it was still on an open channel, he was then able to acknowledge Frank with the good news of Lenny's recovery and safely on his way to hospital.

A young policewoman was left to gather and tag bags containing personal effects from the crash site, before Tommy interrupted her, he decided to take the bull by the horns before any questions were asked of him as to his presence, finding some property among the debris he quickly retrieved the assortment scattered on the floor and approached and handed his find to the woman officer, this was his way of being dutiful as if he was one of the searchers with an open remit to search vehicles, so he quickly rounded onto the Jaguar and began removing items found inside, then attacking the boot of the vehicle as he rather convincingly produced a key for the vehicle from his trouser pocket and opened the boot. The woman officer was nearby but unaware of Tommy's actions, so whilst she was distracted he emptied the boot and took what he needed and handed the policewoman the remainder of the contents, in fact, he left them piled on the ground for her later attention as she was still occupied.

Tommy slowly melted back among others milling around at the scene who were helping walking casualties who were still present, Tommy was able to obtain the hospital details to where the casualties had been taken, realising that he had pushed his luck to the limit and managed an almighty bluff without being challenged and with more people now dispersing from the scene he too decided to slide off and disappear over the barrier and down into the drainage gulley to rejoin Frank who in his absence had made himself quite comfortable whilst hidden in the undergrowth. Together the pals slowly retraced their steps back to the Range Rover and sat for a few minutes in a very relieved state of Europhobia.

"Thank fuck for that Frank we have done it, we have got away with it, I got what I needed from the jaguar," and laughed at how he had found Lenny's mobile phone in the torn headlining of the vehicle. Tommy just sat grinning and staring out the front of the vehicle for no reason other than being very happy at Lenny's safety.

"God I cannot believe all this, I just cannot get my head around it," said Tommy. Frank just sat and nodded,"And you said to me come on down to the countryside for a quiet few days, my arse, this has been a fucking war zone – It's been busier than Piccadilly Circus at least when I home I get a good night's sleep without interruptions old mate," said Frank laughing in jest as Tommy turned the ignition and slowly drew away from the hedgerow towards the gate they entered earlier.

"Thank fuck for that Frank, we've done it mate, we've got away with it, Christ what a bloody day this has been," said Tommy as he and Frank remained transfixed, just staring and thinking.

With the short journey home, Tommy already needed a shower and a change of clothes I need to get down to the hospital and check on Lenny,

"Frank – Are you going to stay here whilst I go to the hospital," said Tommy, "I'll bring the other two dogs in and I'll take 'Raz' with me for the company - he can look after the motor for me," said Tommy already working on his game plan.

"The other thing I need to take care of is letting the girls know when I get back from the hospital, I can't kid myself on this one, can I Frank, there think I am an uncaring bastard if I don't tell them in quick time tonight," said Tommy in earnest of his thoughts, Frank accepted Tommy's decision and nodded in agreement.

"Well you need to get down there to know how bad he is, at least he is out of it and safe, so at least when speaking to the girls you've got answers – I tell you what you are better telling Toni first and let her break the news to Karen, saves you all the tears, they will be down here in quick time they are not going to wait till Thursday mate, you see," said Frank with a masterful performance as a caring fatherly figure giving advice.

Tommy just stared at Frank, thinking on his words, he turned and went off for his shower and change ready for the hospital.

CHAPTER TWELVE
Lenny's In Hospital

Just after eight o'clock the same evening, Tommy arrived at the hospital which was clearly heaving with people coming and going all looking for someone involved in the earlier accident.

Tommy decided to head up to the wards and poke around see what information he could find about Lenny, it wasn't long before he found a nurse to approach, then another and another on his walkabout, none were able to assist him, although advised to return to the reception desk at the 'A & E' dept downstairs.

Tommy continued to ferret for answers when eventually he found the answer he was looking for, due to the 'Data Protection Act' he was initially fucked as they would not give out information, frustrated he managed to blag sufficient details off a member of staff to realise that other than a broken ankle, torn ligaments, internal bruising to his chest and a head wound that was of some concern. He was semi-concussed when they brought him into the 'A & E dept. He was okay and now in theatre whilst they sorted out his ankle injury. He learned also that Lenny was being admitted to a ward later and kept in for observation because of a concussion.

Trying for a cup of coffee from the cafeteria was going to be a long wait and he decided not to queue and to go home, so leaving his details at reception to be noted on Lenny's file as next of kin and was about to leave when he caught sight of the policewoman he met earlier, the clipboard was still in her hand as she glanced up as Tommy waved and acknowledged her from across the hallway.

More people were arriving as he left the main reception area and the place was beginning to buzz, including the arrival of the press and media, he knew it was time to get out of there and home.

On his drive home he stopped off at a pub for a quick drink it wasn't the 'Bull & Butcher this time, but the 'Stag & Hounds' that was close to the hospital, then realised that this was a mistake as others were stopping off with the same idea when leaving the hospital. He left the pub and returned home entering the house.

"Lenny's Okay! Well that wasn't so bad as I expected, it's funny how we all seem to recover quickly from such events, one minute a fucking nightmare and the other sheer relief and orderly, but I don't know if there are any killed, but a lot of people were down there it's going to be a long night for some of them," said Tommy, "Anyway Lenny was in theatre so I didn't see him, he's got a broken ankle, torn ligaments and internal bruising, but he whacked his head so he's got concussion so they are keeping him in for observation and going to put him up on a ward later, so I left my details as next of kin and left – I saw that woman officer down there, clipboard and all doing her bit in collecting details, I waved and left mate, press and media down there all trying for a story," said Tommy, reaching out for the whisky bottle to pour a drink, he whistled and brought all the four dogs a running to him as they each looked up as they moved around him, giving each a good pat and a cuddle as he went down on one knee to recognise their patience and Lenny's absence tonight.

With enough Dutch courage, he decided to telephone Toni and break the news to her about Lenny's accident and to reassure them both (her & Karen) that his injuries although, serious were not life threatening and that he will be remaining in hospital for the foreseeable future.

Frank had already turned in for the night when Tommy decided on his last chore himself, having locked and secured the house he climbed stairs in darkness leaving the downstairs to the four dogs to occupy. Whilst upstairs he decided to visit his office alone to check on his messages and emails, on entering his office he found a blue flashing light had been activated, this is not what he had expected to find, as being physically and mentally tired he wasn't looking for further drama at such a late hour. Now exasperated by the find, he ran through parts of his videotape recordings from earlier in the evening to establish the cause of the activation. It was clear from some parts of the tape movement figures could be seen in the grounds of the house, skimming forwards again he realised that the activity he found was really coming from the direction of the boundary fence. He checked further the infrared sensors at which point they too had been activated by an unknown source.

(Tommy had used sensors which he had inserted into the timber fencing and the wooden stile, so any heavy pressure would, in turn, activate the alarm; this is one of his own designs, so he felt rather chuffed at his workmanship as this was the first time he had seen it activated)

It was clear from the pattern of events the boundary fence was where the unwelcome visitors were accessing the grounds at night-time, when the front gates of the drive were always unlocked with easy access to the grounds, it was the ongoing mentality of those who continued to visit at night and why the house held such an attraction that deepened the mystery even further, especially not having an answer, and yet his hidden secret in the copse and woodland had remained undisturbed. Summarising again that his visitors were probably the young gypsies again as each night more activity was happening and appearing to be more brazen as to their identities still remaining a mystery. Still watching the video tape he counted five figures, so it seems the move around mob handed.

"I don't understand why they have chosen us for their nightly jaunts," he thought,

Still watching the tape and puzzled as to what they hoped to achieve night after night by visiting, even old Ben Witney had not given him a good reason as to why?

The sensor only recorded their movements away from the house, although they did walk around it, they don't appear to have come that close to the building as shown on the graph he had printed out. Even the previous incident with the dogs doesn't appear to have deterred them or could there be another undisclosed reason why they left the house alone when clearly they were out doing burglaries.

On one clip he viewed he saw the outline of a couple lying on the grass nearest the house, it was clear they were having sex from their movements, but was it one of the gypsies or a couple who happened to wander off the track for privacy, you didn't need to be a rocket scientist to know which one was the female, surprised by their voyeurism on their part as anybody could easily have tripped over them like that.

Tommy made do with the results of his find, knowing that he was not about to antagonise his nightly visitors, happy that he had decided to check the videotapes, he did smile on the couple in the grass as he realised that he and Toni did not have the monopoly on sex, he locked up and went to his bedroom.

By morning Lenny was the first thing on his mind, now having rested up and eaten breakfast he decided that a quick visit to the hospital was first so that Frank can see him for himself before he leaves for London later.

At the same time he picked up an earlier text message from Toni which she sent at seven o'clock, reading – 'Both on our way down - see you later – bye Toni'.

It was exactly had he mentioned to Frank that once the girls knew about Lenny they would be down straight away, it was to be expected, he couldn't put them off, with the girls down today he needn't worry about Thursday one job less to do, he thought as he continued to reason out the coming hours and how he would manage once Frank had left was going to be a juggling time, the girls hadn't requested a pick up so he assumed rightly they were travelling under their own steam, he knew he could carry on and deal with Lenny' situation.

"Nice one Cyril – Nice one," (pun) as he thought, smiling in a more happier frame of mind as he continued to busier himself before ten o'clock, before leaving for the hospital. Frank meanwhile had packed his things, having showered and changed his braces to lime green, he surely was about to make a big impression with the nurses and staff at the hospital with such a splash of colour, and such a large lumbering frame of a man and a smile that would have launched a thousand ships, what more could Tommy possibly want with true friendship, I ask!

Later at the hospital, the pals had found their way to the surgical ward having been sent by reception, police activity was still evident and apparent with the numbers of people waiting to be seen in the main lobby of the hospital.

"Coppers everywhere with clipboards," he smirked as they took the lift to the second floor reaching Lenny's ward and the nurses' station.

"Business looks brisk in here mate, I like the style of uniforms Frank, brings back old memories of the nurses home and peeping toms," said Tommy laughing, Frank let out a croaking cough.

"You remember those days Frank," as he joked with his words, before being told off.

"Please keep the noise down," by a slip of a young nurse.

"Whoops, You've done it now Frank," said Tommy whispering.

Within minutes of their arrival at the ward, a petite young nurse with a face full of smiles led them both to Lenny's bedside. He was hooked up to a monitor and attached to a drip feed positioned on a standing frame alongside his bed. Lenny was lying with both eyes closed and was wearing a pair of earphones. Tommy looked at

Frank when the nurse responded.

"He is alright, he's listening to music, that's all," said the nurse as she moved to the bed and touched Lenny's arm.

"Christ I thought it was worse than that," said Tommy.

"No nothing that rest won't cure, please though don't be long he has been very tired since coming up from theatre, it's the drugs' effect," said the nurse as she left them.

Tommy could see the foot bandaged and a large lump trailing upwards towards his right knee, Tommy eyed his naked chest and saw those sticky tags attached to his skin the wires trailed back to the monitor, although, his face was swollen and the bruising was beginning to show him worse for wear as his skin colour was on the change.

Lenny was glad to see them both as he tried to smile, but gave more of a wave of acknowledgement as his eyes followed them both as he just stared without uttering a word to either. Tommy looked at Frank, as much to say should we be worried, by his facial expression.

"How are you mate," said Frank.

"Fucking sore, I ache all over," said Lenny mumbling his words, "My jaw aches,"

"How's your foot," said Tommy anxiously.

"They have done a good job, it's still attached, they let me keep it," said Lenny is a serious tone of voice.

Tommy's face was a picture of torment as he realised that Lenny's last comment was said in typical jest.

"We came down to the accident and I saw you being lifted onto the stretcher when the doc checked you out before they took you away, I filmed it for you as a keepsake," said Tommy.

"You are fucking joking Tommy, you filmed it, you are having a bloody laugh aren't you, how did you manage that for Christ Sake," said Lenny disbelieving his words.

"He's right Lenny, I've seen the video mate," said Frank convincingly.

"You see I saw you, but you didn't see me mate, you were concussed, not only that I found your mobile tucked in the lining and I managed to retrieve everything from the Jag, it's going to be a right off, well damaged it is," said Tommy showing he had been more practical with his time when he got to the scene.

"Bloody hell Tommy you have been a busy boy, did you come last night," said Lenny.

"Yes but couldn't get past reception it was a mad house here, and the Old Bill was doing their bit, outside the media and journalists all looking for a story. Anyway I blagged the information and found you were in theatre so I came home, pointless me waiting," said Tommy

The news seemed to have been well received by Lenny, as it was clear that there had been an atmosphere brewing, but Tommy's last words seemed to have taken the sting out the tail, as Lenny realised that his mate did care and did try to reach him, he hadn't been abandoned. The friends continued much idle chat between them as the nurses went about their duties, although, the situation was not good it was much better than Tommy had imagined, lifting Lenny's spirits, as he became chirpier and lively. Knowing he was in safe hands and was a little emotional that their visit had come to an end, Frank said his goodbyes as he was returning to London later and hoped that he would be in to see him on Thursday otherwise see you at the house, Tim Boyce is coming down with me.

"Give Primmy my love mate," said Lenny as he saw his pals leave the ward.

In the corridor you never mentioned the girls, "Tommy," said Frank.

"No I did that on purpose, let it be a surprise for him later, that will keep all three of them occupied for awhile," said Tommy.

"What about his mobile," said Frank

"No I am going to keep it, for now, he might have some stuff on there that might be a bit dodgy for us, I'll get him a cheap one in town when I drop you off Frank, he can play with that," said Tommy sounding rather organised.

"Lenny was a lucky sod, I haven't heard of any fatal's last night, lots injured and still no cause, strange that," said Tommy, "I would have thought that the police would have known straight away they got all the drivers, they must have spoken with them all by now I would have thought," said Tommy gesturing to Frank as they strolled back to the car park.

"No, I've heard nothing either, I can't believe anyone survived near those tankers and that fucking fire. Well that was enough to roast my balls from where I sat in the vehicle, you could sense the heat radiating from the inferno," said Frank.

"Well I suppose we will find out soon, it's amazing though when you look around and see so many Old Bill here, and yet, like was mentioned the other night in the pub, you don't see them out and about doing what they should be doing – Catching arseholes like us Frank," as Tommy burst out laughing as he opened the doors of the black beast parked up.

"Hey Tommy, watch your language," as Frank began to laugh heartedly as he smacked his knee in delight.

"Right time is pressing back to the house and collect your stuff mate and I'll get you down to the station," said Tommy, "We can grab a coffee and sandwich before the train leaves, so long as I can get back by one-thirty I be alright for time then, I've printed a couple of pictures of the pieces for you to take back and see if you can get an opinion on the jewellery if you can, don't push it though, I've left the envelope in the glove box," said Tommy.

Back at the house Frank soon collected his stuff and tided up, he brought his bed sheets down for washing and left them in the kitchen for Tommy's later attention.

Leaving the four dogs together in the house he locked up and were soon on the road,

"When I've got the girls settled and occupied I'll have a look at Lenny's stuff he brought back from Bristol and I let you know the results on Thursday – Now about Thursday, if the arrangements still stand, you don't have to bell me when you get back to London, so if I hear nothing by ten o'clock Thursday morning then I know you are on your way down – Alright, it's better this way with all the fuck-ups we've had," Tommy.

The choice of Railway station was ideal, no more than twenty minutes drive from the hospital and ten minutes to home, only a small station country station with a little coffee place nearby suited them both rather than Frank rushing in crowds at the much bigger station in town.

Arriving early it was relaxing for both pals to be away from the house and to simply enjoy some normality of just being themselves and to express and bond their feelings. After such a long absence apart and to forge a greater understanding from Tommy's viewpoint in pressing home his determination as never before as to how ruthless he intended to be to succeed with one final last big crime caper, without hindrance or fear of being discovered, and with a greater impetus than ever before, with new meaning but above all their professionalism was at stake, albeit, criminals of some past standing. It very much mattered to both men in how they are perceived among their own.

On arrival of the train the pals said their goodbyes and Tommy watched Frank board, waving as the train pulled away. Tommy was soon driving into town to purchase a new mobile for Lenny, at the same time he had left his mind blank at this time, not thinking or churning over the events that occurred, it nothing more than a quiet interlude of the morning, knowing that he had not confided in Frank about the video tapes from the night before.

During his drive and time alone he was becoming more addicted towards the idea of both girls coming down this morning, knowing he needed company but not in his face every minute of the day that he didn't need. His thoughts turned to Toni, he liked being with her a lot, in fact, more than he was prepared to reveal to her. He knew himself that he needed to keep it in perspective as she had no idea what he was planning in the future and whether she was prepared to accept his kind of lifestyle overall and then of course how he came by his money. He knew that he needed to be a little careful and not to go overboard and in the wrong direction otherwise he will truly screw up any potential relationship he was hoping for.

It was just after one o'clock the chauffeur driven car stopped at the top of the driveway of the house. The dogs alerted him to the sounds outside, looking up the drive from the Kitchen porch he knew the girls had arrived. What followed next was to knock Tommy for a six as Karen ran towards him and grabbed him forcibly by the arm and pleaded for news on Lenny, he reached out to steady the impact as their bodies met.

"Bloody hell girl your have us both over in a minute," said Tommy as he reached out and took hold of her, the driver had placed the bags inside the gate as Toni waved, then turned and thanked the driver before he departed.

Tommy took hold of Karen and provided a reassuring hug and cuddle that all was well and there was no need to panic as he whispered comforting words that he hadn't expected to utter and with such an emotional scene on his doorstep.

Toni remained at the gate, before Tommy was able to move and leave Karen as his attention turned towards Toni and their luggage that needed to be retrieved and brought down to the house. Karen was wiping her eyes as Tommy and Toni passed her with some of their luggage, Karen turned and she too collected the remainder of their things from the gate. By the time she reached the kitchen her mascara had run and smudged down the cheeks of her face, Toni took a tissue and held the back of her head whilst she wiped her cheek,

"There that's much better, you clean up whilst we do the coffee Karen, said Toni grinning.

The girl's luggage had been placed in the hall as the dogs kept padding the hallway just sniffing the air and moving in and out of the kitchen before Tommy ordered them all to lie down and stay still as they were becoming a nuisance probably wondering where Lenny was.

In Karen's absence, Tommy whispered to Toni as he went to kiss and cuddle her, "She's very emotional about Lenny... I'll take your bags up in a minute," as he gestured his hand in Karen's earlier direction. Toni turned and faced him as she outstretched her arms in moving to respond to his approach as his hands touched and held her waist, Toni said.

"You've got two emotional women on your hands now Tommy, be gentle with us both, please," Toni gave an extra hug on his waist and smiled as their faces met and said, "She's been like this since I broke the news to her, it's the not knowing bit about him that makes her so tearful, (pause) When she's been to the hospital and seen him she will pull herself together and settle down. We women are like that, we're fragile creatures, you should remember that," said Toni rather cheekily in trying to deflect away from the emotion that was beginning to make sad their reunion, "So don't make me cry as well, Tommy, let's get that coffee we promised and tell me what you have been up to since we left," said Toni as her head bobbed with a wink as she felt his hand land on her backside, "Steady on boy, I ain't got my saddle on yet," she shrieked out loud at his touch.

The dogs reacted to the shrill of her voice and came padding into the kitchen, tails wagging and Toni reacting and said,

"Bloody hell their tails hurt banging against my legs,"

"I'll shut them in the lounge for a moment, otherwise it will be mayhem and what will the neighbours say," said Tommy in a direct tone of voice.

"What neighbours you on about Tommy, you haven't got any," said Toni at Tommy's remarks.

"Joke, it's just a joke," said Tommy as he followed Toni round the kitchen," What you after big boy," said Toni as she began to laugh and moved quickly out of his way as they both laughed together as Tommy had his tongue hanging out panting like the dogs.

"Stop it, she said, as Toni made the three coffees as Karen finally returned to join them.

"Look drink up and I'll run you down to the hospital, visiting starts at three o'clock," Tommy said to the girls, "I am going to arrange with the insurance company a loan vehicle later, then you can come and go as you like, I'll make sure the insurance covers you both okay, you both got your driver's licences with you," said Tommy as the girls said ,"Yes," to his question, "Good that's sorted then," said Tommy.

The anxious wait for Karen was soon over as the three of them left the house for the hospital, within half an hour they all three entered Lenny's ward, Karen was the first as she rushed to his bed,

Tommy turned and pulled Toni to one side and said, "Come on luv, let's take a walk for a few minutes and leave them to it."

The couple walked back down the corridor and sat in the seated area in the foyer.

"God these places give me the bloody creeps," said Tommy as he flinched as a patient's bed was wheeled past them, he was almost naked with a modest strip hiding his private parts as tubes led from his body in all directions.

Some twenty minutes had passed when Karen

looking for them both and beckoned for them to come, by this time Tommy flashed his eyes and winked at Toni, Karen was buoyant and all smiles, just what Toni had predicted, her thinking was spot on about Karen's mood change once she had seen Lenny for herself.

But her actions was more of fear and disquiet than one of disrespect, neither Tommy or Toni was able to grasp the intimacy Karen shared with Lenny, it remained much deeper than either of them could have empathised and Karen was no longer despondent and her relief showed on her face as she kept touching and kissing Lenny. At one time Karen sat alongside his bed her hand was on his one minute and then the next it had disappeared under the sheet as her hand could be seen moving and stroking his leg. Tommy and Toni made eyes at each other as Toni looked around for prying eyes, she said,

"Right we need to get back and sort ourselves out, Karen," said Toni feeling a little uncomfortable in the way Karen was behaving with Lenny, whispering to Tommy, "she be climbing on him soon," said Toni laughing, "She's got her energy back," as Tommy couldn't stop laughing at her comment.

"We need to go, mate, I've arranged a loan car for the girls, so I need to be back for that," said Tommy breaking into the couples privacy.

Before leaving Karen had promised Lenny that she had taken some time off work and would stay a few days,

"I'll come back later this evening Lenny," said Karen in a happier frame of mind.

Karen hoped that Lenny's stay in hospital would be no more than a couple of days so she would be around to help out at the house. Tommy was somewhat relieved when he heard Karen's intentions as it obviously included Toni in the arrangements, it meant that he could concentrate on his plans and with the girls around life will be that much nicer and more pleasant in the circumstances of Lenny's hospitalisation and great company to enjoy rather being alone with the dogs.

During their evening meal Tommy informed the girls that he had visitors coming down on Thursday and included Frank again as he had business matters to attend to at the house. From the girls' viewpoint neither thought otherwise at his comment about Thursday, no suspicions had been aroused on the face value of his words. The girls were later upstairs unpacking and showering when the loan vehicle arrived at the house, which relieved Tommy as the girls could use that for the hospital visit, the car was only a small family size run around and ideal for them both to use as it wasn't as big as the Range Rover, which he really wanted to tuck out of view as he was uncomfortable to keep show casing the vehicle around the house.

It was from an upstairs bedroom window that the girls watched the dogs being exercised out in the grounds; it was clear to the girls the kind of strength the dogs exerted as they charged around with noses to the ground which had been described earlier like a bloody Hoover. The girls remained fascinated and glued to the glass when Tommy caught sight of them looking out.

Meeting up in the kitchen when Tommy returned, Karen said,

"Where are the dogs? (pause) What're their names,"

"When they're ready they will come back on their own, so I'll introduce you properly – It's a good job you've got jeans on and as long as you two aren't on heat, your be alright," said Tommy jesting.

"Bloody cheek, what do you mean are we on heat, we've just had a shower thank you," said Toni sounding rather cross at his words,

"God you've got more sauce than the gander you,"

"No I don't want any accidents, there very boisterous animals and very strong, I don't want them jumping up, so I would both sit at the table and let the dogs do their bit, you will be alright, it's just they like a good sniff," as Tommy burst out laughing, he thought it hilarious when he said it, but Toni's facial expression was very different.

"You seen how they operate just now from the window, they are hunting dogs, they run in packs," said Tommy.

"Come on you two outside and I'll show you again as to how they behave," said Tommy.

At the front of the house, all three stood together as they once again watched the dogs perform, it was when Tommy noticed the upturned brick positioned on the copse, old Ben had paid a visit and left something for him to find. Calling the dogs back he got the girls to return with them and fill their water bowls, as he quickly made his excuses and left the girls before that took interest in his disappearance. He reappeared as quickly as he had left, although his face rather flushed, the girls said nothing as he went off to use the downstairs loo. It was there that he examined a wax piece of paper with a serial number and a couple of jewellery pouches with a logo emblazoned on them, the two split matches which accompanied the items had been spliced to form a cross. Tommy knew the cross meant to beware, somebody had fingered them, someone was out to do harm, but whom? He wrapped the items in the wax paper and put them back in his pocket as he flushed the toilet on his way back to the girls in the kitchen.

Seven o/clock the girls were about to leave,

"Here are the keys to the loan car," said Tommy, "Now drive carefully," Toni was going with Karen for company whilst she visited the hospital.

"Will you be alright in finding your way and ring me if you need help," said Tommy trying to be helpful and reassuring.

Toni was hoping to share a more intimate and private time with Tommy, whilst Karen visited Lenny, but Tommy thwarted her plans by suggesting they both go to the hospital, then Tommy changed his mind and said,

"I'll take you down to the hospital and drop you off, then ring when you are ready to be picked up Karen,"

Toni's face lit up as if he had read her mind, soon dropping Karen off he drove off with Toni looking much happier as Tommy said,

"Let's go and park up somewhere, let's have a walk," said Tommy.

Toni pointed to a place to park, stopping she was quickly out of the vehicle and beckoned Tommy to follow. As she ducked down through a gap in the hedge, Tommy chose to climb over the gate nearby, but before he could place both feet off the ground, Toni was quickly all over him, he straddled the gate as Toni pulled him towards her as he crashed to the ground, they both rolled over and over as Toni pulled herself up and crawled in between his legs, burying her head into the soft tissue of his belly. Tommy remained on his back just looking down at the top of her head, she then lifted her herself up and reached his lips with a long lingering kiss that she didn't want to go away. It was then that Toni drew back onto her knees and pushed her hands underneath his upper clothes and felt the warmth of his nakedness, back and forth she rubbed his flesh as he laid with his arms outstretched and eyes closed as Toni continued to stroke and move her hands over his upper body.

Toni continued and slowly brought her hands down to his waist line and began to fidget and undo his belt and the flies of his jeans, he lifted up his buttocks to aid her movements as she pulled down his jeans and pants exposing a growing creature of some delight that she had longed to touch, Toni placed her head sideways on his tummy as she reached down and took hold of his member and played with it until it became fully hard, she ran her fingers through his pubic hair and twiddled playfully as she was taking her time not to rush a spurting moment with him. Her green eyes were wide and awesome as her head tilted back to search for his face, her hands kept hold of the warming creature whose tip remained hidden. The hilarity and impact were all so sudden and was real 'hank panky' slap stick stuff that fellows often dream of and now it was happening right before his eyes as Toni was so determined to expose his lower body as her hands continued to pull and peel down his jeans and pants. Laughter began to be raised in a fever pitch as she hurried and pulled as Tommy went to move she pushed him back onto the ground. Having now exposed his lower body and a penis that was like the rock of Gibraltar, she stood over him as she lifted up her dress and pulled down her briefs lifting one leg at a time exposing her pussy lips to Tommy as he lay on his back looking up. Then quickly down on her knees she hovered over his penis and took hold of it as she gently thread it slowly into her as she pulled back on his foreskin as her moistened opening was already greeting him as he began to push in her darkness, she leaned forwards and placed her hands on his shoulders as she began to move back and forth with his penis inside of her, she thought this to be a good seven inches, bigger than she had encountered before as this had been the real first opportunity she had being that close on a face to face (giggling to herself) as she began to work her lower body pressing and drawing on his shoulders as he just lay there with his hands on her waist feeling every move she made., as he lay in the dust of a field with not a care in the world, then slowing her pace as she kissed him passionately and much harder than the first time, she really was going to town on him for all she was worth, this time she really had taken charge of the moment and wasn't going to let anything spoil their intimacy, she wriggled sideway and the back and forth as she was making the most of what she was enjoying with his hardness still up and well penetrated deep inside as she squeezed her buttocks together time and again as he felt her grip on him.

Tommy was very much in no man's land by Toni's ingenuity in the way she controlled the situation, but before they each reached the pinnacle of orgasms, he saw a fast approaching black shape appearing above him in the sky, he grabbed Toni and rolled to one side as she continued to push and fuck him hard, she was holding and gripping him hard as she exploded with her climax, he felt by her sudden jerking that she had her orgasm in his sudden rush to move her. When he heard the first thud on the ground, then a second.

"Toni let go, someone is throwing rocks at us," said Tommy urgently urging her to get off him, she was letting out loud whimpers and sexual noises and was not listening to him,"

"Fucking hell, another rock, who the fuck is doing this," said Tommy out loud.

He broke free of Toni as a fourth rock landed near them as he managed to get to his feet, Toni grabbed her briefs and wiped between legs as she stood and wondered what all the fuss was about, she thought, it's different as she still hadn't realised of the rock throwing incident and the danger they were in. Tommy was off racing to the hedge and gate, still half naked below waist, as he soon heard the sounds of running feet and garbled noises which sounded more than two people were involved, reaching the gate whoever was responsible had vanished, not even the sound of a vehicle driving off, which made him think of the matchsticks and more likely they were gypsies somewhere out there on foot.

Returning to Toni she was more astonished at his actions without realising the situation they had been in which could have been very serious and injuries to both, as he tried to explain the incident, she seemed unphased and still, in a heightened sexual state of mind, he couldn't believe it. She was so gooey eyed as she just wanted to be cuddled, but then he hadn't tried to explain, all he had done was to get up and rush off, realising what a fucking idiot he was in not stopping and ushering her to safety. Tommy was very much focused on Toni's pure frenzy of her physical energy, let alone making love in the open again and so close to the road, as he dressed and helped Toni over the gate, once in the vehicle he began to explain the incident to her at the same time showing her one of the rocks that had been thrown, it was only then that Toni realised why he moved so quickly at the time. As she took her briefs and again wiped between her legs, as Tommy passed a pack of wipes, she was still listening as he spoke about what happened to where she began twisting and turning in her seat, not knowing what she was seeking.

Returning to the hospital to collect Karen was a short journey without words as Toni was feeling the effects of her moment of bewitching sexual madness and Tommy's deep thought as to who their attackers were. With Karen in the vehicle and idle chat on the way home about Lenny, Tommy made no approach on the earlier incident to her, she only mentioned that Lenny wanted to get away for him to convalesce when he left hospital, he seemed pretty down tonight because he couldn't come home.

"I left him the new mobile you bought him and he was pleased you set it with our numbers, so all in all I left a happy bunny wanting to escape his burrow at this time," said Karen laughing as Toni raised her hand back to share a five between them.

CHAPTER THIRTEEN
Night Visitors

Toni had said very little all evening, and Tommy's opinion was more forthright, she seemed to be suffering from the sexual blues. She was warm, cuddly and very affectionate in bed although, he had not really grasped the magnitude of Toni's sexual appetite until now. The way she took control earlier, acting like a piranha. Her performance was incredible, which left him wondering about the future and whether she would expect this all the time. I mean there was poor old Lenny going on about how physically tired he was after forty-eight hours of shagging. So what would it be like to have a permanent relationship with either of the girls, he laughed as he knew he could not keep up with her appetite should she want fucking every night, like all woman they only have to open their legs and men have to get a hard on to meet the occasion, bewildered to say the least but at the same time worrying as to how a relationship could cope at his age and her being younger by some years, would she want more and wander he thought, but what a fuck it was today, feeling very chuffed about the experience but he dare not tell her about his thoughts. Being that adventurous in the way she applied herself to some degree frightened him as he knew once she got her teeth into him she would fuck him dry.

"Fucking hell, what am I going to do," he thought,

Was she like this all the time or only with her customers, he thought wrongly, but irritated on the way she ignored his alarm today and oblivious to the dangers they had faced, and would she listen to sensible conversation in the long term. The whole matter was so bizarre beyond any descriptive he could think of. As Tommy really did enjoy the savouring moments when Toni was on top of him and the way she fucked him hard. Although, what really pissed him off the most he didn't come and not playing his part in fulfilling her. So perhaps the odds weren't quite stacked against him in the way he assumed from the beginning.

Sleeping naked together he watched as she eased back onto her side of the bed, at the same time he saw her roundness of her exposed breasts as the duvet cover slipped and where he became entangled for his efforts. He wanted to take her in his arms and kiss her, and suck each nipple in turn, he wanted to kiss her from head to toe and let her have the experience of his sexual wisdom. He moved behind her as he placed an arm over her body to cuddle up, the tips of his fingers touched her pubic line that lay in the shadows of her flesh. She stirred, she wriggled and sighed all at the same time as they lay together he behind her and a placid penis lay in the crease of her buttocks. Feeling horny and trying to control his thoughts he left the bed and paced the floor of the bedroom naked. Unsettled his mind awash with the all kinds of thoughts especially with the question of the gypsies, unaware of the night and clearly still dark outside he became alert to the sounds of the dogs downstairs, in fact, they were on the landing pacing and padding up and down like sentries out of their boxes, being restless the dogs had sensed something, but what he thought, he left the bedroom clutching his clothes as he left. He remained in the shadows of the landing as he saw three sets of eyes upon him, the dogs were really playing their part in all of this, the fourth dog was laid at Karen's door, perhaps just a coincidence or an omen. He went one tread at a time downstairs analysing his thoughts and staring down into the darkness of the hall, his ears cocked for sounds. Reaching the floor of the hall, he went directly to the downstairs loo and retrieved items he had hidden earlier. Three of the dogs had trailed him down to the hallway and remained silent throughout, not a peep out of them, good training by Lenny he thought, trained them well.

The spliced matches, which formed the cross was the

most troublesome of the items found, he knew the meaning of the message but who did it concern? he thought.

Hearing the sound of breaking glass, and muffled voices someone had entered the house, Tommy remained in the shadows of the hallway listening, the dogs were aroused although, stayed close and alert, none raised a whisper, if he panicked then all mayhem would erupt bringing the girls racing out onto the landing. Tommy moved across to the open door of the lounge and pressed up against the door frame as he listened, it had gone quiet. He felt sure that someone was outside the house. A second and then a third seemed to come from upstairs on the landing. The dogs grew restless as he whispered for calm among them, 'shhhhhhing' quietly, he knew the situation was precarious as he hoped and prayed the dogs wouldn't upset the applecart. He wanted a prisoner? He wanted answers to his thoughts? As he continued to move around silently in the dark, listening for any recognised sound. Then he heard the thunderous roar of a heavy diesel engine start up, then another and then a third engine burst into life, "What the fuck he thought, What's going on outside," he muttered to himself, whatever was happening it was close to the house. Tommy's reasoning went much further, three engines, then three persons? He had to be right, so how many more could there be lurking outside the house? Was it a trap? What were they planning? Why the sound of engines? All these questions raced through his thoughts, vowing not to make the same mistake again, he was not prepared to go rushing out but remained in the darkness of the hallway listening.

It wasn't until Tommy heard the dogs howling did he realise that the house was under attack, it wasn't until the sounds of further glass breaking in the lounge. The dogs reacted alarmingly, their sudden rush and baying calls howled and echoed throughout the house. He knew that it wouldn't be long before the girls would wake from their sleep adding further problems for him and their safety. He acted quickly to investigate, still in the dark he fumbled and made his way towards the broken window. A figure stood outside feeding a long hosepipe through. Realising that they were going to smoke them out by using diesel fumes being piped through the hosepipe, then sudden screams coming from upstairs caused him to run towards the disturbance.

"The girls, Oh! Fuck it," mumbled Tommy;

In haste as he rushed the stairs two at a time, by the time he had reached the landing the dogs had arrived first and the dogs were in action, the figure who entered via the earlier broken window and in haste to escape the dogs attacked him. The figure made a lunge for the window, but to no avail, as one of the dogs caught him on the fleshy part of the thigh, all dogs were attacking the figure standing and struggling to move away from the snarling jaws of the animals.

Tommy managed to control with the help of the girls who now had reacted to the intruder, holding back the dogs, Tommy was desperate to know the identity of the figure.

"Come on you bastard, show me your face, you fucking creature, who are you," said Tommy as he looked in the half-light and saw the face of a young male gypsy.

Tommy did no more than bodily pick him up and threw him back the way he had entered, through the prised open window. Tommy didn't even consider the consequences of his actions he was defending his rights, his property from arseholes. Tommy went to his bedroom and it was empty but the sidelight was left on, then to Karen's bedroom the door was locked, he called in a whisper and tapped gently as he called their names.

"Tommy, is that you?" said Toni in a frightened voice.

Tommy replied as the key turned and the door opened, the dogs rushed him as they went along the landing howling and baying for blood. He explained the circumstances down stairs with the hosepipes. Tommy was less in haste as he went back downstairs and found the lounge filled with exhaust fumes, a hosepipe had been jammed in the window by a wad of material. He knew that the girl's safety was paramount as he called out to dress quickly and come down and join him, in the meantime, Tommy had removed a panel in the downstairs toilet revealing a secret door which led into a passageway under the house. With the girls waiting he fetched his shotgun, torches and dog leads hanging from the kitchen door. Returning to the girls he ushered both into the passage pulling the panel back into place and securing the secret door behind them as they slowly made their way through the tunnel, at the end they wait calming the dogs in the torch light and using the rope to attach their collars, the girls held back the dogs as Tommy slowly prised open a door at the end of the passageway which was more of a large grating that represented a garden ornament from outside. Leaving the girls in the tunnel with the dogs, he emerged with his shotgun and a pocket full of cartridges. His first instinct was to blast both barrels at the first thing that moved, but his ideology was more mainstream thinking for common sense, moving up the side of the house he could hear the sounds of engines, he took the shotgun and fired into the air, using the beam of the torch he found the switch to the outside lights underneath a window sill, now the grounds were bathed in some light as some bulbs were not working but clearly he saw the damage the gypsies had caused to his property and realised that they had brought and used farm tractors to smoke them out, just an unbelievable sight as he reloaded the shotgun he again fired into the air, then again he fired. The gypsies had run off as he slowly searched the side of the house down past the kitchen, then back he came to the tractor and turned off the engine, following the sounds of another engine which he found had been left in the adjacent field and again switched off the second tractor, the third tractor was much further away and appeared bogged down in a trench of sorts, with all three engines now turned off he realised that the Police will now be needed at the house as he couldn't explain this away as juvenile fun but something more serious was at play and of course the girls safety was paramount. He went back and fetched the girls and dogs from the tunnel, replacing the grating he brought them round to the front of the house and sat them down on the grass with the dogs. Two of the tractors had been deliberately rammed through the hedge and into the field, it had to be that each had been rolled down the lane to the house otherwise the engines would have been heard inside the house, and the reason why two were in the field thank god as they clearly couldn't handle the machines without the engines to operate the power steering, he realised they had screwed up. There were too many "If's and buts," about the demise he found himself in and the probability that something would eventually go wrong. Still coming to terms with the events and now having informed the police, he heard what sounded like running water, he went to where the sound was coming from in the hedgerow and found a figure urinating, Tommy let off another shotgun blast and that clearly brought the figure to his senses and left in a hurry, scrambling and climbing the bank to the lane.

Behind where the girls sat another moving figure was seen heading for the grass bank and the lane, Tommy let two of the dogs loose as both were taking their responsibilities seriously as they went into attack mode, it was clear in the beam of the torch the dogs were lunging at the fleeing figure, the dogs showed no quarter as they took bites. It was a cry for help, which made Tommy respond to the girl's calls to fetch the dogs back as it was clear the figure had bite injuries from the dogs. Tommy bellowed at the dogs to return and bellowed and shouted the loudest as the dogs returned to his side, the gypsy was in great pain and was laid foetus like on the ground, Tommy realised on moving closer it was a grown man and not a youth who the dogs attacked. Tommy felt no remorse, as he grabbed the man and pulled him to his feet, in doing so the man lashed out with a kick, Tommy quickly retaliated and thumped him hard in the face, down he went and Tommy left him there ignoring his injuries as he watched him struggle awkwardly to his feet running head first as he stumbled towards the entrance and disappeared into the night, Tommy had by then returned to the girls side and encouraged them to move and return to the house via the front door it was the only house key in his pocket with that he kept with the vehicle fob. He stashed the shotgun behind the lounge door in case of a next time. He went around the house upstairs and downstairs turning on the lights in every room, his anger now subdued as he joined the girls in the kitchen, and waited for a coffee the girls were brewing, his knuckles hurt as he rubbed the back of his hand and realised that we can all fumble for the truth and now the truth had found him. Tonight he knew they would have to be more vigilant than they have ever been at the house, as their lives were very much in danger, without over empathising the need for greater caution. He stood bent over as he leaned with both elbows on the table to Toni seated.

"Gypsies, they were gypsies who attacked us tonight, girls," said Tommy, "The police shouldn't be too long, I hope, be another bloody headache having them running around here," he groaned.

"Why, what's wrong with having them here Tommy," said Karen, she turned, surprised at his comment and looked in his direction.

As the three sipped coffee a Police vehicle arrived in the driveway as the dogs let out their whimpers. Tommy left by the back door and found a lone officer had arrived without any backup as one would have expected. The officer stood astonished and shocked at seeing the first tractor so close to the building with a hosepipe stuffed through a broken window.

Tommy said, "There are two more tractors over the hedge, one with a hosepipe attached, I switched all three engines off, I had to let my shotgun off in the air to scare them and my dogs had a few bites at a couple of them, they were running all over the bloody place."

"I appreciate what you've said but I would tone down your comments about the use of shotgun, the media will make this a very dramatic story as this clearly it is a shocking incident to the point of this being attempted murder, this was obviously well organised in the way this involved farm tractors and where did they steal them from, leave it with me I have to call this in and get help up here, CID will take this over once we can see the ground much clearer in daylight."

"Fuck it, fuck it that's all we bloody need," to himself, he mumbled under his breath.

"In the meantime would you like a coffee, as I need to put my dogs in their kennels otherwise there be chasing your people around and I've had enough surprises for one night," said Tommy in a friendly manner.

"I'll have a coffee please, - Who's in the house? - Anybody hurt?, said the Police officer.

"I own the house and I have two female visitor's girlfriend and friend, more frightened than anything, the dogs protected them, but no injuries between us," said Tommy choosing his words carefully.

Returning to the kitchen for the officer's coffee, the girls sat bleary eyed at the table both clutched coffee mugs as he walked in on them. Rounding up the four dogs he returned them to their kennels. For the police will be crawling all over this place shortly, back with the girls he informed them of the impending melee that will be happening as more police will be arriving.

"The copper outside views this as attempted murder, so he has called for backup, he's on his own," said Tommy, "I'll call him down for his coffee."

Tommy called out and beckoned the officer to the

kitchen door, entering to take the coffee from him, adding milk and sugar, Tommy introduced him to the girls as he turned and waited outside in the porch.

"Others will be here in about twenty minutes," said the Policeman.

Tommy had worked matters over and over in his mind, until he was satisfied with his alibi, that's in case he needed one, he knew the girls couldn't verify his story and the gypsies themselves were certainly not going to lose face and tell tales to the coppers.

"Keep it simple, don't complicate it my boy," said Tommy whispering to himself, "Just basic stuff that's all they need," he griped and murmured to himself, rejoining the girls, he whispered to Karen, "Don't let Lenny know about tonight, he will only worry,"

Toni nodded in agreement to Karen.

"Precise, it wouldn't be fair on him, laying in hospital knowing that the gypsies attacked the house, would it now," said Toni.

Tommy just nodded at the conversation and realised the girls were very much on his wavelength and he felt chuffed that this should have happened at such a time, it gave him greater confidence in the girls.

The three hadn't realised that the time was four-thirty in the morning; it seemed that the incident had been going on all night.

"The dogs were absolutely brilliant, especially when it came to attacking; they knew exactly what to do when the time came. Fucking marvellous they were," said Tommy as he looked at the girls, gesturing an open hand in salute of their performance.

"Anyway girls, I need to have a scout around and make sure, I've seen everything that I want to see – are you girls staying up," said Tommy gesturing lovingly as hc gcntly pinched Toni's cheeks together as he kissed her full on the lips.

"Yes, we'll wait for you to come back, we don't want any more shocks, do we Karen, is the policeman still out there," said Toni laughing and wiping her face with her hands, Karen nodded in agreement

"Yes he's sitting in the police car drinking his coffee, he's waiting on his backup, there's not much he can do until daylight," said Tommy.

He went to leave and turned thinking, hovering, not making up his mind.

"Word will soon get around the village this morning, be lots of nosey parkers having a gander, tractors need to be removed, oh! Sod it I ain't going out anymore," said Tommy.

He suddenly in the kitchen stripped down to his underpants, to the girls' astonishment as he completely ignored their presence, as if they didn't exist.

"Don't worry girls, I know the limits (he raised a finger in their direction with a big open mouthed smile) I just need to get this stuff off me, I am feeling really bloody dirty, I need to lay in the bath and soak," said Tommy with an urgent tone to his voice.

Toni offered to run the bath for him, as Karen suggested that she and Toni add items of their own to the washing machine.

"I can't do anymore, because the police will need to see it as we found it, I can't interfere, I'll leave it to them to sort out," said Tommy as his near naked frame followed Toni up the stairs,

From all the fussing and waiting the time was now an hour later nearing five-thirty on a Wednesday morning with a breaking dawn and weather indicated a beautiful start to the day.

In the bathroom, Toni fussed over Tommy's preparation to take a relaxing bath and rid the diesel smell from his body. Having watched Toni flit around the bathroom organising the suds and bath towels, he had in the meantime slipped out of his underpants and stood behind her naked as she leaned over the bath to check on the water temperature. She turned okaying it was ready, as he got one leg over the side, Toni placed his penis in the palm of her hand, now flaccid and limp, she bent to kiss it,

"Not now later," he said laughing, "It's all dirty,"

Tommy with bath suds up to his neck saw the two girls enter the bathroom and use the large adjoining shower together, he hadn't taken any real notice of what the girls were doing, as he laid back and closed his eyes, now cradled in the warmth of bath water and feeling weak and tired with his energy slowly being zapped minute by minute.

Eventually from the girl's noises in the shower, both emerged wrapped in large towels as they walked past him into the adjacent bedroom and dressed themselves, both wore full body dresses in similar styles and colours with wide flowing hems, he from the bath had a quick fashion show to hand as the girls continued to come and go whilst doing their hair. Both girls ready and Toni waiting for him to finish in the bath, when standing he called out for a towel, entering Toni came face to face with a full hard on, she shrieked out loud.

"Bloody hell Tommy, put that away," laughed Toni as she handed him the towel, he stood on the place mat whilst Toni rubbed his back and shoulders for him, "That feels nice don't stop girl," said Tommy cheekily, "Karen what do you think of a bloke who doesn't know how to be quiet when the queen's not at home," said Toni laughing at Tommy's reaction to her comments.

"I have just come on Tommy, sorry my period comes first," said Toni waiting to see his reaction, he turned and gave her one bloody big cuddle and squeezed her hard as he lifted her off her feet and carried her into the bedroom, "We are one my girl, who cares," he said caringly as he let go of her.

Tommy wasn't fazed about Toni's period, deep down

he was somewhat relieved for nature's intrusion and the rest he hoped to enjoy from her physical activities. He returned to the bathroom and continued to dry himself, although he sported a bloody great hard on when he finally stood naked and shouted for Toni, on reaching the door she shrieked out and laughed,

"Bloody hell Tommy you look like a Greek god," she said, just unbelievable you are, I can't take you anywhere like that," said Tommy with his head bent forward and slightly turned at an angle, an arm raised like a statue and of course a bended knee to complete the picture.

Toni beckoned over Karen, with her finger to her lips, Karen shrieked out,

"Toni how are you coping with that, it's a whopper," and continued to laugh as Tommy was still sporting a hard on, although, he hadn't seen Karen at the door he continued to play act his pose.

"Tommy put that away and get dressed will you, remember the Police downstairs they could be walking in on you at any minute," said Toni urging him to hurry up.

Both girls sat on the bed still giggling about what they had seen, Karen was shocked at the size,

"It's not always like that," said Toni laughing, "It does go down when I don't need it," she continued to laugh as Karen had a hand over her mouth giggling, "Christ Toni, it's a whopper, can you get it to fit," said Karen now in hysterics.

Tommy was completely unaware of the laughter the girls were having at the size of his penis, Toni had even remarked to Karen that it was not only hooded but more brownie than pinkie in colour,

"Because he has kept it in the dark for far too long, it hasn't seen much daylight over the years, apparently – His words not mine," said Toni as her funny comment started Karen off again, it was hilarious laughter at Tommy's unwitting expense.

Back downstairs and now fully dressed all three pals went outside onto the driveway, more police had arrived and much activity was happening all around them, even one of the farmers was present to claim back his stolen tractor.

All three were taken by surprise at the number of police and others present and completely unaware this was happening whilst they frolicked upstairs.

"I suppose we ought to ask if any want tea or coffee Tommy," said Toni as she looked around to ask an officer, it was a sergeant who approached and accepted her offer.

By nine o'clock the sounds of a helicopter could be heard overhead, as the engine noise shook the house and set the dogs barking, as it moved and hovered around as trees danced and swayed in the wake of the downdraft, the pitter-patter of the rota blades created its own echo effect as the house shook and trembled even more so from the air pressure it produced. The noise was deafening from the jet engines. The whole flight lasted a few minutes and then disappeared as it moved away and back into the sky.

The girls provided the visitors with lots of tea and coffee with a couple of brews in the next hour saw them eating their own long overdue breakfast.

By midday, the tractors had been removed and the police had done what was necessary their scenes of crime officers had videoed the area and examined windows for fingerprints and the grounds searched thoroughly, including to copse area.

Finally, one officer remained at the house to take some brief details of the time and the events that had occurred and of course Tommy's biggest concern was providing his name and that of the girls. It was clear that more focus will be on the gypsy camp although, Tommy assumed that they whoever had done a runner and wouldn't be coming back into the area that soon, especially those who were bitten by the dogs and his biggest worry was there was no dead body lying under the window from where he threw the gypsy out.

CHAPTER FOURTEEN
The Barrister - The Meeting

Just after seven o'clock on the Thursday morning, Tommy woke from a deep sleep; daylight crept through the landing window and disturbed him as did the smell of dogs. He had slept on the landing on a makeshift bed outside his own bedroom whilst the girls shared his room for the night. However, it was the rancid flatulent doggy smell that wafted into his nostrils that had the most effect on him. Now fully alert knowing they had got through the night without being disturbed was a godsend. The dogs had remained with him having sprawled in all directions across the landing. Tommy needed to rise and let the animals out with such awful smells on the landing and was beginning to take hold, the dogs ambled around watching him at the same time you could hear those crafty peaky whispering farts, as each dog appeared to be taking it in turns to correlate and orchestrated a symphony between them, whether it was by 'Bach' or 'Strauss' was incidental. They needed their morning constitution as he pushed himself up onto his feet still bleary eyed he went downstairs slowly with a hand sliding and gripping the bannister as he went one tread at a time.

At times Tommy at to hold his breath, the smell was rancid as he was half way down the stairs he realised that he had slept bollock naked and his clothes were back on the landing where he had left them the night before.

"Sod it – Come on boys out you go," said Tommy talking to the dogs as they rushed the open kitchen door, baying and howling as they went.

During their absence he followed the morning ritual of coffee and toast, deciding to take this up to the girls as a morning treat, rather they wait on him. Still naked he carried the tray as he climbed the stairs reaching the landing he placed it on a chair whilst he dressed himself, and then quietly crept into the semi-darkened bedroom. He pushed each foot forward in a sliding motion across the carpet; the girls were still sounding asleep as he found Toni and went and sat on her side of the bed. He blew into her face, she stirred and blinked, her head turned and simply stared at him, not a word uttered still sleepy and his presence not really registering in her thoughts. Now roused she again blinked and pushed herself back up in the bed coming rest on the pillows. Taking the tray from him and still not uttering a word as she watched him draw back the curtains a short way, enough for daylight to bring the sunshine into the room. It was obvious the girls slept naked as strewn over the floor was clothes and underwear, plus two empty wine bottles left on the side and one glass remained quarter filled resembling a urine sample, rather yellowish in colour, with a heavy scented aroma.

Both girls were covered by a flimsy sheet as the duvet lay crumpled where he stood at the bottom of the bed. As curiosity got the better of him he noticed a yellow shaped banana sticking out from under Karen's pillow, she was laying in a forward position on her side facing Toni, so the object was plain to see from where he stood. Bending down he gathered the duvet off the floor and placed on the bed in doing so he noticed it covered two handy looking sized dildo's underneath, one resembled a cave mans pre historic club, covered in bulbous nodules and the other was more feminine and dainty like, in a rather fleshy colour. Surprised at his find he couldn't stand gawping and wondering what he had missed in the night or pure fantasy on his part. Toni's hand shielded her eyes from the bright sunshine, as she picked out Tommy's silhouette at the base of the bed; suddenly she felt the weight of the duvet on her feet.

It was then Tommy left the room and went back downstairs to check on the dogs they needed watering and fed, Toni had not moved with the tray it was still on her lap as she nudged Karen with her foot, Karen began to stir and just lay blinking and gathering herself finally moving after a few moments as she sat up to join Toni, the tray was then laid between on the bed.

"Tommy's treat," she said giggling, "Coffee and toast,"

"He saw the mess then," said Karen with a dry throat.

"I would have thought so, can't miss our clothes they are all over the floor and our knickers are somewhere," said Toni giggling.

"I just tossed mine, just like that," said Karen demonstrating a flicking wrist movement and giggled and giggled.

Back in the kitchen, he realised that his toast was missing from the table.

"The fucking dogs have nicked the bloody toast," he saw and muttered to himself.

Tommy's toast had been left on a plate on the table, with the kitchen door open, it was obvious the dogs had returned on their own accord which made a change for not having to find them. Looking down at their faces as to who was the guilty one made no difference; he made the mistake of leaving food uncovered, and smiled at their bloody cheek as he ended up making fresh toast and drinking the last dregs of warm coffee from his mug.

Minutes later he was back climbing the stairs, reaching the landing and standing outside his open bedroom door,

"Good morning girls," he said loudly, "I've more toast if you want it," as he cocked an ear for a reply, as he re-entered the bedroom, "Do you know girls this is the third time I have been up here," said Tommy laughing out loud, the girls looked startled by his words as they faced each other frowning and puzzled.

Both girls had pillows laid across their tummies with arms resting and their legs lay over the top of the duvet which Tommy earlier had picked off the floor. Again standing at the foot of the bed Tommy realised he was looking at more than he bargained for; the flimsy sheet had not covered their modesty as it did when he first left them, it seemed as if Toni had received a black eye in the crutch and the eyelid was squinting and Karen's crutch was bare and peach like with a smooth fold that presented a delightful smile. Embarrassed, he carried on regardless as if nothing had happened, the girls didn't bat an eyelid, and neither did they make a move to cover their modesty as he stood facing them from the foot of the bed.

He left the bedroom without further words being exchanged between them, leaving the door ajar as he went back downstairs. At the same time pulling on the front of his trousers to make himself more comfortable, he felt horny as his underpants fought in the tightness of the material against his rising devil he was trying to control by which time he reached the hallway.

The night had been without further incident, so by and large he was happy that he could now clean the mess left by the gypsies and get some normality back in their lives, hearing from Karen that Lenny would be leaving hospital as early as next Monday was a good omen for them all.

Ten o'clock came and went so Tommy was confident that Frank and Tim were on their way down, which meant their meeting, could go ahead in the afternoon at the house. At the same time, Tommy had made the girl's aware of the meeting and they decided they would go shopping first and then on to see Lenny at the Hospital, he made sure they were in possession of the loan car keys to avoid any last minute hitches.

A national glass company was called out to the house to repair the window damage, Tommy avoided a local company and potential gossip as well as nosey parker's, no matter how confidential and private one can be people talk and he was not going to be on any local agenda.

So finally late morning Tommy remained alone in the

house, the dogs were settled, the girls shopping and the house was at long last quiet.

Just after midday Tommy had wandered the grounds and was stood by the main gate when a Land Rover pulled alongside him and stopped, Tommy recognised the driver as one of the farmers whose tractor was stolen. With idle chat, he was learning more about the local travellers and the problems they were causing in the local area.

"Why don't the local do something about them, they clearly need sorting out, someone is going to get seriously hurt with them racing up and down the lanes in stolen cars, I met two young gypsies the other night pushing a vehicle up the bloody lane. I had only just left the pub, in fact, I met the local copper Bob Benyon," said Tommy hoping to receive more information from the farmer.

"Bob, yeah, he is a good copper, one of the best, he tries to do what he can but politics plays a big part in all this today, with many losing their marbles in being politically correct, pressure groups wanting to change the world, silly bastards," the farmer retorted,

"It's fear, the locals fear reprisals if they got involved and complained too much, it's the law criminal's are an endangered species and need protecting in this country," said the farmer.

Tommy found his comments funny as he laughed and agreed with the farmer in understanding the local problem, Tommy continued to laugh as he continued to listen to the farmer's words.

"We should be proud like a politicians are, I mean we elect them and they go off and work for themselves in lining their own pockets, criminals are part of the British Heritage, Look if you're fucking different, a migrant or someone scheming for their own ends the world is your oyster, ordinary folk don't matter, we let them get away with it, we are as a nation fucking lazy, we love to whinge and whine all the time trying to put other nations to right," said the farmer now in main stream flow as you could feel his anger in his words.

"Yes I know how you must feel, I had my taste last night, the bastards, I don't suppose they have done with us yet, I expect them to try again," said Tommy looking around him for prying eyes, "You don't know who's around these days, we see movement over the other side of the lane behind you among the trees, we pick them out on the skyline," said Tommy not being too obvious.

"Anyway I best be going, my name is Anderson (Nickname Alec) that's what everybody calls me, my farm is up the lane about two miles, you can't miss my sign 'Apple-tree' get the time and come and visit, we'll chat some more," said the farmer as he checked the lane before moving off.

"Well that was some interesting conversation I must say, at least I am not the only one being bothered by those bastards," said Tommy as he stood rooted to the spot and thinking.

He also noticed some movement opposite in the woods, whether it was a local walking their dog or eyes upon us for other reasons, he saw the silhouette of what appeared to be a large man. Tommy could see his shape standing in among the trees, the figure looked eerie rather than menacing he thought, as he turned and walked back to the house. From the kitchen window Tommy continued to watch the figure, then movement as the figure climbed through the undergrowth to reach the top of the embankment and then disappeared into the field beyond.

"Interesting moment," he thought as he muttered to himself, at intervals he continued to glance out of the window for any signs of life, "Sweep, I need a chimney sweep, I need some bags of soot," he thought.

His idea was to sprinkle soot around key places on the ground in the hope he might find footprints giving evidence of where access to the grounds was most likely, other than down by the boundary fence. He knew they were finding their way onto the property from other places and he needed to know where.

"It was beginning to be like a headache living around here," said Tommy again muttering and muttering to himself, as he had no one he could sensibly speak with about his troubles, without bringing more trouble to the house.

Tommy was finally relieved when he saw just after two o'clock a Maroon coloured 4 X 4 enter the drive of the house; he saw the larger than life figure of Frank sat in the front passenger seat.

"Thank fuck for them," said Tommy hurrying outside to meet Frank and Tim, "Bloody hell, I thought you were coming by train," said Tommy as he greeted the lumbering frame of Frank alighting from the vehicle.

"Thought so too," said Frank, "Trouble on the line just outside London, so Tim decided to drive down, Not a bad journey not much traffic about," said Frank as his arms reached skywards as he stretched and swayed his body sideways to loosen up.

"Nice looking vehicle," said Tommy as he patted the bonnet as he walked round to the driver's door to greet Tim, being greeted by a solid handshake and such a bloody big hug Tommy gave his old mate.

"Tim, you're a bit greyer than the last time we met," said Tommy grinning, Tim touched and patted his head in response.

"That's family life for you," said Tim in a very polite and polished voice.

"How many kids have you now," said Tommy

"Four and all under fourteen, school age, two boys, two girls," said Tim.

"Never thought you would be a family man, with such a busy life in the smoke, Frank tells me you are now based in the sticks," (countryside) said Tommy.

"Come on let's go round the back through the gardens, we'll sit out on the patio," said Tommy, gesturing with his hand.

A short distance from the vehicle Tommy stopped, turned and looked back at Tim,

"You know Tim that is a smart looking vehicle of yours, I am impressed, to say the least," said Tommy as the group continued walking to the rear of the house.

"You know the girls are back, they're off shopping this afternoon and then later this evening will be visiting the hospital to see Lenny," said Tommy.

"How is the old boy," said Frank, "What's happening to him," said Frank.

"Well by all accounts he could be out on Monday, Karen's indicated that she and Lenny are going away somewhere for him to convalesce," said Tommy, humping his shoulders, "Have to wait and see, What their plans are," said Tommy.

"Frank was telling me about the accident and what you two did, sounds a right fiasco you had to retrieve Lenny's things from the vehicle," said Tim.

"Fiasco is the right word, it was a bloody nightmare, I managed to film as much as I could, even with Lenny being taken off in the ambulance," said Tommy, "Well to be honest, it would be the best thing for him to get away, what with our business arrangements and all."

"Yes I see your point, Tommy, that would be better if the two of them took off for awhile," said Frank as he walked in between Tommy and Tim and took the most comfortable chair on the patio.

Tim stood still and just stared at the landscape as he reached the patio.

"I say Tommy is this all yours, very nice indeed, how far does your property go back, (pause) does it include the field in front of us," said Tim with a very inquiring voice, " I am impressed you boys have done well," said Tim laughing and turning to sit down.

"Have you forgotten Tim, you bought this place for us," said Tommy as he laughed smiled at him, "You losing your memory old mate," said Tommy, "You did the negotiations and the paperwork for us,"

"I can't remember," said Tim looking at both of them, "Long time ago dear boy, I didn't know whether perhaps you had sold up and moved on for the more expensive things in life," Tim smiling as he replied.

Tommy invited each to help themselves with the sandwiches and drinks on the table as the three pals spent the next few minutes discussing Lenny's accident; Tim was much more informed with Tommy ending his story of Lenny's situation.

"Anyway I can help with his situation should he need it, especially not being at fault and any personal claims needed for him or the loss of the vehicle," said Tim (pause) always looking for new clients with a grin.

"Right Tim the reason you are here and this being the most important part of the day, as I know Frank's giving you a small brief of what I am doing. (Pause) I have arranged a business venture that's very different to the old days. My staff will be greater in foreigner numbers than of our own. The reason for that is should any of this operation go belly up and Old Bill goes about early morning turn over's, then they are going to be right up the duff. Because our operatives will be telling the truth, they will not know anything; they will be nothing more than drivers acting more as taxi drivers. I still have a number of loose ends to tie up first before I finalise my plans and the final number of personal I will need, at the moment I have around sixty people involved the vast majority from overseas, this is to ensure that we remain virgin and clean to the capers I have planned," said Tommy as he sat with a folder laid on his lap, "I have put a file together with some facts for you," said Tommy pushing the folder across the table to Tim.

Tim remained quiet sipping coffee and thinking, and then his head slowly began to nod, nod, and nodded as his mind digested Tommy's words bit, by bit.

"That's why I have brought you down today and whether I can include you to work on a retainer, although, all your potential clients, will have guilty knowledge none will be an active participant, (Pause) None will be involved directly on the ground and of course, this is on a need to know basis only, none will know the identities of those they are ferrying around, when each caper ends, then everybody from that group moves on and goes their own way home or has accepted the arrangements I have made available for them." said Tommy being very businesslike, Frank sat stony faced throughout just listening and watching Tim's face.

Tommy sat back and waited for a reaction from Tim, focusing on his face for signs of approval, looking for an in-depth sign, but then again Tim is older and wiser with family commitments with a well established Law firm in London and the sticks, Tim never gave much away, he was always the thinker, never flinched and never flapped, always a calm man. A man who never gets flustered but one with a brilliant mind who never rushes and answers in haste.

"First things first," said Tim with a face in deep thought as one could see his concentration, "I assume you are working on a business plan and of course the nature of your expenses, then your cash flow – are you looking for investors? If so, what interest are you offering on the investment? Of course, you must consider the risk factor – insurance on the investment with a small guaranteed return should this fall flat. Merchandise outlets and the guarantees that can be attractive for the investor. You will need to put in place a contract of sorts between parties involved," said Tim as he scribbled on the cover of Tommy's folder.

"Investor's I am not sure about, I could fund the whole operation with Lenny's approval but of course he is not here to voice an opinion, Frank are you able to add anything that Tim has said," said Tommy.

"I have drummed up some interest with a number of private sources without them knowing about our business, so there is a question mark as to a go, go, go, on the offers I could get," said Frank somewhat business-like without the use of a foul tongue.

Tommy was already laughing to himself as to how cultured Frank's voice had become at that moment and watching his 'Ps' and 'Qs'.

"So basically you are able to place interested parties at the table metaphorically speaking, should that become necessary Tommy," said Tim exercising his prerogative on the subject.

"Yes in view of what Frank's said, that's right isn't it Frank," said Tommy looking across at him.

"How long do you intend to keep your foreigners here in the country," said Tim.

"Less than seventy-two hours and then send them packing back abroad," said Tommy, "I do not want any staying over, that's the plan,"

"Oh! My dear fellow Tommy, that is bloody peanuts, so that's another matter resolved," said Tim, then raising his pen to scratch his head (thinking) both the pals focused on him to speak further.

"Due to the current asylum problems in the country today and the loathing by other countries in Europe to aid and assist Britain, we tend not to get the class of people this nation hopes for – what I am trying to say is that as long as you thoroughly vet your root sources in their home countries and they do not belong to any religious or have a political affiliation with known agitators and associated groups, then you are plain sailing so to speak, you need to reappraise those you currently have in mind – I don't need to teach you to suck eggs, Tommy, if you are reading between the lines dear chap," said Tim with a focused view as he stared in

Tommy's direction, "Just keep it tight and sweet, that is all that is required."

"I have already taken that in to account, I have enough trouble around here with the Fucking gypsies, so I don't want to add to my worries," said Tommy standing, "I'll make some fresh coffee," as he left for the kitchen, Frank moved to use the toilet as Tim remained seated enjoying the view of the countryside, which appeared more lush and greener than his part of the world, he thought.

On Tommy's return with fresh coffee they continued to chat and further discuss the forthcoming caper, Tim had agreed a financial retainer fee with Tommy and that would take effect twenty-four hours before the operation starts. It was nearly three hours later when the group moved indoors.

"I wanna keep an eye open for the girls, first I must let the dogs out for a run," said Tommy opening the rear door of the kitchen,

As the dogs wandered out one by one, Tommy laughed they don't seem to be in a hurry, as each stretched leaning first forwards then backwards and then disappeared outside.

"It's much cooler in here Tommy," said Frank as he pulled down on his multicoloured braces,

Tommy just glanced and grinned, Tim made no comment he appeared deep in thought, jotting down notes as he occasionally looked up at the pals. Then completely going off tangent Tim said,

"Have you had your place valued Tommy,"

"No why do you ask," said Tommy responding to Tim's question.

"I would expect this to be of high value in the market, I really feel that you would be rather shocked at what this could command, you should have it valued above all else, for your own affairs as you are both on the deeds, otherwise if something happened to either of you, it could be a costly exercise," said Tim as he faced Tommy, he then turned to Frank looking for an answer, why? – Tommy acted on a sudden impulse to involve him, but it was not Frank's concerns.

Tim's conclusions about the value of the property certainly left Tommy pondering on his words and to consider his advice in the very near future and have the property valued; it would be a wise move and investment on their part.

"You need an upmarket agency and not local one," said Tim.

"Believe me Tim I would never go local, avoid the gossip," said Tommy.

Frank steered the conversation away from the subject of the house and referred to Tim's conversation on the drive down about the changes in the legal system and new ideas, new legislation and all manner of other things.

"Tim tell Tommy about the Crown Prosecution Service and the Poacher – Go on tell him, you see how bloody stupid it's got today Tommy," said Frank encouraging Tim to speak.

"It concerned a poaching offence, where they returned a file to a police officer with a query. The query concerned whether the police officer was able to state, now you need to be mindful that the poacher was arrested with all of his equipment and was armed to the teeth with firearms at the time and he was arrested on private land going equipped in the middle of the night and the birds of game including a dead rabbit was found on his person. The 'CPS' query to the officer was whether the rabbit had rigor mortis and did the dead birds come from that land or elsewhere. The ridicules part of this is the poacher admitted in his statement under caution that he had indeed poached the game birds and rabbit that very night on the land he was arrested on – The 'CPS' did not regard the poachers statement to be adequate to prove his guilt along with other evidence that was confiscated from his on arrest," said Tim, "That is how politically robust and correct the situation has become today, there is little appetite to convict as in the old days hoping to avoid any civil claims, simply the 'CPS' lacks streetwise solicitors who have knowledge of the real world they live in, they are mostly townies who have little time for the countryside, more about the social ladder and wine bars to further their careers, in other words plain and simple bloody lazy people with very lazy minds." said Tim as he finished telling the story.

"Fucking hell Tim, what would they do if they met a real villain like us mate, can you imagine the grief they would have in trying to understand how the mind of the criminal works," said Tommy with a loud laugh and shocked at Tim's story, " I have always believed that the 'CPS' stands for 'Cut Price Services' because they have got to be the most incompetent law agency you could possibly wish to meet, who was the idiot in politics who introduced this, I wonder – I mean let's get real here Tim, the 'CPS' employ fresh faced daisy solicitors who have no real experience of life on the street, they are not streetwise. How many of them actually meet people like me and Frank, they wouldn't have a fucking clue in the real world, they're all juggling and jockeying their lives for climbing the ladder, they don't have the bottle to run a case through court like the Old Bill's prosecuting departments did when they had the responsibility of dealing with criminals – But this business today of the 'CPS' being judge, jury and not the executioner is a fucking joke – To be honest Tim if I ever got shafted by anyone I would not be complaining to the police, I would go for a private prosecution and stuff the 'CPS' – The trouble is with the 'CPS' because it is second rate service then you will only have second rate people apply for the jobs, look at people from your position, Barristers, look at the many politicians in parliament who are from the legal profession – Why, why are they in parliament, because many are failures in their own careers, they either couldn't make a living on their bloody own or were no bloody good in the practice they worked and shown the door, not earning enough money because who wants the hard work of casework, Look Tim you are better placed than I am, when a Barrister Politician loses his meal ticket on election night, how many go back into practice? – They don't, they become advisors to this and that quango until the next election and hope they get re-elected and so the wheel of fortune keeps turning as long as they follow the party line and we are the mugs, the real bloody mugs for keeping them in work. Can you imagine a 'QC' working as a dustman of course not there is no social standing in that mate, but a 'QC' in parliament looks good, this country is well and truly fucked by the poor showing of who we keep electing, as out there we have better," said Tommy now gesturing and waving his hands around and Frank sat on the sidelines grinning to himself as he saw that the old Tommy had now come alive and going full throttle for the country's jugular.

"Tell me, Tommy, where did you learn about the failed barrister racket," said Tim, smiling with enthusiasm at Tommy's statement.

"From your lot, your profession, other legals told me how it's all played out, more like a pantomime of sorts," said Tommy in reply to Tim's question.

"You see Frank, I'm bloody right, tell him Tim," said Tim laughing to himself.

"Well, it has been known and recognised for some years in our profession that this is a general principle of failure, so this goes on among Barristers and Politicians, obviously those elected to parliament tend to be rightly (like Tommy has said) Advisors and the other scam that has been operated among them for years is of course to be consultants," said Tim grinning.

"Listening to you at the moment Tommy, perhaps you ought to stand for parliament, you would make a good appointment, make good television in the afternoons," said Tim cheekily laughing with Frank as he gave a wink to Tommy in appreciation of his words.

"I am amazed by your soap box approach dear boy," said Tim with still expressing a hearty laugh and a handclap, Frank was curled up with laughter, especially with Tommy sounding more like a labour comrade of the present.

Tommy started to dance rather strangely as the others stood and watched him go through his moves.

"Where did that funny dance come from Tommy," said Frank in fits of tearful laughter, "Oh! Dear," he kept repeating.

"My party piece, I walked behind the female warders of course and copied them moving about on the wings," said Tommy still acting out the fool.

Soon after the hilarities had calmed down between them all, the dogs became restless and barked, it was then Tommy from the kitchen window recognised and acknowledged the return of the girls as he spoke aloud, Frank went to the back door of the kitchen and walked out for a cigarette.

During Tommy's absence in greeting the girls, Tim who was in the lounge stood to stretch his legs and flex his muscles, in the recess of the bay window, it wasn't deliberate on his part to be inquisitive or nosey in looking out of the window at the time, but then for reasons unknown at the time, Tim mumbled to himself,

"Good lord, I know that face, yes heavens I do," turning round to speak with Frank he realised that he was alone in the room.

It was much later in the day after having met the girls and neither made comment of having met Tim before, that Tim realised the significance of not being recognised. In the girls' absence Tommy said,

"You look preoccupied then Tim,"

"The young lady Karen, I thought I recognised her, her face is very familiar," said Tim whilst his hand was stroking his chin as he was thinking to himself, trying to remember where he had previously seen Karen.

"What Karen, I doubt it old mate, she's not from these parts, that's for sure and not from London," said Tommy now pondering on Tim's words.

"No it was her face that drew my attention, it's something that's not recent that's for sure," said Tim.

"Not recent, what do you mean Tim," said Tommy.

"Someone I met a few years ago, she is so familiar, obviously I am wrong as she never recognised me," said Tim.

"She has a face that many woman would die for, is that what you're saying Tim," said Tommy laughing.

"I suppose you are right Tommy both are very attractive girls," said Tim.

"I would second that Tim, they are both lovely girls and Lenny thinks the world of Karen, they are good together, they make an attractive couple," Frank adding his two pennyworth to the conversation.

The pals were unaware that Karen was descending the stairs when halfway down, she inexplicably stopped and listened to the wafting gist of conversation coming from the lounge, it was uncanny on her part, but she felt that she was the topic of conversation between the three of them. Perhaps a sixth sense on her part. Although, she did no more than continue down as her eyes met Tommy's as she passed the open door of the lounge heading to the kitchen. Tommy called after her.

"Karen, do you and Toni want me to pour you a drink," said Tommy.

"Yes I'll have one, Toni's still in the shower," called Karen.

"Would you bring some ice back from the fridge," shouted Tommy.

Karen returned to the lounge with ice in hand.

"What time are you both going to the hospital," said Tommy

"Well it depends first if you want a meal, depends on what you fellows want," said Karen.

"Oh! Don't worry about us luv, blimey we can see to ourselves, tell her Tommy they haven't got to worry about us three," said Frank.

Tommy gave her a hug,

"Go on luv, you both carry on with what you are doing," said Tommy, as he reached out and gave her a small peck on the cheek, then handed the drink to her.

Karen took a couple of sips before leaving the room.

"In view of the time Tommy, I would like to pop in and see Lenny for five minutes before we head back, considering the distance if we left by seven o'clock, quick visit to the hospital, dropping Frank at home - I should get home by around ten-thirty," said Tim.

"Well yes, that's fine, we've sorted out the arrangements, there's nothing more for us to discuss at the moment – Except I haven't given you your envelope... let me go and get that now, so I know that's done and dusted with," said Tommy as Frank interrupted,

"Talking of envelopes, I have one for you, Tommy, the details are inside, it's about the photos you gave me, you've got a good result," said Frank, "Perhaps it's your investor," as he grinned at Tommy as he, in turn, stepped back and took the envelope from Frank.

Tommy left the room and went upstairs meeting Toni coming down, they momentarily stopped and kissed each other in passing and then went their separate ways, he was a few minutes in the bedroom before, he joined Karen on the landing she too was about to walk down the stairs, when Tommy mentioned that Frank and Tim would follow them down to the hospital to see Lenny for five minutes before they go back to London.

Tommy noticed how quiet Tim was since meeting the girls, although, he hadn't ignored either of them as it was his style to show bad manners.

"Tommy I must check outside for my notebook, I may have left it on the chair," said Tim.

"Let's have a look," said Tommy to Tim.

Frank has struggled to his feet and slowly ambled across the room, the girls had walked their way to the front door, by which time Frank appeared in the hallway and joined them. Tommy passed Tim the cash envelope in private.

"This last hour you've been rather quiet Tim, are you alright," said Tommy.

"I wasn't intending to be rude old fellow, it's Karen's face it still bugs me, I can see her in my mind but from where I don't know," said Tim, "I suppose on the drive home it will come to me," he uttered to Tommy.

"Are you still thinking about Karen," said Tommy

"Yes, it will come to me in time, and then I'll let you know," said Tim.

"It would be interesting, I hope it's not matrimonial or bus loads of kids, that would put the mockers on it for Lenny," said Tommy jokingly.

"No I am sure it's none of those things, I am confident it's relevant to my work – I have been very busy on immigration affairs during the last few years, up and down like a yo-yo for the government," said Tim.

"She is not an asylum seeker Tim, she's English through and through, like me and you," said Tommy.

"Never mind old chap, I could be wrong on the subject," said Tim.

Walking back through the house to the hallway and the waiting group, who left by the front door, within minutes the two vehicles were slowly manoeuvring up the drive. Tommy watched as both vehicles accelerated and disappeared from view as Tommy ushered the dogs back in the house and closed the front door. Alone in the house, Tommy began a clean and tidy up around him and only the sounds of the hall clock and dogs yawning and scratching could be heard. Eventually unwinding in the lounge to watch television, Frank's envelope remained where Tommy had left it unopened on the drinks cabinet, his neglect consumed by his interest in television. It didn't seem more than five minutes since everybody had left for the hospital, when Tommy heard the sounds of a vehicle on the driveway.

"Christ there back what's this about," said Tommy muttering to himself as he left the chair and walked to the front door for an answer.

He waited at the open door, no one appeared, and he closed the door and went to the rear kitchen door, still no presence of anyone. He left the rear porch and walked down the side of the house back towards the front, he found Toni standing on the edge of the lawn, and Karen was still seated in the vehicle. Toni heard Tommy's footsteps and turned and walked towards him.

"What's a matter, Toni," said Tommy sounding bewildered in his tone.

"Wait a minute Tommy, I'm waiting to see if an old man passes the gate entrance," said Toni seemingly rather concerned about the man.

"Why what's up with him," said Tommy looking in the direction of the entrance.

"Well I saw this old fellow standing up the road from the entrance, we were following Tim's vehicle, as I came past he stood on the verge to let me go by and when I looked in the rear mirror, I couldn't see him standing there, I know I was close to him, but I don't think I hit him, so I waited for him to show and he didn't so I panicked and came back to see if I could find him, so I am waiting to see if he comes past the entrance, he was going that way," said Toni now worried and confused.

"Where about's was he when you saw him, (pointing) over there," said Tommy facing Toni.

"Yes in that direction but on the opposite side of the lane," said Toni now very concerned, "Bloody hell where could he have gone, he was stood in the shadows (Pause) you could hardly see him when we approached," said Toni now beginning to sound tearful as she described the old man.

Tommy realised that she had seen old Ben Witney and why Toni couldn't find him, Ben had ducked through the gap in the hedge as he came across the lane after the girls returned to the house. Old Ben had climbed the bank and was in the copse opposite. Tommy went looking for the old man (Old Ben had watched the couple from the undergrowth and saw Tommy walk into the lane) within minutes both men found each other and the mystery solved; Ben was safe and well and had no brush with Toni's vehicle. Tommy got Ben to wait whilst he returned and reassured Toni of Ben's welfare (the excuse - he was looking for mushrooms?) and to get the girls away and back on their journey to the hospital. Seeing the girls off for the second time Tommy popped into the house for a few moments, then returning and headed back to the copse and old Ben, Tommy bunged the old man fifty quid for his troubles. Old Ben mentioned the previous night's attack on the house and the injuries some of the gypsies received for their troubles. But they were bad blood and would cause Tommy more trouble and he needs to beware as they intended to do him harm, some were from another family who had been drinking that night and helped the young ones out from his camp, they managed to steal the tractors and caused a lot of damage to some vehicles they used to push the tractors through the lanes until they reached the top of the hill and free wheeled down to your house. Ben mentioned that the Police had been buzzing their camp with the helicopter in the early hours. The young ones were sleeping out in the fields, as they had been drinking and shagging some of the local girls from the next village over the ridge. They had stolen a couple of vehicles which they brought back; they were racing around the field in the darkness and crashing into each other for fun they abandoned the vehicles in the hedge. One of the local girls got hurt and broke her leg, she is in hospital.

Tommy realised there clearly is a lot of infighting among the fraternities and clearly no one strong enough to control the young ones they have no respect for each other, it was madness in the extreme and that was troubling, to say the least.

Tommy mentioned the big man in the hedge he saw at lunchtime, pointing in the direction of where he was seen. Old Ben called him the 'Postman' a man who delivers trouble; he lives and breathes trouble as Old Ben continued to explain more about the man as a 'USER' anybody can get him to do their dirty work for them. He is not a traveller, he is a 'Gorger' (lives in house) he speaks a lot to the 'Gavvers' (Police) he hangs around the travellers but he is not trusted, the young ones take the piss out of him, he tries to be hard but he is getting on now, because he is a big man it makes people afraid of him, he is always creeping around and being nosey, he does a bit of peeping on the courting couples that park up in the lane at night.

Eventually, Tommy was the first to leave Old Ben and return to the house, sometime later Old Ben and (fifty quid richer) would have crept back onto the lane and headed back to the gypsy camp further up.

Toni was alone on her return from hospital, she had not gone as long as he had expected, and she closed the kitchen door behind her as she entered as she faced Tommy.

"Where's Karen," said Tommy looking surprised at her appearance.

"Karen's gone with Frank and Tim," said Toni as she removed her coat and left it over the back of the chair, turning to make herself a coffee.

"What do you mean she's gone with them, what for," he cried out, Tommy was beginning to feel concerned and as this was rather bizarre especially reflecting on Tim's earlier conversation about her.

"When we got there tonight, Lenny's up and about with some nurses helping him, then a doctor spoke to and apparently he can come home on Monday as we earlier thought. So, (Pause) Lenny and Karen have decided that they want to get away as soon as possible (Pause) agreeing between them and on the spur of the moment Karen decided to get a lift back with Tim, he would drop her off at St. Albans on the way back – Karen was going to speak to her family for the loan of their summer cottage on the Norfolk coast. She's going to stay overnight with her family and drive back to her place to pack some things and then to drive back down in her car on Sunday, so organising her time away and then back for Lenny on Monday morning once he has been seen by the doctor. She will pack and organise Lenny's things for him on Sunday when she gets back," said Toni as she took hold of Tommy's hand, he looked shaken by the rushed decision that had been taken by Karen and Lenny.

"And that's it, so you only have me around for the time being," said Toni.

"Christ what a bloody shock you've given me, I wondered what the bloody hell had happened you coming back in quick time and alone, so she's already on her way back with the boy's, said Tommy still confused at the news.

"Yes, she's gone, they're on their way back to London," said Toni.

"I don't fucking believe it," said Tommy laughing and scratching his head at the same time.

"Lenny was going to call you, I said I would tell you, that's why I'm back early," said Toni, "Just me and you now, Tommy." as Toni cuddled up to Tommy and rubbed his back as he rested his arms over her shoulders, "I'm bloody confused, that's all," said Tommy.

It was very late when Tommy took a phone call from Tim.

"Karen, I remembered where I had seen her before. About four years ago in Essex there was a number of people involved in a big drugs bust which was dealt with by Customs Officer's, Karen was there she is a Customs Officer Tommy, she was with the drugs squad at the time," said Tim in his usual quiet manner.

Tommy remained stunned at the news and echoed a muttering 'thank you' as he came off the phone; Tommy accepted the news without making any further comment as Toni was sitting nearby, he put on a brave face as he turned and said,

"They're all home safely, that was Tim letting us know, Karen was dropped off at her parents place, after Frank's drop off, so that's good, with the house locked up we can get up those apples and pears ourselves me darling (speaking to Toni) said Tommy trying to be jovial in spite of the bad news.

They both called it a night and climbed the stairs to bed.

CHAPTER FIFTEEN
Feelings And Emotions

Around eight o'clock Friday Morning Toni used the bathroom, on her return a few minutes later Tommy was stirring. Toni sat on the edge of the bed, having raised and rested her leg on the mattress. Whilst she eyed Tommy's naked figure slowly he began to move and fidget before finally waking, he caught Toni's stare. She leaned over and kissed gently, then again and parted. Tommy realised the urgency of her kiss, as she again kissed him for a third time, as each kiss lasted longer than the last. However, this morning, Toni was different, she was much quieter than usual, her face appeared to be hypnotic as if mesmerised. Her eyes stared and focused on his nakedness, as with a gentle softening smile that welcomed his day. Tommy sensed the change in her, the green of her eyes were wide and inviting with a glint that was caught by the daylight in the room. He felt the intensity of her loneliness, if that were her feelings at the time. She seemed distant and vacant to her surroundings, as he reached out and pulled her down on top of him. Their eyes remained focused on each other without a blink between them, he felt that Toni was searching for answers, but what answers was she looking for? What did she want from him? She turned and laid her head on his tummy as she gently ran the palm of her hand in gentle strokes over his flesh. He ran his fingers up and down her spine as she flinched at times as she felt the goose bumps with his touching, still wondering what ailed her at this time. Tommy didn't want to disturb her thoughts as they lazed together, content just to lay together, he felt calm and nice at their togetherness, although, not unduly worried by her quietness.

Toni responded to his touches, she twitched her shoulders as his finger circled on a sensitive area. It seemed ages before the couple finally moved, as she lay on her back alongside him, her eyes stared at the ceiling. Her breasts gently moved up and down as she breathed, her nipples lay flat and blended against the apex of a darker ring, the petite size was a beautiful shape to admire. Each stood alone and perfect for her naked contours, a slim waist and a small neatly trimmed pubic area that had been cropped close to her skin. Her manicured hands and painted lacquer matched those of her toes, attached to her small size feet.

Tommy knew that Toni was dreams come true, although, he felt that he hadn't quite reached the deep sense of feeling that she perhaps was seeking from him. They neither had sought to inquire of their past and former lives of each other. Their beginning was a business arrangement and now it seemed that this was perhaps not enough for Toni, could she be wanting more? Especially now Karen and Lenny are now officially a couple, could this be jealousy on her part as to what Karen had achieved.

Tommy didn't have an answer as they continued to lay and laze naked together this very morning without any words being spoken between them. Knowing how vacant and distance Toni seemed to be.

"Penny for your thoughts," said Tommy whispering to her.

Toni just looked and smiled as Tommy repeated his words,

"Penny for your thoughts," he said for the second time of asking.

"Mmmm, I'm thinking," said Toni.

"What about," said Tommy quietly?

"All, lots of things," said Toni turning her head towards him.

"What things, tell me, I'm interested (Pause) I'm listening just try me," said Tommy intent on knowing more.

"About my life," said Toni still looking up into his face.

"This is about Karen and Lenny, isn't it, you aren't happy," said Tommy showing some concern for her feelings.

"To a degree," she replied quietly.

"Come on then, I'm all ears, what's troubling you," said Tommy in a mumbling whisper.

"What am I doing? Where am I going? Things like that," said Toni.

"And, so what is it? – What's the matter at this time?" said Tommy.

"Oh! I thought I had come on again this morning, but it's too early, it makes us women like that sometimes moody – I had a slight tummy ache in the night, I feel drained and exhausted this morning, I think it was a reaction to the Old man, thinking I had run him over yesterday, that really scared me," said Toni as she laid her hand on his thigh and began to stroke his leg as they laid side by side.

Toni's eyes continued to stare into Tommy's face as with her giving him a smile as she recognised his facial signs of showing an inquisitiveness of her words and thoughts as her eyes darted around his face at the same time of him looking down at her. She continued to scrutinise his face, his forehead lines, crow's feet around the eyes even the crease of his mouth came in for attention as did the lobes of his ears, as she raised the back of her hand and gently stroked his face, as he suddenly took hold of her hand and bent over her and passionately kissed Toni full on her lips, this time the kiss lingered and continued with their lips locked together and Toni's fingers of one hand twiddled and stroked his hair at back of his head and around his neck.

"Aren't you going to tell me then or are going to keep me in suspense," said Tommy anxiously waiting for a sign from her.

"Well it's a lot of things to do with me Tommy, I have moments like this then I sit and reflect on my life of the past and where I will be in ten years time from now, what will I be doing? Possibly not what I am doing today that's for sure, I need a change of direction, I need a new challenge to my life," said Toni as she became more enthusiastic about Tommy's concerns, does he really care?

"Is it Lenny and Karen's situation that got you feeling like this," said Tommy now wondering if this is a reason of sorts,

"Has something been said by Karen," said Toni inquiring further to the way she was feeling.

"No, but I am also capable of picking up vibes from other people and their situation has moved rather fast in the last week and now what with this bloody accident, and Karen and Lenny going away – Me and Lenny have been together for the last five years in this house with little change, along the way we have grown our own interests during those years, now it's all beginning to change, so you are not the only one who's thinking about the future," said Tommy grinning down at her,

Toni continued stroking his face, when Tommy's hand grabbed her wrist and pushed it down to her side, as he again leaned over and gently kissed her, their lips pressed together showing some real passion from him, more of an urgency as on his part. Tommy saw right deep into her face and saw the small red veins in the whites of her eyes as he continued to focus his attentions and that close to her. Slightly lifting her head as he slipped an arm under her neck, he turned and adjusted more of his position, as with the hand on the other arm he ran the back of his hand over her breasts, and tummy in slow deliberate strokes, then a finger circled the base of her breasts as he continued to look into her face for answers. All the time Toni lay and felt his touch stroking her flesh and how nice it was to enjoy quietly his touch as she at one time closed her eyes, with occasional squints in staring into his face.

How caring he was?

How friendly he was?

And the kind of lover he was?

But who was Tommy really?

She thought? And was perhaps the biggest question to be answered from her searching questions. How could two men live a life in recluse and not be a couple of queers?

What business were they in?

Did they have a family of their own?

Had they been married?

Was he married?

Did he have any children?

Does he want Children?

Children, Children, Were her biggest concerns for Toni, as sadly she could not have children due to her earlier years of extreme sexual activity which left her barren and caused years of mental and physical torment and which now returns to haunt her in such a dreadful way of realising her fears of experiencing a real growing relationship and now in her thirties would this be a burden with Tommy and would she fall at the very first hurdle of trying.

"Look, your thoughts are about us, right, so please listen to what I have to say – You are comparing relationships? (Pause) You want what Karen's got? – Although, little did you know that you have it already? – Are we an item or not? – Is our situation any different to theirs (Pause) Think about it? (Pause) It's only the accident that has brought them closer together, that is the only difference – So what I am telling you is gospel babe, I am not going anywhere, you can stay and hang onto my shirt tail or go back to the life you have today –

We are more than friends in my book and well fucking lovers at the same time you are a bloody man eater, my balls are still hanging on the fence from the other evening, you sucked me dry darling, the point is I might not be as romantic as Lenny or others, but believe me I really truly care about you and love the times we have spent together (Pause) more than you can possibly know." said Tommy in a real change in his voice that really grabbed Toni's full attention.

"I want you around for as long as you want it, I am not the one who will push you away, I have business to sort out in the coming months and after that I shall have more time, in fact as much time as you want to share with me," said Tommy with a reactive and gentle tone to his voice.

Not shying away from Toni, but being clear as to his feelings and her decision to decide on the relationship she sought from him, Toni's face lit up in a way that remained very private to them both, it was that moment of truth that all couples seek and never sure of the final answer, a real tenderfoot acceptance in their lives and being together.

"So I am not selfish in ignoring you, perhaps in the way you feel at the moment, it's not about take, take, take and fuck her hard, it flows much deeper in my veins as to who you are and what I want, and it seems that we both want the same things out of life," said Tommy with an emotional tear in the eyes and a taint to his voice.

"Oh! Dear (she sighs). You're right, I was laying here thinking about us, but more about how we would develop, I know nothing about you (Tommy interrupted her)

"So who are you, my girl? – remember what I said when I first spoke to you, can you remember my words about confidentiality. Right, was I right? (Pause) Your visit was a business arrangement; none of us at the time would have believed that a relationship was going to happen between Karen and Lenny and now us as well, you came at a time when we needed to change our lifestyles and you girls sub consciously were also looking for the same things, nature has played a quirk of fate on the four of us in bringing our chemistry to flow and make our situation more emotionally charged and involved than we had planned for in the beginning, it's our time now to grab it whilst we want it to happen," said Tommy his voice was now on a roll with such a smooth tongue, Toni was intently listening and loving every minute as she hung on every word he said.

Toni was excited and looked more alive and flushed as she moved and turned to talk to him,

"I see the point you are making Tommy, but from a woman's point of view, there are unanswered questions – How do I know that you are not married with a house full of children or have you ever been married, is their children and where are your family? Are your parents alive? Brother and Sisters? You know normal things that couples share together," said Toni being serious, Tommy burst out laughing as he suddenly realised the very nature of what was troubling Toni.

"You belong here with me my girl, is that bloody plain enough," said Tommy.

In recent years Toni's parent retired to France, that was the nice bit, but the awful bit was when things go wrong and you end up wanting the comfort of your parents, even when you have a cold and you have no one to turn to like you do and a girls relationship with their mums is always special, that's what she missed about her parents absence being able to pop down the road or the next town to drop in for a tea or coffee, you know what I mean, that is the hardest part of being apart hoping they are safe and well and not ending up with a telephone relationship as she has with her parents and what she wants to avoid happening to her. Her sisters have children and families to look after and this she loves to be a part of, Toni realised she had the choice to come and go and share with the children, leaving them she had no responsibilities towards them but always she would be their aunt wherever she was in her life, the children's aunt?

"I have not been married – I have no children and no children that I aware of," said Tommy funning with Toni.

"What do you mean about children, not being aware if you have any," said Toni frowning and screwing her face in dismay at his answer.

"It's a pun darling, I am a man of the world – I am not a bloody virgin am I, accidents happen only to find out years later when a knock comes at the door, hello dad – You know what I mean a Pun is a pun and nothing more I do not have children," said Tommy alarmed as to where this conversation was going with Toni.

"Sorry I wasn't thinking Tommy," said Toni realising she had hurt his feelings.

"Sorry sunshine, I'm not trying to make mountains out of molehills – I am trying to show you cannot change the past but only move on with your futures, whatever is behind us is incidental, this is between us – Is it going you make any difference in the way we feel about each other, is it," said Tommy, inquiring about their present relationship.

"I want to know more of the man than the stranger who made love to me," said Toni pointing a finger at him.

"Touché' – Your right, you are so right, I have no wife or children, I am a single man and does not want children at my time of life, I need more of a wife and lover than just a sexual companion to share my life, I need a bloody soul mate to share my life with, someone who loves me for me and me only, someone I can occasionally fuck and get drunk with and bloody laugh with, without getting a fucking bollocking," (Pause) Tommy then raised a pleading voice – Catching her by surprise, "So Toni are you that bloody woman, if so, say yes out loud so I can fucking hear you, put me out of my misery please girl, Are you listening, are we on the same wavelength," said Tommy as he finally reached a point where enough is enough and again plunged in with a passionate kissing session that went on and on and on, when Toni finally managed to push him to one side as she came up for air, "Christ Tommy," said Toni rather shocked at how amorous he had become and soon she had joined the passion that glued them together, bodies writhing and moving as each kiss, each gasp of air reached new heights as they continued kissing and kissing. When Toni pulled Tommy on top of her as the kissing continued, with both hands she pushed and parted her lips and said, "Tommy, fuck me, Tommy fuck me, be gentle with me, but fuck me I want you inside of me, I want to feel you," as she felt around and found his semi-limp penis was far from aroused and not ready to do her feelings justice.

Tommy did no more than covert her naked body with one lingering cuddle and his head resting at the side of her neck as he kissed and pecked gently. Toni was underneath him and yet she had hold of this limp manhood the female weapon of destruction, she pulled on it and he squirmed a little as she was now in full flight of urgency she wanted him to fuck her as she kept crying out to fuck her, her legs continued to open and shut in quick succession, teasing him in the only way how. Toni knew that she was so moist and ready for any man to fuck her but she wanted Tommy to rise and shine, he was struggling in the process of not concentring like Toni wanted, but she changed tack and touched him more gently and kissed him in the process and found that it worked as he was beginning to rise to her occasion. Finally Tommy triumphed in rising to the occasion and gently penetrated Toni's vagina with many gentle movements that made Toni whimper her feelings were loud as Tommy pushed his member right up to the hilt, in fact, he dragged a pillow across the bed and got Toni to raise her buttocks as he placed not one but two pillows underneath her body as he had decided and intend to go as deep as nature would allow him in satisfying Toni's sexual needs, she was hot, she was moist, she wanted to be fucked by him, Toni was going for broke as she clung on around his neck with her legs around his waist with her ankles locked hard against his bodily movements in pleasing her, as Tommy lifted himself up and moved Toni was glued to him his penis was well and truly buried deep inside of her, the thrill was real passion as she felt his real gentleness in the way he took her, so kind, so gentle and of course Toni was able to take the most from his penetration as she began to feel herself moving and writhing as she too was coming and encouraging Tommy to ride with her as he did his utmost to come and let his cream dribble into her silky lining as they both lay one on top of the other in total sexual satisfaction, it was the heighten moment of what Toni wanted from Tommy, it was the real Tommy making real love to her and not just a man having sex, Toni felt it deep as to how her emotions suddenly found that lasting feeling having been filled by man which left her with a warm belly that would last her days in the warming of their love together. Their touching, their love making finally blew away the cobwebs that had stood in the way of their feelings and new relationship.

Finally, after some minutes, they both stirred and Tommy decided he would be the first in the shower, as Toni remained in her lazy sexual moments of satisfaction.

Tommy had showered and dressed as Toni still laid naked on the bed with tissues stuck between her legs as Tommy left the bedroom, for the next hour Tommy had entered his man cave in the copse and was rummaging through various boxes and found different types of equipment which he placed in a cardboard box. Tommy was on a personal mission. At the same time, Tommy checked on his final arrangement he had made earlier, then finding an email needing his attention and concerned the storage yard he owned. Confirming the alternations he requested had been completed and the various gantries and hydraulics he required were now in place, including the raised platforms and extra storage facilities.

Finally, Tommy sat back in his chair and realised that his arrangements had been completed, he tapped, he hummed as he went through the last half-hours work, checking and rechecking for any mistakes. Toni was already downstairs by this time, although not perturbed by Tommy's absence as she brewed fresh coffee.

By two o'clock the couple had entered the Bull and Butcher public house, Toni was not aware of Tommy's ulterior motive of visiting at this hour of the afternoon, and neither was she aware of the cardboard boxes in the boot of the vehicle, with only a handful of locals in the pub, Tommy soon found Judy stokes the licensees wife, he reminded her of his previous visit when he was introduced to Bob Benyon the local Policeman.

"I wonder if I might ask a favour of you, I have some boxes to leave your local policeman and I would rather trust you with them and not the local station to give to him when he is back off his course," said Tommy hoping she would agree to his request.

"I don't see why not, you say you have them with you," said Judy

"Yes that's right I have them in the car," said Tommy, also keeping an eye on Toni's return from the loo.

"Bring them round to the back and I'll call my Dan to take them and store them on Bob's return," said Judy.

Judy was speaking with Toni whilst Tommy brought the Range Rover round to the back door of the pub and met with Dan, handing over the cardboards boxes he returned to the bar and joined Toni. By this time Tommy saw Toni in a different light, she hadn't asked questions about their pub visit, this did seem out of character with Tommy.

(Tommy had placed numerous gadgets, listening equipment, walkie-talkies, digital camera with tripod and other surveillance equipment and hoped that the policeman would find the items of interest and help him with his tasks against the gypsies and give him an edge over them)

By three-thirty o'clock Tommy and Toni returned to the house having been shopping and a visit to the hospital to see Lenny. Toni felt more involved as she was now playing her part alongside Tommy; they acted and seemed a couple. Although, they both kept hidden their past history from each other, it still remained a mystery of the real unknown for both of them; it was a day of touché' neither a winner, but now as one.

CHAPTER SIXTEEN
Alone And Together

Come Saturday morning with breakfast over and now gone after nine o'clock when Tommy and Toni took the dogs down to the field adjacent the patio at the back of the house. The dogs when lose went in all directions crisscrossing each other's tracks as their noses remained to the ground sniffing and following the scents they found.

Sat together on the ground Tommy and Toni watched as their eyes traced the movement of the dogs racing around the field, Tommy's thoughts became preoccupied and turned to the 45 acres of pasture land purchased with the house. It also included among the picturesque landscape a wide deep gulley that remained hidden from general view on the property. Months earlier, tons of soil had been delivered and placed around the ridge of the gulley with a future purpose of burying vehicles and equipment used in his forthcoming crime caper. The mounds of earth would be bulldozed from around the ridge of the gulley onto the hidden vehicles below, not one trace of evidence would be left to be found by the naked eye, this would be the final epitaph and resting place of his crime caper buried deep forevermore from the authorities and prying eyes, only a new landscape to be found of grass and weeds from the ground and air.

Time today had no importance for either of them, from their heart to heart the day before both were more relaxed and comfortable with each other showing a change in their personalities as to their togetherness in having begun to clear the air, although, Tommy had been drip feeding Toni antidotes of his past life and in doing so waited for her reaction but her questions never came she just listened intently without compromising further her judgement and preconceptions of him. Perhaps now both could move on their relationship and be the couple they wish to be and only time will be their witness.

Gone after ten o'clock by the time the dogs had been called and the couple returned to the house, having settled the animals, Toni brewing fresh coffee and Tommy having fetched the newspaper from the hallway which he spread across the kitchen table to read the headlines, both sat quietly drinking their coffees.

Toni mentioned that she was intending to bring down the bed sheets and duvet covers for washing with so much physical activity having taken place between the two couples since their arrival, Toni decided to retain her standards of hygiene throughout the bedrooms, with Karen returning for the one night on Sunday and Lenny's absence was long term from the house that both bedrooms needed to be aired.

In the meantime, Tommy had disappeared to his man cave in the copse, intent on checking and rechecking equipment and planned schedules, he wasn't about to miss a trick.

During his absence from Toni's company he pondered and chewed over Tim's findings about Karen, having decided that he would not mention this to Lenny or approach Karen at his discovery. But Toni was a different ball game she must know of Karen's position, then again did it really matter he thought as he continued to mutter to himself, then realising that it didn't as not all her customers were planning a major crime caper like he and Lenny were planning and what damage would this cause to their budding relationship. Tommy came to the conclusion that he couldn't make the problem go away, but certainly he could bury his concerns for the time being as neither Karen nor Lenny were going to be around for awhile, so there were no obvious dangers in raising the matter at this time, let sleeping dogs lie he thought, why stick his neck out at this time.

By midday he was back in the house, Toni was still upstairs as he thought, working on a bloody good spring clean of the bedrooms and long overdue at that. From the lounge he made a number of phones calls, one especially to Frank; he confirmed the booking of a hotel conference room the following Friday adjacent Heathrow airport and those on the list were English drivers who would be attending, a couple flying in from Spain and Italy, so slowly his plans were coming together and he needed to be a bit crafty with Toni now moving into the house on a more permanent footing and next Friday was an ideal opportunity to drop her off at her place whilst he fronted the meeting at the hotel. Toni would then have the opportunity to pack more of her things to bring back with her, with time apart that morning would be ideal without any pressure being applied by him, Toni would be able to pick and chose her clothes and personal items and collect her post at leisure and arrange for her neighbours to keep an eye on her place whilst away. He decided to tell her of the London meeting later and his thoughts of taking her with him to drop off and leave her at her place to collect clothes and personal items and he would return after the meeting to collect her. This would also show further his commitment to her for the long haul of wanting a relationship and to establish her greater presence at the house as he had suggested that she retire from her present career and to let him support her.

Later Tommy climbed the stairs with two mugs of fresh coffee he was going in pursuit of Toni; she sat in their bedroom, with a foot resting on the edge of a chair painting her toenails. A towel lay before her on the floor; she looked up as she saw him place the coffee down on the dressing table nearby. He went over and sat on the bed, she blew a kiss, smiling he put the mug on the floor, raised both arms and laid back on the bed.

"There that's it," said Toni having finished her toenails.

She looked over and saw Tommy was fully stretched out on the bed his eyes closed; Toni just stared and sipped her coffee from where she sat. The smell of coffee blended with the new freshness of the room, having renewed the sheet and duvet cover he laid on. Their behaviour showed much contentment between themselves, he on the bed and Toni drinking from a mug and the hours of the day was their day to share with each other now alone and together.

Karen's return tomorrow (Sunday) would be her preparation to pack Lenny's things, clothes and personal items he would need to cover their time away whilst he convalesces from his injuries. Travelling to Norfolk on the Monday once Lenny has been seen by the doctor for his final once over, and then their journey would begin from the hospital and not return to the house for their goodbyes. Tommy was happy about this arrangement as he wanted no further drama to their leaving.

The next day (Sunday) Karen arrived late at the house, with Toni's help the two of them organised Lenny's clothes and personal items, ready for him and Karen's eventual drive to her families cottage in Norfolk. It was near to midnight by the time the two girls had finished organising and packing his things along with Karen's. Tommy had remained out of the way having watched television for most of the evening. Before Karen went to bed she came back downstairs and congratulated Tommy on his choice of a good woman, jokingly smiling as she made the comment, but was very sincere in the remainder of the conversation and so happy that her good friend Toni and Tommy had officially become a real item as relationships go, she was excited for the pair of them and couldn't wait to tell Lenny in the morning.

"Such wonderful news to sleep on," said Karen.

By eight o'clock next morning (Monday) Tommy and Toni said their farewells to Karen as she was early in packing the car and now ready to leave for the Hospital, declining breakfast; she clearly was excited to be holidaying with Lenny today and looking forward to their drive to Norfolk, as neither having agreed a return time it was more about Lenny recovering from his accident and their time alone together was all that mattered to her.

The quietness of the last 48 hours had brought home to Toni the peace and the calm she was experiencing in and around the house, even with Tommy coming and going about his business around the house she remained unperturbed by her long spells alone. It was like an act of cleansing when she compared and considered the hustle and bustle of her previous life she left only weeks past.

She felt amazing and free in ways that she couldn't describe to herself let alone another and as it so happened she found torn pieces of paper with scribble left on the kitchen table this particular morning.

She looked closer as some pieces were on the floor which she bent down and retrieved, curiosity got her reading the words and then like a jigsaw puzzle she spread the pieces across the table and began to piece together and slowly realised that it was a hand written poem of sorts, the contents were erotic and featured women as the subject.

"The old bugger," she muttered to herself as she looked towards the open door of the kitchen, could it be Tommy's writing, Tommy's poem she thought?

"Oh! My god, could it be his writing," she said out loud, then placed a hand over her mouth and laughed in her palm, and laughed, and laughed.

Toni remained shocked at what she had read, having now pieced together the whole poem, which was clearly an erotic verse that read as follows.

Beyond the Sea

I stand on land and seek that somewhere, way up in the sky,

Then if only I could fly,

If only to caress and touch the stars as I pass her by,

As I seek that somewhere, Way up in the sky, on land or Beyond the Sea,

But I do get by without a cry,

As from the inside I look out,

As she passes by,

As my strengths ebb and flow within my veins and always a smile upon my face,

As she is out there somewhere,

But not beyond the moon,

But to a tranquil place of our design,

For to seek is to find and find is to touch as we entwine,

Among the clouds like peppercorn,

So listen to my music,

Listen to my song in the absence of our times,

As you will surely glow when touched by my caress upon your naked flesh,

As I will be there,

Somewhere in the mists of time,

As you pass me by,

As I reach out and gently touch your sensitivity and your femininity

As you emerge from sweet sleeping dreams and pecking kisses upon your mouth,

As my whispers reach your ears,

As you awaken to your passions that quiver from inside,

As I want to leave my feelings deep inside,

Whilst your Pudenda holds me fast while we rhythm and rhyme

In the closeness of our time, somewhere,

As I am the man from nowhere who came from far

Beyond the Sea in search of you,

As she is somewhere, alone out there,

So where is she?

She is alone out there, somewhere.

Toni sat back in the chair and was very much lost for words, she read twice more the verse that left her shaken and stirred. She had gone all weak at the knees when she stood to stand and remained like some giggling schoolgirl at the surprise of her find as she leaned on the table for support.

"Oh! My god, it can't be true," she remained giggling to herself when she left the kitchen to find Tommy in the lounge,

Listening to bird sounds with his eyes closed, he was in deep in concentration as she approached his seated figure. She tapped him on the knee for attention his eyes opened and blinked several times whilst looking up into her face, he was startled at seeing Toni in front of him holding pieces of torn paper in her hands as she gestured about the writing and who wrote the verse.

"I did," said Tommy, (Pause)

"Why what's wrong," said Tommy.

"It's beautiful, I have nearly fallen over as it has made me go weak at the knees," said Toni quietly.

"Well that's your bloody fault for being nosey," said Tommy, laughing.

"Did you really write these words, Tommy," said Toni pleading with him to be serious for one moment.

"Yes I did, I wrote it for you, I can express myself more that way," said Tommy, "And another thing I can't keep fucking you like we have day after day, I am bloody drained of energy, So I decided to write the verse to compensate for not being able to keep up with you, I am knackered from all this fucking, you are younger than me, anyway remember what I said about women you've only got to open your legs wide, we men have to work at it to get it to attention if you women want the business, we have to get our heads in the right mode me darling," said Tommy more on a lecturing roll, then he burst out laughing, it was hilarious to see Toni's face in astonishment, "Anyway, I forgot all about the bits I had torn and left on the table, so you found it, it was to be a surprise for you," said Tommy as he continued giggling.

"It's a lovely way to find your surprise," said Toni, "So where is the finished verse," as she handed him the torn pieces.

"Well, to be honest, I have written several for you and I was deciding on which one to give you," said Tommy in a more serious voice.

"Yes I have them in my folder," said Tommy.

"Bloody hell you men, why can't I have them all, instead of the one," said Toni astonished at Tommy's thinking.

"Well I didn't want to go overboard with my words of thought," said Tommy, rather taken back at her words, and said

"Alright, alright, alright I'll give them to you, I had written them for you, I mean one a day just like the doctor ordered," said Tommy as he joked and laughed.

"Go and do some fresh coffee, and while you do that I sort the verse out," said Tommy as he stood and kissed Toni before she left the room.

In Toni's absence Tommy fetched his folder that laid on a bookshelf, so by the time Toni returned with the coffee he handed her three erotic verse to read, she by now was excited and went and sat in the bay window to read quietly in the daylight. Tommy had sunk back into the armchair and waited in silence to her response of his writing.

Some minutes passed when he heard sighs, gasps and whimpers, Tommy was wondering if she was having a self-inflicted orgasm at the bay window, as he giggled at the way she sat, with her knees drawn back and her arms resting on them like a book stand as she gripped the paper.

(Verse With No Name)

In her presence of her own femininity
She needed to be laid in the manager of love
She needed to be loved and cherished
She needed to be understood
Her femininity was in deep flower
And her love nest needed to be touched
She was ripe for the love of man
She was ripe to be plucked upon a millstone
As she grinds her sexuality into a rather
Exhilarating moment of deep fulfilment
That man can reach in their togetherness
Of touch and move upon her frame
As man lifts high her buttocks as he goes
Deep inside her frame of womanhood
She murmurs, she wimps, she moans
She gyrates' her emotions in her movements
As he laid between her thighs, movements
That they shared together as orgasms expelled
From their bodies as they writhed together
As they touched and cuddled bodies stuck as one
In those final, after moments of real tenderness
Which they shared together in dripping perspiration

All Things Nice

Sugar & Spice is all things nice

As from the shadows I heard her giggles

Then she appeared - All Sugar & Spice

Giggling femininity as I stood and watched

More gooey eyed as she was sprite and glowing

As her natural beauty oozed her sexuality

She was on heat and ready to perspire

She was all things nice as Sugar & Spice

And all things that I wanted to touch

To feel, to hold, to cuddle and kiss

And to be close and dream awhile in her warmth

As her natural beauty remained captivating and yet

She was unaware of the effects she had on man

As her giggles continued out loud

Just feet from where I stood

She glanced like a true English Rose in full blossom

Like a goddess as she stood in the light

That came from the skylight above – a Halo of feelings

Where mans endowment stood proud and upright

Ready to slide and enter her Silky lining and do

Justice to the moistened femininity she oozed

By taking her from behind in gentle pose

Of the thrusts that I imposed upon her femininity

As I pecked her neck and caressed her breasts

Then she reached fulfilment as we came together

In the rhythm and rhyme of natures orgasm of life

As she was not to be left behind by sexual famine

That frustrated her beauty and womanhood that

Needed to be cherished by man for all her worth

As I rode her high and low in her deep channel

As I listened to her murmurs, grunts and whimpers

As I fucked her hard, but slow and teasing
As we fucked until we stopped exhausted.

———

Tommy could see that Toni was at times just staring out of the window, he began to fear that perhaps he had gone over the top with his writing and that perhaps each was too personal in the way he expressed himself sexually and also in the deep seated feelings that he found too difficult to say face to face, but in time he knew he would learn much from Toni as she was well balanced and certainly broad-minded in what they achieved sexually, (thinking of his balls being left on the fence the other night) he sniggered quietly and not daring to move he just had to be patient and take his punishment like any good man (he laughed to himself)

Tommy saw Toni had finished reading and remained just staring out of the window, she never moved like a statue, a figure set in stone, he left the armchair and went to her side at the window and rubbed her shoulder.

Toni turned and faced him crying, tears rolled down her cheeks, he began to apologise profusely realising as he thought having screwed up, he again apologised to her.

"Stop bloody apologising Tommy, I am so happy at what you have written, the verse is beautiful, so beautiful, I am so bloody shocked you big ape to realise the saying about 'judging a book by its cover', well it's much more than that Tommy, you are a silly sod, I love them and written for me, now I know what goes on in that head of yours," she said still crying.

As she pulled herself up and stood cuddling Tommy, with her arms around his waist and her fingers locked together as she pressed her head to his chest, he placed his arms around her body and both stood locked together for ages and ages, and then parted. Toni dropped her skirt to the floor,

"I need to clean up I am so wet down below, god can you smell me, those dogs will be chasing me if I don't soon take a shower, bloody hell I never thought such words would work into multiple orgasms's I am so shocked at my own behaviour, I had plenty of wet moments when I use to ride horses, always keeping clean underwear with me, but this, I am so giddy and light headed, you're going to have to carry me upstairs Tommy before I faint and fall down on the carpet," said Toni in a light hearted moment as Tommy felt the creeping panic beset his mind thinking that she wanted to fuck again.

"I'll come up stairs with you and I'll take a shower, on one condition though," said Tommy to Toni.

"And what would that be," said Toni.

"Just the shower and no fucking please, I am knackered," said Tommy, "I'll give you a lovely cuddle on the bed afterwards, but just a cuddle," he said as he grinned.

"I promise, I promise, I'll leave you alone, good job I brought my own toys with me," she turned and faced him as she laughed and scooped her skirt from the floor and then stepped out of her briefs.

Tommy followed her naked arse up the stairs to the bedroom, feeling somewhat chuffed at his own performance and now knowing the power of his words give women orgasms, what more does a man want – 'Rest and sleep', crossed his mind as he muttered under his breath.

Later still wrapped in bath towels after showering together the couple lay on the bed and cuddled up as steam swept in and swirled around from the open door of the bathroom as they lay fast asleep.

CHAPTER SEVENTEEN
Heathrow Hotel Meeting

Seven o'clock Friday morning a saloon car turned into the drive of the house, the occupants are the two awaited security officers Tommy's hired for 12 hours of duty, whilst he and Toni are in London for the day.

The comforts of the Range Rover made driving much easier travelling down the motorway and of course, his first port of call was to drop Toni off at her place as arranged and then to return later after his meeting to collect her. With time on her hands, Toni can decide on what she needs in terms of clothes and personal items, make a few phone calls, and speak to neighbours about keeping an eye on her place at her own leisure.

Finally, he came off the slip road alongside Heathrow Airport and drove into lush surroundings of a large Hotel. Already intense activity was in play as people were boarding a parked coach, and another was off loading passengers and hotel staff were off in all directions with luggage being loaded on and off waiting trolleys. He drove to a point beyond the entrance to a large rear car park sign posted for patrons only.

Dressed in a light grey suit, with a blue shirt, maroon coloured tie and well polished brown shoes, carrying a large business brief case of the same colour he entered the foyer and approached the reception desk. He was directed to the fourth floor where he would be met by a member of staff assigned to him for the duration of his conference meeting. Greeted by a staff member and shown the conference room already prepared for his meeting, ten places had been set with notepads and pencils, silver trays with glasses upturned with capped water jugs, fruit juices. Tommy was already impressed by the greeting and presentation of the room, first to arrive, jacket off and hung on a peg he was soon over to the window and stood watching the hubbub of comings and goings at the hotel.

Around ten-thirty o'clock Tony Markham was the first to arrive and enter the room accompanied by Frank Boxer, as the minutes passed more arrivals of Bomber Harris, Andy Cole, Charlie Spateman, Billy Bone along with his two nephews (Harry & Ginger) and Phil Cruickshank and Martin Hayes. With handshakes and numerous 'cor blimeys' well said the introductions came to a halt as the group settled around the table, as Tommy stood to open the meeting and began his first statement of intent.

"Right first things first, as you know the jobs planned are not to rekindle the 'Old Firm', for many months I've planned a very big caper in the West Country. In order that it comes off and through our Frank initially to see if I could obtain confidential services, and I mean confidential services and Frank has done me proud on this one that's why you are all here today, as some of you will remember what it's like being captured, well that is not going to happen this time, I do not intend to get fucked over.

My proposals here today have been researched for months, during the course of the morning I'll hand you each a portfolio on the five targets I have chosen.

(Now one of us is missing and I want to make mention of Lenny, a couple of weeks ago he was involved in the big motorway accident he got knocked about and ended up in hospital, he's okay and on the mend. He has gone off for a few weeks to convalesce with his girlfriend, but nevertheless, Lenny has a part to play in this)

Now what's discussed in this room today, Lenny will obviously not be aware of you all by name and I have not had time to bring him up to speed, however, Lenny will run the last decoy job on the night.

Lenny did all the reconnoitre and I managed to salvaged with Frank's help all the stuff Lenny managed to video, I got down to the scene of the accident and recovered everything before the 'Bobbyjacs' removed the Jaguar. As that is a right-off, we need a new car.

So how I have arranged this is you will be in charge of a team as driver's and spotters, for security sakes you will the only ones to know what's going on, so if any of your members are captured, they can't put names to faces, none of your identities will be known to your teams and visa versa, I must be hard on this factor alone, we can't afford any mistakes at any cost. Any questions at the moment," said Tommy looking around the table.

"Where is the muscle coming from Tommy," said Bomber.

"Well firstly there is no muscle on this caper, all your teams have been researched and selected and are on standby for the big day. I only want brains, therefore no weapons at any cost, it's not needed, there is not to be any violence, I can't stress this enough and I want to make absolutely clear, no violence otherwise we are stuffed and I ain't letting months of work being fucked because someone is not listening and is fucking careless. This is to be done with the least hassle as possible," said Tommy again searching the faces around the table to be absolutely clear.

Intermittent words of agreement echoed round the table, eyes nodded with a head roll from some. Taking a green coloured folder from his brief case, Tommy flicked through the pages, stopping and folding back some pages that he held fast.

"I'll read the list from the ground we have covered so far, stop me if you have questions," said Tommy in a well meaning voice, get in involved if you have to, which he emphasised to the group.

1.   "Locations have been well planned and well organised for access to and from the places we are targeting. All of which are on the video's that I have with me (tapping his brief case) these I'll show you later,"

2.   "All transport and equipment will be provided I have a pool of seven drivers to do the basics, some of these drivers are now and will continue to drive over the chosen routes until they can find their way blindfolded.

A hand went up and a Tony Markham spoke.

"What do you mean English drivers; we are English unless you've got an Irish surprise ay Tommy."

A few chuckles from around the table, as it was clear they sat with confused faces and Tommy was beginning to feel that his message was not getting through to them.

"At the moment I want to leave it like that, you will understand when I explain the bigger picture to you all," said Tommy.

3.   I have local authority plans for all the targets, and I have them here for inspection. Details have also been marked down as to whether there are any security guards, alarms etc and that has all been done for you," said Tommy again looking up at the group.

4.   "I have marked a much larger map that I want you to look at, you'll see I've marked where possible the 'T.Ks' in red (Telephone Kiosks) that is like looking for a needle in a haystack, also the nearest dwellings to the targets have also been checked for any cameras and that applies to the streets as well, street lights are marked in green. I also have some Ariel shots taken above the locations, so the layouts are much easier to focus on, the shots are recent and I will have these updated twenty fours before the off," said Tommy, again the faces became more intent of his words, it was beginning to come together at last he thought.

5.   The most important aspect of the nights capers will be down to these headlines and why this is

happening for us – (Tommy held aloft the news paper with the headlines reading – 'PUBLIC OUTRAGE AT POLICE PHONES') well I must tell you now this job hinges on these phones going down on the night, so I have arranged for some specialist help in that area to make sure it happens, I'll leave the paper on the table if any of you want a read," said Tommy after a good hour the group broke off for refreshments that had been laid out for them earlier, "and remember no smoking - if you want a quick fag go downstairs please," again said Tommy commenting on the Hotel rules.

After a 20-minute short break and returning to their seats with sandwiches and drinks, Tommy waited for the group to settle down before he resumed the meeting.

"First up Frank has an envelope for each of you, you have all got the same amount for coming today and the beginnings of your retainers as I can assure you all it will be a handsome pay day for us all," said Tommy hoping this will make them more attentive.

"Now your transport will be provided as I've already said, each vehicle will have its own bag of goodies, radio's, mobile phones, plus a bleeper for the team leaders, this is for emergencies should there be a need if anything goes wrong. Obviously, I'll be the one in the know on that side of things should we need to abort any target. Team leader will then bell me for an update but at the same time to withdraw from the area completely for your own safety. The portfolios will show you where to assemble with your timetable of events. The times are only a summary, not exact, also included are the places of rendezvous when you complete the jobs.

Now before you say how do we get there Tommy? – that is where your drivers will come in, I mean you can drive yourselves but the drivers must remain with you at all times they have many times practised the routes, your drivers have the knowledge of the areas and for

Christ-sake remember, no friendships this is business other than getting you there and getting you out that's all that's needed no personal questions or comments or again asking who they are, as they will not play ball they have my instructions as the same as you, alright do you understand me," said Tommy flicking through the remaining pages of his folder.

"This is where young Harry and Ginger come into it, they are using motor cycles on the night and will act as couriers between targets or what may be required on the night to fetch and carry," said Tommy –

Both lads sat back with big grins realising how important their jobs were going to be on the night. Tommy continued to explain the details of the jobs; slowly he covered all the minute details, with few interruptions. Frank looked contented now realising that he was Tommy's Lieutenant. After speaking for nearly a further hour, Tommy reached a point where he needed to explain the team layouts.

It was Tony Markham who said out loud,

"This is fucking brilliant Tommy, fucking brilliant, I can see where you are coming from and the protection you are giving us from Old Bill, brilliant," as he sat back and grinned tapping the table with a pencil.

"I'll hand out these folders for you to see the list of names they are your teams on the night," said Tommy.

"Fucking hell Tommy, foreigners it might as well be in code, how we gonna understand them," said Andy

"Easy they all speak English we are in the European Union boys, those names have been chosen by them, so their real names are no go areas, also you may not be aware but some are females who will be taking part," said Tommy, as the group appeared restless at the news of foreigners being involved. He remained momentarily quiet.

"Just hang on a minute and I'll explain the reasons why I have chosen the majority of foreigners from abroad. Point one, times have changed I want a job well done with the best in the business and that's what I have achieved, I have a total of twenty-eight from abroad and all highly skilled at what they do. Now think about this for a moment, when the news breaks next day about these jobs, the government is going to go fucking crazy in wanting results, so the management of Old Bill are going to get their ears clipped over this and in turn that will come down through the ranks, alright. Now because I have chosen the West Country - Old Bill will be looking for names in the West Midlands and the cities, Manchester and Liverpool, Leeds, so there onto a duff mission. I have not touched the Met for the simple reason if it's on their patch then there be lots of early morning turnovers, should any of you get caught up in this you are clean, you have no idea of any of the operatives involved or the fucking targets, you are just team leaders with a vehicle and driver, you are untouchable do you hear me, untouchable. But to be on the safe side I have retained some insurance should any of you run into trouble, but god help anyone who fucks up with a big mouth or spending big numbers in cash on your manor, no flashing the wallets let others pay for your nights out." said Tommy really getting home and emphasising the need for care.

"None of your fingerprints will be found on any of the equipment, vehicles, Old Bill will not know what they are looking for, now is this beginning to sink in and why I have the foreigners on board. The teams will arrive twenty-four hours before the off, I have mentioned hotels booked but I have not identified them at the moment, the drivers nominated will look after them, you don't have to worry Okay. Soon as the targets have been hit and successful the arrangements are that the teams are sent packing, sent home, I have provisional bookings for some, others chose to visit family some have legit businesses so all this fits like a glove. Those leaving the UK are to be back in Europe by 8 o'clock on the same morning as the targets were hit. So by around nine o'clock on the morning after some businesses will open up and all hell will be let loose, I'll give you a few minutes to check your folders as you see I have not identified targets they go by numbers for the moment," said Tommy eager to move on and close the meeting.

Over the remaining time as Tommy was clock watching knowing he must be away by three o'clock the latest. The group gave him the green light and realised that there was more to come and he had their safety in mind was good enough in placing their trust in him. It was an exciting prospect of utilising some forty people on the ground to pull off a massive crime caper in one night.

"I have no fixed date arranged as yet, I need to be sure that it has been well scrutinised before I decide with Frank," said Tommy with both hands leaning on the table.

The group acknowledged Tommy's last comment as clearly, it was the day and date they all waited on.

"One more thing Tommy," said Billy, inquiring as he spoke, "What's with the word 'Bobbyjac' I've rumbled what it means, but some of us wondered what was behind it," as heads began to nod around the table.

"Well as I said before, times have changed and so have we over the years, Old Bill is a thing of the past, that was around when 'Fabian' was still at the Yard, so I thought up a new name that was more in keeping with our times. You think about today and what coppers have to do, I mean can you imagine waking up one morning and not seeing a 'Bobbyjac' around, it would be fucking frightening thinks about it. They get a lot of stick from some pretty weird groups these days and all those bloody do-gooders to contend with. What with legalised kidnapping of children for sexual purposes you wonder what the fucking hell is happening out on the streets, the government really don't give a fuck mate they are only in it for what they can get out it, we ought to have a Minister of Common Sense overseeing and prevailing, so I chose 'Bobbyjac' as the 'JAC' is French, get it EU,"

Tommy stood back and gave a loud laugh that echoed in the room, some of the others laughed with him. Bringing the meeting to an end Tommy reminded them to wear the caps they wore coming into the foyer, so disperse and keep your heads down please avoid the cameras,"

Tommy joined Frank and Tony on the last lift going down, "Yes I left a good tip on the table," said Tommy, "Good," said Frank smiling.

"Honest for a moment I didn't think it was going to run for everybody, but as Tony said, fucking brilliant, you did a great job and none of us has details of the targets or the teams, that is fucking brilliant, to say the least, outside the Hotel the three walked to the car park and said their goodbyes, Tommy told Frank that he was off to collect Toni from her place, and informed him that they were an item. He also whispered to Frank that Karen was a Customs Officer, Tim fingered her from a drugs job he did some years back. So I have not told Lenny and nor am I going to – I am going to leave them on holiday and just forget about them.

By seven o'clock in the evening, Tommy and Toni had arrived home with time to spare and unpacked her luggage from the Range Rover, holding back the dogs as they entered by the front door.

Tommy approached the two security guards who were still present at the house and thanked them for their support and patience and gave them each fifty quid for their services. He watched them drive off as he went back into the house and let the dogs out for exercise. Finally, he sat in the kitchen drinking fresh coffee with Toni agreeing to leave her luggage until the morning, before they turned in for the night as the dogs settled.

CHAPTER EIGHTEEN
'Crimes Galore' – Set To Go?

Early Wednesday morning Frank and his nephew Harry were the first down for breakfast. Their presence at the house was arranged on the spur of the moment, Tommy had chosen Friday night to be the go ahead for the crime spree, so bringing both to the house two days earlier was a godsend for Tommy to finalise his final briefings for the crime teams. For some reason, he had changed his mind from his comments made at last Friday's conference meeting in London when asked by the group for the start date.

Frank went over Harry's route with him was the primary motorcyclist and courier for all the drivers on Friday night. With overnight bags left in the hall as both waited for their transport to arrive, Frank watched from the bay window, as Tommy sat close by in quiet conversation.

With Frank and Harry's departure, it was around one o'clock when the team bus arrived (12-seater) with his couriers on board, bringing together the group was the culmination of his plans and to go over any teething problems and any thoughts individuals may have had on the plans. Tommy was long impressed with the professional approach of his couriers as he handed each an envelope containing their bonuses and congratulated the group on their presentations with further bonuses to be given when the operation was finished.

Toni had been gone with the dogs before the group arrived, way down by the river the four dogs were doing their usual runs and ferreting and sniffing, as she was stood looking at the rippling water and rubbing her tummy at the same time, reflecting on her thoughts of her first outdoor sexual encounter with Tommy in the long grass of wild flowers. Like all girls hoping that the romance of any relationship never goes away, the touches, the kisses and those long afternoon cuddles over a weekend when it's a time for relaxing and there is only the two of them in private.

Toni at the time of leaving the house was unaware that she had been watched from the undergrowth high on the opposite side of the lane facing the house. The gypsies had arrived during the mid-morning and had monitored the comings and goings at the house. 'Leafy' and 'Bailey' had slid down the bank and slipped quietly across the lane into the woodland close to the house and sat waiting for the moment to make their move towards the house. By this time Toni had gone way beyond the boundary fence into the field below and was clearly out of sight by the two gypsies who ran to the side of the house, in turn the two youths attacked the air vent fixed into the brickwork of the house with screwdrivers and a small jemmy they had brought with them. The third gypsy had stayed put from where the other two had left him on the opposite side of the lane, he watched ready to whistle should there be movement from within the house. Eventually, the two youths went back the way they had come taking the air vent with them and leaving a nine by nine-inch hole in the brickwork of the house. Their reasons were unknown at the time as causing the damage offered no explanation as to what would follow in the coming nights of traveller activity and the vengeance they sought on the occupants of the house.

Tommy had remained in the house in the absence of Toni and the departure of Frank and Harry unaware of the gypsy's presence in the grounds. By the time the couriers arrived at the house the travellers were long gone, and Toni returned after two o'clock to a house full of guests unaware of the reasons for the visit and four lively dogs in tow was a problem she foresaw, instead of bringing them into the kitchen she took all four down to the kennels and locked them up after feeding and watering the animals as all four were well and truly knackered from the exercise.

Tommy was soon to greet her on entering the kitchen,

"Trying to do a brew up, me darling," said Tommy as he laughed.

"What you mean Tommy is would I do the coffees and teas," said Toni as she walked under his face and looked up as she passed.

"That is what you want, isn't it," as Toni began to laugh at him.

"Yes you are right – Please Toni, take care of it for me," said Tommy in rather a sheepish way for having his motives caught out.

Eventually with the couriers now all back on their bus having been well briefed by Tommy, Toni stood behind him at the front door and said,

"I hope you are not going to disappear for an hour now they are leaving," he heard her laughter behind him as he turned, Toni stood with arms folded, he laughed and said,

"I was going to quickly check around the house," said Tommy, but with Toni's questioning him disappearing and she reminded him that she had already been around the house and grounds earlier with the dogs, so Tommy soon put that idea to bed and came back into the house with his arm around Toni's shoulder.

Another two days to the off as Tommy heard the chimes of the clock, the time piece reminded him that time was all he had left for the rest of the day other than sitting down with Toni to enjoy an evening meal and share a few glasses of wine between them, inside of himself he was unbelievably excited at the way his plans had come together, in military style he thought. Toni noticed how relaxed and jovial he seemed this hour as they ate together at the kitchen table, then being reminded about the absence of the dogs, remember to bring two in when we have finished dinner she remarked.

"I am going up later for a shower Tommy and staying

up to watch some telly," said Toni as she stared across the table at him with a smile and a wink.

Tommy couldn't help but laugh at the way Toni expressed herself and a smile that made him feel wanted.

"Good idea that shower and telly," better staying up Tommy thought.

This would suit his needs being able to slip into his office no excuses in having to disappear, realising that Toni was not aware of the secrets of the wall panelling on the landing nor was she aware of the forthcoming crime operation, knowing he would soon have to address both issues with Toni.

Later when Toni was showering Tommy had opened up the office, leaving the door wide open, as he got down to business first checking the security cameras, eventually seeing the two gypsy's approach the house from the woodland. The camera was unable to pick them up so close to the building, however, he watched minutes later leave the same way they came, one of the travellers was carrying something so it was clear that he would have to check in the morning, then realising that he may be able to see from the window. He opened the window and leaned out to look down, not sure, he decided to use a selfie-stick with his mobile and film the outside wall of the house. Checking his mobile he saw the darkened patch in the brickwork below, it was ages before the penny dropped for him.

"The bastards have come back and stolen the fucking air vent, they're mad, what is it to them?" said Tommy as he stood up from his seat and paced the floor.

"Incredible they came right under our fucking noses," said Tommy,

As the anger in his voice could be heard as it echoed from the office. That was when Toni from the bedroom door saw a light coming further down the landing corridor, she went to be nosey and indeed this is how she became to be introduced to Tommy's world of criminality and the impending planned operation. Her hair still damp from the shower as she used a towel to dry and listen to Tommy at the same time describe the new world she was about to embrace. From his swivel chair he looked the business as he laid both arms on the desk in front of him and leaned forward as he spoke with Toni, she was still looking down to the floor as she continued towelling her hair dry.

In truth Tommy had planned and hoped that Toni would find him and make an entrance to his criminal world of operations, it meant what her eyes captured was less for him to tell her, the value of common sense is a wonderful thing, so is hindsight, either way Toni appeared comfortable and relaxed at what she had seen and been told.

Eventually Toni let the towel slip to the floor and sat dressed in a flimsy housecoat that hid nothing from one's imagination, she pushed herself back into the chair and raised her knees and placed both feet on the edge, knees together and ankles splayed out, still naked under the garment and hopefully she was looking for Tommy's nightcap as it was plain for him to see between her open legs that she was minus underwear, she was teasing him, she was really laying this on thick, she was in her own way telling him without words but actions that she didn't care what his business was nor how busy his working days, she was not bothered as her interest was him – 'Tommy the man', that is all she wanted after their long talk the other day and their feelings about each other was made clear to both and of course her raptures over his writing still had her on another plateau that she never knew existed in the sexual sense and her man took her to his special place hidden deep in his mind, words, words, words how beautiful he wrote such erotic verse for her.

Tommy decided to leave the office and take a shower before he continued his monitoring and sending emails, he needed to be sure that all his operatives were over in the UK by Thursday as planned, the next couple of hours ought to see everybody contacted and him through for the night. Toni followed him out onto the landing and came behind him and thrust her arms around him and hugged him close, Tommy continued walking as Toni was on tiptoe trying to keep up with him, he felt the warmth of her face pressed into his back as she continued to hug him tight. In the bedroom, her grip loosened as he turned and kissed her nose and gripped her tightly around the shoulders, then stuck his nose into her hair as he sniffed, and sniffed the fresh smell left by the shampoo.

"Well I better have my shower and freshen up my girl," said Tommy, "Friday is going to be a busy day with long hours into the night, I'll need some help if you are up for it, lot to do in the office mate, after that Lenny and I are free to live out our dreams, are you coming," said Tommy still holding Toni round the shoulders.

"Still want me then," she said smiling.

"Too bloody right, mate you are not going anywhere, without me," said Tommy.

Feeling rather boisterous as he turned and flung Toni up and over his shoulder, patting her bum at the same time as she squealed, he went over to the bed and laid her down on her tummy, then reached down grabbed her waist and dragged her back up onto her knees, her arms outstretched, her hands pressing down on the bed. Tommy had pulled her back to the edge of the bed, at the same time he lifted up her flimsy garment and placed a hand between her legs and gently moved back and forth in a stroking motion, at the same time he felt Toni pushing her pubic line into the heel of his hand. He listened as she let out her whispering sighs and said,

"God Tommy are you going to fuck me doggy," said Toni as her breathing became louder as she was working herself against the palm of his hand.

Tommy remained silent and then withdrew his hand and pushed his torso hard against her naked buttocks as he held her by the waist and simulated a doggy style motion, then stopping and placed his hand back between her legs and felt how wet and moist she was. He raised the bar himself as he had a right storker, hard and ready to plunge into her darkness, with both hands he gripped and pulled apart her naked cheeks as the worming machine was wobbling and prodding her flesh trying to find her hidden entrance, Toni reached under her and took hold of his wobbling stork.

"Bloody hell Tommy are you using one of my toys or a broom handle, where did that stork come from," said Toni.

As she rubbed the tip of his penis against her lips and gently the member slipped into her pussy. Tommy pushed hard right up to the hilt as both bodies touched and gyrated together as Tommy again took hold of her waist and moved her body back and forth on his member, Toni's grunt and deep raucous sounds echoed loud in the bedroom, she was really going for it, when Tommy withdrew and splashed his remains over her backside and said,

"Right we both need a shower," said Tommy laughing.

As he pulled Toni up off the bed still gripping her waist he pressed her body into his chest as with her feet off the ground she thrashed her legs as he carried her into the bathroom, she excited and squealing as they roll played. Together in the shower.

"Bloody hell Tommy you were a big boy tonight, I was shocked at the size, what have you been feeding it," said Toni grinning as she wiped the water from her face as she looked down and felt him.

"I've been feeding it with love, I have a one to one talk with it each morning, me and the old fellow have this understanding that I must service you with pride, nothing more, nothing less is the order," said Tommy giving out one of his big belly-laughs.

As he took hold of Toni and kissed as they stood together under the shower head, oblivious to time the kiss became a long lingering moment that even surprised Toni in how suddenly Tommy became turned on and so arduous in fucking her doggy style which made a change from her doing all the work, we are a partnership.

"He's learning fast this man of mine," she muttered to herself.

Eventually, the couple parted and dried off, back in the bedroom, Toni boiled the kettle for coffee, she had earlier in the day put milk into the small drinks fridge kept on a side cabinet in the room, ideal rather than going back and forth downstairs as they had been doing. Tommy realised that he was being given a females education and which was long overdue and so was the years alone without sharing female company and now ending on a beautiful choice of woman. Tommy kept chuckling to himself as if he needed to pinch himself as to the difference Toni had made to his life in such a short time.

Sat drinking coffee together Toni was the first to speak to her gorgeous partner as she put her coffee down, stood and walked over to Tommy and immediately sat astride him, holding his face with both hands she slowly ran her cheek against his and brought her lips to his for one long lingering kiss, a kiss of real passion as she ran her fingers through his hair, he was still holding the coffee in one hand, the other laid on her waist.

"This is strange for me, you are some real horny female Toni, you know on first relationships all couples behave differently in private, we all act like bunny rabbits fucking the doe like crazy in every which way we can, because of the newness and the excitement of being greedy with each other, think about it for a moment. All couples are very touchy in the beginning, we are all up for a quickie and that is where we go wrong, it's about satisfaction, fellows don't bother with foreplay, it's all about lifting your skirt, pulling your knickers to one side and banging you against the kitchen sink before mum gets home or do it standing up in an alleyway," said Tommy as he nodded to her.

"Oh! Tommy your are so bloody funny in the way you tell it, a quickie is a quickie the only problem with that is walking off with a wet pussy, weak at the knees and wobbly legs," said Toni as she leaned back on his lap and continued speaking,

"I like quality rather than quantity,"

"Hold on a minute you are getting both, quality and quantity," said Tommy in a hilarious grin.

"So you are getting it both ways literally me darling," spoken with a big grin.

"So what are you saying about fucking like bunny rabbits," said Toni.

"Well it's true, we fuck like that in the beginning, because relationships are mostly couples living apart, like courting if you get my meaning, knowing where you can do it often it's the bloody car being laid on the back seat or bending over the back of the passenger seat, it's the rush of adrenaline we can't get enough of each other, then as time moves on the fucking gets less because we become more stable in the way we feel, more so when you move in together, if you get my gist," said Tommy

"How do you know all this Tommy are you some kind of counsellor," said Toni laughing.

"No you silly sod blokes talk and brag just the same as women, in fact women are the worst, that's why their men often end up fucking their best friend, because they talk too much about the leg over's there getting and their friends want a taste of the action to compare the proof of the supper and to see what they are missing in their relationships," said Tommy appearing to be very knowledgeable on the subject.

Toni couldn't stop laughing to herself; as he is so funny with his words.

"You speak as if you have been a fly on the wall," said Toni

"The proverbial cake and eat it syndrome, curiosity killed the cat, it's the knowing bit that makes other women chance their arm in their excitement of knowing who is the best lover, who fucks the best," said Tommy indicating that women talk more to friends than men do, drink brings out the worst in the men folk in telling tales.

"With a quickie you haven't got commitment, have you, do it and fuck off, whether you carry on with the person is up for debate, you've now had a taste of the forbidden fruit, do you the man want more of the same or go elsewhere for a new model," said Tommy pulling a strange face at her.

"For Christ sake Tommy you talk as if all women are from the scrap yard, choosing a new model, if it moves and fucks to your liking then keep it otherwise put it back where you found it," said Toni,

"I am shocked at what you have said," said Toni as she sat silent just staring into his face.

"No listen up I am just outlining what I have seen and experienced being in a man's world you listen to their stories and the storylines are all virtually the same, I personally find it embarrassing when you meet some of these women knowing what their men folk have said and described, that is not my scene, my lips are sealed," said Tommy, spoken with a serious tone to his voice.

"Look I will tell you a story about me personally feeling the sexual vibes of another she was confused at the lack of intimacy and the sexual famine she found herself suffering. Well, I gave her and husband a lift to a social event. Anyway, when I dropped them off back home later that night, the English rose came and kissed me for taking them, if her husband had not been present, I would have returned the kiss and much more, I would have taken her into the shadows of the house and by the time she went indoors she would have been weak at the knees and her underwear hidden in her pocket, having brushed off the brick dust from her clothes. I would have fucked her standing up, I would have had her arse in my hands as I lifted to penetrate her, her lips and mouth would be pressed into my neck as she held my flesh with her butterfly pecks as she would have been held fast on my old man as I gave her the fucking she long desired," said Tommy, "What I am trying to say, is you don't have to belong or be married to another to have the greatest fuck you have ever experienced and the giver of the fuck could be the ugliest man in the world. It wouldn't matter for the woman; it was about the experience as most men finish too quickly and make a right balls up of it for the woman. It takes females about forty-five minutes to really get going and the blokes are a spent force, so you can understand why there are so many affairs and comparisons. Sex is the easy bit, love making is something else," said Tommy he was well away with the time ticking late going way beyond his thoughts.

Toni moved off his lap and stood looking down into his face as he looked into hers, she gave a final kiss and took the mug from him and placed it on the side with hers.

"I don't know what to say Tommy, you have taken the wind out my sails in more ways than I could describe, you really are a thinker and I can now understand where your writing verse comes from, you are obviously very observant and a good listener, the more I chew on your words the more I can see where you are coming from, it resonates with some of my experiences," said Toni still thinking and pondering on his words.

"It's late and I need to get back to the office, are you coming or staying here," said Tommy, "It's getting late and I never intended to fuck you tonight or to sit talking like we have," he said grinning, "But very nice nevertheless,.."

"You were the one doing all the talking Tommy," said Toni as she gave out a loud laugh that remained as she continued speaking,

"No I am not poking fun, it's a conversation I never expected and at such a late hour. After fucking me like you did, you are still awake, most men would have fallen asleep by now," said Toni still laughing.

"Yes I am coming with you, just tell me what you want doing," said Toni.

She changed the subject as the couple returned to Tommy's office, having both stepped over the two sleeping dogs that lay on the landing, no movement from them only their eyes following the couple.

Tommy asked Toni to tick the boxes as he read out the ones to tick, he sat behind his desk, and Toni stood in next to nothing flimsy garment,

"Are you cold, the heating will be going off soon," said Tommy.

"No I am comfortable, after that seeing too you gave me I am on fire," said Toni and she turned and grinned at him.

"Right tick the first three boxes to your immediate left and put a cross in the next on the same line as the first tick – great, it's coming together. Toni whilst I am doing my emails, would you flick through the security monitors and see if we have any visitors," said Tommy engrossed in what his emails were revealing.

Going to the operation board he marked off the vehicles and checked they had been stored in their respective locations, cars had been divided into three areas and the Lorries were together, and stored separately at another location.

His operatives were all tucked up at their different accommodations, drivers close by for the off and the team leaders contacted and informed of the time the operation would be ready for the off. Excitement was beginning to build, Toni screened all the monitors and saw nothing untoward on the videos.

Back to the board, Toni added more ticks, crosses and written updates on the board. Tommy had supervised the charging of the batteries for the radios and mobile phones, one wall was covered in red and green lights from the charging units all banked together, he got Toni to layout out the five storage boxes on the long bench and took from Tommy a pile of stationary to be divided up and placed in the boxes. Tommy sat still just staring at the board on the wall, thinking.

"Well girl, that's it until tomorrow night, let's get off to bed," said Tommy.

As he moved behind Toni to usher her out of the office, she waited on the landing as he closed up the office, she saw how secret it was from prying eyes, knowing at last Tommy was trusting her, as he came up behind her and laid a hand on her backside as he felt her cheeks, she reciprocated by placing her hand behind her and held his as they both returned to the bedroom and bed, both slept naked as they cuddled together.

CHAPTER NINETEEN
At Last - Everybody Is On The Move

Friday afternoon Tony Markham had left his coastal hideaway and travelled inland with his English driver 'Snowy', down the motorway they travelled at speed heading towards the Bristol Dock area, arriving just after six o'clock having made good time.

'Snowy' picked their way through the maze of dingy back streets of the dock area, arriving at a large old water-front building, clearly some sort of warehouse. Pulling up at the rough painted double doors with a locked wicker gate, he walked over the cobble stones, click, click, and click as his heels echoed the sounds of his walk towards the doors.

A flap opened on the service door, then a loud band and grating sounds heard as the two large doors parted, 'Snowy' returned to the vehicle and drove through the gap into the building, doors when closed behind him as Tony saw other members of the team already waiting inside as a sea of faces stared in his direction, as he leaned back in the vehicle and lifted out a large brief case, 'Snowy' fetched a large box from the boot of the vehicle.

Maria the Spanish and only female operative of this eleven man team had taken charge, having arranged a variety of comforts for the waiting team. Other members consisted of four Spanish and Italian males, and his two English companions Doug and 'Snowy' and obviously they had made their own introductions and were now known to each other.

The Spanish and Italians arrived the day before and been conveyed to their hotel by 'Snowy' details had been prior arranged and booked, the group was left in the care of Doug, who picked them up next morning (Friday) and by mid afternoon Doug had driven the mini bus to their present location.

Maria, the only girl present, would act as interpreter should her services be needed for any reason. Tony made it known to her that he would speak slowly whilst doing the briefing.

"Right, now first on the agenda are there any problems, I hope you were all comfortable with the arrangements," said Tony.

"Yes fine," as replied by Maria.

"Snowy' and Doug will be you throughout the operation tonight; they are there to aid and help you, including the transport for drop off and pickup. When you are finished and all together you will be taken to the port as arranged and seen off safely, except for 'Gino' and 'Salvatora' both have other plans.

"Now another matter that concerns me, before you left your homes, did you receive your money from the local contact and are you all happy with what you received and the arrangement made when the proceeds have been sorted, I hope you realise how generous the payments have been," said Tony looking around at everybody.

"Our bonuses will be paid in the same way," said Maria.

"Exactly," said Tony.

Maria nodded to the others in acknowledgement of his comment.

Turning to Doug,

"You've checked everyones passports - I take it there okay?"

"Yes that was my first job when they arrived," said Doug.

"Driver's licences," said Tony

"Yep done them as well and sorted out insurances," said Doug

"Brilliant," said Tony, "Right if we settle down I will show you a video of the target outlined for tonight and explain what we have to do, okay," said Tony, he spoke throughout the running of the video pointing out certain points to be noted, explaining a compound and surrounding area and adjacent buildings, ending on the security offices where the night crew work from. Maria, do our friends have any questions?" said Tony.

"Yes only one, Franco says there is to be no violence Si, the guards will not be harmed," said Tony as he gestured 'NO' with his hands.

The group broke off for refreshments, during which time 'Snowy' opened up the box and laid out the equipment contained inside for the group to see and understand that walkie-talkie's had ear pieces including the mobile phones and he stressed that there was to be no idle chat at any time, conversation must be kept to a minimum.

'Snowy' now had to depart for another appointment with the next team elsewhere in the city.

Tony used the floor of the warehouse showing a floor chart and a practical demonstration using Dinky cars; with nimble fingers he pushed the toys around the floor chart explaining their strategy.

––––––

Second Team

By eleven o'clock the same morning at a separate location, Frank and his Dutch companion Rudi who was laid on the back seat of the vehicle just gazing at the sights, Frank pulled into a parking space opposite the main foyer of the hotel. Both approaching the front of the building was greeted by the doorman, who opened the main door as they entered the foyer. Inside they found two girls at their rendezvous point, Frank introduced himself and bent to pick up one of their cases, Rudi moved forward to collect the other case as all four left the foyer as the doorman held back the door as they left the building. With both girls comfortable in the rear of the vehicle and Rudi front passenger Frank drove off. On their journey, Rudi nudged Frank and told him the girls thought him rather handsome for an older man.

"Jesus that's all I need," said Frank.

Tapping Rudi on the shoulder, one of the girls spoke in English,

"You understand Dutch."

"I am Dutch," he replied,

Both girls smiled and looked at each other.

"Girls can we please keep this in English as arranged," said Frank.

Nearing midday Frank pulled into the car park of the 'Trout Restaurant'

"Right everybody meal time," said Frank, "There is no rush nice and steady please,"

Turning with a glass in hand he asked the girls if they were looked after at the hotel last night.

"Yes Very good, no problems," said Inga

"Good now your cases will stay in the car after dinner I will take you up to the house. Everything has been taken care of, your housecoats and things are in the car as arranged, do you have any questions since I last spoke with you," said Frank.

"No, no we understand what we do, except Yan has something to say," said Inga.

Frank waited for her comment, 'Yan' smiled cheekily at 'Inga', facing Frank she said,

"If we have to keep the Policeman, how do we entertain him, I think maybe seduce him if he is nice looking, okay,"

Frank almost choked on his wine in disbelief, the girls giggled with hands across their faces; Rudi tucked into his meal and didn't utter a word.

Tony – First Way

'Snowy' having arrived back at the warehouse just before ten 'clock at night informed the plans were now finalised and within the hour they would be on the move. All personal belongings to be left for return pick up.

Just after eleven o'clock (pm) from the bowels of the building emerged three empty vehicle transporters, driven by Doug, 'Snowy' and Gino, following in the mini was the reminder of the team, belching diesel fumes left a heavy trail of fumes as the convoy moved away from the building.

Without lights the clank of metal could be heard as the vehicles travelled over the cobbles stones heading towards the centre of Bristol, the fifteen-minute journey saw the convoy turn off into a side street, which led alongside a vehicle compound of a large Marketing Agency and stopping some three hundred yards beyond the perimeter fence. The middle aged security guard sporting a large beer belly sat in the security post and only glanced up as the convoy travelled past. The guard was obviously a happy soul as it was plain to see his disinterest in the passing vehicles as he clearly had his eyes on the television as he settled back in the chair, clearly a man of a lazy disposition as much had been said about this particular guard and was often the brunt of many practical jokes, Tommy had been able to obtain much about the man and personality. Not having raised any suspicion from the security guard, the transporters were slowly lined up facing the security fence, using only the windscreens to see from in manoeuvring the vehicles, in judging the overhang above the top of the drivers cab as each needed to be placed over the fence which was topped by barb wire, fluorescent markers had been tagged on the fence to show where each vehicles position was located.

The drivers stepped down from the cabs and stood in the shadows of the vehicles, checking watches the three moved off across the open waste ground towards the derelict council garages, Doug walked into the garage that had the rear wall missing, this allowed access into the vehicle compound at ground level, the missing wall had been camouflaged by a canvas sheet covering the missing section of wall, this also gave access to the garage forecourt at the front of the building where 'Salvatori' was met in the waiting mini bus with the remainder of the team in situ.

The mini bus with the three transporter drivers slowly drove from the area back past the guards' station, who could clearly be seen watching TV.

The team would return much later that night as the scene had been prepared without the hindrance of the security guard.

––––––

Frank Was On The Move

Just after midnight Frank and others drove to a wooded area on common land. Freewheeling across the grass Frank made a 'U' turn seeking his rendezvous point. From with the woodland, a light flashed, young Harry, Frank's nephew emerged from the darkness to greet them.

"Everything is all set, I've checked the house a couple of times and only five cars have passed in the last hour, no signs of 'Old Bill' actually I've had a good reception on the radio up here, so it's all good," said Harry.

"Marvellous, we're doing alright for time. Where do we park the vehicle?" said Frank relying on Young Harry to show them.

Pointing,

"If you reverse back over there, then you're facing the road for a quick exit," said Harry.

Reversing back into the woodland and outside of the road, Frank went round to the boot,

"Give us a hand Harry," said Frank.

By now Rudi stood by the passenger door of the

vehicle, listening to the conversation between Frank and Harry. Harry pulled from the vehicle a camouflage netting to cover the vehicle. Still sitting in the vehicle were the two girls on the back seat, the netting blotted out the twilight of the night sky and left the girls in total darkness.

"Time for another listen," said Harry to Frank.

As they both went into undergrowth to where Harry's motorcycle had been hidden, he picked up the headphones left on the seat, in a whisper he got Frank to listen as clearly Harry had been monitoring.

"Not long I've got another five minutes here, and then I have to shoot off to town, now when I get to town I'll call you on the bat phone. I'll wait twenty minutes after my call, if 'Boobyjacs' come past I will bell you. That's as long as I can wait on this one, Frank. I've another two trips before I get back to the farm, does that sound alright?" said Harry.

"Yeah, yeah that's fine by me, but don't rush your luck and leave yourself short of time, Remember I've got Rudi here," said Frank.

"Yeah I know that, but I don't want the 'Old Bill' coming with a small army, I just want to cover your tracks," said Harry.

"Okay, that's set then I'll get the girls over to the house while you are still here," said Frank.

Rejoining the others Frank informed the two girls they were moving onto the house with Rudi, he grabbed the girl's bag from the vehicle, as the four quietly moved along a footpath through the woodland which ran close to the road, still in the woodland Frank halted and pointed to the large detached house that was directly opposite. The silhouette of the house could be seen against the backdrop of the night sky and it was big in terms of actual size and clearly a house of some substance.

"Easy does it now, no noise and stay close to Rudi,"

said Frank referring to the two girls.

All four broke the cover of the trees and crept across the damp grass onto the hard surface of the driveway that led up to the building. Momentarily the group listened for any sounds and movement before Frank moved to the back of the house, taking five strides to the patio and the large window that confronted him, finding young Harry's mark on the glass, Frank whispered to Rudi,

"How long will it take you to get in, only I want Harry away ASAP," said Frank.

Rudi remained silent and stepped past Frank, taking the tool from round his neck, with professional expertise in seconds he removed the glass and wrapped it in cloth and stood the item against the wall.

"Bloody hell," Frank murmured in disbelief, he knows his stuff alright this Rudi.

He quietly ushered the two girls through the opening into what appeared to be a large room, possibly a large lounge in the way shadows outlined furniture by the nightlight.

"Right girls off you go and close all the curtains in every room," said Frank.

The girls left the room as his attention turned to Rudi,

"I want you to place the empty wine bottle on the table with wine swished around the glasses as if used, I am off to find the kitchen," said Frank.

The taps in the kitchen both worked, water had not been turned off, nor had the electric in this unoccupied property, the owners were aboard on vacation, so the property had been acquired for the benefits of the one night in working a number of deceptions on their intended victims. Guests had all been prior selected and invited due to their wealth and backgrounds and were shortly to arrive unaware of the elaborate sting that had been organised especially to fleece them all on the night.

"Have you organised the bedrooms," said Frank when he went in search of the girls.

"Yes we jump on the beds and ruffle the duvets, so we leave a little untidy in some of the rooms," said Yan, excited by the proposed ruse that would later greet some of the guests.

Frank was still wearing his surgical rubber gloves as he stood by the open window and radioed Harry in another five minutes he could go.

"Come on girls show me the bedroom," said Frank as the girls led the way.

On entering the bedroom selected by the girls, Frank looked around and saw the girls had done a good job of making out they occupied the room.

"Rudi can you remove the door handle from the bathroom," said Frank,

Seconds later he entered the bathroom and closed the door behind him, he rattled the handle and obviously it wouldn't open. Rudi let Frank out.

"That will work nicely," said Frank.

Leave the door ajar Rudi and replace the unscrewed handle onto protruding bar that operates the door lock, by which time when both men turned, 'Yan' was naked on the bed, propped up by pillows, 'Inga' stood in front of a full-length mirror as the housecoat was about to be wrapped around her naked frame.

Rudi smiled, his eyes touching every part of the girl's anatomy, Frank felt a little rattled with himself, Rudi sensed how uncomfortable he was and pushed him out of the bedroom onto the landing. Pulling himself together Frank knocked and entered the room again.

"Here you are, keep this safe the pair of you," said Frank to the girls.

He handed the screws to the door handle and part of a lever purposely broken off the handle. 'Yan' was still naked as she continued to move around the bedroom, it was clear that both girls were completely uninhibited and so relaxed in their own skins.

Rudi was downstairs unlocking the front door, the house alarm had already been immobilised by young Harry earlier. Soon expecting their nominated guests to arrive, the trap was now set.

The girls had the protection of the bathroom should any men be to over amorous in their attentions on either of the girls, providing Rudi the opportunity of removing the individual from the bathroom and now a victim of blackmail, it was a question of silly actions pay high dividends in avoiding publicity and payments never fail.

———

Tony – The Team Returns

During the early hours of Friday morning Tony returned to the car park and the parked transporters, assembling quietly inside the derelict garage, the four Italians were the first through the opening with Tony in the lead, the first of the expensive vehicles had been selected and was ready to go, each vehicle, in turn, was silently pushed over the hard surface of the compound to the hidden section of the derelict garage which had now been exposed for the vehicles to be rolled through the building onto the car park beyond. The pushing manpower finally managed each vehicle, in turn, to be lined up behind the lower section of the transporter aided by a rope pulley loaded three vehicles onto each of the three lower decks of the transporters.

The Spanish quartet had been building a platform from the upper overhang of the transporter in linking the upper deck of loaded transporters inside the compound, the final push of the operation was nearing completion as the Spanish and Italians teams worked closely together to move vehicles from the compound across the man made bridge, to their positioned loaders, three times the teams extracted two vehicles from each of the opposing transporters in the compound to their side of the fence.

Tony brought the group together once again in the shadows of the transporters and waited the ten minutes required, meanwhile 'Snowy' had crept to a position where he was able to observe the security post, it was clear the guard seen earlier watching television was fast asleep at his post, with only a small light for comfort.

Doug, 'Snowy' and Gino were soon climbing into the cabs of the vehicle transporters, simultaneously the engines came to life, eventually moving off in the opposite direction to the security guards post. Down through narrow streets in convoy heading out onto the arterial roads that would take them away from the Dock area and the City suburbs, the mini bus followed at some distance behind having picked up Maria who had been secreted near the guards post in the event of her services being required to distract the guard, fortunately she wasn't needed as the guard never left his post. 'Snowy' knew of Maria's location earlier when he went to check on the guard, but left her in situ until they were ready for the off.

Ten miles out the convoy of vehicles turned off onto a small narrow lane which took them down to a large farm building, the doors of the three steel containers nearby swung open and the top tier of the transporters were lowered having been emptied of cars minutes earlier at the lower level and each of the two vehicles removed from the top were rolled into the containers and secured to the floor ready for the off. The container Lorries were driven by Doug, 'Snowy' and Gino some miles deep into Wales, to the ferry port that shipped to Ireland once the vehicles were loaded onto the ferry, new drivers took charge of the container consignments and Doug, 'Snowy' and Gino were driven back to the farm building by 'Salvatori' who had travelled up later to bring them back in the mini bus.

Meanwhile back at the farm building, Tony had the

group working tirelessly in secreting the nine remaining vehicles underground. Each vehicle had to be lowered by hydraulic equipment into the basement of the farm building, team members were fascinated by the detail that had gone into the operation, and the basement area under the farm building had been purposely created to hide vehicles, the hydraulic lift remained part of the normal farm equipment and would not have looked out of place to prying eyes. The barn floor was reinstated as per the use of the farm building and none the wiser as to what was hidden in the building. On the arrival of the mini bus and all team members present, it was time for them to disperse, the three transport loaders were to be driven to a car park on route and abandoned, and the three Arctic trucks were driven back in the direction of the Mansion house and parked in a field where Doug took charge of the vehicles and 'Snowy' was waiting with another mini bus for the group to arrive in their mini bus. Swapping vehicles and driven by 'Snowy' the nine foreign operatives were driven away and taken to their respective rendezvous and each their departures home bound. 'Snowy' drove the empty mini bus back into London where a close source later that day returned the vehicle to the garage lot it had been borrowed from and a nice little earner was paid for the loan of it.

Meanwhile, Doug had driven the three trucks and mini bus into the deep gulley and aligned all three close together as daybreak came upon him; he used the parked digger which had been left for the sole purpose of pushing the mounds of soil onto the vehicles below so in order to bury them once and for all and never to be used as evidence in the future, should that ever happen.

When completed Doug went into the bushes and donned his motorcycle gear, and removed the camouflage that had been laid over his machine, leaving the field for the last time he sped off and travelled some distance before finally stopping and making contact with Tommy at the house. After the call Tommy was walking around in euphoria, Toni was bemused in the way he behaved just one the one phone call what was he going to be like when the others call him,

"God help him," she thought muttering to herself and grinning.

So the first of the operations were now a success and he needed to wait patiently on the others to make contact and provide the news he so longs for and hopes no failures.

———

Police Station

With the crackle of the radio and the clatter thud of a telex machine, the young woman leant over the desk of the Police Station and said to the duty officer,

"I'll leave my things here, I'll see if my lift has come, yes," said the woman,

In fact 'Joelle' was another foreign operative from Europe brought over especially to reconnoitre the movements of the local police, outside and away from the Police station she called her contact, she had a brief conversation to confirm that the officer was indicating to her that the Police phones were not working as they should be, 'Joelle' had reported cattle straying and causing chaos so she took refuge in the Police station as these animals were rather frisky and wandering all over the place.

'Joelle' returned to the Police station foyer and spoke with the young officer on desk duty, he was eager for such an attractive companion at such a late hour of the night, she thought he looked really pissed off with all the interruptions, as his radio crackled for the umpteenth time,

"Delta one, go ahead with message," said the Policeman.

"Yes, go ahead with message," he replied for the

second time.

"I have found the barn fire at Dingle top, would you call fire service and tell them of location, I will hang around until they arrive," said an officer on motor patrol.

"Not able to telephone, phones are playing up, use force radio and get central control to call fire service," said station duty officer.

"Jesus, yes alright leave it with me," said the patrol officer.

'Joelle' watched the extra minutes tick away; quietly she picked up her things and was gone from the Police station into her waiting car,

"Christ girl I thought you were staying the night," said the driver.

"Don't be silly, I was listening to the radio messages about a barn fire at a place called Tingles Tip," said Joelle.

"Barn fire yeah, I think that is one of ours," said the driver.

Back to base was a short run, having relayed the fire incident back to their contact, in turn, contacted Tommy at the house.

"Do we have any arrangements for a barn fire at a place called Tingle Tips," said the contact speaking to Tommy, he laughed and said,

"No that's Dingle Tops, that's our way about half an hour from here, that is gypsy country, it's not one of ours tonight," said Tommy.

"I thought so," said the contact.

"Leave that one with me and I make sure, nothing was planned up there, anything else," said Tommy to the contact.

"Yes there's fucking cows everywhere in town and the phones at the nick are also down," said the contact laughing as he relayed his news.

"I can imagine the sight of those cows everywhere trampling over gardens, that is good news about the phones they have been down nearly two hours now, we're doing alright if we keep going like this," said Tommy ending his call to the contact.

The Police Panda car arrived in the High street nearing its junction with Bridge Street with two officers as occupants, using their vehicle to block off part of the street in order to usher the cattle into a more confined area. Both officers walked facing the cattle with arms outstretched trying to shoo the creatures back down the street, a few odd cows remained and appeared stubborn not wanting to move, budging inch by inch one officer got within touching distance, when with a sudden turn and gallop the animals were off running, this started a chain reaction and they all went wild, the going was getting difficult underfoot with fresh dung dropped everywhere, the smell wafted in the air and steam could be seen rising from some cow pats.

In startling contrast, both officers came together in the middle of an alley way, they decided on plan two to keep together the herd, suddenly the sounds of hooves running on cobblestones got louder behind them, they watched in horror as more of the cows re-entered the junction behind them. Their parked Police Car came in for some rough handling as it was bumped, pushed and buffeted as the herd charged, both officers laughed in panic, desperately they tried to move out of the way of the charging herd, but the slimy ground beneath their feet took them both off balance as they fell to the ground, now their uniforms were splattered and saturated in cows shit, their legs strained as they tried to clamber forwards and out of the path of these charging animals, finally they reached the safety of a niche in the adjacent wall of a nearby building now taking refuge as the animals stopped and just milling around, when a familiar voice could be heard entering the alleyway, their sergeant appeared in the company of two locals who had come to assist them.

The sergeant stood with his torch beam on the two officers now covered in cows dung, he tried to put a brave face on the situation without being too serious about their general state of their uniforms.

"Don't worry lads the night's not yet over," said the Sergeant.

"Oh! Bollocks Sarge, this is no sodding joke, why did you let the others down here, you could see the panda parked up the top, we're never going to get the fucking things back. Do you know where they have come from because we bloody don't, listen to them?" said one of the officers from the Panda car.

In the darkness, you could hear their sounds and bellowing with the clatter of hooves on the cobblestones.

"Look we have got them trapped at the moment, they can't go anywhere," said the sergeant.

"No sarge only in the fucking drink," replied by another officer.

That one comment the joviality stopped, the sergeant's voice turned to panic, his smile gone from his face, realising the dangers the tables now turned on the sergeant.

"You never know sarge, they might all try and swim to Ireland," said an officer.

"Less of your bloody lip Dave, let's get down there and make sure that none had fallen off the Warf," said the sergeant.

As predicted, some of the cattle had fallen into the water and now measures were needed to rescue them, other night workers on the Warf had left their warehouses and had come to assist the Police officers, it was understood by the workers that the cattle had escaped from the slaughter house pens. With the assistance of the Port Authorities cattle in the water were finally rescued and considerable Police time had been used on this one incident.

From across the opposing Warf two figures from a warehouse had stood in the shadows of the building and watched the shenanigans occur with the Police, the two men had been responsible for letting loose the cattle from the abattoirs pens, laughing and shaking their heads they returned to the wicker gate of the warehouse and disappeared inside, both men were waiting for Tony to return having made arrangements for them to join the second team, as the first had now finished and dispersed for home.

Another Job Well Done

Through the night there was much coming and going to the house, Frank spent his watching hours overseeing the operation with occasional walks in the grounds, as 'Yan' and 'Inga' were very busy girls and it was obvious their male's companions were smitten by the girl's attention. Rudi had been busy in the house as the card games had paid dividends throughout the night it was more like a conveyor belt of activity that reached fever pitch by dawn and the invited guests were trickling away from the house. Eventually, just the team remained and a check over the house was needed to reinstate as much as they could possibly achieve in the time remaining. The door handle to the bathroom was screwed on, beds and all bedrooms checked for tidiness, which only left for them to round up bottles and glasses and other removable items used in the house deception, Frank was full of smiles with so much money and expensive gifts and jewellery collected from the ever throng of people who descended and some of the visitors were compromised by the girls and were quick to pay up and leave the premises. So finally leaving by the same way they entered following the same route back into the woods and undergrowth, reaching their camouflaged vehicle, packing up their bits and pieces they had brought with them, Frank drove slowly out of the shadows of a breaking dawn rather quickly and back onto the main road and away. Rudi had texted Tommy at the house with a very successful job well done.

Arriving back at their dispersing point, Frank had already arranged for the pickup to be made for the girls and Rudi to be taken to a coastal location for them to travel home.

CHAPTER TWENTY
Up, Up And Away

Approaching the cross roads, 'Bomber' Harris throttled down to turn right into a narrow road leading off the main highway, manoeuvring the large pantechnicon round into the junction, Following his given instructions he continued in low gear, driving through the suburbs of sleepy village for some three miles, then turning right onto a large recreation ground, headlights swept over the lush grass, then picking out a number of parked vehicles dotted along the edge of the grass.

The entourage of which led up to a large house set back from the road, 'Bomber' halted the vehicle alongside an empty house. Two passengers accompanying 'Bomber' climbed down from the cab, both males dressed in smart overalls walked casually to the side entrance of the house. Running parallel to the entrance was a boundary wall of the large house. Charlie and 'Biscuit' had expected to observe the property from their current position.

It was then a small crowd appeared on foot through the large Iron gates of the property, one could hear the excitement which echoed in the calm night air, with so little breeze noise carried far. On seeing the group both men moved back into the shadows of the hanging Ivy that partially protected the Iron railings and the adjacent wall that fronted the entrance to the property.

On passing one of the crowd stopped, a man turned towards the two concealed figures in the Ivy, both remained reverted to the spot, had they been spotted, to their relief and apparently to the man himself, the sound of gushing liquid could be heard as the inevitable had happened, the man decided to take a piss then and there and under the noses of the two figures hiding.

From a distance a voice calls out to the man to hurry,

"Come on Phil we are waiting," said a male voice

"Can't you lot wait five bloody minutes," said Phil in a gruff voice.

Losing his concentration the man gripped the railings with his left hand as support, his urine flowed and covered the path, trickling back down the gradient towards the man, steam glistened and chased the man.

"Sod me, my bloody shoes," he said murmuring.

'Biscuit' felt like reaching out and throttling the fellow, as he grappled with the zip on his trousers. The man moved away to join the waiting group, hearing vehicle doors slam and engines start and sounds of laughter dying as the vehicles drove away. Both men came from under the Ivy and ferreted and weaved their way under the shadows of the high wall, more sounds of laughter and frivolities could be heard coming from the grounds of the house.

In the meantime 'Bomber' had climbed onto a fixed bunk behind the seats in the cab, pushing back a sliding hatch in the rear panel, he spoke to two girls who remained in seclusion in the back of the vehicle.

"Just a few more minutes then we'll be off," said 'Bomber'

The girls nodded as he closed the hatch and lay back on the bunk.

In the alley opposite, Charlie whispered to 'Biscuit',

"Well what do you think, seems alright?"

"Yeah I think the party is a goer having done a good job, we might as well go back mate and get organised," said 'Biscuit'.

Seconds later a feint tap on the cab window and both men climbed in to join 'Bomber'. During their absence of the two men, the line of parked vehicles around the grass edge began to disappear, 'Biscuit' sat cursing and swearing at the timc.

"I saw it happen," said 'Bomber'

"Fuck me I am covered in the bloody stuff, steamy

and smelly," said 'Biscuit'

With that Charlie and 'Bomber' began to laugh, 'Biscuit' sat stern faced as he tried to repeat the story, his hands gestured his anger. Easing back into the comforts of his seat, 'Bomber' lifted the hand set of the radio telephone in the cab and dialled a number, the familiar voice of Tommy answered the call, Tommy acknowledged the call sign given by 'Bomber', "All's well on the night, a further call when the birds have flown, time in hand thirteen minutes," said 'Bomber'.

"Bloody marvellous, look after the time and good luck," said Tommy.

Replacing the handset, he turned on the ignition and gently brought the vehicle to life, edging slowly from the kerb, they travelled past the large house on the left and moved a couple of hundred yards up the road and pulled the vehicle close to the boundary wall of the house, 'Bomber' eased down reducing the vehicles movements to a snail's pace, then stopped the lorry, lights off, the occupants sat in silence waiting for a response to their presence by the security staff at the house it never came after some fifteen minutes of waiting the two men decided to go, slipping quietly from the cab, both climbed up the side of the pantechnicon reaching out for the top of the wall, they both walked carefully along the ridge of the wall. Midway along the roof line of the vehicle body, both pulled on a fixed hinged platform (giving the appearance of shelf fixed to a wall) climbing onto the platform, 'Biscuit' slid back a hatch in the roof section of the vehicle body and descended quietly into the body of the vehicle, Charlie remained on top of the roof, releasing a couple of canvas straps fixed under the canopy of the roof, which supported two pairs of stilts, each one was passed by 'Biscuit' through the roof opening for Charlie to stand both pairs up against the wall inside the grounds of the house.

Both men had by now reached the inside floor of the vehicle and joined the two girls seated on a sofa, their strong facial features, high cheek bones, blonde hair and blue eyes portrayed their origin of German birth.

Hidden by a curtain at the back of the vehicle was an array of surveillance equipment, glancing at his watch Charlie held up his hand towards the girls for the off, both girls went behind another curtain and soon emerged in jump suits and head gear. Charlie was busy with headphones glued to his head, listening for signs of life from the house as the girls made themselves ready. Charlie by this time was using the onboard video camera as he scanned the area and signs of security guards on patrol would be of interest if he could locate them on the property.

Both the girls 'Uli' and 'Monika' were making ready to leave the comforts of the vehicle, Charlie had seen the last remaining house visitors leave by the front entrance, but still no signs of the security patrol. Charlie gave the girls the off signal as they both climbed the ladder to the roof of the vehicle, the interior lights inside the vehicle body had been momentarily switched off, as Charlie returned to the monitoring screen, 'Biscuit' closed the roof hatch.

On the screen Charlie saw both girls standing on the side platform attached to the vehicle body, the girls now prepared their final move away from the parked vehicle, 'Biscuit' was amazed to see the girls loom higher than the wall in the light of the night sky as they stood unaided on their stilts. Both men were enthralled at their lithe figures which stood out on the monitor against the backdrop of the night sky. Both girls moved off in the grounds of the house and out of sight of the mounted camera on the roof of the vehicle, it meant that Charlie and 'Biscuit' had to sit and wait, 'Bomber' had become aware that the girls had gone from the vehicle, via the open intercom of the vehicle.

Tommy had been relieved that the girls had entered the ground of the house without a hitch; he was content to have received the call to that effect. Using the wall chart on the wall of Tommy's office he continued to chart the progress of the teams involved, the wall looked more like a bookies forum, showing very favourable odds. This for him was the worst time of all, playing the waiting game was not really his style; he was always in the thick of things. Toni had earlier been busy but more or less sat quietly as Tommy paced the floor at times showing signs of his growing impatience, in many ways spooking him to the waiting silence of the office.

Both girls had been gone ten minutes and already they had reached an area of the house where they saw glimmers of light protruding through the drawn curtains of a number of upper windows. Both girls were members of a German Circus troupe their main act was walking on stilts, very professional in approach to their work as trained gymnasts, with such fit a lithe light weight bodies the girls were able to move like prowling cats, felines without the purring as they moved silently on the outside of the building. From head to floor the girls had donned a camouflage that represented hanging Ivy as neither stilts could be seen underneath unless touching the fabric.

The girls had moved round to the opposite side of the building, finding the darkened alleyway that led between the wings of the two buildings at the back of the house. The girls arrived at where they needed to be, waited intently on the expected arrival of one of the patrolling guards; from their high position and looking down they had stood alongside a down sewer pipe that was connected elsewhere to other pipe work for waste water. It provided good extra , minutes lapsed when a beam of light was seen as it swept over the ground and then disappeared, then the beam of light reappeared and was somewhat erratic as it swept the ground closer to the girls, it was then the girls saw the trail in the air of what was obvious to them as the guard was drawing on a cigarette as he patrolled now it was for them easy to track his position for as long as the cigarette lasted.

Finally the guard had disappeared as 'Uli' moved from behind 'Monika' removing the canvas strap attached to her stilts she placed round her companions waist looping and making a foot stirrup, 'Monika' was now braced to take the extra weight as 'Uli' climbed the extended stilt snake like as her lithe figure slowly edged upwards to a window, with gentle manipulation she forced open and eased her body through the window, as her stilts remained with 'Monkia' and now it was her turn to be pulled up and through the window with their extended stilts left propped under the windowsill outside.

Now both girls were on the upper attic floor of the house, sweating the girls peeled of their outer clothing, leaving the jump suits near to the open window wearing only their briefs the girls moved to the outside of the room where a narrow staircase led down to the landing area, laughter and voices of excitement could be heard drifting along the corridor from the opposite end of the house.

Eventually the girls went down onto the landing in search of their target being the annexe which was off the main landing, the interior of the house was deceiving in size with many doors leading off, some were cupboards and storage areas others were bathrooms and bedrooms of various sizes, in one of the bedrooms the girls were kept prisoner whilst a couple had entered and quickly locked themselves together in a flurry of hurried emotion and grunting noises they parted and left the room just as quickly as they had entered, both girls had stood hidden behind the floor to ceiling curtains, it was 'Monika' who caught her toes in a pair of ladies briefs on the floor, it was obvious in haste of leaving the bedroom the woman had left her underwear behind, 'Monika' removed the garment from her foot and placed the briefs on the floor of the landing directly outside the bedroom door, bringing scandal to the household, she smiled at 'Uli' for the devilment of her actions.

Having now browsed and searched all the rooms on the upper floor the girls had sought and found their intended targets in most of the bedrooms allocated to the members of the Jewellery and Diamond Association, prior inside knowledge had been a godsend being spot on for the girls to amble quietly collecting as much of the proceeds as they could possibly find. Whilst leaving one bedroom a shadow was cast on the opposite wall of the corridor, someone was approaching in their direction. 'Uli' quickly turned and pushed 'Monika' up against the wall thrusting her breasts against hers, with one hand fumbling through her companion's hair giving the appearance of two lesbians, the lone figure of a woman passed without taking notice of the two girls in the doorway, 'Uli' whispered,

"That must be the guys wife, Christ if that's her," not finishing her conversation.

They had no time to waste, fetching the case from the bedroom they quickly left the landing and climbed the narrow staircase back up to the attic, with the door closed they felt safe. Helping each other on with their jump suits and their bodies hot with the stress of almost being found out was now more urgent than ever for the girls to leave by the window and get back to the vehicle. Everything found in the case and more of the many pouches collected from the many bedrooms visited were being stuffed into each other's backpacks, with hands-free, 'Uli' was the first to the window, repeating their descent down in the same mode they had climbed to the window. Outside in the darkness they realised they were some minutes overdue, as they made their way back through the garden and out onto the vast lawn, reaching the woodland they edged slowly through to the boundary wall, both panicked as they had come to rest in the wrong location, with some urgency the girls climbed up on top of the wall and worked their way back carrying their stilts with them, dogs could be heard barking in the distance. Finding the vehicle the girls relaxed as

'Monika' was the first to climb onto the overhanging side platform, then sliding back the roof hatch she peered down into the depths of subdued lighting and the smiling faces of Charlie and 'Biscuit' looking up as she climbed down the ladder and greeting cuddles from both men 'Ul' was soon follow down the ladder. 'Biscuit' quickly climbed back to the roof to secure the girl's stilts and then slid the platform back into the body of the vehicle and closed the roof hatch.

Soon 'Bomber' was given the nod to move off slowly without raising the neighbours interests as they travelled for a short distance without lights, then finally Bomber's driving became more normal as he accelerated away from the house travelling back the way they had arrived through the narrow lanes and through a sleepy village heading towards the main road and on to the farm building hide away.

The Pantechnicon finally arrived at the farm, Frank was the first to greet the five members of the team, with moments of back slapping and handshakes as Frank moved 'Bomber' from ear shot of the others and filled him in with the details and success of their operation.

"A bloody dream the girls, I don't know how they managed on stilts," said 'Bomber' laughing.

"Give over mate fucking stilts what's this a fucking circus," said Frank

"Yes mate you are right," said 'Bomber' the girls are from a circus, as his laughter got grip of him.

"That's unbelievable mate," said Frank still not sure as to whether his leg was being pulled, "Fucking stilts, unbelievable."

Gathering the group around him, Frank outlined the final task before they parted for home, holding aloft small containers he explained that each would hold some of the precious stones that would fit in the capsules, 'Bomber' appeared with a large basket that housed pigeons, it didn't take long to attach the capsules to their legs and let fly the birds.

From the group's location, the sky was beginning to lighten as dawn was approaching with fine weather looking more likely for the day. The group waited on the arrival of the driver who collected the two Frenchmen from another operation.

(The two Frenchmen 'Pierre' and Jean-Luke were pyrotechnic specialists brought into the operation to leave the local area with a blitz of raging and shooting colour along the Motorway cutting. Again it all hinged on whether Tommy's audacious plans had succeeded and that's exactly what happened, having covered the high ground of the cutting with a mass of fireworks all linked and fed back to a timer hidden in the shrubs. It had taken most of the night for the French lads to achieve their target of laying out the fireworks, and their driver remained secreted off road in a field nearby ready for the off).

With quick handshakes between 'Bomber' and Frank and stares from the remaining group waiting to leave as the Pantechnicon was reversed up to one of the large farm buildings, all the bits and pieces found and all the odds and ends left over from the operations were all brought together and placed into the rear of the vehicle body, along with motorcycles. The two Frenchmen arranged for their fire bombs to be placed at strategic places throughout the building and a new vehicle body had been transferred onto the chassis of another truck, with some adjustments to the interior of the vehicle body it was now ready to be used as a people carrier. One of the English driver's had driven off with the Pantechnicon, the remaining driver was waiting to drive the converted people carrier away with the four girls, Rudi and the two Frenchmen, with the final goodbyes now said by each and a night full of excitement and surprises throughout the Bristol area, without the razzmatazz to send them on their way.

Frank, Charlie, 'Biscuit' and 'Bomber' remained at

the farm waiting on young Harry to pick them up and drop them off at their prearranged locations on route back to London.

The motorway journey went through a hillside cutting followed by a steep gradient, it was whilst reaching this point that the occupants burst out laughing as the hillside was ablaze of colour it was an awesome sight and truly a fitting send off for a good nights work. As the vehicle accelerated and moved out into the fast lane as cheers and whistles were rapturous as they congratulated each other as Frank made the last phone call to Tommy, as he too could hear the noise they were all making, "I need not say anything further my old shiner, we are heading home and alls done and dusted, only the farm building to go up in smoke shortly,

"By Tommy and you take care of your lady, catch up with you in the week," said Frank shouting down the phone.

Young Harry was a pace setter with a nice steady drive back to London.

CHAPTER TWENTY-ONE
The Gypsies Vengeance

During the early hours of Saturday and twenty hours after Tommy's audacious success having pulled off one the largest Crime sprees in history, gypsies returned in their numbers, mob handed and intent on taking revenge for the early attack on them at the house.

Tommy and Toni were the only occupants known to have been in the house at the time, it was assumed due to the time recorded on the report received by the emergency services that they would have been asleep at such an hour, as the house was in darkness at the time.

A petrol tanker had been manoeuvred into place at the top of the drive; the vehicles near side had been positioned at an angle facing the house. The growing crowd of gypsies was attributed to the accompanying vehicles and passengers that followed the Petrol tanker down the lane. The stupidity of the travellers was clear to be seen in the pushing and shoving that occurred among them in deciding who was going to open the valves on the tanker first.

Known among the travellers as 'Leafy', the boyish looking figure suddenly emerged and run beyond the watching crowd to the tanker and began to open the first valve, petrol began gushing at some force hit and splayed across the ground, two more valves opened and the gushing repeated as the liquid could be heard by the mob standing in the lane, it was more in silence as the petrol could be seen as a silent moving flood heading down in the direction of the house, at times the petrol shimmered in the night sky as moving clouds cast moments of shadows and then cleared as moonlight caught the moving flood, it was more than eerie as it began to sink in with some of the watching standing mob in the lane at what they had unleashed.

Another young traveller entered the cab of the vehicle

from the passenger side, suddenly the vehicle shunted forward; the two gypsies who had been with him were stood close to the offside rear wheels of the vehicle as they waited for their friend to jump clear of the cab. He never emerged as he had managed to turn the front wheels in the opposite direction towards the house, in doing so the passenger door closed on him and one of the gypsies standing close to the rear wheels was caught by their clothing and dragged across the ground, eventually his clothing gave way, but sadly he became a victim as the wheels of the tanker ran over one of his legs, he let out a horrendous scream, frightening sounds panicked among the waiting mob. The moving sounds of the vehicle could be heard as it crushed the gravel under its weight as it slowly rolled down the drive, the youth in the cab of the tanker had panicked and his actions set off the alarming scene the waiting mob was witnessing. Gypsies rushed to the traveller with the leg injury and dragged him back to the lane and waiting vehicle, he and a small group made off.

'Leafy' the instigator of the unfolding drama had run back to the gate of the house, he was saturated in petrol and clearly the skin was beginning to burn from being caught in the gushing fuel he was attempting to remove his clothes, when from nowhere a spark set off a chain reaction across the ground as the flame intensified as it raced towards the house. Petrol had reached the house and flowed following the contours of the building, when with an almighty bang a massive orange ball of flame roared skywards, illuminating all in sundry including the faces of the watching mob standing in the lane. Such was the force that the mob dispersed in panic going in every direction imaginable, some racing to parked vehicles, some ran back up the hill; others climbed the bank opposite to reach the open field beyond. The noise intensified and it was not clear as to what had happened to the gypsy youth who earlier climbed into the tankers cab and whose actions had caused the massive fire ball. The tanker had reached the side of the house as the momentum and weight propelled the vehicle as the near side scraped along the brick wall of the house. By now the vehicle was covered in roaring flames from front to back of the vehicle. The heat from the fire could be felt by the dispersing mob in the lane, 'Leafy' was finally helped away from the scene, having discarded some of his clothing in the lane the full extent of his injuries remained unknown.

The final horrific explosion from the tanker sent shock waves for miles and disturbed many in the village below, blue lights of the fire engines could be seen weaving their way through the narrow country lane at pace only to be met by a catastrophic scene when they arrived at the Mansion house. Fire had reached the roof level on the kitchen side of building and was rapidly spreading as more petrol aflame had followed the house contours on the opposite side of the building and was beginning to increase its ferocity as flames in part licked the brickwork, dancing up trying to reach anything that was combustible in it growing path. During the whole fracas the house remained in darkness, only the howls of dogs could be heard in between the roars of the growing fire as it now had engulfed the whole of the house, flames reached skywards as sparks flew in every direction.

Fire crews stood in the shadows of the horror which greeted their arrival as fire hoses first trained on the tanker to quell the rage, some firemen washed down the driveway to dilute the petrol that had seeped into the ground. The smell of fuel was rancid as rubber and plastic became very acrylic and acidic in the atmosphere irritating eyes and breathing, as fire crews donned their breathing apparatus for safety.

Villagers began to appear in a state of undress and nightwear all concerned at the raging fire and the explosion that had shaken the whole village, others remained in the village looking up into the sky as orange plumes could be seen tailing off into the night sky. Lots of opinions were being offered by some of the watching crowd, as fire always seems to attract a cross section of society dying to know how it started and were there casualties involved, ghoulish and gruesome talk at times.

The car park of the local pub the Bull and Butcher had become the focal point for the growing gathering of locals. Traffic cones were now being placed by the first Policeman to arrive, comments among the crowd were of the opinion that it had to be the Mansion house, 'Marshall Green' –

"Oh! my god," cried a voice, "It had to be there is not any other building up there,"

Speculation was now rife as Judy and Dan Stokes opened the pub doors and asked for volunteers to set tables for tea and coffee brews for the emergency services. Group of locals had soon organised themselves into a helping hand of assistance, with buckets of water for washing hands as it soon came into play as some firemen had been brought down to the car park for resting up from the awful smells that hung in the air, as it was a blessing that the night air remained calm with little breeze to increase the fire.

Back at the house, the roof had collapsed in parts as clouds of long streams of sparks flew up into the air and hovered and swirled around before caught by the breeze to disperse. Then more sounds of crashing brick and masonry could be heard and seen collapsing inwards and outside the building as chunks fell to the ground. Fire fighters were well entrenched in fighting the fire with many personal and many hoses trained on the building, but sadly the Mansion being an old building was disintegrating before their very eyes, it was self-destructing under intense heat with the whole roof now demolished and much of the wall construction destroyed, little was beginning to remain as the former building resembled a pile of burning embers, many of the fire fighters had stood back as more of the walls collapsed adding to the pile already established inside the building. It was then that a group of firemen watched in horror, it was dreamlike as horrors go as among the burning debris appeared the silhouette of a moving object, illuminated by the red hot embers, the elongated head, neck and chest rose up and pointed skywards as if being dragged along by the fire, like a flaming dragon.

"What the hell is it," shouted one of the crew, others came to look and stared at the moving shape.

"Oh! Christ, it's a dog," said another fireman.

The shape continued to struggle as if to breathe as it fought death in its path, when as suddenly as it appeared the creature fell back into the fire and disappeared from view, from those watching it was a horror story of a kind that one could not describe as all the animals body and shape had not been seen. The group of fire fighters just stood in silence and turned and went about their fire duties sickened by the creature's demise.

By daylight more Police had arrived at the property as the fire was now under control, with numerous sightseers coming and going as most of the emergency services were now down the hill in the car park of the local public. Food was being cooked and served to the fire crews as other locals made the many brews of tea and coffee.

A huge heavy lifting vehicle came trundling through the village and parked up on the edge of the village, the driver had been sent to assist with the tankers removal. Other experts in petroleum had arrived to aid the fire crews as concerns were expressed as to whether further explosions could occur by removing the tanker at this time, as it was necessary to open up the top covers so that foam could be inserted into each of the fuel compartments.

As the morning progressed more emergency crews arrived, some already scrapping back burning timbers and sifting through for any signs of the property being occupied on the night of the fire.

By midday it was clear that nothing remained of 'Marshalls Green', the building had been completely raised to the ground and the known occupants of the house had not appeared at the property, as the immediate landscape to the house was blackened and imparts now barren where shrubs and trees once grew were now burnt to a cinder.

No bodies were found in the debris and yet it was known that the house had been occupied and at some time in the afternoon villagers had left flowers at the gate assuming that the occupants had perished in the fire.

The whereabouts of Tommy and Toni was in its self a mystery as some hours later quietness stood over the remains as fire crews continued to dampen down the last of the burning embers as steam rose and spat back at them. It was only later that the crews were informed that a body had been found in the cab of the tanker, the identity remained unknown as the body was unrecognisable.

The remaining mob of gypsies had been quick to disperse to the point where some had completely left the area within minutes of leaving the scene. It was rumoured also that the gypsy with legs injuries had been taken many miles away for treatment and of course, a yarn told to the hospital about how his leg became broken, (road accidents are frequent) but whatever the truth he apparently received the treatment required, with a leg in plaster for his troubles. 'Leafy' became just another casualty on the night, his whereabouts remains unknown to the authorities.

CHAPTER TWENTY-TWO
'Marshalls Green'

Sunday midday Karen and Lenny were nearing the end of their journey home, it followed the day after the house fire at 'Marshalls Green', both were completely unaware of the tragic events that had befallen the building the day before.

About to enter the lane when a 'Police No Entry' sign confronted them, wondering what had taken place and the reason why they couldn't travel further, Karen had to stop the vehicle, it was then that Lenny noticed a number of parked vehicles in an open gated field. He indicated to Karen to pull in off the lane and park up, at that moment two elderly woman with dogs approached the gate heading back onto the lane, quickly leaving the car Lenny beckoned to and called out,

"Excuse me but do you know what's happened and why the Police sign, we want to drive up the lane," said Lenny indicating some concern to the ladies.

"There's been a very nasty accident, it's terrible, the Mansion house on the hill was burnt to the ground during the early hours of Saturday, real nasty business," said one of the ladies.

Lenny reeled back at the news, shocked and stunned at what he had been told.

"How do you know," said Lenny, "Do you know what caused it."

"We don't know, do we June, we went up and had a look, such a fine old house, it's such a shame," said June's friend.

"Was there anybody hurt do you know," said Lenny holding back his emotions.

"We don't know do we June, there was a dog apparently found dead," said the elderly lady.

"Are there many people up there now do you know,"

said Lenny.

"Yes the Police and fire officers are still there and people standing at the gate as flowers are being left by visitors who have heard about the fire," said the lady.

Lenny thanked the ladies and returned to the vehicle, once inside he burst into tears, he was sobbing his heart out.

"Oh! My god Lennyyyyyy, you are frightening me, what's wrong, what's happened," said Karen as she faced Lenny for answers.

Still tearful and holding back his emotions,

"Jesus Christ the house has burnt down during the early hours of yesterday. No one has yet been found, but one of the dogs was found dead," said Lenny as his chest heaved with every breath.

Karen screamed at the news, gripping the steering wheel as she cried out,

"Oh! My god, it can't be Lenny, what about Tommy and Toni, we've got to find them," said Karen she and Lenny just sat and stared out the window of the vehicle, numbed and shocked at the news.

Lenny's was ashen-faced, he couldn't speak as he left the vehicle, first leaning his back against the vehicle then pacing up and down, trying to understand the picture and the events that'd happened.

Karen left the vehicle and joined him; she was shaking as she spoke,

"Lenny we will go and find out for ourselves, won't we," said Karen.

"Can't we walk from here," said Karen as she leant on Lenny's shoulder, "can't we get to a position up there," as Karen pointed across the field to the opposite hedgerow.

Lenny agreed with her, locking and leaving the vehicle the couple walked across the field to the hedgerow and disappeared into the undergrowth. From their position sounds of radio's could be heard, obviously the sounds of the emergency services still on scene. From their position it was apparent their view was obscured and they would need to move closer, as they crept forward keeping inside the hedgerow Lenny stopped and realised that the house ought to be seen from their new position. His heart sank as he told Karen, edging down the bank using the shrubs and more undergrowth as support to cover their movements, they moved along the boundary fence and stopped both sitting on the ground listening. The smell of burning was in the air and the radio sounds were much closer, including movement and voices. Lenny realised the elderly ladies had been correct about the house fire, he clenched his fist and banged the ground in despair, Karen was still crying as she searched for a tissue from her pockets.

"What are we going to do Lenny, what about speaking to the Police and telling them that we also are from the house," said Karen now concerned as to what the truth really was as Lenny appeared reluctant to speak with the Police.

Lenny could hear the beating of his heart as he drew breath as he was really struggling with his thoughts.

"I feel I am suffocating, we need to go back, my mind is scrambled, I just can't think, oh! Fucking Christ what the hell has happened here," said Lenny now beginning to really search for answers.

Karen hadn't said a word she was too shocked she felt lost and confused and was not communicating properly with Lenny, Lenny realised that they needed to get back to the car quickly as Karen was appearing to go into shock, he rushed as best he could in the circumstances encouraging Karen to keep up with him as he held fast her hand eventually reaching the safety of the vehicle. He put Karen into the passenger seat as he took the vehicle keys away from her.

Lenny decided to drive to the local pub, on arriving the car park was full of Police and Fire crews, mingling with many of the locals from the village.

Leaving Karen in the car Lenny went into the pub for a brandy for Karen; he purchased for himself a coffee brew then returned to the vehicle. Karen had rested her head against a rolled up coat trying to close her eyes at the same time to shut out the horrors of the fire. On Lenny's return, she sat sipping the brandy to warm her; Lenny was sipping his coffee when clearly both their minds were elsewhere struggling as to Tommy and Toni's whereabouts, as none of this made any sense to either of them.

Lenny decided to leave Karen in the vehicle whilst he mingled with the locals and listened to their stories, it wasn't long before he engaged a local man who appeared to know the area very well, he mentioned that a dead dog had been seen in the fire and appeared to upset a number of the fire crews who witnessed the creature appear out of the flames and then fell back and disappeared. Then he mentioned what he had seen and wasn't sure if his eyes were playing tricks on him, he thought he saw the movement of two dogs in the woodland above the house and with a blink of the eye they had vanished. Lenny was sure that at least two of the dogs were alive, but which of them managed to escape and which died in the fire. Lenny went back to Karen and told her to stay put as he was going to have a wander up there and see if the story about the dogs was correct, he knew if they were alive he would find them, could Tommy and Toni be hiding too in the woodland, he had to know as he walked off up the hill towards the house. Eventually going beyond the house to the copse, Lenny found his way into the woodland and secreted himself in the undergrowth, whispering the names of the dogs, hoping they would come and find him. He remained well hidden as he was able to see some of the fire damage below and able to note that the house was in total ruins and truly raised to the ground.

Moving through the woodland he came back to the opposite fence away from the house and to his amazement found one of the dogs laying in the grass, Lenny was hesitant but the dog heard his movement and raised its head, it was 'Solo' who crawled towards him, acting as if the animal had behaved badly, appearing afraid, but soon in his arms cuddling and patting him making the dog welcome at the same time he spoke in calming whispers so as not to over excite the animal and draw attention to himself. Solo appeared to be uninjured although very nervous as the dog wouldn't stop shaking as he tried to calm the animal with the kindness he had always shown his animals. Realising there were still two to find and whether they had survived, but it wasn't long before he caught sight of the missing dogs down in the high grass of the meadow down near the river. Encouraging 'Solo' to follow him as he went seeking the other two dogs, he walked as if he was out exercising his dogs like other locals in the area. With the company of 'Solo' at his side, he whistled hoping to attract the other two dogs to come to heel. Finally, he greeted the other two dogs 'Raz' and 'Taz' they too appeared to be uninjured although very apprehensive about his presence, so giving each a reassurance cuddle and to let them know he was back to take care of them. Walking down to the river's edge he encouraged the dogs to walk with him as he headed back to the car park. None of the dogs had collars, so he had to improvise using baling string he found along the pathway to try and make sufficient leads and collars to keep all three together and not to run havoc nearing the pub. He managed to attract Karen who by this time had been searching for his return, seeing him peering through the hedge of the field they had earlier parked in, she left the vehicle to meet him, both remained out in the open for others to see them without drawing attention to themselves by hurrying the dogs, it worked by a slow approach as they managed to get all three dogs into the vehicle, somewhat relieved he went in search of some biscuits that he could give them, all three had drank from the river on the way back so thirst was not the concern.

Eventually leaving the dogs to settle Lenny and Karen entered the pub, sitting by a window overlooking the car, it was on both their minds to reflect on what to do next and realising the enormity and the task ahead to find ways of sorting this mess out, he knew that he was being backed into a corner as Karen expected him to speak to the authorities, unbeknown to her Lenny was scared stiff of such a move. Lenny's mind worked overtime as he roughed out an explanation hoping that he would be able to convince Karen about the reasons why he couldn't approach the Police, he had no idea that Tommy had activated his crime caper and could only be described as an absolute success on Tommy's part, having pulled off such audacious crimes as neither he nor Karen had seen the news or read the newspapers.

"Karen, look I need to talk to you, obviously I have a lot on my mind but there is something that I want you to understand and why I can't speak to the Police at the moment. Many years ago, well if the truth be known, we served a prison term and released five years ago and why we are where we are today. Tommy and me left our past behind and to start over like we have, at the same time Tommy wouldn't want to speak to the Police, he is very tight with personal details and I wouldn't want to interfere with his affairs at the moment as no bodies have been found at the house, only one mentioned was the person found in the tanker cab and that is not going to be Tommy. But how did that vehicle get close to the fucking house, it smells gypsy to me and that's another reason why I don't want to be identified at the moment, we have the dogs everything else has gone, all our personal gear and effects burnt and destroyed. But what is missing is Tommy's Range Rover at the house, he would have left that on the drive if they had been out at any time," said Lenny,

Now really waiting to get it in the neck as he felt this is where her true loyalty and friendship will surface if she is genuine about a relationship with him, she certainly cares, but is that enough for her?

"But what about Toni and her family," said Karen, "They need to be informed – please, they must be told,"

"But there is nothing to be told, no bodies have been found, so later it must be down to the authorities to inform her family, It would be wrong of us to do so, we don't know if they died in the fire, they could hiding out somewhere like us," said Lenny with a pleading voice, then he realised that Karen had not made mention of their criminal past and that confused him as to why she hadn't.

"Look what I can do is to inform Frank in London and let him speak with one of our legal contacts to act on behalf of Tommy, being one of the legal owners of the house, we don't know if it was an accident, whether it was the gypsies or whether it was caused by some other factor that we haven't considered, it could be murder, so I don't want to expose us, when it's not necessary others I can pay will do that for me and it's all about being confidential as solicitor client privilege," said Lenny now beginning to think more clearly at the seriousness of what could happen if they were identified as being from the house.

Agreeing to Lenny's proposals, Karen opened her handbag, fumbling for her diary she removed some of the contents from the bag. A piece of plastic fell onto the table, Karen hadn't noticed, Lenny picked up the plastic and began to fiddle with it as he spun it through his fingers, then glancing at the plastic he saw a photograph on one side, he saw a picture of Karen, reading the print on the plastic he saw she was a Customs officer, Karen was busy with her diary as Lenny held up the plastic warrant card, she looked up and took it from him. Neither spoke but each stared into each other's faces waiting for answers as to his find and Karen concerning Lenny's Criminal past.

"Before you say anything, Lenny, Do you remember when we first met, it was you who said we wouldn't talk about our past, so I wasn't going to say a word," said Karen.

Pulling an envelope from her bag and handing it to Lenny,

"I want you to read this letter, you will see it's my resignation from the service, I was going to post it on holiday, check the date on it, that's all. What difference does it make?" said Karen as tears rolled down her cheeks as she stared into his face.

Lenny reached out and squeezed his hand over hers holding the letter, he pushed her hand away saying,

"Put it away, point taken Karen, no questions asked," said Lenny.

Lenny nodded and suggested they make a move,

"We are going to need somewhere to stay and we have three dogs with us, times pressing so we are likely to be stuffed for accommodation tonight, Do hotels allow dogs, cross my palm with a big banknote and pray, I say what you," said Lenny as he reached out and gave Karen one huge cuddle before driving off.

POSTSCRIPT

Three weeks later, Police constable Bob Benyon returned to duty in the village having been on a course.

(Twenty years service and he was in the process of rebuilding his life after a recent separation).

He had gone to 'Marshalls Green' Manor House, the significance of his visit and how he would be drawn into a future conflict was not apparent to him, unaware that his path had crossed previously with one of the occupants, later to find that a parcel (a gift) awaited his presence at the local pub and had been left in the care of the licensee's wife Judy Stokes. The Manor House will become a place of many secrets and mystery will be second fold as to the whereabouts of the occupants of the house.

———————

A.E. Snelling-Munro

An indentured apprentice to the motor industry who, on completion, entered the Police service as a full-term career.

Since retirement, he is now an established inventor with many concepts to his name.

Interests include serious DIY, family history and writing - including verse and lampoons and the idiocies of British politics.

Available worldwide from

Amazon

_____

www.mtp.agency